I0554309

A Mage's Mentor

Book One of the Ucksil's Folly Trilogy

Stephen Jarocki

Book Cover by Pat Jarocki

Map Illustrations by Stephen Jarocki

Library of Congress Control Number: 2025905911

ISBN 978-1-967540-00-6 (paperback)
ISBN 978-1-967540-01-3 (hardcover)
ISBN 978-1-967540-02-0 (ebook)

First Edition: 2025

CONTENTS

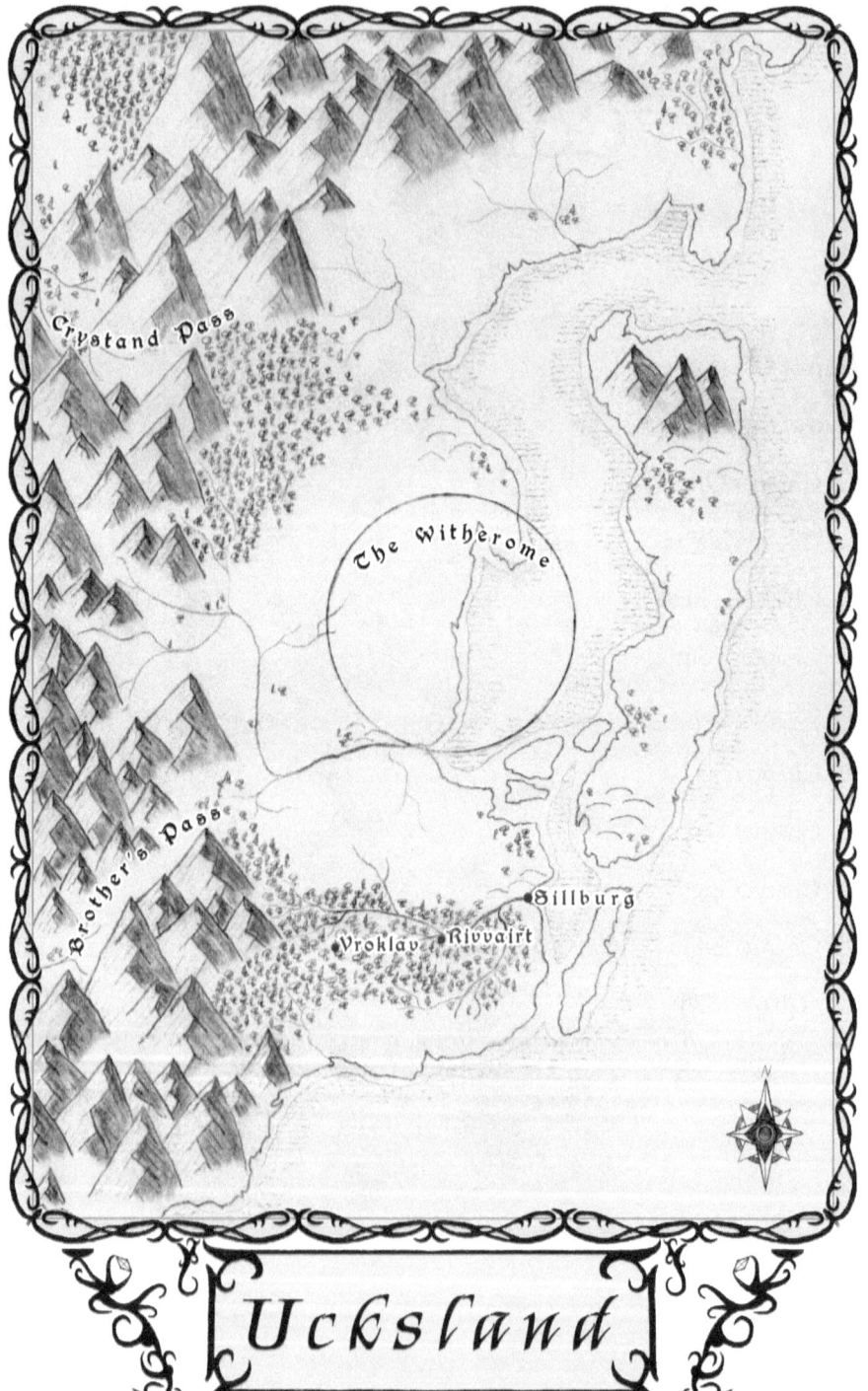

Crystand Pass

The Witherome

Brother's Pass

Sillburg
Vroklav • Rivvairt

Ucksland

Sillburg

For Luke,
Who supported the dream

CHAPTER ONE

Sinccah clutched her mother's pendant. So many years had passed. It was time to learn the truth.

A sharp wail echoed through the mountain pass. She grimaced as she let the pendant fall back onto her chest. The wailing continued unabated. Her hands clenched into fists as she fought to avoid showing her discomfort. The sound was wretched, and the memories it brought back were even worse. If only the mountains would fall on them so that she might be free of the hideous sound. It'd been going on forever, minutes probably, but forever all the same.

She glanced toward the infant who was producing the wailing and watched as his mother tried vainly to calm him. Sinccah turned away and tried to redirect her focus toward something else, anything else. She looked up at the towering mountains on either side of the narrow pass. Between the jagged stone faces, large patches of fir trees clung desperately to the steep walls. She tried to fixate on these, to pick single trees out of the distant forest. It was no use; her mind raced back to the unpleasant memories of the last several years. The smirking faces of Lady Dove's children crowded into her mind. Spoiled brats, both of them.

A lull in the wailing allowed Sinccah to pull her thoughts back to the present. She glanced over the cobblestone road she was traveling on, which cut deep into the surrounding rock. In spite of winding through the mountains, it was one of the widest roads she'd ever seen. Centuries of rockslides had reduced its width significantly, but it remained impressive.

She turned her attention to the modest caravan that was plodding down that road. The small cart where she sat brought up the rear of this caravan. It was pulled by a pair of massive goats and also carried the wailing child and his parents.

The young couple had been kind enough to let Sinccah ride with them after she'd stumbled over some rocks the day before. A fresh bout of wailing caused Sinccah's gaze to snap back to the child. His mother shuffled him onto one of her arms before reaching up and returning a few stray hairs to her sandy-blond bun. She shifted her weight as the cart bounced over a stone. Grimacing slightly, she glanced around in distress. Her eyes met Sinccah's. Sinccah tried to offer a sympathetic smile, but she couldn't hide her own discomfort and it ended up appearing judgmental instead. Both women looked away awkwardly.

Sinccah grimaced. She hadn't meant to appear so rude, but it was hard to resist the emotions that came with her torturous memories. A fresh cry rang out. She frowned as her head flopped forward. It was just like when she'd been working for Lady Dove. How did anyone stand this?! She brushed away a few long straight strands of auburn hair that had fallen in front of her eyes. Maybe she ought to just leave. If only she could use her healing magic on herself! Her lip curled upward. Technically, it could be done, but all the manuals had insisted it was quite dangerous. Something about using magical energy to alter the body that was producing it. Certainly not worth it here.

She sighed as her hand twitched nervously to her mother's pendant. Instinctively, her fingers began to rub the intricate engravings. Then, noticing her fidgeting, she dropped the pendant. She stared at the rounded golden disk as it dangled in front of her dull beige shirt. She really needed to stop playing with it whenever she got nervous. The pendant rotated slowly, reflecting the rays of the setting sun. The engravings had always amazed her. All around the outside, dozens of tiny yarrow flowers had been expertly carved. She smiled. Even though she must have inspected this pendant hundreds of times, the minuscule petals seemed to reveal more and more detail each time she looked at them. Sorrow suddenly crowded in and began to taint her thoughts. The corners of her mouth tugged downward. She blinked some moisture out of her eyes before shaking her head. She'd never really known her mother. It had been so long, and she'd never learned what happened. Had something taken her mother, or had the woman never cared to begin with?

Her gaze slowly drifted to her left foot. She wiped her eyes before pulling it into her lap to inspect her ankle. Pulling back the tattered brown hem of her pant leg revealed that the swelling from the day before had subsided somewhat. She probed the area with her finger. It didn't hurt to touch it anymore; perhaps her injury had healed. She moved her foot back to the floor of the cart and tried putting some weight on it. It still hurt, but it was manageable.

The wailing grew louder and higher pitched. Sinccah felt her mind being pulled toward the past. No, she couldn't go there again. She began searching for an excuse to give to the child's parents, some reason why she needed to get off the cart. This couple had been kind to her, so she didn't want to offend them with her actions, but she couldn't bear it anymore. Her eyes wandered to the right side of the path. Through the scraggly trees, she saw a small trickle of water that flowed lazily eastward. Her eyes darted upstream as she thought back to the start of the expedition. That was it! A powerful mage was leading the caravan, and she did want to speak to him before they reached their destination. She leaned forward to tap on the cart driver's shoulder.

"Hey," Sinccah said loudly over the wailing, "thanks for the ride, but my foot is feeling better now, and I wanted to talk with Vistimmot, so I'm going to head up there now."

"No problem," the man said as he turned to her. His face featured a kindhearted smile and was framed by a mat of dark brown hair and a scraggly wisp of a beard. "Feel free to come back if your ankle starts bothering you again."

"I appreciate the offer," Sinccah said as she grabbed her pack and hopped off the cart onto the rough rocky path. "Thanks again for the ride." The man waved at her before turning to his wife. Sinccah walked briskly away from the cart, every other step causing her a brief stab of pain. She fought through it and quickened her pace. She soon passed by the group of travelers who had been walking in front of the cart. There were six of them, each carrying a large pack and excitedly exchanging plans for what they would do when they got to Sillburg.

As Sinccah passed them, she began to ponder what she would do herself. Obviously, she needed to figure out why her mother had disappeared. In order to do that, she would need to talk to Ucksil. He was somewhat related to her after all, so he'd probably be willing to help her get established. He might even know what had happened. She grimaced. It was probably naive to think that way. She'd be fortunate to find anyone in all of Ucksland who knew, and it almost certainly wouldn't be the first person she talked to. She sighed. Still, she could hope.

She breathed in deeply as her gaze wandered into the mountain peaks. If all that failed, maybe Ucksil could help her find the mage who owed her family a favor. Her aunt had assured her this great mage was living somewhere in Ucksland, so he shouldn't be that hard to find. Hopefully, the mage would be willing to teach her more magic. Perhaps she could even become a great mage under his training. A look of determination formed on her face. She was sick of being a nobody. No matter what happened, this was her chance to change that.

She began fidgeting with her pendant again and a thought slipped into her mind. Perhaps she could find her mother. Maybe it was foolish to even consider such an idea, but a part of her still held out hope. It had been forever since she'd heard from her mother, so it was unlikely either of them would be able to recognize each other. Still, she had so many questions and couldn't help but hope that maybe, somehow, she might find her.

Sinccah noticed she'd passed several more groups of people while she'd been pondering her future. Additionally, she'd finally gotten far enough forward that the child's screams could only be heard distantly. Hopefully, the child's father had been genuine with his offer. If the wailing ever stopped, it'd be nice to stop putting so much stress on her ankle. She looked up at the massive peaks that flanked the caravan. Even though the summer was drawing to a close, large patches of snow still decorated the gaps between the tallest points. Her gaze drifted between the rocky peaks. Most of the Mountains of Spiirige were already behind them. Only two large mountains remained: the two brothers for whom the pass was named: Jelmont on the northern side, and Nelmont to the south. Each of these jutted slightly from the main range, which made the space between them comparatively flat. She marveled at the size of Jelmont. It wasn't the tallest mountain in the surrounding range, but the unobstructed view from the mighty peak to the flat base was nothing short of incredible. Her eyes darted over to the smaller brother: Nelmont. It was fairly short compared to the other mountains she'd been traveling through, but it was impressive all the same. She followed the patchy trees upward until she found herself staring into a bright-green patch of grass that formed a collar for the rocky summit.

Sinccah stumbled over a loose cobblestone. She caught herself with her injured foot and grimaced at the sharp spike of pain. She breathed in deeply before pressing forward. As she did, her mind thought back to the couple. They seemed like nice people. She frowned as she realized she hadn't bothered to learn their names. Hopefully, that wouldn't cause problems later.

She continued toward the front of the caravan, passing a handful of other carts and several groups of people on foot. As she tried to squeeze between two smaller groups of people, an excited squeal sounded right beside her, and the small arm of a young girl was suddenly thrust nearly into Sinccah's face. She recoiled at the motion and the sound, but she found her eyes following the girl's arm toward the mountain stream. A scowl quickly formed on her face as she determined that the child was simply pointing at a small bird that was hopping between the nearby rocks. Really?! All this over some silly bird? She didn't have time for such nonsense. She stepped forward and set her hand on the girl's arm. Pushing it downward, she stepped through, giving the girl an annoyed snarl as she did. The girl cowered before burying her face in the cloak of another traveler.

Sinccah rolled her eyes and quickened her pace, avoiding the judgmental glances from the girl's companions. Her face curled back into a snarl. Children. She breathed in deeply and shook her head. The next set of travelers rode in an ornately carved carriage. They were the only people in the entire caravan who gave the impression of wealth; all the other travelers were simple craftsmen or farmers. Apparently, they were looking for a new opportunity in Ucksland. She began to wonder whom the elaborate carriage belonged to—perhaps some rich merchant who was carrying on trade over the mountains, or maybe even a nobleman who simply had some business to attend to.

She tried to think back to the start of the expedition. Had there been anyone who truly looked wealthy? As she drew near the carriage, her eyes were drawn to a horseman who was traveling alongside the carriage. He was a young man, not more than thirty, with a weathered look that told Sinccah that this probably wasn't his first trip over the mountains. His hair was snarled together into a ratty brown mass, and his eyes moved around nervously. First, he would look intently at the carriage, then his eyes would dart off the path into the mountains. He fidgeted with an unstrung bow, occasionally reaching for the quiver that was strapped to his saddle. Sinccah hadn't noticed that her pace had slowed as she had been thinking about the carriage, and she soon found that she had been walking between the horseman and the carriage for several seconds. She wondered why this man was here, as he seemed far too nervous to simply be heading over the mountains. Suddenly, he turned toward her with a deep scowl.

"Move along," he said gruffly.

"Oh, uh, sorry," Sinccah stammered, "I didn't mean to stare."

"I don't care," he said dismissively.

"Ah, right," Sinccah replied, "I was just wondering—"

"None of your business," the man growled. His mouth curled into a snarl, and he thrust his chin forward. "Ealch."

Sinccah recoiled at the vulgarity, then scowled. While such a term would've brought horror in Lady Dove's court, it was only reasonable to expect such words in the wilds of Ucksland. "Sorry," she mumbled as she quickened her pace to get ahead of both the horseman and the carriage.

After a few seconds of rapid walking, she turned to look back at the horseman. It seemed he had resumed his previous rhythm of nervous glaces. His eyes briefly met hers, and he scowled at her again. Sinccah spun away and moved to the other side of the path so that a cart would block her from his view. As she did so, she became aware of the gurgle of water. She looked up to see the path in front of her had begun to slope gently downward, taking the small roadside stream with it. Her eyes were instantly drawn to the large swath of terrain that now stretched in front of her.

Ucksland. They'd nearly made it over the mountains! Her gaze swept over the vast land. On her left, she noted an enormous expanse of flat land, which the maps had called the Plains of Shoon. To her right was Sirlwood, the great forest of southern Ucksland. Near the border between the two, on the southern edge of the open land, the River of Sorrow flowed away from her toward the distant sea. She paused for a moment to marvel at the sight, but the sound of footsteps behind her pushed her back into motion. As she walked, she looked over the portion of the caravan that was still in front of her. Several dozen people traveled on foot with large packs on their backs. They were dotted with a handful of people riding horses, and perhaps twenty carts pulled by various animals. In the very front was Vistimmot, the powerful old mage responsible for keeping the caravan safe from dragon attacks. He sat tall atop a large horse and truly had an aura of confidence. Sinccah had talked to him briefly before the caravan had set out, and he'd made a vague offer to teach her some magic during the journey. Hopefully, he'd meant that.

Sinccah spent the next quarter hour trudging through the front half of the caravan. As she neared Vistimmot, she made an effort to stop limping. It hurt to walk, but she couldn't let this mage see that. Not when she needed to make a good impression. She walked somewhat stiffly up behind the old mage. He wore a simple outfit. Had it not been for the golden circlet he wore beneath his thin silver hair, he would have been nearly indistinguishable from the commoners who accompanied him. Sinccah jogged up alongside him.

"Excuse me, Vistimmot?" she said with far less confidence than she had intended.

Vistimmot brought his horse to a halt and turned to Sinccah. "Ah hello, young lady!" he said with a gentle smile. "What can I do for you?"

Sinccah looked up at the tall mage, finding it suddenly hard to get her words straight. Now that he was facing her, she could see his old eyes looking at her with a kind expression. He wore seven fist-sized gems on a belt that ran from his shoulder to his hip. The gems were each a slightly different color and were arranged to transition from a vibrant green at his shoulder to a deep blue at his hip. Sinccah recognized these as maggni: small gems used to store magical energy. Even the royal arch-mage who had attended one of Lady Dove's banquets had only carried five. Just how advanced was this mage?

"When we were first setting out," Sinccah finally managed with as much optimism as she could muster, "you said you would teach me some magic. I was hoping now would be a good time for that."

Vistimmot gave a knowing smile. "Of course, but first, what is your name?"

"Sinccah."

"Alright, Sinccah, what do you want to learn about?"

"Well," Sinccah answered, barely managing to contain her newfound excitement. "I heard you were something of an expert on fire magic, so perhaps you could teach me some of that?"

"An expert?" Vistimmot said with a chuckle. "Is that what they call me? I suppose I have picked up a few things over the years. Is there anything in particular you want to learn?"

"I don't really know any fire magic," Sinccah responded, "so just about anything would be fine. Do you think you could teach me a fireball spell?"

"Do you have much experience with projectile spells?" Vistimmot asked as he urged his horse into a walk.

"No," Sinccah admitted, her excitement waning as she began walking to keep pace with the mage. "I can only do shield spells and some basic healing."

Vistimmot turned to her suddenly. "Don't be so hard on yourself! The correct use of shield spells is very complicated, and any proficiency in healing magic is no small accomplishment. If you can manage them, you are already a fine mage. However, if you are not experienced with ranged magic, it would likely be better to start with a flamewisp. It is a simple utility spell, but it will help you with all future fire spells."

"Oh," Sinccah said, trying to hide her disappointment. "I guess I was hoping to learn something more impressive."

"Perhaps we will get to those." Vistimmot said gently. "We still have at least three days until we reach Sillburg. That should be plenty of time for you to learn something *impressive*."

The additional emphasis on the last word rekindled Sinccah's excitement. "You think so?" she asked hopefully.

"Of course!" Vistimmot said with a smirk. "They don't call me an expert for nothing!"

Sinccah tried to remain composed but found herself chuckling at the eccentric old mage. "Thank you," she said smiling. "Where do we begin?"

"Well ..." Vistimmot said thoughtfully, "I think it would be best if we—"

Sinccah gasped as she took a wrong step and pain shot through her ankle, causing her to stumble to her knees.

Vistimmot jumped from his horse. "Are you all right, Sinccah?" he said as he reached out and helped her back onto her feet. "Are you injured somehow?"

"I'm alright," Sinccah said with a grimace. "I tripped on the path a few days ago, and apparently my ankle hasn't quite healed yet."

"You're pushing yourself too hard," Vistimmot said sympathetically.

"I wanted to learn some magic," Sinccah said stubbornly. "I'm not going to let a sprained ankle get in the way of that."

"I see you are persistent," Vistimmot said with a knowing smile. "That's an admirable trait in a developing mage. You'll do great things if you can keep that attitude."

"Really?" Sinccah asked with a hint of pride.

"Of course," Vistimmot replied with a fresh smirk, "supposing that you consider what I do great. First, however, we are going to get your ankle patched up."

He turned to a boy sitting in the ox-drawn cart just behind them. "Young man! How would you feel taking the reins of this expedition?"

The boy's head jerked up. "You really mean it, mister Vistimmot sir?"

"Yes, just help this young lady onto your father's cart for me."

The boy beamed as he leapt from the cart and ran to help Sinccah. She cringed at the boy's excessive excitement but handed him her pack before hobbling to the cart herself. The boy helped her climb on before sprinting to Vistimmot's horse and excitedly clambering into the saddle.

"Look Dad!" he yelled, gently nudging the horse forward. "I'm leading the caravan!"

The boy's father smiled as he waved at the boy. He then turned to Vistimmot, who was climbing into the cart himself. "Thank you, sir," he said, "I didn't realize you overheard my son's earlier request. Is there anything else we can do for you?"

"Nah," Vistimmot grunted, "it is my pleasure. The temporary use of your cart will be more than enough."

"Very well," the man said, "you have use of it as long as you need it."

"Excellent," Vistimmot said before turning to Sinccah with a satisfied grin. "This will be a better environment for teaching anyway." His expression changed as he looked at the scowl Sinccah now wore. "Is something wrong?"

"Somewhat," Sinccah said. She lowered her voice and leaned closer to the old mage. "Isn't it a bit foolish to let a boy lead the caravan like that?"

Vistimmot gave her a puzzled look, "What ever would be the problem with it?" He gestured toward Sinccah's foot, and she pulled it up onto a couple of bags that sat between the two of them on the cart.

"It's just ..." Sinccah said before her voice trailed off. Vistimmot put his hand on her ankle and she could feel the subtle pain of healing magic. "What would happen if the caravan were attacked right now? That boy isn't going to know what to do."

"No, I suppose he won't," Vistimmot said as he took his hand off Sinccah's ankle, "but I'm hardly out of reach. Besides, do you see how happy he is?"

"Sure," Sinccah grunted as she pulled her foot from the bags and tested it on the floor of the cart. "I just don't think the boy's happiness is worth the risk to the rest of the caravan."

"Sinccah," Vistimmot said softly, his face turning to one of pity, "are you always this bitter?"

"What?!" Sinccah said angrily. "How can you even ask that?"

Vistimmot's face contorted into a sorrowful frown. "My apologies. Perhaps I can clear something up for you." He gestured toward the mountains on either side of the path. "We are currently in the steepest part of the pass. For the next several hours, there are no ways on or off the road. The only potential risk to the caravan right now is dragons, and if they attacked us, it would matter very little where exactly I was."

Sinccah bit her lip. "I guess that makes sense."

"I shouldn't have intruded like that," Vistimmot said with a frown. "Your personnel matters shouldn't be my concern. However," he said, a faint smile returning to his face, "for me, there is nothing that brings back good memories like joyful children."

"I guess I don't share that sentiment," Sinccah said flatly. "Most of my memories of children come from my time working as a nurse-mage for Lady Dove."

"You took care of a noblewoman's children?" Vistimmot asked.

"Yes," Sinccah spat, "and it was awful."

"Sorry to hear that," Vistimmot sighed, "but I would encourage you to keep an open mind. Not all children are raised thinking the world bows to them."

"Perhaps," Sinccah grumbled, her voice tinged with annoyance. "I guess I just don't care for them."

"Fair enough," Vistimmot said, "but enough personal discussions. I think it is about time we started learning some magic."

———◄○►———

Sinccah clenched her eyes closed, trying desperately to concentrate. She felt a tingling on her fingertips, and—heat? Her eyes shot open and beheld a small wisp of fire dancing above her outstretched hand. She'd done it! The flame suddenly withered and died, leaving Sinccah to drop her hands to her sides as she slumped in exhaustion.

"Nice work!" Vistimmot exclaimed as he clapped his hands together. "You just successfully cast a flame spell!"

"Yeah," Sinccah responded, her mental fatigue robbing her voice of the excitement it would've had otherwise. She'd been working on casting that one spell for the last three hours, and it had certainly taken its toll.

"You did marvelously," Vistimmot said with a kind smile. "Merely casting a brand new spell after only a few hours of training is quite impressive. You must have had an excellent teacher!" The old mage chuckled warmly, and Sinccah couldn't help but smile. Vistimmot had continued his curious mannerisms throughout the entirety of the magic lesson. He was certainly a bit odd, but Sinccah couldn't help but find him endearing.

"Thank you," she said as she sat up straight. "I honestly didn't think your teaching offer was genuine, but I really appreciate all this."

"I understand," Vistimmot said as he leaned back and looked up the road. "And it is my pleasure."

"Do you normally give magic lessons to your fellow travelers?" Sinccah asked.

"Oh yes," Vistimmot said as he turned back to Sinccah with a thin smile. "I started giving out lessons a bit ago, and I haven't stopped yet."

"Really?" Sinccah said in surprise. "How many students have you had?"

"One so far," the old mage said calmly as his smile deepened.

Sinccah shot a glance at Vistimmot, who began chuckling. "So just me," she said.

"What can I say?" Vistimmot said as he held up his hands in mock surrender. "Knowledge of this sort is valuable. I'm sure you were surprised that I was giving it out for free. There are not many left who still do."

"Mages used to offer teaching without charging for it?!" Sinccah blurted out.

"Yes," Vistimmot said with a sigh. "But that was long ago, before the rebellion. After that, everyone got more careful, and the free exchange of ideas all but died. I suppose it makes sense. Had there been fewer mages, the rebellion wouldn't have been so costly."

"Oh?" Sinccah said, her curiosity piqued. "Do you remember the rebellion?"

"I wish I didn't," The old mage answered. His face suddenly contorted in pain. "Back then I was still young, still learning the ways of magic myself. I don't want to relive those memories." He shook his head before turning to look up the road once more. "The king was right though, something needed to be done to stop future bloodshed."

Sinccah gazed intently at the mage as he stared down the road. She hadn't really thought about how old he must be, but if he had vivid memories of the Son's Rebellion, then he must be nearly seventy. Perhaps even older. She began to wonder what had caused him to take up work guarding caravans after starting his life like that. Particularly if he had terrible memories from the rebellion. As she opened her mouth to ask, she thought better of it. It was probably best to avoid opening the old man's wounds. Maybe she could direct the conversation in a different direction.

"Is that why you have extra maggni?" Sinccah finally asked. "Because you're not actually a part of the royal mages?"

Vistimmot turned slowly back to her. "Correct. By the time they were formed, I was already capable of teaching myself."

"Wasn't there a large group of people like that?" Sinccah asked, her curiosity getting the better of her.

"There was once," the old mage said, showing no discernible emotion. "Over a couple of decades, the group slowly merged into the royal mages until there was basically no one left."

Sinccah looked at Vistimmot in amazement. "But you never did?"

"No," he said cautiously and deliberately, "I never did. I never quite agreed with their policies of restricting who could learn magic. Particularly spells like the ones you know." His voice became more agitated. "What harm would it do the world to have more healers and protectors in it?"

"I guess I never thought about that," Sinccah admitted. She paused briefly as the cart lurched over a rock. "Does it bother you that I asked to learn a fireball spell?"

A faint smile returned to Vistimmot's face. "Being a protector is more than just casting shields."

Sinccah gave him a confused look. "Aren't there better spells for incapac-
itating people than fireballs?"

"Of course," the old mage responded, his usual smirk returning. "But you
did ask to learn a fire spell."

"I'm not sure I understand," Sinccah said as she tilted her head slightly.

"Do this for me," Vistimmot said as he leaned in. "When you do learn how
to cast a fireball, from me or from anyone else. Use it for good."

Sinccah's mind raced. Of course she could do that, and she intended to,
but what did he mean by using it for good? Did he have something particular
in mind? Her eyes darted to her feet. "I don't know if I can do that."

"Oh?" Vistimmot said as he leaned back into his seat.

"I need to ask a question first," Sinccah said as she looked at the old mage.

"Of course," Vistimmot replied, a faint smile spreading across his face,
"but I doubt I know the answer better than you do."

Sinccah tried to figure out what he meant. Eventually, she gave up and
asked anyway: "What exactly do you mean by using it for good?"

"If only I could answer that," Vistimmot said knowingly. "How about this:
promote kindness, not cruelty, and kinship, not conflict."

"I think ..." Sinccah said softly, "I think I can do that."

"Excellent," Vistimmot said as he turned to look up the road again.

"But," Sinccah continued with a sly grin, "I only have to do that while
using the fireball, right?"

"Well," Vistimmot said quickly as he turned back with a look of concern,
"that isn't exactly what I—" His eyes met Sinccah's, and the two started
chuckling. He regained his composure. "Perhaps I've taught you too much
already."

"Perhaps." Sinccah said, retaining her sly smile.

"Well," Vistimmot said as he gestured toward the path in front of them,
"it appears the mountains are opening up again. I best make sure the caravan
doesn't go astray."

"Oh," Sinccah said while trying to hide her disappointment. "I suppose that makes sense. Thanks again for the magic lesson, and ..." she paused, "for everything else as well."

"Young lady," the old mage said with a kind smile, "it is my pleasure."

As Vistimmot started to stretch his legs in preparation for standing, Sinccah blurted out a question. "Can we do this again tomorrow?"

"Perhaps," Vistimmot responded. "It depends on the state of the roads after we leave the pass. If everything is calm, I'll teach you some more. Otherwise, once we reach Sillburg, there's a book you can look for. It might be hard to find with the royal mages always confiscating them, but their reach is limited in Ucksland. Regardless, it's called *A Maze Ablaze*. It was the book I learned the most from when I was around your skill. Besides," he chuckled to himself, "it has a healthy emphasis on fire magic."

"Thank you so much!" Sinccah exclaimed. "I'll be sure to see if I can find it."

"Of course," Vistimmot said with a nod. "For now, you should get some rest. You clearly need it."

Sinccah smiled. Finally, she would have the opportunity to learn powerful magic. She couldn't even remember how long she'd been dreaming of this.

The man in the front of the cart suddenly lurched backward. "What the ..." he muttered.

Sinccah and Vistimmot turned to follow his gaze. On the side of the road stood a half dozen jagged black structures. Sinccah's eyes widened as she realized they were the burnt remains of wooden carts.

"The work of dragons, no doubt," Vistimmot mumbled as he rose to his feet. He let out a soft sigh before calling out: "Young man! It seems I have need of that fine steed once more!"

Sinccah watched the old mage return to his horse and climb into the saddle. He led the caravan cautiously around the charred remains. As they moved past, Sinccah shuddered. She'd never given that much thought to dragons before. She glanced cautiously into the sky, the sharp mountain peaks taking on a distinctly more foreboding feel. Were dragons lurking among them? She glanced back at

Vistimmot. The old mage would be able to keep them safe, right? Her eyes suddenly caught a flash of white from among the burnt wreckage. Was that a bone?! She lowered herself deeper into the cart as she scanned the charred remains. The fire must have burned out days ago. Did that mean the dragon was gone?

A few agonizing minutes passed as the caravan slowly drifted past the blackened site. The pace quickened slightly as each group of people came to the other side. Sinccah once again scanned the sky. As she lowered her gaze, she found her eyes darting between dark patches in the mountains above her. Nothing stirred. Clearly, whatever dragon had done this hadn't stuck around. Feeling somewhat safer, she settled down in the cart. Her mind danced between excitement over her new mentor and fear of the dangers of Ucksland. Eventually, her mental exhaustion got the better of her and she drifted from consciousness.

A sharp crack roused Sinccah from her light sleep. She looked up to see the sun just beginning to dip below the tall mountains behind them. Rolling over and sitting up, she glanced toward the front of the caravan. The boy had rejoined his father at the front of the cart and had just hurled a small rock into a stone outcropping that partially blocked the path. A scowl slowly formed on her face as the boy reached down, grabbed another small rock, and threw it against the rocks.

As he reached toward the seat to grab another stone, Sinccah let her annoyance be known: "Can you stop that?" she hissed.

The boy spun around as fear swept over his face.

Sinccah forced a smile onto her face. She took a sharp breath before trying to make her voice sound sweet: "You don't want the dragons to hear you, do you?"

"No, ma'am," the boy responded, cowering slightly.

Sinccah could see the boy's father glance back at her judgmentally. Foolish boy. She frowned. It didn't matter. She squeezed her eyes shut before shaking her head and glancing up at the mountains. The peaks of the two brothers were already behind them. Trees had become more common, and the terrain had started to level out. Her eyes were drawn to the dark patches on the eastern side of the mountains where dragons might still lurk. She pulled her gaze away and turned back to the road. Just in front of the cart she was on, she could see Vistimmot sitting tall atop his horse. She thought back to their lesson. He had been so encouraging throughout, even though she certainly hadn't been that impressive. After all, she had only barely cast a weak spell after three hours of careful instruction. There was no way she'd even be able to cast it again without more of his instruction. Even so, the old mage had continued to encourage her. For some reason he seemed to believe in her.

Her mind started to drift as she wondered why. It didn't make sense for such a powerful mage to take on a student he'd just met, and what was all the talk about doing good? He didn't even know her; how did he know she wouldn't just use the spells he'd taught her for evil? Perhaps she could just ask him. Would that make everything awkward? Maybe. However, she couldn't think of a better option. She got up, hopped off the cart, and walked briskly up beside him.

"I see you're up," Vistimmot said as he turned to her with a smile. "Hopefully, your time was quite restful."

"It was good," Sinccah said with pleasantness that was slightly marred by her annoyance at the boy for waking her, "but I have a question for you."

"For me?" he said with a smirk. "Are you sure you can't find a better mage to ask?"

Sinccah shook her head. "I could probably find a saner one, but you seem to be the only mage around."

"Now now, young lady," Vistimmot chuckled with his usual grin. "From where I am sitting, I see two mages."

"Oh," Sinccah said in mock surprise as she turned to scan the caravan behind them. "Actually though," she said, turning back to the old mage, "I'm quite sure you're the only person who can answer it."

Vistimmot tilted an eyebrow. "Perhaps you think too highly of me."

"That isn't what I meant," Sinccah said as she shook her head in amusement. "What I mean to ask you is this: why did you decide to teach me? I know you and I are the only mages in this caravan, but I'm nothing special, and you don't even know me. Why would you even bother?"

Vistimmot looked up at the mountains that surrounded them. "Perhaps I know more about you than you think."

Sinccah pulled away. "What do you mean?" she asked, suddenly wary of the old mage.

"Your pendant," Vistimmot said as he gestured toward Sinccah. "I've seen it once before."

"What?!" Sinccah exclaimed. How was that even possible? She'd had the pendant since she was five. How had this old man seen it?

"Your mother gave that to you," Vistimmot said with a kind expression, "didn't she?"

"Well," Sinccah stammered, "yes, she gave it to me nearly twenty years ago, and …" her voice drifted off as tears threatened to form in her eyes. "I …" she started before bowing her head. "I never saw her again after that." She cringed slightly as she moved her hand in front of her mouth. She'd said too much.

"Sinccah," the old mage said. Sinccah felt a hand on her shoulder. She looked up to see that Vistimmot had dismounted and was now standing in front of her with tears in his eyes. "I'm sorry to hear that she never made it back to you."

Sinccah pulled away and returned her gaze to the ground. She didn't want this conversation, but she needed answers. She breathed in deeply. "I never even knew her," she said softly. "Why did she leave me?"

"Sinccah," Vistimmot said again.

"Why didn't she come back?!" Sinccah screamed. She cowered slightly as she felt the gaze of the other members of the caravan falling onto her.

The old mage put his hand on Sinccah's shoulder again. "Sinccah," he said softly, "I don't quite know why she left you, but I'm sure she did everything in her power to come back to you."

"So she's dead?" Sinccah cried. She looked up at Vistimmot, her eyes probing for resolution.

"That," Vistimmot said sorrowfully, "I don't know. When she came back from giving you that pendant, she went north to speak with the goblins. She never returned. In the years that followed, I started hearing stories about the goblins in the area going crazy, but I never could figure out what really happened."

Sinccah shook her head as her face twisted in sorrow. "She left me for goblins?"

"I'm afraid it's not that simple," Vistimmot said as he gestured down the path. Sinccah looked up to see that the first few carts of the caravan had already passed by. She started walking after them. Vistimmot joined her, leading his horse.

"What do you mean by that?" Sinccah asked as she turned toward the old mage.

Vistimmot sighed. "You don't know about your father, do you?"

"No," Sinccah said, "I never knew him."

Vistimmot nodded. "I'm not sure your mother truly did either."

"What!" Sinccah exclaimed.

"I never met your father," Vistimmot said with a hint of anger. "From what I heard about him, I don't know that I would've wanted to. He was obsessed with the seas. In particular, he was set on being the first captain to return to Tempouriah."

Sinccah nodded stiffly at the mention of the continent to the south. Sea captains had been attempting the voyage for centuries, at the cost of thousands of lives.

"It seems to me your mother and father couldn't have wanted more different things," Vistimmot continued. "Your mother loved this island, and your father wanted nothing more than to get off of it." He shook his head. "I'm not quite sure what she saw in him."

"How did you know my mother?" Sinccah asked suddenly.

"Oh!" the old mage exclaimed. "I suppose I've gotten ahead of myself. Your mother and I used to guard caravans over this pass together."

"Really?" Sinccah asked in surprise. "Just how long have you been doing this?"

"Ever since the rebellion ended," Vistimmot said, a twinge of sorrow coloring his voice.

"Oh," Sinccah said awkwardly. "Did you meet my mother in this pass?"

"Not quite," Vistimmot said with a chuckle. "It was in Crystand Pass to the north. I had already been doing this for nearly three decades when I met her. She was coming over the pass to try to meet with goblins. At the time, I tried to discourage her. After all, the relations between goblins and humans were even more strained in those days. It seemed she was successful though, as she was often traveling back and forth over the mountains."

"So you got to know her by guarding the mountain passes?" Sinccah interjected.

"Yes," Vistimmot replied. "Over time we became something of partners. Seeing as she was traveling over the mountains anyway, I figured it would be better for both of us if we worked together. After all, the dragons were far more aggressive back then."

"My mother fought dragons?" Sinccah asked in shock.

"Why yes!" the old mage said with a smile. "Several times even. She had such precise knowledge of shield spells. It honestly put me to shame."

"I never knew any of that," Sinccah said sadly.

Vistimmot put his hand on Sinccah's shoulder. "You hardly had an opportunity."

"I suppose so," Sinccah admitted. "Where does my father come into all of this?"

"Ah yes, your father," Vistimmot said with disappointment. "Your mother must have met him when she traveled down south. She was trying to get the support of a noble family so that she could continue her research with the goblins. As far as I can tell, they fell for each other almost instantly. For nearly a year, she didn't return to the mountains. I'm not sure exactly what happened to her during that time, but when she finally did return, she had changed. She was broken somehow. Apparently, your father had set sail for Tempouriah under the cover of a storm. I guess he thought that would protect him from dragon attacks."

"Captain Ekkmund was my father?!" Sinccah exclaimed.

"So you do know of him," Vistimmot said sorrowfully.

"I think everyone does," Sinccah said with dismay. "He was considered the greatest fool of the last few decades. Who sails into a raging storm to avoid dragons? I never thought my father was that Ekkmund."

"Your aunt never told you?" Vistimmot asked.

"No," Sinccah replied, "she never really talked about my parents after my mother disappeared. Though," Sinccah paused, "I don't think she ever mentioned him. Even when I was younger, he never seemed to come up."

"It is possible your mother never even told her," Vistimmot suggested. "From what I can tell, he set sail just after you were born."

Sinccah turned to the old mage in shock. "Really? He just abandoned my mother and me to attempt that foolish voyage?"

"That's how it would seem," Vistimmot responded. "His decision completely crushed your mother. When I saw her next, she had already put you in the care of her sister. She told me she didn't think she could raise you herself. She figured your aunt and uncle would do a better job than she ever could."

"Oh," Sinccah said in dismay. "So she abandoned me because my father abandoned us."

Vistimmot stopped suddenly and turned to Sinccah. "She never meant to abandon you. That much was always clear to me. I'm not sure why she did what she did nor why she insisted on going back to the goblins. Whenever we met, she would talk about you and how she needed to finish her research so she could finally stay with you. Apparently, she had learned a great deal about what happened after the Withering but could never quite piece everything together. Wherever she brought it up, she would always make it sound ominous, as if some great doom would come upon the island if she didn't figure it out."

Sinccah frowned. "I doubt her academic research was worth abandoning me."

"It's not my place to say if her actions were justified," Vistimmot said sorrowfully. "However, you should know that she worked tirelessly to make sure your aunt would be able to take care of you. For five years after you were born, she went back over the mountains constantly to make sure her sister had everything she needed. I'm confident she wanted to come back to you after she figured it all out."

Sinccah shook her head in disbelief as the pair resumed their walking. "My aunt never told me any of that."

"Perhaps ..." Vistimmot said sorrowfully before pausing for a few seconds, "she also felt abandoned."

Sinccah turned to Vistimmot in surprise. "I didn't think about that. It ..." her voice trailed off. "It would actually make a lot of sense."

"I feared as much," the old mage said with a sigh. "Perhaps now you understand the answer to your initial question."

Sinccah had already forgotten what she had first asked. She started thinking back. "Oh," she eventually said. "Yeah, I guess I understand why you were so willing to teach me magic."

"Good," Vistimmot said as they finally overtook the first cart in the caravan. "If you are feeling up to it, we can probably have another lesson tonight."

"I would love to," Sinccah said cautiously, "but you've given me a lot to think about, so I don't know."

"I understand," Vistimmot said. "You still have an hour or so to think about it. Tell me what you decide when we stop for the night."

"Of course," Sinccah said as she smiled at the old mage, "and thank you. If I had known you knew so much about my mother, I would have sought you out far sooner."

"You sure?" Vistimmot said, his face slipping into a sly grin. "I'm a pretty difficult mage to find." He alternated raising each of his eyebrows in quick succession.

Sinccah laughed. "I don't know about that."

"Honestly," the old mage said with a short sigh, "had I known how, I would've found you first."

Sinccah smiled. "Well, I'm glad we stumbled into each other."

"Indeed," Vistimmot said with a grin, "but next time you might want to avoid spraining your ankle to do it."

"You're very funny," Sinccah said, trying hard to sound upset.

"I'm honored to hear you think so," Vistimmot said with a bow. His face suddenly became more serious. "Did you ever find the message your mother left for you in that pendant?"

"There's a message?!" Sinccah exclaimed. "Where?"

"I'm not sure," Vistimmot said with sudden excitement, "but after your mother gave it to you, she told me it had a message hidden inside a secret compartment. Perhaps you should hop back on the cart and figure out how to open it."

"Sure," Sinccah said as she pulled the pendant in front of her eyes and began to study it with newfound interest. "Are you going to join me?"

"Unfortunately, no," Vistimmot said as he looked over the road in front of them. "We're exiting the pass soon, so I must be alert for threats. Do let me know what you find though!"

"Of course," Sinccah said as she walked back to the lead cart and climbed on.

The boy on the cart, apparently having forgotten the interaction they'd had earlier, turned to her as she climbed up. "Are you a friend of mister Vistimmot, ma'am?"

"Uh, somewhat." Sinccah answered, trying not to show annoyance at the boy's interruption. She looked intently at the pendant, inspecting every flower petal with newfound urgency.

"Do you think he'll let me ride his horse again?" The boy asked loudly.

Sinccah looked up at him as a scowl formed on her face. "If you don't mind," she growled, "I'm a little busy at the moment."

The boy's father turned to him. "That's enough questions for the young woman. I'm sure mister Vistimmot would be happy to answer your question himself when we set up camp tonight."

The boy looked briefly dejected but quickly returned to optimism. He turned to his father. "Do you think he'll let me ride again?"

The father shot Sinccah an irritated glance before turning back to his son. "I suppose we'll have to wait and see."

⸻◆⸻

Sinccah squinted at the pendant. That flower petal looked different. Didn't it? She moved the pendant closer to her eyes. No, nothing special about it after all. She let the pendant drop to her chest as she flopped backward into her seat. How was this secret chamber so hard to open? She'd been at this for almost an hour already and her eyes were sore from the intense strain. Had Vistimmot played some joke on her? No, he wouldn't do that, would he? It didn't make sense. He was a bit odd and certainly liked his jokes, but this would be too cruel. After everything they'd just talked about, there was no way he'd try something like that. Still, perhaps it'd be good to ask him if he knew anything else about the pendant. It really couldn't hurt. Sinccah looked up. Vistimmot was leading the caravan from much farther forward than he had previously been. He might not even hear her if she called to him. Besides, he had talked about how dangerous the area was. It'd be best to avoid distracting him.

Her gaze drifted from the path. A few minutes ago, they'd left confines of the sharp mountain slopes, and they were now traveling through the steep foothills. Sinccah looked into the trees that now flanked the path. They had already gotten quite thick, threatening to engulf the path entirely. She stared into the dark patches between the trees, where she could still see the terrain sloping upward to meet the mountain slopes. Already the sun had begun slipping behind the mountains, and the light was starting to dim. The forest was looking unnaturally ominous.

She shook her head, grabbed her pendant, and held it up. The light of the setting sun gleamed off the metallic face into Sinccah's eyes. She squinted as she inspected the metal disk. One of the flowers near the top suddenly stood out at her. It seemed to be surrounded by small wisps of golden flame. She turned the pendant and the illusion vanished. Had that section of the surface seemed brighter than the rest? She quickly rotated the pendant, and the appearance of flames returned. It certainly was brighter, but the glow was not on the flowers, like Sinccah had expected, but in the space between them. She began feeling around this area with newfound excitement. Perhaps it hid some sort of switch that opened the secret compartment. She ran her finger over the nearby flowers. They didn't feel any different. Did that mean there was no switch? But why would this space look different, then? She turned the pendant slightly, studying the golden flames that now seemed so clear. Did the flames mean something?

Suddenly, an idea came to her. Perhaps the flames were calling for heat. Some metals expand when heated. Maybe this pendant used that to hide the compartment. She pressed her thumb onto the gleaming flower. The heat from her hand should warm the metal somewhat. For several minutes she squeezed the pendant. It didn't seem to change. Perhaps the flames were actually calling for fire, or at least a much greater heat. She thought back to her lesson with Vistimmot. A simple spell like that would work. She held out her hand and tried to concentrate. It was no use. She was too excited. There was no way she could cast a spell she barely knew without more focus. She looked up at Vistimmot. He had drifted closer to the caravan. Certainly one of his spells could warm the pendant up enough to open it. Assuming that her idea about fire had been correct.

She watched the old mage glance about quickly through the trees. The distant whinny of a horse sounded from behind her. She turned to see that the horseman from the carriage was slowly riding toward the front of the caravan. A feeling of unease swept over her. Something wasn't right. She jumped from the cart and looked into the trees. She caught a glimpse of movement as a dark figure dashed between two of the trees.

"Vistimmot—" she started to call out.

"Who goes there?!" Vistimmot suddenly exclaimed as he projected a shell of shields around his person.

"Nobody move!" a harsh male voice called from in front of Vistimmot. Sinccah turned quickly as a few dozen men dashed onto the road from under the trees. In a matter of seconds the front of the caravan was surrounded. Sinccah looked at Vistimmot, who had calmly dismounted and was standing in the middle of the road. In front of him, a pair of cloaked figures emerged from behind a fallen tree. She glanced around; the caravan was trapped. The trees were far too thick, and the surrounding terrain far too uneven, so their only escape route was back through the mountain pass. Hardly a viable option.

"Very good," the harsh voice continued. It was now clear that it came from one of the two cloaked figures who stood in front of Vistimmot. "Now, if you would be so kind as to hand over your valuables, that would save us a great deal of time."

"Gillopp," Vistimmot said slowly, not betraying any emotions. "I didn't think you and your filth still came this far south."

"Silence, old man!" the other figure on the road yelled in a harsh, but noticeably female, voice.

The first figure, apparently Gillopp, turned to the other. "It's alright, Mikcalla," he said confidently. "The old fool simply wishes his end to come sooner." He raised his hand, and the men surrounding the caravan pulled up bows and nocked arrows. Sinccah fidgeted. Vistimmot needed her help; she was a mage after all. Admittedly, she didn't know any offensive spells, but she had become quite proficient in shield spells, maybe she and Vistimmot could take on these bandits!

"You're a fearsome group," Vistimmot said calmly as the shields around him dissolved, "but I'm afraid that you picked the wrong caravan to rob."

"You think you're so strong, do you?!" Mikcalla screeched.

"Oh no," Vistimmot said with a smirk, "but this caravan is almost entirely peasants. We are hardly carrying anything of value."

"We'll see about that!" Gillopp said, taking a step toward Vistimmot. "I think you'll find the content of this caravan is plenty valuable."

"I very much doubt that," Vistimmot responded. "I know how far you must've come to get to this pass."

"I'm sure you'll more than make it worth our while," Gillopp said arrogantly.

"Oh?" Vistimmot asked. "Perhaps you were right to come here. Maybe I really can make it worth your while. Are you looking for money? Or would you prefer renown?"

"We have no interest in your fake promises!" Mikcalla shouted. "Your words are nothing but rot!"

"Now, now, sister," Gillopp said as he held his hand in front of Mikcalla. "I do quite enjoy these dialogues with our victims."

"They're certainly not fake," Vistimmot said slowly, "but it appears you'd rather take the scraps these poor people have."

"You're forgetting something, old man," Mikcalla hissed. "You're leading this ealched caravan."

Vistimmot gave the two bandits a look of mock confusion. "You flatter me," he said grimly, "but I'm afraid that your estimation of me is incorrect."

Gillopp let out an amused snort.

"Step aside, wither-headed old fool!" Mikcalla shouted. "You're dead!"

"Is that so?" Vistimmot said, anger now clear in his voice. "We shall see about that."

"Shoot him!" Gillopp shouted. The surrounding men drew their bows and unleashed a flurry of arrows.

"No!" Sinccah screamed. She watched the arrows sail toward Vistimmot, but just before reaching him, they deflected off walls of faint yellow light that had suddenly appeared. One of the arrows sailed past the old mage and stuck his horse. The poor creature whinnied in pain as it bolted into the woods.

"Is that all?" Vistimmot asked. He spun suddenly, two balls or red fire issuing from his hands. The first struck a group of three archers who had been nearest to him. The spell exploded into flames, enveloping the men completely. The second was directed straight at the two bandits in the road. The spell exploded in front of them, and flames quickly wrapped around the pair, obscuring them from view. Screams filled the air as the three archers were caught in the blaze. As the fire died down around them, only one was still moving, and he merely rolled around on the ground, continuing to screech in pain.

"Keep shooting, you stupid clods!" came Gillopp's voice. Sinccah turned to where he had been. Both the bandit leaders were still standing, untouched by the flames.

"You'll have to do better than that, you ealched old man!" Mikcalla shrieked and threw a ball of white light toward Vistimmot. The spell and the second round of arrows arrived at nearly the same time. Once again, they were blocked, but this time the old mage staggered as the white light struck his shield.

Sinccah glanced between the bandits. She needed to do something! A gust of wind swept over the battle, and the scent of burnt flesh filled Sinccah's nostrils. The smell nauseated her, and she staggered forward against the cart. She pulled herself together and squinted through the smoke at the group of archers nearest to her. If only she knew a spell that she could use to attack them! A few more fireballs struck the bandits, and several scattered into the trees for cover. The trees nearest the road were already alight, and the bandits scrambled past them into the deeper forest. Sinccah looked at the bandit leaders, who still stood in the middle of the road, apparently able to block Vistimmot's spells with their own shields.

"Just die already!" Mikcalla screeched. She threw a flurry of spells toward Vistimmot. The old mage turned quickly as he threw up shields to block the spells. Sinccah noticed a group of archers as they poked out from the trees and loosed their arrows at Vistimmot. She squinted her eyes and projected her own shield spell to deflect the arrows. There was no way she would leave Vistimmot alone in this fight. The arrows deflected harmlessly off her shield. She felt her energy drain with each arrow. The shield had been too far away. If she really wanted to help, she would need to get closer, but if the bandits targeted her, she was dead. If only she had some of her own maggni! Then she could replenish her spent energy and use her shields from safety.

A group of bandits charged out of the trees with swords drawn. As the charged, Mikcalla threw another round of spells at Vistimmot. The spells were synced with another volley of arrows, which Sinccah managed to block with a set of shield spells. Vistimmot staggered as his shields absorbed the spells, but he still swept his hand toward the charging bandits and launched a ball of red fire. The spell exploded on a shield just before it reached the bandits. Sinccah could see Gillopp stagger as it hit. Pounding hooves sounded behind Sinccah, and she turned to see the horseman from the carriage ride quickly up beside her. He pulled his horse to a stop and drew his bow. Sinccah's eyes widened in horror as he aimed at Vistimmot and loosed. The arrow caught Sinccah off guard and flew by her. She whirled to look at Vistimmot. He hadn't seen the arrow! She threw up a shield at the last moment. The arrow shattered on the shield and its splinters fell harmlessly at Vistimmot's feet. Sinccah staggered as the shock of the arrow against her shield drained most of her energy. It had been a poor shield. She knew she needed to deflect the arrow to preserve her energy, particularly at that distance, but she hadn't had the time. The full force of the arrow was nearly too much to her. She collapsed against the cart, struggling to remain conscious.

The horseman turned toward Sinccah. "You're helping him!" he roared. He drew his bow and aimed it at Sinccah. "You'll die for that, wretch!"

Sinccah looked up in desperation as the horseman released his arrow. As it neared, she managed to throw up another shield that barely deflected the arrow. Apparently, it wasn't quite enough. The arrow sliced into her arm and she cried out in pain as she collapsed to the ground. The shields had taken too much from her: she was exhausted. There was no way she could cast another spell without fainting. If only she hadn't spent herself on the flamewisp! Her vision suddenly blurred and she felt herself drifting from consciousness. No! She couldn't fail now. Her vision cleared somewhat, and she looked up at the horseman. He was pulling another arrow from his quiver. A set of red explosions lit up the corner of Sinccah's vision as another round of fireballs exploded on some unprotected bandits. Screams again filled the air, briefly distracting the horseman. He turned back to Sinccah and drew his bow. Suddenly, a rock struck his horse, and it reared, throwing its rider to the ground.

Sinccah rolled under the cart and looked toward Vistimmot. The charging bandits were nearly upon him. He blocked another set of Mikcalla's spells and turned toward the incoming bandits. Sinccah watched as he released his own flurry of spells toward his attackers. Each spell was blocked by a well placed shield. Vistimmot turned toward the bandit leaders and threw a bright white spell at them. Simultaneously, he tossed two more spells toward the charging bandits. The first spell exploded on a shield, but the bright spell had disrupted Mikcalla and Gillopp enough that the second spell sailed into the first of the rapidly approaching bandits. The spell exploded into a cone of fire that engulfed the entire group.

"NO!" a voice screeched. Sinccah turned her head to see the horseman had recovered from his fall and was now staring at the explosion. He started running toward Vistimmot. "You wretched monster!" he screamed. "That was my brother!" He stopped to shoot his bow. Vistimmot glanced toward the sound of the man's yells and quickly deflected the arrow. He flicked a single white spell at the horseman before turning back to the bandit leaders. The horseman tried to leap out of the spell's path, but he hadn't been fast enough. The spell struck him in the shoulder, and a sickening crack echoed off the mountains. The horseman fell to the ground, shrieking as he grabbed his shoulder.

"Charge!" Gillopp called out. Sinccah turned to see him and Mikcalla rushing toward Vistimmot. The remaining bandit archers released a storm of arrows that sailed toward the old mage. Vistimmot cleanly blocked the arrows once again, but Sinccah could see he was tiring. She wondered if his maggni had finally run out, or maybe he couldn't draw the energy from them fast enough. She tried to crawl toward him, but her vision blurred. She squeezed her eyes shut, and a series of explosions sounded, followed by the screams of many men. A massive explosion suddenly rang out, and for a moment, everything was quiet. Then the screams returned. Sinccah looked up to see Gillopp standing over Vistimmot, blood covering his sword. All around them, she saw the writhing bodies of burning bandits. Gillopp stooped and picked up a round object: Vistimmot's circlet. The old mage had fallen. Sinccah wanted to scream, she wanted to do something, anything, but it was too late. Her dizziness returned, and she let her head flop to the ground.

"I'm so sorry, Vistimmot," she said quietly as tears started pouring down her face. "I couldn't help you." As she lay on the ground quivering, she could hear the bandits approaching the cart.

"How was that old coot so powerful?!" one of the bandits exclaimed.

"I don't know!" Mikcalla yelled. "Why didn't you stupid morons follow the plan?"

"Yeah, why didn't we charge to our deaths also!" another bandit called out.

"Silence!" Gillopp shouted. "There will be time for discussion later. For now, we have spoils to take." Sinccah looked up as Gillopp walked to the fallen horseman. "Jarnick," Gillopp said, "what valuables does this caravan hold?"

"Almost nothing," Jarnick groaned. "A rich merchant has a carriage in the back, but everyone else is broke."

"I see," Gillopp said as murmurs spread through the gathered bandits. "Well, you clods should make sure to grab it before we leave." A large group of bandits walked past Sinccah into the rest of the caravan. She could hear them extorting the other people she had been traveling with.

"The girl," Jarnick growled as he grimaced from his wounds. "The ealching girl under the cart needs to die."

Sinccah gasped. She looked out as Gillopp turned to her. She tried to crawl away, but her body was too exhausted. Gillopp walked up to the cart.

"Please, sir," the man whose son had ridden Vistimmot's horse said, "don't hurt the boy, he was scared, that's all."

"Shut up." Gillopp commanded. He reached under the cart and grabbed Sinccah's arm. She tried to pull away, but it was no use. She closed her eyes, and the bandit leader dragged her from under the cart.

"Let me kill her," Jarnick growled as Gillopp dropped Sinccah on the side of the road.

"No," Gillopp said flatly. He kicked Sinccah in the side. "Roll over," he snapped. Sinccah remained motionless just to spite him. He kicked her again. "I said." He grabbed her shoulder and rolled her onto her back. "To roll over." Sinccah opened her eyes and looked up at the gruff bandit. She tried to muster a look of defiance, but her face wouldn't cooperate.

"Does she have anything valuable?" Mikcalla asked as she walked up beside Gillopp.

"She had a golden pendant on earlier," Jarnick grunted.

"Oh, does she?" Mikcalla said as her face twisted into a smile. She bent down and began searching Sinccah.

"Please ..." Sinccah muttered as she struggled to avoid fainting. "My mother ..."

"Oh!" Mikcalla exclaimed as she straightened up with Sinccah's pendant dangling from her hand. "This really is a good find! I'll be taking this one." She looked down at Sinccah judgmentally. "I'm so sorry," she said mockingly. "I'll make sure to take good care of this." Sinccah tried to sit up, tried to protest, but it was no use. She closed her eyes, desperately hoping this was all a bad dream. She knew it wasn't, but facing the reality of the situation was too hard. Jarnick would get his way and the bandits would kill her. What reason did they have for doing anything else?

"I want her dead!" Jarnick yelled.

"And why is that?" Gillopp asked disdainfully.

"She blocked my arrow!" Jarnick shouted. "If not for her, we could have killed the ealching old man before he butchered—"

"Oh," Gillopp said flatly, "you want to protect your ego after your poor aim and inability to follow orders nearly cost all of us our lives. My answer remains the same: leave the girl alone. We don't kill for no reason."

"Oh sure," Jarnick said angrily, "you throw away forty men to kill an old mage, but then you have the gall to claim you aren't a wretched killer."

Sinccah cracked her eyes open again and glanced quickly between the two men.

"Jarnick," Gillopp said slowly, a subtle rage building in his voice, "I think you are forgetting who's in charge here."

Jarnick's face contorted in anger. "How—"

"Silence!" Gillopp commanded. He stooped and picked something off the road. He held the object toward Jarnick. "This is your bow?" he asked disdainfully.

Jarnick's face trembled in rage as he slowly nodded.

Gillopp waved another bandit over and handed him the bow. "You can have it back once you've learned how to use it." He turned back to Jarnick with a fierce glare. "Do you understand?"

"Yes, sir," Jarnick growled.

"Then we're agreed," Gillopp said forcefully. "Mikcalla, why don't you make sure our friend Jarnick gets back to camp safely. We wouldn't want him succumbing to his injuries." He turned toward the caravan. "We'll finish looting what we can and get out of here before Ucksil's men show up."

Sinccah's eyes slowly drifted closed as the bandits around her dispersed. She could hear Jarnick murmuring to himself as she faded from consciousness.

CHAPTER TWO

Sinccah became aware of subtle bouncing beneath her. She was moving. Her face twitched. She was in a cart, and that cart was rolling, presumably fairly slowly. A dull pain throbbed in her arm. She felt the rough texture of a cloth being rubbed against the skin near her arrow wound. Suddenly, the pain spiked as she felt the cloth tighten. Her eyes shot open. Kneeling beside her was the young woman whose infant son had been wailing. She was in the process of tying off a bandage around Sinccah's cut.

The woman recoiled at Sinccah's sudden movement. "You're awake!" she said excitedly, returning her hands to the bandage to finish tying it off. "We weren't sure you were going to make it."

Sinccah's face contorted in pain. "What happened?" she wheezed.

"The caravan was attacked!" The woman exclaimed. "They killed the old mage who was guarding us and looted everyone!" The woman started breathing heavily. "I suppose you knew all that already, didn't you?"

"Yeah," Sinccah said as she tried to sit up. Her head started pounding, and she gave up on the attempt. "I couldn't save Vistimmot." she said sorrowfully as she closed her eyes again. An awkward silence fell between the two women.

"I'm sorry," the woman said softly. She took a deep breath, then perked up slightly. "I, uh, never introduced myself when we first met. I'm Iszailliah." She gestured over her shoulder. "That's my husband, Filwurn, and little Aardinn."

Sinccah squeezed her eyes closed. "Sinccah," she replied

"Was Vistimmot a friend of yours?" Iszailliah asked tenderly.

Sinccah opened her eyes to look at the woman again. "Yes?" she said cautiously. She felt tears welling up in her eyes. "I want to believe he was," she continued.

"He and my mother were old friends, and ..." her voice drifted off as she choked back sobs. "I think he actually cared about me." Tears continued to flow as she mourned the loss of the old mage. He had been planning to teach her magic—she shuddered—and tell her what her mother had been like. That was all gone now!

"I'm so sorry," Iszailliah said sympathetically as she placed her hand on Sinccah's. Sinccah waited for her to continue, but Iszailliah just sat there with her head down and eyes closed.

"How long was I unconscious?" Sinccah asked.

Iszailliah startled. "Oh, uh, it has been nearly two days now."

"What?!" Sinccah exclaimed, pulling her hand away. She looked up at the sun. It was just beginning to brush the tops of the mountains. The peaks looked so distant now; little more than a jagged blueish-gray silhouette. The spells she had cast must have taken everything out of her. She was fortunate to have survived at all. She glanced quickly at their surroundings. They were in a forest, presumably the same one she'd noticed when she had first caught sight of Ucksland. The trees here were thinner, greener, and appeared friendlier. Over the edge of the cart, she could see that the road had become quite smooth, and the surrounding terrain was almost completely flat.

"Here," Iszailliah said, handing Sinccah a water skin, "you must be thirsty."

Sinccah turned back to Iszailliah and started to lift her hand to take the outstretched water. A spike of pain in her arm reminded her of the wound, and she let her hand drop. She tried to sit up and found her body somewhat responsive. She reached out her other hand and took the water. "Thank you," she said, suddenly realizing how thirsty she was. "What happened after the attack?" she asked before taking a drink.

"Well," Iszailliah started, "when the bandits first showed up, we saw a lot of light coming from the front of the caravan. Apparently, our mage took down quite a lot of them before they got him." Iszailliah stopped. "Sorry, you probably know all of that better than I do." She let out a sigh as she hung her head.

Sinccah could tell the poor woman was struggling, and recalling the events of the attack wasn't helping. Sinccah shook her head. If she were being honest with herself, she wasn't doing any better. "It's alright," she said softly. "Just tell me the details as you remember them."

Iszailliah looked up, and a pained smile appeared on her face. She looked back down before continuing. "After all the explosions of light, a handful of armed men came through the caravan. They extorted everyone and took anything that might have been valuable." Tears formed in her eyes.

Sinccah eyes widened. "Is your family alright?" she asked urgently as the cart suddenly lurched.

Iszailliah wiped her tears on her sleeve. "We're fine, thank goodness." She gestured toward the front of the cart where the child was lying peacefully in his father's arms. "But the brutes took everything of value!" Iszailliah held out a quivering hand. "Even my husband's tools! They're priceless," she said softly as she hung her head. "Made in Tempouriah before the days of Rilmn and passed from father to son ever since."

Sinccah felt a stab of guilt. If only she had been able to do more. She could have stopped this. "I'm sorry," she said, "I wasn't strong enough."

Iszailliah recoiled slightly. "What are you talking about?"

"I tried to save Vistimmot." Sinccah said sorrowfully as she bowed her head. "If I had been stronger, he wouldn't have died." Her face contorted in sorrow. "You wouldn't have lost anything."

Iszailliah put her hand on Sinccah's again. "You did your best," she said tenderly. "The people at the front of the caravan told us that you had been very brave. I can't imagine getting involved in that fight."

"But it wasn't enough," Sinccah said angrily as she once again yanked her hand away and buried her face in it. "I should have been able to do more." She pushed her hand up her face and began running it through her hair in frustration.

Iszailliah folded her hands together. "You still tried at least," she said kindly. "That's more than I would've been able to do."

Sinccah looked into the young woman's eyes. What she was saying was true, but it didn't excuse her failure. "I just wish I could've done more."

"I understand," Iszailliah said as she looked down. "I think it's fine to be upset, but this wasn't your fault. There's only so much you could've done."

"I suppose so," Sinccah said, trying not to betray the fact that she still didn't really believe it. "What happened after the bandits robbed everyone? Did they just leave?"

"Not exactly," Iszailliah answered as she started shivering. "As they were extorting everyone, they noticed a dragon flying overhead." Her body shuddered violently. "The brutes all fled into the woods! They abandoned us to our fate!" She bit her lip as she tried to calm down. "We all scrambled forward, but the dragon never attacked. It just circled slowly overhead for what felt like hours."

She sighed as the cart creaked sharply. "I guess it must have only been a minute or two though, because the monster was already gone when my husband and I got to the scene of the battle. We saw ..." Iszailliah's voice drifted off. She inhaled sharply before continuing. "We saw all the burned bodies," she said quickly. "We tried to pass them as fast as we could, but as we rushed by, I noticed you lying by the side of the road. At first, I assumed you were dead like our mage. I even lamented your fate to my husband. He was the one who insisted that we give you and our mage a proper burial. We had just been talking to you after all, and the old mage really gave it his all trying to protect us. We recruited a few other folks to help bury the mage. We gave him a proper grave and covered it in stones. But obviously we didn't bury you—because when we picked you up, we noticed you were still alive, so we took you with us."

"No one else in the caravan noticed me?" Sinccah asked dejectedly.

Iszailliah held her mouth agape as she looked at Sinccah. "I ..." she started awkwardly. "I guess I don't know. Maybe the other members were more eager to get out of there?" she suggested. "I think the dragon had everyone spooked, so they probably just rushed past."

Sinccah sighed. "I guess that would make sense. I just thought someone would have been more worried about me. I had just been talking to a man and his son ..." her voice trailed off as she recalled the way she had spoken to the boy and the looks his father had given her.

"Was this son still a lad?" Iszailliah asked.

"Yeah," Sinccah answered. "He couldn't have been more than ten."

Iszailliah nodded. "They came by after they learned you were still alive."

"Oh," Sinccah said, her spirits rising somewhat. "When did that happen?"

"At the camp that night," Iszailliah replied. "Everyone was talking about what'd happened, and apparently the two of them heard we'd picked you up and that you were still alive. That is actually their water skin," she said, gesturing toward Sinccah's hand. "They also brought your pack." She pointed to the bundle lying next to Sinccah. "The man said the bandits didn't take anything out of it."

"I suppose I should thank them for that," Sinccah said, still feeling a little sad about the fact that only the very last cart of the caravan had bothered to check on her.

"A lot of people were talking about your bravery," Iszailliah said as she leaned closer, "casting shield spells to keep the mage safe. I didn't even know you were a mage."

"Not a very good one," Sinccah said as she shook her head before lowering her voice. "I basically just transcribed manuals."

"Better than me," Iszailliah said with a thin smile. "It would be amazing to learn magic someday."

Sinccah looked into Iszailliah's excited eyes. She thought back to the kindness Vistimmot had shown her. "I, uh ... could maybe ..." she mumbled

"Oh no," Iszailliah said with a short laugh. "Don't try to teach me anything right now. I'm sure that would take far too long. Besides, you need to rest. You just spent the last couple of days passed out. There's no way you should expend your energy teaching me!" She turned around and grabbed a small pouch. "Here," she said, "there is some food in here; it should help you recover."

Sinccah took the pouch. "Thank you," she said.

Iszailliah nodded. "No problem!" she exclaimed. "I'm just glad we could help." She started to get up. "Now if you'll excuse me, I think my husband would appreciate a break from child duty."

Sinccah reached out and grabbed the woman's hand. "Iszailliah," she said with a pained smile, "you and your husband saved my life; if there's anything I can do for you, let me know."

"Of course," Iszailliah said cheerfully. "But for now, you should try to rest. I'll be back in a couple of hours to change your bandage."

"Thank you," Sinccah said as she slumped back, "Thank you for everything."

———◄○►———

The next few hours passed fitfully. From time to time, Sinccah nodded off as her body frantically tried to recover from the exhaustion she'd forced upon it. During the periods when she was conscious, her mind fixated on the events of the battle. If only she'd already been at Vistimmot's side. If only she'd noticed the bandits sooner. If only she'd paid more attention during her studies at the academy. Perhaps it would've made all the difference.

She thought back to how the battle had started. Vistimmot and the bandits had seemed to know each other. They certainly hadn't been friends, but they'd known each other's names. Sinccah began to ponder this. Why had the bandits come down to this pass? What was all this talk about Vistimmot making it worth their while? Did Vistimmot really have some way to do that? Or was it just a ploy to gain him more time? Perhaps it had all been another of his jokes.

Tears started running down Sinccah's face. There were so many things she still wanted to ask the old mage: about his past, about her mother, about magic, about the pendant. The pendant! Her hand darted into her chest but returned empty. She held her open palm in front of her eyes. Of course. The bandits had taken it. She had finally uncovered a real link to her mother, and now it was gone—snatched away as she lay helpless. She closed her eyes and combed her fingers into her hair. She closed her hand into a fist, grabbing a handful of hair. A scream threatened to escape her, but she suppressed it. She would only be more wretched if she alarmed the rest of the caravan.

Sinccah felt something touch her clenched hand. She opened her eyes to see Iszailliah sitting next to her. "Are you alright?" Iszailliah asked.

Sinccah lowered her hand. "Not really," she said, brushing away the hair that had fallen into her face.

Iszailliah put her hand on Sinccah's bandage. "Is it because of your arm?" she said urgently.

"No," Sinccah replied. "My arm is fine. At least, as fine as can be expected." She wiped the tears out of her eyes before moving her good arm to her chest. "It's just that I lost something very precious."

"I understand," Iszailliah said sorrowfully. "When my father passed away, I could hardly bear it. I see this Vistimmot meant a lot to you. Perhaps he was even something of a father to you."

Sinccah burst into tears. "If only I could've done something!" she screamed.

Iszailliah put her arm around Sinccah's shoulder. "It's alright."

Sinccah continued to sob. "I wish he were still alive."

"Of course you do," Iszailliah said and she squeezed Sinccah's shoulders. "You cared about him."

"I wish I'd never even met him!" Sinccah cried.

"I'm sure it feels that way," Iszailliah said softly. "I know the two of you had only just met, but try to remember the good times."

Sinccah thought back to the old mage's jokes and found a faint smile slipping onto her lips. "I guess so ..." she started to say before the image of Gillopp's bloody sword forced itself into her mind. She started sobbing anew.

"It's alright," Iszailliah said again. She bowed her head, and silence fell between the two women, broken only by Sinccah's periodic sobs. A flock of birds took offense to the presence of the caravan and took to the air as they let out a series of disgruntled cries. Sinccah watched as they slowly disappeared into the dimming sky.

After a few minutes, she turned back to her companion. "Thank you," she said softly.

Iszailliah smiled gently at her. "No problem." She pulled her arm off Sinccah's shoulder. "If it's alright, your bandage could use a change."

Sinccah looked down at her arm. Already the outside of the cloth had taken on a faint reddish hue. She nodded. Iszailliah began to untie the old wrapping. As she did so, Sinccah gazed in the direction the birds had flown. For a moment, her eyes settled on the closest of the mountains. "What did the dragon look like?" she asked quietly.

Iszailliah glanced up. "What did what look like?"

"The dragon," Sinccah answered. "The one that flew over the caravan."

"Oh, ah, yes," Iszailliah mumbled. "It was, uh, dark blue. Some of the other folks said it was a smaller one. One fellow even claimed that it was female."

"It was that close?" Sinccah asked in amazement.

"Apparently," Iszailliah answered as she squinted in the direction Sinccah was looking. "The man said he could tell it was female because it had a pointed ridge running down its chest. I guess only the female dragons look like that."

"I see," Sinccah said, her gaze still fixed on the open sky. "Did you see where she went?"

"No," Iszailliah replied, clearly flustered. "Well somewhat, I guess. It seemed to be flying south. Why do you ask?"

"Just curious," Sinccah said softly. "I wonder why she chose not to attack us."

"Oh," Iszailliah said as she tied off Sinccah's bandage. "I don't think any of us know. Maybe it thought we weren't worth the fight."

"Perhaps," Sinccah said with a wince. "I always thought dragons were more aggressive than that."

"I did too," Iszailliah said quickly. "Though, I'd never seen one before, so I'm hardly an expert."

"I suppose I still haven't seen one," Sinccah sighed as she turned back to Iszailliah. "It would have been a fascinating experience."

"If you say so," Iszailliah said, shaking her head. "If you ask me, it was downright frightful. I don't think I ever need to see one again." She paused. "Are you one of those mages who can cast that spell?" she asked suddenly.

"Which one?" Sinccah responded.

"The one that turns dragons into humans," Iszailliah answered quickly. "Apparently, it's how most dragons are killed."

"No," Sinccah said softly, "I don't know the dragon spell. It's far beyond my skill."

"Oh," Iszailliah said awkwardly. "I just thought you might be a dragon hunter since you seemed so interested in the dragon. I hear a lot of mages come to Ucksland to hunt dragons."

"Unfortunately no," Sinccah lamented. "Only the most powerful mages know that spell."

"Ah," Iszailliah replied. "I didn't know."

Sinccah nodded as silence fell between them. She shivered as a ray of sunlight slipped through an opening in the trees and washed over the cart. After a few seconds, she looked past the young woman to her husband. "What brought your family to Ucksland?"

"Oh," Iszailliah said, suddenly regaining some of her composure. "My husband is a carpenter. His brother owns a lumber mill over here. I wasn't particularly keen on getting into business with that man, but he said there was a lot of opportunity. Apparently, crowds of people are coming over the mountains these days, and they all need places to live."

"That makes sense," Sinccah said. "How do you feel about living so far from the capital?"

"I felt a lot better until now," Iszailliah lamented. "Ever since the attack, I can't help but feel like my family is never going to be safe here. The Witherome was one thing, but at least it doesn't move. Bandits and dragons are another thing altogether."

"Understandable," Sinccah said with a sigh.

"Why did you come to Ucksland?"

Sinccah looked down at her chest. "I'm not sure anymore," she said frankly. "I thought I might be able to figure out what happened to my mother or maybe find someone to tutor me in magic, but ..." Her voice drifted off as the tears returned.

"I'm sorry," Iszailliah said. "I'm sure you'll find something."

Sinccah's eyes widened as she inhaled sharply. She continued to stare downward. "I sure hope so."

A faint cry sounded from the cart in front of them. "Well, duty calls," Iszailliah said as she raised herself to a crouch. "Your arm is looking a lot better now. You should be able to start using it again soon."

"Thank you," Sinccah said. Iszailliah smiled before turning away and crawling toward the front of the cart. Sinccah turned to stare into the darkening sky. What *would* she do when she got to Sillburg?

Sinccah looked out over the stretching caravan. They'd left the forest and now moved through the southernmost edge of the Plains of Shoon. To her right, the trees of Sirlwood still kept the travelers company, and the road periodically slipped under the shelter of the outstretched branches. On the left, the plain stretched on for what seemed forever. Thick patches of tall grass rippled in the light breeze. She leaned back and stretched her shoulders. She'd fallen asleep after Iszailliah had left and hadn't woken until the next morning. It was a shame too. She had hoped to talk to the father at the front of the caravan while everyone was stopped for the night. Her gaze drifted toward his cart. Honestly, it wasn't that far away, and she was feeling considerably better; she could probably just walk up there. Her attention moved to the sun as it slowly rose in front of the caravan. This would be the last day before they came to Sillburg.

She turned to Iszailliah, who was sitting behind her in the cart, tending to her son. "I think I'm going to walk for a bit." Sinccah said.

Iszailliah looked up. "Oh, you're feeling that well already?"

"Well enough," Sinccah replied. "I was thinking it would be nice to talk to the folks at the front before we reach Sillburg."

"Alright," Iszailliah said as her son let out a short whine, "I'm sure they'd appreciate seeing you awake."

Sinccah looked down as the child began to squirm. "Uh, Iszailliah?"

"Yeah?"

"I gave you a rude look when we were coming out of the pass," Sinccah said quickly. "I'm sorry," she sighed. "I was a little on edge. It was supposed to be kindhearted, but I'm afraid it didn't come across that way."

"I understand," Iszailliah said with a knowing smile as she attempted to soothe her son. "The sound of wailing doesn't exactly ease my mind either."

"Right," Sinccah said sheepishly. "I just feel bad about it after everything you've done for me."

Iszailliah let out a brief laugh. "It's alright," she said. "And we were more than happy to help you."

Sinccah looked into Iszailliah's kind eyes. "Thank you," she said. "I just really want you to know how much I appreciate all this."

"No problem," Iszailliah said cheerfully, "Now get going, or we'll reach Sillburg by the time you leave!"

Sinccah shook her head with a smile as she hopped off the cart. As she took the first few steps, her body cried out in protest, but it was overruled. She pressed on and soon found the movement refreshing. A rustle sounded to her right, and she glanced over to see a rodent fleeing into the trees. Her smile deepened as she turned from the trees back toward the road. The smile quickly vanished as she began an all too familiar path toward the front of the caravan. Thoughts began pouring into her mind, replaying the events of the attack. She walked past the same group of six, who now walked with worried glances and grim faces.

She noticed the little girl who she had pushed aside. The poor child no longer looked excitedly at the surrounding beauty. Rather, she walked with her head down and her shoulder pressed against the people who walked beside her.

Sinccah felt her face start to contort. A feeling of dread threatened to overtake her. It was hard to not feel that something awful would happen when she got to the front once again. She recognized these thoughts as irrational, but it did little to soothe her mind. Her eyes darted to the trees as the rustling of a small bird snatched her attention. She put her head down and started walking faster.

A picture began to form in her mind: Vistimmot sitting atop his horse, extending a hand toward Sinccah as she reached the front of the caravan. Suddenly, he was engulfed in a swarm of arrows, and the image vanished. Sinccah gasped. It was only her mind playing tricks on her; still, she couldn't keep letting her mind wander like that. She began to think that this walk had been a massive mistake. It probably would've been better to just stay with Iszailliah. Perhaps then she could've avoided this awkward journey. She looked down at the road and focused on the pebbles she was walking over. The caravan must be quite close to Sillburg. Already the road had taken on a truly paved look. It was smoother than she would've expected. And old. Very old. So much so that the stones had been worn smooth. Her eyebrow arched. She hadn't really expected these lands to have good infrastructure. After all, Ucksil had only founded the city of Sillburg a couple decades ago. If she were being honest, she hadn't expected anything more than a collection of shacks.

Out of the corner of her eye, Sinccah suddenly noticed an ornate wheel. She looked up to see the merchant's carriage. Somehow, the fancy carvings looked beaten down, perhaps even damaged. An uneasy feeling began to creep up on Sinccah, and she quickly spun around. There was nothing there, only the space where the horseman had been riding when she first walked up. She shivered as she pushed herself to walk faster. The image of his enraged face and drawn bow tried to force themselves into her mind. That horrible man had been working with the bandits the whole time! They must've planted him in the caravan to scout for valuables. Her mind raced back to her pendant. If only this bandit hadn't been here, then the others might not have even noticed it. Sinccah suddenly realized how silly this thought was. Of course the bandits would've checked her for valuables anyway. She clenched her fists. When Ucksil learned about their attack, he'd certainly send men after them. Clearly, a raid like that would greatly discourage new settlers coming over the mountains. Sinccah quickly grew hopeful. Maybe she could join the troops to track down these bandits. Once they found them, she'd be able to get her pendant back.

"Dad," a boy called out. Sinccah could sense apprehension in his voice

Sinccah looked up. She was already at the front of the caravan. Apparently, her pace had been far faster this time. The boy from earlier was sitting at the back of his father's cart, wide eyed and mouth agape. "Uh, hello," Sinccah managed.

The father turned to look back. "Sinccah? Wasn't it?" he questioned.

"Yeah," Sinccah said as she jogged up to the cart. "May I join you?"

"Sure," the father responded flatly. He slowed to allow her to climb up, then turned back toward the road. "Everyone was quite concerned about you."

"So I heard," Sinccah said. "I'm sorry I wasn't able to talk with you last night. I must've been quite exhausted."

"It would've been nice," the father said quickly, "but I suppose you did what you could."

Sinccah felt her muscles tense. Was this man scolding her for not talking to him sooner? "Here," she said as she held out the now-empty water skin. "Iszailliah said this was yours."

"Ah, yes," the man said as he took the skin. "I hope it helped you somehow."

Sinccah nodded. She looked at the father. His face was tight and his eyes looked heavy. She leaned closer. "How are you holding up?"

The man's eyes widened, but he continued to gaze straight ahead. "I'm fine," he said somewhat gruffly. "This trip has been hard on everyone, but it'll be over soon."

"Of course," Sinccah said. "Honestly, this trip has been a real nightmare."

The man shook his head. "It wouldn't be so bad if it were just me," he said as he turned to look at his son. "But the poor boy will be scarred forever by this experience." The boy had his head hung, with his legs dangling off the back of the cart.

Sinccah looked into the man's pained eyes. "Oh—" she started

"If only we'd brought more guards," the man said bitterly. "The old fool clearly wasn't enough."

Sinccah was stunned. This man had seemed so friendly toward Vistimmot before the attack. He'd even let her stay in his cart on Vistimmot's request. She studied the man's snarling face. "I don't know how we could've predicted such a large group of them," she ventured softly. "This was clearly an abnormal attack."

The man's snarl deepened. "Perhaps," he said stiffly. "We still should've been more prepared. I mean, we only had one real mage. What were we thinking?"

Sinccah felt his words stab into her. She wanted to cry. She wanted to scream at him. She wanted to tell him that Vistimmot had died defending him. He could at least show a little respect! Instead, she softly asked a distracting question: "Did you see who threw the rock?" The man squirmed in his seat but didn't reply. Sinccah figured he might not have understood, so she continued: "When the bandit with the horse, Jarnick I guess, was about to kill me, someone hit his horse with a rock. Did you see where it came from?"

"Yes," the man replied coldly.

Sinccah shifted in her seat. She felt the sudden urge to flee, but she wanted to confirm who had saved her. "Did your son throw it?"

The man lowered his head and hunched his shoulders. "He nearly got himself killed for it."

"I'm so sorry," Sinccah offered. The man waved his hand and turned away. Sinccah glanced around awkwardly. "I think I'm going to head back to Iszailliah now." The man seemed to nod. "Thanks for all your help," she said before jumping from the cart.

Sinccah ran to the edge of the road. She fought back tears as she watched the man and his son continue forward until a tree hid them from her view. Her mind raced. She fell to her knees as the tears overcame her resistance. Did all the other members of the caravan feel the same way about her? Did they think her efforts were pointless, merely increasing the risk to each of them? She thought back to Jarnick's rage. Had her actions only caused more harm to the people in the caravan? She had been trying though. Didn't that count for something? It was always like this. No one ever appreciated all the effort she put in for them. She wanted to scream but instead slowly pushed herself to her feet and began to plod along with the caravan.

The man's harsh words played over and over in her mind as she walked. She was a real mage, wasn't she? Vistimmot had told her she was. He'd even told her that her skills were impressive. Her face contorted in sorrow as a picture of the kind old mage's face appeared in her mind. It didn't matter what Vistimmot thought of her now. He was dead. Tears returned to her eyes and began running down her face. If she'd been stronger, she could've saved him. If she had been a *real* mage she could have saved him.

A resolute frown formed on her face. Next time she'd be better. Next time she'd be good enough. She'd put in the effort, learn the spells, become powerful. She'd honor Vistimmot's legacy by becoming as great a mage as he was. Perhaps even greater. She thought back to the flamewisp spell he had been teaching her. It'd be a start. She held out her hand and tried to focus on the instructions Vistimmot had given her. As she continued to walk along the caravan, she felt a renewed sense of purpose. She'd master this spell—and every spell that came after.

⊰◦⊱

Sinccah held out her hand as she finished casting the spell. She looked down at her palm. Nothing. Still no fire. She let out a sigh as her shoulders slumped. This spell had been eluding her all day. She'd already cast it with Vistimmot. Why was it so hard to cast again? A look of pain formed on her face. If only the old mage were still here to help her. It was probably something simple she was messing up. He'd be able to tell her what to do differently. Or at the very least, encourage her, tell her that she was doing well, and insist that she'd be a great mage someday. She looked up as tears started to form in her eyes. She wanted to believe Vistimmot had been right about her. She wanted to believe she could actually become the great mage that he'd told her she was. Doubt surged into her thoughts. She wasn't a great mage, and she probably never would be. Even this simple flamewisp spell had stumped her.

She sighed. During her time struggling to cast the spell, the caravan had continued toward Sillburg. Sinccah had done a pretty good job of keeping up with everyone else and was still near the middle of the caravan despite pausing frequently to focus on the spell. She'd considered going back to Iszailliah, but she didn't want to feel needy. She began to look around dejectedly. The forest was still distantly visible, but it no longer encroached on the road. Instead, the terrain had gotten rougher, and they were now surrounded by small hills. She noticed a small cluster of wooden buildings that stood near the road. They must be quite close to Sillburg. Some movement caught Sinccah's attention, and she looked over to see an old man pulling a small hand cart. He was coming down a small path toward the road. It seemed the caravan wasn't the only thing headed to Sillburg today.

Sinccah turned her focus back to the ground. The old man reminded her of Vistimmot, and the pain of that memory hurt. Still, Vistimmot had believed in her, so she couldn't give up. She stopped, closed her eyes, and tried to cast the flamewisp. Still nothing. She sighed. Clearly she'd forgotten some important piece of the casting sequence. She'd probably need someone to teach her everything again. She thought back to her time with Vistimmot. He'd mentioned a book to her. It had a name that sounded fiery, and the old mage had told her it had a healthy emphasis on fire magic. Perhaps if she found a copy, she'd be able to determine what she was doing wrong. She'd have to ask about it in Sillburg. Hopefully, there wouldn't be any royal mages around to question her about it. Otherwise, she could look for the mage her aunt had told her about. He owed the family a favor, so it might be possible to convince him to help her.

Hushed voices started rising behind Sinccah, and she turned around as the source of the whispering passed her. In the distance, just beyond the end of the caravan some twenty mounted men were approaching. Each of them wore metal armor and carried a large array of weapons. A pair of banners fluttered behind them as they rode. Sinccah recognized the symbol that each bore as the Charlok, the symbol of the kingdom. These must be Ucksil's men! They'd certainly help with the bandit situation. She started jogging toward them. She needed to report the raid the caravan had suffered.

Sinccah and Ucksil's men reached the end of the caravan at around the same time. Most of the mounted men continued past Iszailliah's cart, but two of them split off from the group. Sinccah stopped to watch them approach. The first was a middle-aged man who had a shining crest in the center of his breastplate. His wavy black hair was peppered with a few light patches, and his face bore the clear sign of many days without shaving. The other man was younger, perhaps a little older than Sinccah. He was less elegantly attired and had shoulder-length light-brown hair that, though clearly not quite properly kept, gave his smooth face a charming, rugged look. The first man called out to Iszailliah and Filwurn as he and his companion approached the cart.

"Greetings travelers!" he said with a smile. "What brings you to this fair city?"

Filwurn turned to the man and pulled the cart to a stop. "Hello, sir!" he said excitedly. "We're here to settle these lands."

"Very good!" the man responded. "I'm Dreekadack, captain of the Sillburg guard. I trust you found—"

"You're the captain of the guard!" Iszailliah interrupted.

"At your service," Dreekadack responded with a short bow.

"Our caravan!" Iszailliah nearly shouted before taking a deep breath. "Our caravan was attacked in the mountain pass!"

Dreekadack frowned, his face turning serious. "What happened?"

"Well," Filwurn started, "we were traveling through the Brothers Pass, and just after we got over the mountains, a large group of bandits attacked us. They killed the mage who was guarding us and looted everything."

Dreekadack's face hardened. "Did you get a good look at them?"

"I didn't myself ..." Filwurn said as he noticed Sinccah stepping up beside him. "But Sinccah here," he gestured, "she was with our guard when the bandits attacked. She can tell you more."

Dreekadack turned to Sinccah as she walked up to the group. "Is that true?"

"Yes," Sinccah answered quickly. "Vistimmot and I were talking shortly before the attack. I ..." her voice drifted off. "I saw everything."

"Vistimmot," Dreekadack said with a nod.

Behind Dreekadack, the younger man's eyes widened, but he didn't speak.

"Yes," Sinccah replied as her face contorted in sorrow, "but the bandits killed him." Sinccah felt tears forming in her eyes and briefly turned away. She took a sharp breath to compose herself, then glanced back at the captain.

"Grave," Dreekadack said grimly. "We must proceed with caution." His eyes bore into Sinccah. "Can you describe your attackers?"

"Yeah," Sinccah said as she tried to keep control of her face. "They were led by two bandits: a man named Gillopp and a woman named Mikcalla."

Dreekadack frowned. "Gillopp's band." He shook his head. "Quite infamous, but not generally this far south. Crystand Pass has long been their mark."

"You're going to go after them though," Iszailliah said suddenly.

"Certainly," Dreekadack said firmly. "Though this group has proved elusive in the past."

"So they are going to get away with this?!" Filwurn shouted.

"No," Dreekadack said resolutely. "Not if it is within my power to prevent it." The corner of his lip twitched upward. "Still, this is a poor time for such a development. We are stretched thin." His face contorted into a frustrated frown as he glanced northward. "I will deal with this threat, but it'll take some time."

Iszailliah glanced at her husband with a worried look. He looked back with a helpless expression. Sinccah inhaled sharply. "Is there anything I can do to help?" she offered.

Dreekadack's gaze snapped to her. His eyes darted over her, taking her in. "Perhaps."

"Right," Sinccah said awkwardly.

"Firstly," Dreekadack said loudly, "you must fill in the details of the attack. Tell me everything. I'll deliver the information to Ucksil."

Sinccah nodded. "I was actually hoping to talk to Ucksil myself."

Dreekadack slowly arched an eyebrow.

"He's a relative of mine," Sinccah replied. "My aunt told me he'd be able to help me get established in Ucksland."

"Ah," Dreekadack said slowly. "Very well. You may join me." He straightened in his saddle. "Do you ride?"

"Uh," Sinccah stammered, "a little."

He motioned to the young man waiting behind him. "Your horse, Carrimar." The man dismounted and gave a slight bow as he gestured to his horse.

Sinccah jogged over.

"My lady," Carrimar said as he flashed her a dashing smile. He then crouched and formed his hands into a platform. Sinccah stepped onto it, and he helped lift her into the saddle.

"Very good," Dreekadack said as Sinccah rode up beside him and the two started to ride forward.

"Stay safe, Sinccah!" Iszailliah called out.

"You too!" Sinccah replied with a nod of farewell. "Thank you for everything!"

Iszailliah waved. "Come find us again when you are finished talking to Ucksil!"

"I will," Sinccah said as she turned away. Dreekadack gave her a nod, and the two pressed their horses into a trot and headed down the road.

CHAPTER THREE

After an hour of riding, Sinccah and Dreekadack still hadn't reached Sill-burg. She'd just finished filling him in on the details of the attack as well as the information Iszailliah had told her.

Dreekadack wore a thoughtful look. "So they were after Vistimmot."

"Yeah," Sinccah responded. "I was thinking the same thing. What I don't understand is why. Certainly Vistimmot was a powerful mage, but it doesn't seem like these bandits had any reason to come all this way just to kill him."

"Indeed," Dreekadack said. "Perhaps he caused them grief during his time in Crystand." He frowned. "Though, that would've been many years ago."

Sinccah frowned as she mulled over the events of the battle. "I think someone paid them."

Dreekadack tilted his head slightly. "What makes you think that?"

"Just the way they were talking," Sinccah said thoughtfully. "They seemed to think that Vistimmot being there made their attack worthwhile. In particular, they said that after he told them they wouldn't get anything valuable from the caravan."

"Strange," Dreekadack said as he shook his head. "Gillopp and his band have never been killers. Certainly aggressive and cruel, but they almost never kill."

"Gillopp did tell that other bandit to leave me alone," Sinccah mused.

"Exactly," Dreekadack responded. "They spared your companions as well." He frowned. "Except Vistimmot."

"That makes it more likely they were paid to kill him," Sinccah said, a hint of anger showing in her voice.

"Perhaps," Dreekadack said slowly. "But there remains the financial concern. Vistimmot was a powerful mage, and from your account, it sounds like they lost over two dozen men in their attack. Only fools would expect any better. The reward must have been great."

"I suppose so," Sinccah said as she looked down at her saddle. "Is there anyone in Sillburg who has that kind of money?"

"No," Dreekadack answered. "Lord Ucksil and the Beatrunds are the only people in all of Ucksland with that kind of wealth, and none of them stand to gain from this."

"Sure," Sinccah said. She had no idea who these Beatrunds were, but Dreekadack certainly knew the people of Ucksland better than she did. She glanced up. "So we're forced to assume that the bandit's patron is from Rimstid."

"Perhaps," Dreekadack said slowly, "but such an employer would first have to find them, which would be difficult without an existing presence on this side of the mountains."

"Sure," Sinccah responded, "but they certainly don't live in Ucksland, whoever they are."

Dreekadack's frown deepened. "Or the bandits acted on their own. We can't forget the potential for a deep seated grudge."

Sinccah gave him a doubtful look. "I don't think—"

"I still think they were paid," Dreekadack interrupted, "but it would be foolish to exclude any potential options."

"Right," Sinccah said, feeling somewhat agitated as she felt the chances of the bandits being caught slipping away. The fiends had her pendant! She couldn't let them escape! Her face curled into a snarl. "Do we even need to figure out their motivation?"

Dreekadack lifted his chin. "Technically, no. However, if a patron exists, we'll need to proceed with much greater caution. Merely removing minions will do little to stop such a powerful force."

"I suppose so," Sinccah said with a sigh.

"Regardless," Dreekadack asserted as he straightened in his saddle, "we can't remain passive. Had the dragon attacked, it would've been the death of the whole caravan. Likely most of the bandits as well. Their reckless actions are just as incriminating as a complete slaughter. Justice must be done."

Sinccah's eyes widened. "The dragon was that dangerous?" she stammered, suddenly feeling foolish for romanticizing the situation to Iszailliah.

"Yes," Dreekadack said solemnly, "Without a mage capable of bringing it down, you were all helpless. Perhaps you could have fled, but dragons are adept hunters. You're incredibly fortunate the beast chose to pass you by."

Sinccah squirmed in the saddle. "Why do you think she left us alone?"

"She?" Dreekadack questioned, his eyebrow arching.

"Oh," Sinccah said awkwardly, "one of the people in the caravan said the dragon was female. Something about a ridge on her chest."

Dreekadack leaned toward Sinccah, his hard eyes boring into her. "You have no idea how close you were to fiery death."

"I uh ..." Sinccah started before the seriousness of Dreekadack's expression caused her voice to drift off.

"If you were close enough to see a dragon with that much detail," Dreekadack said slowly, not breaking his stare, "then it was close enough to see that your mage was dead. That dragon let you live."

Sinccah's mind raced. "I had no idea," she managed to say as she realized how precarious that day had been. She'd nearly died twice over: first from the bandits and then from the dragon.

"It's alright," Dreekadack said and he pulled away from Sinccah. "Your ignorance is forgivable. Besides, you were unconscious at the time, so there was nothing you could've done."

"I guess so," Sinccah said, still somewhat in shock at everything that had happened. "Why would a dragon do that?"

Dreekadack grunted. "I wouldn't know. The decisions those monsters make are impossible to understand." His eyes narrowed. "All I can say is this: your experience is an anomaly. If you ever see a dragon in the wilderness again, you'd better hope you can hide."

"I understand," Sinccah said softly. "Thanks for the advice."

"Of course," Dreekadack said with a slight bow. "Glad to be of service."

Sinccah nodded, then nudged her horse to the side of the road to make way for a small group of people. Several of them waved to Dreekadack as they passed. Sinccah glanced between the people and Dreekadack. "How long have you been the captain of the guard?"

He smiled, welcoming the change of topic. "Nearly ten years now, but I've been serving this town for far longer. In fact, I guarded Sillburg before the town even got its name."

"So you've been here thirty years?" Sinccah asked.

"Closer to fifty actually," Dreekadack said with a proud smile. "My parents were among the first settlers to come to the settlement that would eventually become Sillburg. Back then, it was little more than a pile of rubble leftover from before the Withering."

"You've spent your whole life in Ucksland?" Sinccah questioned.

"Since I was a young boy," Dreekadack answered. "Sillburg will always be home for me."

Sinccah frowned at the mention of home. She'd never had a real home. Not since her mother left. "That's impressive," she said awkwardly as her thoughts continued to pull her mind elsewhere. She suddenly felt her hand reach for her pendent only to close around empty air. Her face contorted in pain.

"Are you alright?" Dreekadack asked.

Sinccah's head jerked up. "I'm fine, just ..." her voice trailed off. She inhaled deeply. "Just thinking of my own home." She grimaced, it wasn't exactly a lie, but she didn't want to tell this man the whole story either.

"I understand," Dreekadack said without noticing Sinccah's grimace, "Many travelers who come over the mountains get homesick." He turned to her with a slight smile. "I'm confident that, in time, you'll discover the true beauty of Sillburg."

Sinccah forced her face into a polite smile. She was skeptical about the captain's assertion, but it was probably best to change the topic. "Of course," she said with fake cheerfulness. A few seconds passed in silence.

"Have you seen my mother?" Sinccah suddenly asked.

Dreekadack startled at the spontaneous question but quickly recovered. "Perhaps," he responded carefully. "What's her name?"

"Neirith."

Dreekadack leaned back as he gazed into the sky. "I can't say I recall that name. Did she spend a lot of time in Sillburg?"

"I'm not actually sure," Sinccah said quickly. "She spent a lot of time in *Ucksland*, but she tended to live farther north. She was a mage who studied the goblins."

"How old would she be now?" Dreekadack asked.

"A little younger than you," Sinccah answered. "Though, if you'd seen her, it would've probably been over twenty years ago. She would've had light-green eyes like mine and thin chestnut hair." She frowned. "I'm not sure what style she would've worn it in."

Dreekadack nodded thoughtfully as he looked into Sinccah's eyes, "I can't say I remember anyone like that."

"Oh," Sinccah said with a twinge of disappointment. "I guess that isn't a surprise."

Dreekadack bobbed his head toward Sinccah. "I apologize for my ignorance. It's likely she rarely visited Sillburg." He straightened. "It's admirable that she studied goblins, though. Twenty years ago, they were quite hostile."

"So I've heard," Sinccah said with a sigh.

"Perhaps they were calmer up north," Dreekadack observed. "Around here, the pesky creatures have been an incredible nuisance."

"They used to be that big of a problem?" Sinccah asked.

Dreekadack let out a soft snort. "They're a problem now." He breathed in deeply. "The last decade has been remarkably peaceful, but that changed last year when they formed the Rakniv."

Sinccah tilted her head.

"It's a collection of goblin villages along the southern coast," Dreekadack explained. "They've always been an issue, but now they're more coordinated." He shook his head. "And growing. Open conflict may be inevitable."

"Oh," Sinccah said glumly, "that explains why you're stretched so thin." Her lip curled upward as she remembered the bandits' smirking faces. If Sillburg wasn't equipped to chase them down, would they get away with this?

Dreekadack shook his head. "During another time, we would've been well equipped to deal with this threat, but this year, it'll be far more difficult."

"Sorry," Sinccah offered.

Dreekadack held up his hand. "Nothing for you to be sorry about. You were a victim of the attack not the cause of it." He lowered his hand. "Unfortunately, a new threat is hardly what Sillburg needs right now."

"I understand," Sinccah said. "I'll do whatever I can to help."

"Very good," Dreekadack said with a brief smile. "A shield mage like yourself would be quite useful in the coming days."

Sinccah nodded. "I hope so."

The two continued riding without further conversation, leaving the land silent, save the sound of the horses' hooves and the periodic calls of nearby birds. In front of them rose a massive hill that was covered in scraggly bushes. For half a minute, they skirted around the base. Suddenly, the road narrowed and sliced through the hill. As they turned and rode through the gap, Sinccah studied the ancient stone walls that were vainly trying to hold back the sides of the hill. At one time these walls must have once been more than three stories high. However, the top portions of the wall had long since collapsed onto the road, leaving just enough space for Sinccah and Dreekadack to continue riding abreast. What little remained of the old wall was crumbled and beginning to bulge inward as though it might give way at any moment. Sinccah glanced nervously at the thin bushes that clung desperately to the walls of stone and earth that surrounded her. There wasn't much left that could realistically collapse, but it was a distressing trek all the same. She shook herself and tried to focus on her destination. Her mind danced through images of what the city must look like. She began thinking about asking Dreekadack about magical books, but he suddenly held up his hand as they rounded a bend in the road.

"Miss Sinccah," he said as he swept his raised hand in front of himself. "Welcome to Sillburg."

Sinccah looked downhill where he was gesturing and beheld the city. It was huge. Far larger than she'd ever imagined. Perhaps even larger than her hometown of Kinscue, which was itself a provincial capital. Her awe became more measured as she looked closely. The whole city was surrounded by a short stone wall, which contained a massive area. However, the wall was crumbled, and the space inside was nearly empty. Much of the land between her and the walls was covered in rolling farmland and dotted by the occasional farmhouse. The city itself was split by a large river that ran nearly straight east into the sea. Both sides of the river contained a similar sized area. However, the northern side couldn't have had more than a hundred buildings in it, many of which were clustered around the remains of a large gate that faced west. From what Sinccah could tell, this was the only gate in the northern half of the city.

Her gaze followed the low wall southward. It stopped at the river, where it was propped up by the remains of a large stone tower. The far side of the river had a similar tower, though this one was considerably less crumbled. Sinccah's eyes continued to drift south, along the wall, until they came to a ruin of a single tower. Beyond it, she saw another gatehouse. This one was in far better repair than the rest of the low wall, though it had clearly seen better days. Another few dozen wooden buildings clustered around the outside of the gate. Far behind the gatehouse towers, Sinccah could see an imposing keep with an additional layer of tall stone walls in front of it. By the state of these taller walls, Sinccah could tell that they contained the real Sillburg, and the fractured low walls were merely the ruins from long ago, before Ucksil had come to Sillburg.

"Shall we?" Dreekadack asked as he nodded toward the nearby gate.

"Of course," Sinccah said excitedly. Finally, she'd reached Sillburg.

Sinccah and Dreekadack continued down the road toward the city. After a few minutes, they came to the northernmost gate. On the right side of the opening, a small banner fluttered in the breeze. On the dull gray cloth, Sinccah could see the Charlok, an eight-tongued half-sun that was to be flown in all the king's lands. Her brow furrowed. Royal law required the banner to be much larger. Additionally, the wavy black line that was supposed to run under the orange half-sun was entirely missing. Weren't the banners also supposed to come in pairs? That was certainly the case back in Kinscue. What kind of city was this? She turned her attention from the banner. A handful of people were milling about the buildings just outside the gate. Several of them turned and waved as Dreekadack approached.

"Captain Dreekadack!" a tall young man in weathered armor called out.

Dreekadack rode up to the speaker, who stood in the center of the road. "At your service," he said cordially.

"Ucksil requested your presence immediately," the man answered.

"Very good," Dreekadack said with a nod toward Sinccah. "We're on our way."

The young man looked at Sinccah. "What brings you to Sillburg, miss?"

"Dark tidings, I'm afraid," Sinccah said grimly.

The man turned to Dreekadack. "What happened?" he asked, worry now tainting his face.

"Bandits," Dreekadack answered flatly. "Gillopp's group attacked a caravan in Brothers Pass."

"Ah," the man said with a frown, "you best get going then." He gave a slight bow as he stepped out of the road.

Dreekadack and Sinccah rode past the collection of buildings. Here Sinccah could see that a shallow ditch ran around the city near the base of the wall. She followed Dreekadack across an earthen causeway that rose over the ditch toward the crumbling gate. As they rode through the large stone arch, Sinccah gazed at the wooden doors that hung open in the gateway. At least these were fairly new, unlike everything else she'd seen so far.

Upon reaching the far side, they were greeted by a few dozen more buildings. Most of them appeared to be simple houses, though a couple of the larger ones might serve as some sort of barracks. Beyond them, Sinccah saw a large flat area that was covered in farmland with occasional farmhouses rising above the lush crops.

Dreekadack gestured over the fields to a low wall that ran along the coast. He quickly started to point out features and explain the state of repairs. Sinccah listened politely as they rode but didn't pay a great deal of attention. Her gaze was drawn to a massive gap in the coastal wall, where she could see the glint of light on the ocean waves.

A frown formed on her face as her eyes darted across the rest of the wall. A few more ruined towers dotted this fortification, and it finally ended in the collapsed remains of a gigantic tower that stood on the bank of the river. At this point, the river had widened significantly such that it could hardly be considered a river anymore. She could still see the remains of the river's current in the swirling water, but it had dissipated significantly in the arrowhead-shaped bay.

Dreekadack noticed her attention shifting and began pointing out features on the far side of the river. There was another massive tower, which stood on a short cliff. This one was in better repair but still looked poorly maintained. From this tower, another wall ran westward along the top of the cliff to an even larger tower. The cliff ended there, but the wall continued along the river, spanning the entire town.

Dreekadack called Sinccah's attention back to the largest tower, which was apparently equipped with a ballista powerful enough to bring down a dragon. Directly under this tower, there was a collection of large buildings and some simple wooden piers. A small fleet of ships were clustered around these piers, which Dreekadack described as the life-blood of Sillburg. Most were small fishing craft, but a few larger vessels were present as well. Between the wall and the river's edge, at least a hundred buildings were situated.

After finishing his brief description of the docks, Dreekadack suddenly stopped and gestured toward the towering keep that rose on the far side of the piers. "Sillburg keep," he said proudly. "Magnificent, isn't it?"

Sinccah turned to see the broad smile that now adorned his face. "Of course," she said quickly before glancing over the scattered buildings that stood beside the water. "How many people live in Sillburg?"

Dreekadack's smile deepened. "A few thousand for now," he said, "but more come over the mountains every month."

"I see," Sinccah said, thinking back to Iszailliah and her comment about people needing houses. It was clear Filwurn's skills would indeed be in high demand. Sinccah looked out over the open space again. "This town is nearly empty," she said slowly.

"It will fill up quickly," Dreekadack said proudly. "Ucksil's generous leadership is attracting scores of new settlers."

Sinccah dipped her head to the side. "Sure."

"Besides," Dreekadack continued, "the empty space is merely an opportunity. The ancient walls may be worn, but they still afford new settlers a great deal of protection while we work on repairs."

Sinccah nodded. She'd already read up a bit on the history of Ucksland before she left Kinscue, but it couldn't hurt to humor the captain. He seemed so passionate about this city after all. "Do you know much about the city that used to be here?"

"Of course," Dreekadack replied calmly. "It was called Ciltonneah. Before the Withering it was a major city, larger than every other city on the island, save Mithroan, the ancient capital."

Sinccah turned and gazed solemnly northward. The ruins of Mithroan weren't all that far from here. She'd never seen them herself, but the stories spoke for themselves. The city had once been majestic, a jewel to crown the whole island. But that was long ago, before the Witherome engulfed and destroyed the entire city, leaving everyone who survived to flee in terror. It was now a strange and harrowing place. She turned back to Dreekadack. "Do you ever think about all the people who used to live here?"

"Occasionally, yes," Dreekadack responded, "but my primary concern is for the people who live here now."

"I guess I meant all of Ucksland," Sinccah said softly. "Long ago, almost everyone lived on this side of the mountains." Her face contorted into a frown. "Then the Withering killed them."

"Not everyone," Dreekadack noted. "It left the ancient people leaderless, but many were still able to flee."

Sinccah's lips tugged downward. "I can't imagine what those people felt," she said softly. "Fear must have run completely rampant."

"True," Dreekadack responded. "However, we now know their primary fear was largely unfounded."

Sinccah rocked her head from side to side as they rode past a couple of people haggling outside a nearby building. "Fair enough," she admitted. She looked at the captain, who was sitting tall on his horse with a proud smile. "What happened to Ciltonneah during the Withering? Was it caught in the deadly radius?"

Dreekadack frowned. "No," he said flatly. "Some claim that the Witherome changed in size erratically during the days after it formed, but I doubt it ever came so far south." He shook his head. "I'm sure it was still a frenzied flight. They, unlike us, didn't know what to expect from the Witherome."

"Yeah," Sinccah said slowly. "They had no way of knowing what would happen."

"Tragic," Dreekadack said solemnly. He paused and let his gaze drift over the city. "If only they'd been less frantic in their flight. Perhaps some people might have remained and our ancestors would have been spared the costly voyage to come back."

Sinccah nodded. The Voyage of the Suns. A bold venture that sought to exterminate the dragons once and for all. It was impossible to say the expedition had truly succeeded, but it had brought people back to the Withered Isle.

"They could've just lived over the mountains in Rimstid," Dreekadack continued. He paused as a frown crept onto his face. "What would Sillburg look like if humans had been here for the last thousand years instead of merely the last couple hundred?" He turned to Sinccah with a renewed smile. "An idle thought."

Sinccah dipped her head in acknowledgment, then silence fell between the two of them. They continued south for a few minutes, periodically passing the occasional citizen as they drifted toward the river. As they drew near, Sinccah's eyes were drawn into the swirling current. The river was massive, but it didn't flow all that quickly. Her gaze snapped to the single bridge that crossed it. On either side of the river, enormous blocks of tall stone stood. They were worn down but still holding up well. In the river itself, some thirty stone pillars rose over the lazy waters to serve as supports. Between them, a rough wooden bridge had been constructed. Sinccah glanced down the river and saw two sets of similar stone blocks. Between the two sets of stones, she could see worn stone pillars dotting the river. Ships glided through these ruins as they drifted to and from the docks.

"Ancient Ciltonneah had a lot more bridges," Dreekadack said.

Sinccah turned to see him gazing down the river. "Each set of blocks was a bridge?"

"Yes," Dreekadack answered. "This wooden one," he said, gesturing in front of them, "was built just over forty years ago. Someday we'll rebuild the original stone bridges and the Cille will once again be conquered." He smiled. "Someday soon."

Sinccah nodded and the two continued onto the bridge. As she rode, she stared down into the swirling waters of the Cille. They had a certain beauty to them. Peaceful, but still on the move. As her gaze danced over the water, her mind began a swirling of its own. Thoughts of Vistimmot, her mother, the bandits. She'd finally found someone who knew about her mother—her face contorted in sorrow—only to have him snatched away along with the hope he'd given her. She shook her head as she pulled her gaze from the water. It was no use to focus on such things. She looked up at the towering keep. Soon she'd talk to Ucksil. He'd make everything right.

As the two companions reached the end of the bridge, they continued toward the gate that stood just in front of them. A few people waved at Dreekadack as they passed through the handful of buildings in front of the cracked wall.

"This is Sillburg proper," Dreekadack said as he gestured toward the gate. "While some settlers have chosen to build elsewhere, most of the population lives within these gates."

Sinccah glanced over the wall at the keep. "So everyone is clustered in a small section of the old city?"

"Well," Dreekadack said with a smile, "I wouldn't exactly call it clustered."

"What do you mean?" Sinccah asked as they passed through the gate. Her question was quickly answered as she beheld the buildings in front of her. "They're so far apart," she said as her wide eyes darted between the sporadic buildings. Though the area didn't have any gigantic empty spaces like the other side of the river, there was still a great deal of open space. "These have to be over ten times farther apart than any city I've ever been in."

Dreekadack's smile deepened. "Unlike in the stuffy cities elsewhere, when you choose to live in Sillburg, you get plenty of land to call your own."

Sinccah looked past the houses. Between them and the keep, another wall stood. This one was taller than the outer wall, and Sinccah could even see a few men patrolling on top of it. The wall had a gate directly in the middle that was flanked by large towers on either side. It sat upon a small rocky ridge that ran smoothly across the entire town, reaching from the clifftop tower that stood over the docks to a similarly sized tower in the southwestern wall. Her gaze drifted to her right and she passed a couple more towers before coming to a western facing gatehouse, presumably the same one she'd seen from the hilltop. From here, the wall ran north into a large tower that was connected to the very wall she'd just passed through to form a rough triangular space.

Her gaze drifted back to the small crowds that moved around between the buildings. "Each of these people owns all the land around their house?" Sinccah questioned.

"Ucksil's rule is very generous," Dreekadack responded. "Someday we'll run out of space, but when we do, these brave people will have property of tremendous value."

"I suppose that's one way to lure in settlers," Sinccah said slowly, trying to avoid sounding doubtful again.

Dreekadack smiled. "It has been working wonders."

Sinccah smiled sheepishly as a small group of people passed them, waving enthusiastically at Dreekadack. "These people seem to have a great deal of respect for you," she said softly.

"Hmm?" Dreekadack questioned before realizing what had been said. "They do indeed. Hopefully, my actions will continue to merit that."

Sinccah nodded as they continued through the buildings toward the keep. Far more people occupied this space, and the sound of bustling business soon filled her ears. A few people called out to Dreekadack, and he responded to each of them with a quick nod. Sinccah kept to herself but couldn't help feeling like many eyes fell upon her. After several minutes of winding through the townspeople, the companions rode through the inner gate. After passing through, Sinccah finally got an unobstructed view of the keep. It was massive, larger than any structure she'd ever seen. Her mouth slid open as her eyes widened.

"The true stronghold of Sillburg," Dreekadack said, noticing Sinccah's gaze. "I'm sure you agree it's more impressive up close."

Sinccah turned to look at the captain. "So that's why the outer walls look so dismal."

Dreekadack frowned, but his smile quickly returned. "We're working on that."

"I understand," Sinccah said with a thin smile. "It hardly makes sense to repair the entire wall when everyone living here could fit in the keep."

"Come now," Dreekadack chuckled. "We have more people than that, and more settle with each passing month."

"Of course," Sinccah said respectfully.

The two continued past the handful of buildings that stood in the courtyard around the keep. A large group of people were milling about, many of whom appeared to be some sort of guards. Sinccah noticed that their armor was not nearly as nice as what she was used to in Kinscue. Most of the men around her wore light gambeson and mail with only a few pieces of metal plate, generally on their arms, head, and shoulders. Though all the armor looked somewhat similar, none of the guards in front of her had a matching set.

"Dreekadack!" a voice called out.

Sinccah turned to the source of the voice. It was an older man in his mid-sixties. His eyes bore a firm look, and half of his face was covered in a thick gray beard. His attire was clearly of high quality but wasn't so expensive as to be gaudy. He strode confidently down the steps leading into the keep.

"My lord," Dreekadack said as he dismounted to give a deep bow. "I apologize for the delay. There were some," his eyes darted to Sinccah, "complications."

"I assumed as much," Ucksil said flatly. He turned to Sinccah. "Who is this?"

Sinccah dismounted and gave a similar bow as Dreekadack. "Sinccah, my lord."

Ucksil eyed her with interest. "Sinccah?" he said, raising an eyebrow. "Have we met before?"

"Not exactly," Sinccah said quickly. "I believe I saw you at your brother's wedding."

Ucksil's brow furrowed. "You must have been quite young." He brushed his fingers through his beard. "Ekkmund's daughter?"

"Yeah," Sinccah admitted as she fought off a wince.

"Ah," Ucksil grunted loudly. "That fool."

Sinccah grimaced but managed to continue. "Your brother married his sister, yes?"

"Indeed he did," Ucksil said with a chuckle, "I suppose that means we are related." His face turned more serious. "I was saddened to hear about your father going mad," he said sympathetically.

"It's alright," Sinccah said while trying to hide how disingenuous her assertion was. "I never even knew him. He left shortly after I was born."

"Right," Ucksil said quickly. "Give your mother my greetings next time you see her." He spun away toward Dreekadack. "I must know these supposed complications you spoke of."

Dreekadack started talking, but Sinccah had stopped listening. Her head sank as her mind was dragged back to thoughts of her mother, of the abandonment she felt. The image of her pendant being taken forced itself into her mind. She clenched her fists as her face soured.

"... that is why Sinccah is here," Dreekadack said.

Her head jerked up. Dreekadack was gesturing toward her, and Ucksil looked on with a grim expression. Sinccah tried to force a pleasant expression onto her face, but it seemed stuck in a pained smile.

"Don't worry," Ucksil said as he gave a nod toward Sinccah. "I will make sure those brigands pay for what they did to you. You are family after all."

"Thank you, my lord," Sinccah managed.

Ucksil gestured toward the keep. "Step inside. You can both enjoy some refreshments as you fill me in on the details."

CHAPTER FOUR

Ucksil got up from the heavy table and walked slowly toward the nearby balcony. Sinccah slumped her shoulders. She'd just finished telling Ucksil everything she knew about the attack. Dreekadack had also gone through the speculations that he and Sinccah had been discussing on their way to the city. Sinccah nervously tapped her fingers against her goblet as she waited for Ucksil to speak. Dreekadack sat next to her with his gaze fixed on Ucksil's back.

Sinccah picked up her goblet and took a sip. As she returned it to the table, her eyes wandered around the sparsely furnished room. The large table where she and Dreekadack sat took up most of the center of the room. A single bookshelf stood against the wall behind them, and a large chest sat next to it. The walls were adorned with some fairly plain tapestries, and the floor was covered in a rough rug.

Ucksil spun around. "We can't let this attack go unanswered," he declared. "The impact on morale will be too high."

"I agree," Dreekadack said, "However—"

"The goblins," Ucksil interrupted. "They'll need to be dealt with. How was the meeting?"

Sinccah turned to Dreekadack, who now wore a deep frown. "Poor, I'm afraid," he said, shaking his head. "Twelve chieftains attended, but the Rakniv leaders scorned the meeting, and only one of them came." Dreekadack's lip curled upward. "And he spent his time trying to convince the others to turn on us. Unfortunately, all I could do was maintain our current status."

Ucksil frowned. "As expected."

Dreekadack nodded. "Last week, three more houses were torched. They're getting bolder."

"I know," Ucksil said grimly as he walked back to the table and sat. "We must find a way to satiate these goblins."

A silence fell on the group. Sinccah glanced around awkwardly as the two men glared at the table. "Is there any way you could ally with some of the friendlier villages?" she asked. "Or at least talk to them individually to explain the situation more fully?"

"You don't know any goblins," Ucksil said slowly, "do you?"

Sinccah was taken aback. "I uh—" she started, sinking into her chair.

"My apologies," Ucksil said as he stood back up and walked toward the balcony. "I meant no offense."

Dreekadack watched his lord walk onto the balcony before turning to Sinccah. "Goblins tend to have a strong sense of kinship," he explained in a hushed voice. "Fighting some of them, even in self-defense, runs the risk of inciting all of them."

"Oh," Sinccah mumbled.

Dreekadack nodded. "That's the trouble with it. Our hands are tied until they do something even other goblins find reprehensible. If we attack before then, we might find ourselves at war with every goblin in Ucksland; perhaps the whole island."

"I understand," Sinccah said grimly.

"Yes," Dreekadack said with a deep frown, "We will bring your bandits to justice, but it will take time. First we need to deal with these rogue goblins."

Sinccah's eyebrows arched. "Are the Rakniv goblins the only hostile ones?"

"Mostly," Ucksil answered as he turned around and walked back to the table. He loudly planted his hands on the smooth wooden surface and leaned forward. "Sillburg has long relied on trade with the more favorable villages." His lips tugged downward. "We are more self-sufficient now but not completely. Depending on such a fickle race has long been concerning, but we must endure it a little longer."

"I understand," Sinccah said awkwardly as she tried to hide her embarrassment. "I'm sorry for my ignorant question."

Ucksil nodded. "That's alright," he said flatly as he leaned back. "There remains the issue of the bandit attack. The mages you described were clearly formidable. We will need to match that. Unfortunately, I cannot spare my mages for this task." He opened his mouth to continue, but stopped suddenly as his gaze passed over Sinccah.

"I understand," Sinccah said dejectedly. "As the ruler you need to make hard decisions."

Ucksil frowned, then raised his eyebrows. "The bandits," he said softly, "did they take anything of yours?"

Sinccah grimaced. "Yes," she said carefully, trying not to reveal too much. "They took a golden pendant that is very precious to me." She looked down as she tried to hide the tears that threatened to form.

"I see," Ucksil said and he straightened up. He moved a hand to his chin and thoughtfully stroked his beard.

"You have a plan, my lord?" Dreekadack asked.

Ucksil squinted at Sinccah before turning to his captain. "We need someone to investigate the bandit situation. Perhaps find their lair. However," he continued, pointing toward Dreekadack. "You are not available for this task, and neither are any of your men. The goblin threat is far too great."

Dreekadack nodded. "Of course."

"We must send word to the king and make sure the caravans come with more guards," Ucksil said flatly.

Sinccah sank lower into her chair as Dreekadack frowned. The captain lifted his hand from the table. "I fear such an action would incite undue fear."

Ucksil leaned onto the table again and stared at Dreekadack. "Explain."

"We can't imply we are too weak to defend ourselves," Dreekadack said quickly. "The people are already uneasy, and such an action is sure to erode confidence in your rule."

Ucksil breathed in deeply. "You make a fair point, captain." He frowned. "Still, we cannot allow people to die. I'll craft a message."

"Yes, my lord," Dreekadack responded. He shook his head. "We must have more mages, but we don't have the months needed for their recruitment."

Ucksil straightened up to stroke his beard once again. "Your insight is astute, captain."

Dreekadack dipped his head in acknowledgment.

"Still," Ucksil continued as his lips tugged downward, "it must be done." He shook his head. "Yet they are so tediously demanding."

"I fear we have little choice," Dreekadack said with a frown.

"I could maybe ..." Sinccah started before the two men turned to her suddenly. "Uh," she stammered. "My aunt told me there is a powerful mage living in Ucksland who owes my family a favor. I might be able to convince him to help."

Ucksil raised an eyebrow. "Who is this mage?"

"Uh," Sinccah said quickly, "Beilbauk, I think."

"Hmm," Ucksil said slowly. "He is a powerful mage and not currently in my service." He paused. "You said he owes you a favor?"

"Yes," Sinccah answered. "My aunt gave me very specific instructions for how to redeem that."

Ucksil began to walk around the table toward the chest. "That sounds promising."

"My lord," Dreekadack said quickly. "Beilbauk is a risky choice. You are well aware of his insane schemes."

"Perhaps," Ucksil said as he stopped and turned to Dreekadack, "but we lack alternatives." He continued to the chest and began fishing through some keys that were tied to his belt.

Dreekadack breathed in deeply. "Perhaps it is worth the risk." He turned to Sinccah with a kind expression. "Are you sure you want to do this? Sillburg would be grateful, but Beilbauk is a mage from older times. To his type, the offer of a favor is much like an oath. You are sacrificing much."

"I understand," Sinccah said with determination. "There's nothing I want more than to get my pendant back." She breathed in deeply. "There's no telling what those brigands are going to do with it."

"Most likely hawk it to the highest bidder," Dreekadack noted.

Sinccah's face hardened. She wouldn't have much time. She had to get Beilbauk's help and fast.

Ucksil grunted as he tried one of the keys. The lock sounded a sharp mechanical click before the light creak of the lid's hinges proclaimed Ucksil's success. He began loudly digging through the chest's contents.

"Very well," Dreekadack said softly. "Just don't go the way of Kollrum. Don't let finding these bandits become your obsession."

"Of course," Sinccah said without taking the time to really think through if she meant that.

"Here you are," Ucksil said as he appeared behind Sinccah and tossed a small bag onto the table in front of her. The bag made a distinct clink as it landed.

"What's this?" Sinccah asked.

"Your first payment," Ucksil answered. "Consider yourself an officer of Sillburg."

"My lord," Dreekadack protested, "she didn't really volunteer for that."

"It's alright," Sinccah interjected. "I can do this," She picked up the bag and inspected the contents. A smile formed on her face. A few dozen sivs. Not a lot, but it would be enough to get her started. "I've always wanted to be part of something bigger," she said in a barely audible voice.

"Very good," Ucksil said with a smile. "Your first task will be to recruit Beilbauk. Report back when that is done, and we can discuss the details of tracking down the bandits."

Sinccah nodded. "Of course," she said excitedly, "do you know where Beilbauk is living these days?"

"For that," Ucksil said quickly, "I'll direct you to my captain." He gestured toward Dreekadack. "In the meantime, I have other matters to attend to."

Dreekadack stood to give Ucksil a bow and Sinccah followed his lead. Ucksil gave them each a short nod before turning away and leaving through one of the room's large doors.

Sinccah turned to Dreekadack. "You know where Beilbauk lives?" she asked hopefully.

"Not quite," Dreekadack admitted. "He has long resided in a ruined tower near the southern coast." He gestured Sinccah to a map on the table and began pointing out locations. "If you follow the road out the southwest gate, you should come to a small settlement named Rivvairt. Really just a collection of houses around a tavern. If you ask about him there, you should get better answers. I hear he visits the town from time to time."

"Alright," Sinccah said, "I'll start there." She stood to leave.

Dreekadack held up his hand. "Wait," he said quickly. "I should warn you; the people living in Rivvairt have become increasingly resentful of Ucksil's rule. Be careful around them."

"Right," Sinccah responded with a nod.

Dreekadack frowned. "You don't have to do this. Your road will be dangerous."

Sinccah smiled. "Don't worry about me," she said confidently. "I want to do this for Sillburg, but more importantly for myself. I'm not going to give up this opportunity to prove myself."

"I can send some of my men with you," Dreekadack offered.

"I'll be alright," Sinccah insisted.

Dreekadack smiled weakly. "I'm sure you can handle yourself, but the wilds of Ucksland can be quite deadly, particularly down south, where the Rakniv lurk. Are you sure you don't want help?"

"I'm sure," Sinccah replied resolutely. "I would hate to rob Sillburg of its defenders."

"Very well," Dreekadack said, lowering his hand. "Can I be of any service before you depart?"

Sinccah thought for a moment. "Well, yes," she replied. "I wanted to ask if Sillburg had any books for learning magic."

Dreekadack's face fell. "Not really," he sighed. "I'd tell you to talk to the city's mages, but I can't imagine them being helpful." He shook his head. "The only place you might find success is at the parchment shop, but the crazy old woman who runs it can be difficult."

"I see," Sinccah said. "I guess I'd still like to give it a try. Do you know where her shop is?"

"Just outside the courtyard's southern gate," Dreekadack said. "It has a fancy sign out front."

"Thank you, Captain," Sinccah said with a smile.

Dreekadack nodded. "One more thing," he said before Sinccah could turn away. "There's a horse trainer who lives near the southwest gate. He has good stock, including a particularly fine one that just became available. Ucksil has an agreement with him to allow mounts to be rented for official business. It might be a good use of your newfound payment."

"I'll make sure to take a look," Sinccah said.

"I need to warn you, though," Dreekadack continued, "the owner is a shrewd man. He will most likely try to swindle you. My advice is that you talk to his wife. She's considerably more pleasant to work with and should give you a hefty discount."

"Will do," Sinccah replied.

Dreekadack stood and gave Sinccah a slight bow. "May fortune favor you on your quest."

"May fortune favor you as well," Sinccah said, then turned and walked briskly out of the room.

⚬

Sinccah looked up at the setting sun as she left the keep. It had just begun slipping below the wall in front of her. Had she been too rash volunteering for all this? Why had Ucksil even let her? Was the situation with the Rakniv goblins really that bad? Probably. It would certainly keep Ucksil and his men tied down. It might be impossible to even get men to go after the bandits. She frowned. Perhaps if she found them quickly enough, the goblins wouldn't be a large enough threat? She shook her head. There was a lot she didn't understand, but at least she was doing something worthwhile. That was what she'd always wanted, wasn't it?

Her lip twitched upward. It didn't matter. She needed to get moving. But first she would need supplies, particularly a weapon. She couldn't afford to be helpless again, not with the dangers of the road ahead of her. Beyond that, she needed to be ready for when she finally found the bandits. Her face hardened. She wouldn't merely be an onlooker the next time they met. Her eyes darted to her left. She didn't have any experience with traditional weapons, so her best chance was finding a magic manual at the parchment shop.

She walked around the keep to the southern gate. On the other side, she found a collection of buildings. The road split almost immediately outside the gatehouse, with several forks winding through the buildings in front of her. The main branch of the road continued to her left before turning south toward what almost certainly was another gate. She glanced over the buildings. They appeared to mostly be houses, though she could see that some were workshops and stores. Turning to her right, she saw an elegant metal sign. The font was excessively fancy, and in the dimming light, Sinccah didn't bother to read it. This must be the place. She walked up and knocked on the heavy wooden door.

The door opened a crack, and a raspy voice issued out. "Who's this?"

Sinccah cringed at the harsh sound. "Uh, my name is Sinccah," she managed to say. "I was told you were the one to talk to if I wanted to purchase a book."

The door opened the rest of the way to reveal a short, plump old woman. "Yer told correct," the woman said loudly, her rasp mostly vanishing. "Come in," she said, turning to walk into the surprisingly well-lit building. Sinccah tentatively followed, stepping onto a thick rug that covered most of the floor. "Fortunate of you to come by just now," the woman said as she walked to a small desk and sat down. "It's almost my bedtime."

Sinccah glanced around, squinting in the bright light, which emanated from a lamp on the woman's desk. The room was filled with piles of paper. On the far wall, a few bookcases stood with books carefully arranged such that the books on the far left were tallest and those on the far right were shortest. Could the book

Vistimmot mentioned be among them? Sinccah turned back to the old woman. "Thanks for taking the time," she said, trying her best to be polite.

"So what exactly you looking for?" the woman asked flatly.

"Well," Sinccah said with a hint of sweetness in her voice, "I came to see if you have any books that teach magic."

The old woman squinted at her. "You don't look like them royal mages."

"Ah, no," Sinccah said as smoothly as she could manage. "I try to keep a low profile."

The woman stuck the side of her lip out. "'Fraid I don't got much of that," she said before getting up and limping to the bookcases. "I mostly got history books, you see." She ran her finger across the tops of several of the books. After a few seconds of silence, she grabbed two small books off the shelves and hobbled back to her desk.

Sinccah stared at the books. This could be her chance!

"Let's see," the woman said as she sat down and inspected the books. "This one here is about healing magic."

"I know a bit of that," Sinccah said as she stepped closer, her eyes darting between the two books. "But it would always be good to learn more."

The old woman grunted. "Looks to be just an introduction, though."

"Oh," Sinccah said disappointedly, "I probably don't need that then."

The woman nodded and began to leaf through the other book. "This's a beginners guide to light magic."

Sinccah perked up. Light magic could be used to blind attackers and worked at a reasonably long range. It wasn't exactly what she'd call a weapon, but it'd certainly be better than nothing. "That sounds useful," she said quickly, a little excitement showing in her voice. "How much would you charge for that?"

The old woman closed her eyes as she exhaled loudly. Then one popped open. "First things," she said dubiously. "I need to see your signet."

Sinccah tried not to panic. Of course the woman would ask her for proof she was a royal mage. She knew it had been unlikely for her to be allowed to buy a magic manual without one, but she had been hopeful. "Of course," she said with fake confidence. She smiled pleasantly as she reached into her pouch. She widened her eyes. "I'm sorry, it seems I left it with my companions."

"Too bad," the woman said gruffly. "Until I see a signet, you're not getting nothing magic from me."

"I understand," Sinccah said with a calmness she didn't feel. "I'd go back and fetch it, but I'm afraid my companions still want to head out tonight, and I can hardly ask them to wait any longer." She started walking toward the door. "Thank you for your time, ma'am." She opened the door and stepped out, turning briefly to nod at the old woman, who wore a dubious frown. "Good night," Sinccah said sweetly as she closed the door.

She sighed as she walked briskly back to the main road. Sure, the whole thing had been a long shot, but it had been worth the try. Now she'd be forced to buy a sword or something. Her shoulders slumped. Not that she'd be able to use it properly. She walked back through the gate into the courtyard around the keep. On the upside, she hadn't told any obvious lies that would cause the old woman to never trust her again. After all, someday she might actually need to buy some paper. She let out a brief laugh in spite of her frustration.

She still needed some kind of weapon, so she might as well look for someone who'd sell her a blade. Beyond that, she still needed to pick up the rest of the supplies she'd need for her trip. Or maybe take a look at the horse Dreekadack had mentioned.

She left the courtyard through the gate she had first come in from. From there, she slipped through a meager crowd toward the last glimpses of the setting sun. Hopefully, everyone would still be open to business this late. She would also need to figure out where to spend the night. Presumably, there was some kind of inn where she could rent a room, but she didn't really want to pay for that. Perhaps she could locate the other members of her caravan. They were certainly finding themselves in the same predicament. It was quite likely they would choose to simply camp out in a less populated part of town. Ideally, she'd be able to join them in that.

A friendly voice suddenly called out from her right. "There you are!"

Sinccah turned to see Iszailliah walking briskly toward her. "Hey," she called back as she stepped off the road. "I was just looking for you!" She frowned slightly. It wasn't exactly true, but close enough.

"How did your talk with Lord Ucksil go?" Iszailliah asked as she stopped next to Sinccah.

"It was …" Sinccah started, a pained smile forming on her face. "It was interesting."

Iszailliah tilted her head to the side. "What does that mean?"

"I learned that everything is a lot more complicated than I first thought," Sinccah replied, shaking her head.

"Lord Ucksil will do something about the bandits," Iszailliah said with a hint of desperation. "Right?"

"Certainly," Sinccah said cautiously. "That's the particularly complicated part."

"What do you mean?"

"I volunteered to help deal with the bandits." Sinccah said softly.

Iszailliah's eyes widened. "Isn't that incredibly dangerous?"

"Yes," Sinccah said slowly as she tried to muster up additional confidence. "But there are several steps that I need to take before we actually go after them."

"What do you mean?" Iszailliah asked.

"Well," Sinccah answered, "we're going to need at least one powerful mage to match the two bandit mages, otherwise there's no point going after them."

"So," Iszailliah said as she directed her gaze at the ground, "I don't mean this to be cruel, but I don't think you quite qualify."

Sinccah furrowed her brow.

Iszailliah quickly continued. "Not that I think you're weak or anything, I'm sure you're great, but those bandits sounded really scary and—"

Sinccah held up her hands. "That's not what I meant," she said, shaking her head as a smile crept onto her face. "There's a mage who lives near the southern coast who has connections with my family. Ucksil wants me to find him and see if I can get him to help."

Iszailliah inhaled deeply. "Ah," she said before pressing her lips together. "I guess I made a bit of an assumption."

"It's alright," Sinccah said as she stepped closer. "For what it's worth, you're right; I'm not a powerful mage. Not yet at least."

Iszailliah looked up, a faint smile appearing on her face. "But you will be someday," she said confidently.

Sinccah smiled, then glanced around. "Where's the rest of your family?"

"They're still on the far side of the river with the rest of the caravan," Iszailliah replied. She gestured in the general direction of the river and the two women started walking. "My brother-in-law was supposed to meet us at the gate when we arrived, but he got here pretty late, so he's talking to my husband now."

"Ah," Sinccah said awkwardly, "he owns a lumber mill in the area, right?"

"Owned," Iszailliah said with sudden sharpness. "Apparently, he had to sell it a few months back to pay off his debts."

Sinccah frowned before turning to Iszailliah. "Weren't you counting on him to help your family get established?"

"Yes," Iszailliah said bitterly. "It seems he thought it more important to squander everything away instead of saving it to help us." She paused, then continued with a much more angry tone. "The only reason I agreed to come to Ucksland was because he promised to help us!"

"That's horrible!" Sinccah exclaimed as the two slipped between a couple of buildings and continued walking toward the gate that would bring them to the river. "Do you know what you're going to do now?"

Iszailliah's face contorted. She opened her mouth to speak, but no words came out. Instead her mouth started quivering. She pressed her lips together as a tear slipped from her eye. "I don't know," she finally said in a voice that was scarcely audible.

"I'm sorry," Sinccah said as the two came to a stop once again.

"I don't even know how to get started," Iszailliah cried out softly. "The bandits took so much from us. My husband doesn't even have the tools he'd need to get a reasonable job." She held her shaking hands in front of her, then slowly curled her fingers together as she brought her hands to her chest. "We're going to end up destitute!" Iszailliah covered her face with her hands and started sobbing.

Sinccah stood awkwardly for a few seconds, not sure how to respond. She reached into her pouch and fidgeted with the bag of coins Ucksil had given her. She was going to need this money. Yet this woman and her husband had saved her life. Her mouth tugged downward. Just like she'd failed to save Vistimmot's. She grimaced. The old mage had told her to promote kindness. Was this a situation that qualified? She shook her head. It was the absolute last thing she wanted to do, but at least it would pay back her debt to this couple. "How much would you need to buy some new tools?"

Iszailliah looked up, wiping the tears out of her eyes. "I'm not sure," she said softly. "Why do you ask?"

Sinccah pulled the bag out of her belt-pouch. "Ucksil gave this to me," she said softly as she opened the bag and poured a dozen or so coins into her hand. "It's my first payment for helping deal with the bandits." She held out the silver coins to Iszailliah. "It isn't a lot, but it should be enough to help you get established."

Iszailliah looked at Sinccah, mouth agape. "I ..." she stammered. "I couldn't. That's your payment. I can't take that from you. You're going to need it for your journey."

Sinccah stepped closer to Iszailliah and pushed the coins toward her again. "You saved my life," she said with a pained smile. "It's the least I can do."

Iszailliah widened her eyes before turning away from Sinccah and staring at the ground. "That was just ..." her voice drifted off. "We were just ..." She turned back to Sinccah with a pained smile. "Are you sure you aren't going to need this?"

"I'll be fine," Sinccah said softly. "You need this more than I do."

Iszailliah sniffled. "Thank you," she said weakly as she took the coins and transferred them into a pouch on her belt. She looked up at Sinccah with tears running down her face.

Sinccah smiled faintly. "I suppose this makes us even."

Iszailliah smiled tearfully, then stepped toward Sinccah and embraced her. "Thank you so much."

Sinccah awkwardly put her arms around Iszailliah to return the embrace. "It is my pleasure." A tear formed in her own eye as an image of Vistimmot appeared in her head. That's exactly what he would've said. She missed the old mage, but she wouldn't let his kindness die with him.

Iszailliah pulled away. "I need to get back to the caravan. My husband isn't going to be happy if I keep him waiting too long."

"Fair enough," Sinccah said as she glanced into the sky. It was probably too late to expect any shops to be open, and she'd rather avoid dealing with people who'd been starved of sleep by her presence. She started after Iszailliah. "I was planning to spend my night with the caravan anyway."

"Why's that?" Iszailliah asked.

"The rent is cheaper," Sinccah said flatly. The two women shared a laugh as they slipped through the gate. They grew silent as they climbed onto the bridge and crossed the river. On the far side, Sinccah found a makeshift camp the members of the caravan had set up.

Iszailliah left in search of her husband, and Sinccah settled at the edge of the camp. She eased her pack from her shoulders and pulled off her bedroll. Glancing around, she located a flat grassy area where she unrolled it, crawled under her blanket, and closed her eyes. After a few seconds she opened them again. She wasn't exhausted anymore, so it'd be good to practice the flamewisp spell she'd been learning. Tears threatened to form in her eyes as she remembered the fate of her mentor. She would master this. For him. She rolled off her mat, held out her hand, and focused on the details of the spell. The nuances of the casting process were still foreign to her, and she couldn't quite recall the exact steps. It was fine; she'd certainly be able to work through it.

For the next few minutes, she tried repeatedly to cast the spell. Each attempt resulted in failure and a large drain on her energy. She grumbled to herself as she gave up for the night. The casting process was more complicated than she remembered, and she was clearly missing chunks of it. She rolled onto her back and looked up into the night sky at the expanse of stars. A smile formed on her face. She'd often spent the night outside gazing at such wonders.

Her eyes were drawn to the two moons currently visible. There was Ahkia, the evening Scern, shining in a near-perfect circle. Beside her was Weilka, the smallest of the moons, whose rare visits denoted the start of each week. Their largest sister, Phosa, had yet to rise, but it wouldn't have been more than a sliver this time of the month anyway. She grimaced as her childhood pushed itself into her mind. Back then, she'd dreamed of her mother returning to lead her off on an epic adventure. Perhaps it was a foolish dream of a child, but a part of her was proud. It was exhilarating to finally be on that adventure but so very bitter to have lost everything she'd had from her mother along the way. In spite of her failure, a look of determination appeared on her face. Sure, a lot of things had gone wrong, but there was always tomorrow to do better.

Sinccah shifted restlessly. The excitement of her coming journey had made for a rather sleepless night. She turned over and looked into the eastern sky, hoping to see the sun peeking over the horizon. A scowl formed on her face as she discovered that only a small band of predawn light was visible. Close enough. She rolled off her sleeping mat onto the hard ground. In the dim light, she briefly attempted to roll up her mat and blanket but quickly decided to bunch everything into a ball and shove it into her pack instead. She would deal with rolling it nicely later. A faint cry sounded behind her, and she turned to see Iszailliah tending to her son.

Sinccah walked over as she slung her pack over her shoulders. "Hey," she said softly.

Iszailliah turned to her. "Good morning," she whispered back. "Heading out early?"

"I think so," Sinccah answered. "I have a few things I need to pick up around town, so I figured I'd get an early start."

"Alright," Iszailliah said with a hint of sadness. "I suppose this is goodbye then."

"For now, yes," Sinccah said softly. "I'll see you when I get back."

"Maybe," Iszailliah responded. "We might not settle in Sillburg."

"Oh?"

"Apparently," Iszailliah said slowly, "the mill my brother-in-law used to own still has a need for skilled carpenters, so we're planning to head there tomorrow."

"I see," Sinccah said. "Are you planning to settle there?"

"If my husband can get a job," Iszailliah answered. "We also need to talk to Lord Ucksil about our land allotment."

"Of course," Sinccah said with a nod. "When I talked to him, he seemed nice enough."

Iszailliah eyed Sinccah curiously. "Your talk with him went that well?"

"Not exactly," Sinccah said with a short laugh, "but he did seem to have a genuine concern for the people who live in Ucksland."

"Alright," Iszailliah said softly. Her son quickly began to raise his voice until it became an ear shattering wail. Iszailliah grimaced before turning to Sinccah with an apologetic smile.

"I'll still try to come visit you after I return," Sinccah said quickly before turning to head toward the river. After a few steps she turned back and waved to Iszailliah, who looked up quickly before waving back.

When she reached the river, Sinccah crouched and splashed some of the cool water into her face. For a few seconds, she wiped the grime off her face before giving it another splash. She let out a slow sigh as the water dribbled off her chin. A thin smile formed on her face. It was a good thing she'd left Lady Dove. The absurd noblewoman would've had a fit if she'd seen her children's nurse-mage looking so unpresentable.

She took a deep breath as she glanced across the water. It was going to be a busy day. She'd need to visit the horse trainer first. At least if she had a mount she'd be able to run away from threats. She sighed. It might make up for her lack of a weapon. Besides, it'd make the whole journey faster, which she'd need if she wanted to find the bandits in time. She straightened and walked briskly toward the bridge. As she drew nearer, she noticed a boy standing beside it. He was hunched over beside the river, staring at the ground. Sinccah's eyes widened as she realized this was the boy from the front of the caravan.

She stepped up beside him. "Hey," she said softly.

The boy didn't move. Almost like he hadn't even heard her.

Sinccah shuffled her feet awkwardly as the water gurgled and splashed. "I, uh," she mumbled. "I wanted to—"

A loud grunt sounded behind her and she spun around to see the boy's father. He wore a disapproving look and promptly gestured for her to leave. "You've done enough harm already," he growled. "Leave him alone."

Sinccah shuddered, wrapped her arms around herself, and slipped past the man onto the bridge. As she crossed, she thought back to everything that had happened in the pass. She hadn't done any real harm to the boy, had she? It was unfortunate the boy had seen so much death in the attack, but it wasn't as though she could've done anything to change that. The poor boy had probably saved her life, though. It was a shame he was suffering so much for his act of bravery. She shook her head and continued over the river and into the city proper.

By the time she could see the southwestern gate, everything had gotten much brighter, so she knelt down to properly pack her sleeping mat. As she did so, she looked over the building that stood just inside the gate. It was a two-story wooden building with stalls on the bottom floor. On the back side, it had a small fenced area that a few dozen horses occupied. She stood and continued to the entrance. As she rounded the corner, she saw a couple of boys scurrying about and a tall, powerful, middle-aged man who seemed to be giving them instructions.

Sinccah approached the man. "Hello," she said in a friendly voice.

The man looked surprised for a moment but quickly donned a warm smile. "What can I do for you, ma'am?"

"Ucksil has given me a task that requires travel," Sinccah said confidently. "I need a horse for the next couple of weeks."

"Well," the man said with an elegant bow. "It appears you have come to the right place. I raise the finest beasts in all of Ucksland."

"So I've been told," Sinccah responded. "Captain Dreekadack said you had a particularly fine one at the moment."

The man grinned. "I'm proud to say I will not disappoint the fine captain's recommendation." He turned to one of the boys. "You heard the woman! Get going!" The boy gave a short bow before scrambling to the far side of the building.

Sinccah watched the boy run off. She probably wouldn't be able to afford the nicest horse this man had. Still, she wanted to appear more confident than she was. She turned back to the man. "Have you been in the horse business for a long time?" she asked courteously.

The man smiled proudly. "I have indeed. Ever since I took over for my late father."

"You seem to be doing quite well," Sinccah said as the boy returned with a remarkably beautiful horse. This horse stood tall and walked confidently, each step causing its speckled gray and black coat to ripple over its powerful muscles. Sinccah resisted the urge to look impressed.

"Beautiful, isn't she," the man said as he took the bridle from the boy. "She comes from a long line of dragon-chargers."

Sinccah nodded, still trying to project knowledge she didn't have. "She's magnificent," she said calmly. "How much would you change for such a fine steed?" A grimace threatened to form on her face. She was going to make a fool of herself. Horses had never really been a topic of interest to her, and she didn't know enough to talk prices with this man.

"Right to business I see," the man said with a chuckle. He breathed in deeply, taking on an appraising look. "Since you're in Ucksil's employ ..." His voice drifted off as he glanced upward and started mumbling. "For this fine beast, for two entire weeks." His eyes snapped to Sinccah, and he donned a warm smile. "I wouldn't dream of charging fewer than forty sivs."

Sinccah nodded as she pretended to think about the absurd price. She didn't have that kind of money. Ucksil had only given her thirty-five, and that was before she'd given over a third of them to Iszailliah. "I'm disinclined to go quite that high for a horse," she said with fake confidence. "Even such a fine horse as this one."

She wanted to scream. There was no way this man would quarter the price just because she asked, but she didn't want him to instantly know how much money she had.

"I understand," the man said calmly as he waved the boy back over.

"Do you have anything else?" Sinccah asked, her facade threatening to break.

"Just one," the man replied calmly. He gestured to the boy, who darted toward a nearby stall. A moment later the boy reappeared, leading a rough looking horse that seemed to have some sort of limp. The man pointed at the horse. "I'm afraid that's the only other beast I have."

Sinccah fought against the urge to give this man a look of disdain. She wasn't stupid. This horse was nothing but an insult. "I see," she replied as annoyance started to show in her voice. "I'll think it over." For a few seconds, she stared at the poor horse as she tried to come up with some way to smoothly transition into what she needed to say next. Eventually, a somewhat compelling lie formed in her mind. She forced her face back into a smile and turned back to the man. "Is your wife around? My aunt wanted me to check in with her about—"

"I'm afraid not," the man interrupted with a twinge of sorrow that Sinccah found dubious. "She hasn't been feeling well."

"Oh," Sinccah responded. "I'm actually a healer, I'm sure I could—"

"No need for that!" the man exclaimed dismissively. "I don't want you to trouble yourself."

"It wouldn't be a problem," Sinccah insisted.

"She'll be fine," the man said forcefully.

Sinccah gave him a hard look. It was obvious he was lying, but it didn't seem like he would be interested in admitting it. "Very well," she said as she gave the man a slight nod. "I must be off then."

The man offered Sinccah a smile that verged on mockery. "Come back if you ever change your mind." He gestured toward the first horse. "Though, I can't promise such a fine beast stays here."

"Of course," Sinccah said with a forced smile. She turned and walked slowly away from the man. After walking past a few more buildings, she ducked behind a large house and let out her breath. She really wasn't cut out for these kinds of situations. The man had certainly been trying to overcharge her, so she'd done well to avoid that. Surely he had more than two horses, right? Had mentioning Dreekadack been a mistake? Had faking confidence been a mistake? She shook her head. It didn't matter; she wasn't going to go back.

Unfortunately, that left her distinctly lacking an effective means of transportation. Now her journey was going to take forever, and the bandits would be long gone by the time she went after them. She ran her hand through her hair and reached toward her neck. Her head slumped forward. She had always fidgeted with her pendant in times like this, and its absence stung. Thoughts of her mother assailed her mind. A sigh escaped her as she let her arms drop to her side. Her face hardened. She still had more than enough money for provisions, which was all she strictly needed. If she had to walk everywhere, so be it. She'd get her pendant back, and while she was at it, she would bring the bandits to justice for what they'd done to Vistimmot.

The sound of pounding hooves suddenly caught her attention. She turned toward the road. The sound was still distant but getting closer. A child's playful scream sounded behind her and she spun to see a pair of small children chasing each other through the alley beside her. The little girl was trying to look backward at the young boy who was chasing her, making her movement erratic. She raced past Sinccah toward the road just as the hoofbeats were nearing.

"Slow down!" Sinccah called out harshly, but the little girl continued her reckless flight. Sinccah grimaced. Why did this have to happen right now? She cast a small shield spell at the little girl's feet. As the child lifted her foot to take another step, it caught on the shield, and the girl fell forward. Sinccah quickly dissipated the shield before it could drain much of her energy. The girl tumbled to the ground beside the road as an armored horseman raced past toward the keep. Sinccah let out a disgusted growl as she walked to the fallen girl, who was pulling herself onto her hands and knees. Why did children always act so foolishly?

Sinccah scowled down at the girl. "Little miss," she said sternly.

The girl looked up with tears forming in her eyes. She started to cry as she held up her arm. Sinccah looked at the girl's outstretched hand, which bore the most minor scrape that had ever existed. She could heal this, but it really wasn't worth her time. Sinccah frowned, then sighed as she held her hand over the child's. Better to just take care of it rather than risk upsetting someone's parents. She closed her eyes and cast a healing spell. The girl's eyes widened, and she stared up at Sinccah, mouth agape.

"You should watch where you're going," Sinccah said as she opened her eyes and glared at the girl.

The girl's head sank downward as she caught Sinccah's gaze. "Swory, ma'am," she said through missing teeth.

The boy ran up and tapped the girl on the shoulder. "Got ya!" he said before turning to run away.

"Young man," Sinccah said forcefully. The boy stopped and turned back to Sinccah. "Is this your sister?" The boy nodded glumly. "In the future," Sinccah commanded, "don't push her so hard. She could've gotten hurt." The boy nodded again while avoiding eye contact. Sinccah helped the little girl to her feet. "Are you alright?" The little girl nodded. "Good," Sinccah said sternly. "Be more careful next time." The two children nodded quickly before turning and running toward the road.

Sinccah signed. Hopefully her warning would keep them out of trouble for at least a couple of minutes. She shook her head as memories of Lady Dove's little brats tried to force their way into her mind. Suddenly the wailing of a small child rang out. Sinccah grimaced before rolling her eyes. Apparently, her hope had been in vain.

A flash of metal caught Sinccah's attention and she looked up to see an armored man walking briskly down the road. He looked to be a guard and was likely on his way to the gate. Sinccah glanced at the sword hanging from his belt. She was going to need one of those as well. Her mind returned to the task at hand. She still needed to pick up a few items before heading out. She would certainly need some provisions, and perhaps some additional survival tools. Enough time had been spent moping about. She stood up straight, breathed deeply, and then stepped back onto the road. Not having a horse wasn't going to stop her from completing her assignment.

CHAPTER FIVE

Sinccah stood on the hills southwest of Sillburg and looked back at the sprawling town. Finally, she was on a real quest. It wasn't quite what she'd intended when she'd first set out from Kinscue, but she couldn't help but feel a sense of fulfillment. At long last, she was doing something that really mattered. She turned toward the sun as it continued the process of slowly escaping the ocean's cold grasp. All things considered, she'd gotten a pretty early start. It had taken less than an hour for her to locate and purchase everything she needed. She reached to her side and fidgeted with the hilt of her new dagger. Ideally, she would've bought a proper sword, but after buying provisions and some basic survival tools, she'd run a bit low on money. Perhaps that was for the best. She'd never been trained in swordplay, so it would've probably been a waste anyway.

Sinccah shrugged to adjust her pack and started walking. She breathed in deeply, taking in the crisp morning air. As she walked, she began to think ahead to her destination. It would take her most of the day to reach the town Dreekadack had pointed out to her. In the meantime, she'd have her thoughts entirely to herself. For half an hour she continued along briskly, enjoying the beautiful scenery of the flourishing countryside. During this time, she was almost entirely surrounded by fields with crops just ripening for the harvest. Occasionally, she'd find her eyes drawn to the farmhouses that dotted the rolling cropland. Quite a few people were already out working. Whenever they noticed her, she'd give them a friendly wave, but she was careful to avoid getting into a conversation.

Soon the road on which she traveled became more overgrown. Presumably, she'd finally reached the end of the farmland that surrounded Sillburg and was headed into the real wilderness. Trees began to pop up along the road, and after less than fifteen minutes, the remains of the ancient road were entirely encased in forest. The trees made her uneasy, as memories of the bandit attack came pouring into her mind. Her hand instinctively reached for her pendant, the absence of which made her discomfort even sharper. Of course, it was ridiculous to think that those bandits would be anywhere nearby. If what Dreekadack said was true, then they'd probably spent the last few days traveling north toward whatever lair they lived in. Sinccah began to ponder how she might track them down. It'd be a tough task. The northern regions of Ucksland were almost entirely uninhabited, and it'd be quite difficult to find anyone in such a lonely land. Hopefully, Ucksil would provide enough men to make the search feasible.

A soft buzzing sounded to Sinccah's left. She turned to look at the source. A small yellow insect was flying by. Sinccah watched as the insect bumbled its way to a small group of tiny flowers and landed on one of them. She smiled as she gazed at the insect. Sometimes nature could be a truly lovely distraction. She stretched her shoulders and adjusted her pack. Unfortunately, she really didn't have that much time for distractions. She turned from the flowers and pressed deeper into the forest.

For another hour she traveled uneventfully, save the periodic interruption of largely unseen wildlife. As the sun continued its daily ascent, Sinccah came to the remains of a large stone bridge that spanned a medium-sized north-flowing river. The bridge looked very similar to the bridge in Sillburg: its base was made of ancient stone and the actual bridge of relatively fresh lumber. Stepping onto the end of the bridge, Sinccah looked down into the rapidly flowing water. She might as well stop for a brief rest. She walked tentatively down a shallow hill to the bank of the river, struggling somewhat to avoid tripping on the vegetation. Upon reaching the river, she removed her pack and crouched on a stone outcropping to begin refilling her water skin.

She closed her eyes and enjoyed the soft gurgle of the water. She thought back to Iszailliah and her family. Hopefully, they'd be alright. The money she'd given them should be enough to get them settled in. She frowned. If only the bandits hadn't taken so much from that poor family. Particularly the tools! They probably wouldn't even sell for that much, but their loss had cost Iszailliah and her husband dearly.

Sinccah's face hardened as she pulled the filled skin from the water. She'd track down those brigands and make everything right once more. Naturally, she'd get her pendant back and finally figure out the message her mother had left her. But she'd also make sure to get those tools back. They were family heirlooms after all.

A soft splash sounded from within the river. Sinccah turned to see a tall bird wading warily away from her. She smiled. She'd seen similar birds in the streams around Kinscue, but it was always nice to see another one. Her mind quickly turned from her hometown to thoughts of her mother. There was a great deal that had never made sense about her disappearance. Sinccah leaned back from the river and sat on a large flat rock. All her memories from that time were fuzzy. She'd only been five, after all. Even so, she could clearly remember that her mother used to visit fairly often. She frowned. Once every few months wasn't really that often, but considering the trip over the mountains that had to be made, it was reasonable. Perhaps when she recovered the pendant, it would finally become clear.

She shook her head. If only she'd known about the message a little sooner or been a little faster in figuring out how to open the pendant. She sighed. It was too late for such thoughts. Her mind pulled up an image of Vistimmot as he coached her in the art of fire spells. She bit her lip in frustration. The flamewisp spell had been eluding her ever since. She held out her hand and tried to focus on the spell once again. As she slowly retraced the steps Vistimmot had taught her, she felt a strange sense of calm. She could do this. She would do this. She finished the spell and opened her eyes. Looking at her hand, she saw a wisp of flame. It was incredibly faint. So much so that she started to doubt if she'd even seen it at all. She closed her eyes to try again.

The snap of a twig caused Sinccah's eyes to snap open. She twisted around toward the source of the sound. Nothing appeared to be moving, but whatever had made that noise must be fairly large. She stood slowly and put her pack back on. A soft rustle sounded behind her, and she spun around. As she did, she caught a glimpse of a gray-green hand retreating into a nearby bush. Her eyes widened as her mind started racing. Was that a goblin?! She backed slowly away from the offending bush before spinning around and darting back up the hill. At the base of the bridge, she stopped and looked suspiciously at the location where she'd just been standing. She didn't know a lot about goblins, but the ones she used to come across in Kinscue had always been bitter creatures. Dreekadack had said that many goblins in this area were peaceful, but she didn't want to risk it. She turned away and started walking briskly across the bridge. After a few steps, she looked over her shoulder. Near the bush where she'd seen the hand, she could now see a short, hunched-over creature. The goblin dove back into the nearby foliage and disappeared. Sinccah had seen enough. Regardless of how peaceful this creature was, it was time to leave. She turned away and sprinted over the bridge.

After a few minutes of running, Sinccah doubled over against a nearby tree, gasping for breath. She really wasn't cut out for this kind of excitement. As her breathing became more regular, she calmed down. It was alright; the goblin had seemed far more afraid of her than she had been of it. And honestly, if it came to fighting, she was quite a bit larger than the goblin. She could probably have beaten it.

"Excuse me, miss," a voice from behind her called out.

Sinccah spun to see a group of three men, each dressed in the robes of the royal mages. One was older, perhaps in his late fifties. The other two were younger, probably in their early twenties. "Greetings, sirs," Sinccah said as she held out her hands face up and gave a short bow.

The oldest of the men walked up to Sinccah. "A fellow mage," he said as he extended his open palms to return the greeting, though he notably failed to return the bow.

"Yes," Sinccah said, somewhat excited at the opportunity to speak to some mages again. "I used to be a student in Kinscue."

"Ah," the man said dismissively, "a former student," he continued, his voice dripping with disdain. "Did the training prove too taxing for you?"

Sinccah grimaced. She felt a strong urge to punch this brat in the face but instead offered an honest reply: "I wasn't able to get much out of the lectures."

The man laughed. "That does explain your present situation. I was wondering why a young woman such as yourself would be sprinting through the wilderness."

"Well actually—" Sinccah started, desperate to defend herself.

"No matter," the man interrupted. "My apprentices and I are tracking down a goblin and are low on time. I don't suppose you have seen one recently."

Sinccah's mind lurched. Of course. She'd just seen a goblin. That was why she'd been running after all. Her face hardened. After such rudeness, these men didn't deserve her help. "I can't say I have," she lied.

"A shame," the man said and he waved his hand arrogantly. "I suppose I wouldn't expect anything more from a dropout."

Sinccah's face warped in anger, but she held her tongue. Ucksil needed a mage to go after the bandits. Even though this man was being incredibly rude, he might still be useful. The sooner she could go after the bandits, the better. "Do you work for Ucksil?" Sinccah asked with forced pleasantness.

The man jerked his head back in disgust. "That fool?" he sneered. "I would never bring myself to work for such an idiot."

"Oh," Sinccah said as calmly as she could. "Why do you say that?"

"The blob of uselessness thinks we can live at peace with the goblins," the man spat. "As though the last couple of centuries taught him nothing. Goblins exist to be tricked and exploited. Nothing more."

"Ucksil is only trying to do what is best for his people," Sinccah insisted.

The man laughed again. "You go ahead and think that," he said mockingly. "Don't come crying to me when he proves you wrong."

Sinccah bit her lip and stared at the ground. Clearly this man hated Ucksil, so his opinion was likely warped beyond recognition. Ucksil certainly wasn't perfect, but he did appear to be trying his best. "I won't," Sinccah said with more confidence than she felt.

"Good," the man said with a chuckle.

Sinccah's head snapped up. "Do any of you know a mage called Beilbauk?"

"A friend of all the crazies, I see," the mage replied with a snort. He shook his head. "I've heard of him."

"Do you know where he lives?" Sinccah asked.

"No," the man scoffed. He raised his chin pompously. "Now if you'll excuse us," he said, gesturing toward the two men behind him. "We have a goblin to catch." Sinccah frowned as the three men walked past her, each giving her a disapproving look.

Sinccah glared into their backs as they walked away. She was sick of getting pushed around like this. Sick of having to put on a show for people who certainly didn't deserve her courtesy. Her lip twitched upward. "I hope your search is fruitful," she called out dryly. The men turned back to scowl at her but kept walking.

Sinccah shook her head as she continued westward. She was glad she hadn't helped those mages find their target. Honestly, she was a bit upset at herself for not deliberately leading them astray. Perhaps it was better this way. She didn't really need to make enemies right now. She frowned. It probably didn't matter: she was working for Ucksil, so if these men hated Ucksil, they would probably come to hate her as well. No wonder Ucksil was so resistant to asking the royal mages for help with the bandits. She sighed as she looked up into the increasingly overcast sky. Clearly there was a lot more intrigue in Ucksland than she'd thought.

⚬

Sinccah stumbled over an outstretched root. The road had long since been overrun, and the footing was becoming more and more treacherous. Either that or she'd wandered from the path entirely. She looked up and squinted into the misting rain that had started almost an hour ago. A scowl formed on her face. Just how far away was this town? In the dim light, she caught the gleam of a faint light. Was that a lantern? She began walking faster, and the light became more bright and distinct. Her shirt suddenly caught a snag, and she turned to free herself from the briars where she'd been caught. As she escaped their clutches and turned back, the light had vanished. She pounded her fist onto a nearby tree. Just what she needed: a fickle light to lead her astray. She leaned against the tree and rested her forehead on its rough bark.

A horse snorted in the distance. She turned to see a single cloaked figure riding through the trees. The rider vanished behind some underbrush before reappearing a moment later. Whoever this was, they seemed to also be heading west. Sinccah shook herself off and started running after the figure. She opened her mouth to call out to the horseman, but as she did, an uneasy feeling swept over her. She had no idea who this was. They might not even be human. Her pace slowed, and she continued following the figure silently.

As Sinccah tailed the cloaked figure, she once again saw lights, this time several of them clustered together. After a few more minutes, the trees abruptly ended. Here the terrain sloped upward slightly into a short bump that was capped off by a pile of loose stones. She watched the horseman climb over the rubble-covered hill and continue through a small field of stumps toward a collection of warmly-lit buildings. Sinccah leaned against a tree to catch her breath as the figure rode up to the largest of the buildings: a two-story structure on the nearside of the town. A boy appeared from beside the building and seemed to be greeting the traveler. The boy then took the figure's horse and vanished into an alley. The figure stood outside the large building for a few seconds, then threw back his hood to reveal a head covered in long red hair and a thick beard. He walked confidently through the door.

Sinccah exhaled deeply. This must be the town Dreekadack had told her about. Presumably, the large building was the tavern. It'd taken her the entire day, but she'd finally made it. She crept out of the trees and climbed the slope. At the top, she stopped to inspect the stones. Clearly they'd once been bricks, though by this time, almost all of them had been shattered. She glanced sideways and noticed the stones continued in the line until the darkness hid them from her view. She wrapped her cloak around herself more tightly and continued through the stumps. Her gaze was drawn to the buildings. With the exception of the tavern, nearly everything looked freshly built. As she entered the cluster of buildings, she turned her attention to the tavern. The sound of loud voices from inside slowly became clear as she approached. She grimaced. This crowd would probably be a collection of thugs. She paused as she came to the door and gazed along the buildings. Besides the tavern, there had to be at least fifty buildings. Hardly the small collection Dreekadack had implied. The roar of laughter sounded from inside the tavern. Sinccah inhaled deeply, brushed her hair out of her eyes, pulled her hood over her face, and opened the door.

She winced as the din instantly became much louder. She slipped through the door and took stock of the room. On the far side, a large man stood behind a sturdy counter. Between her and the counter was a small collection of perhaps ten tables. Most of these tables were surrounded by people, none of whom seemed to acknowledge her entrance. She finally let herself exhale as she searched for an open table. Seeing one in the far right corner of the room, she walked briskly over and sat down.

"You shoulda seen the look on the ealched fool's face!" a burly voice called out. Sinccah looked up to see the red-headed man she'd been following. He was leaning against the counter as the other patrons looked on with interest. "He seemed so surprised to see me!" the man continued in a mocking tone. Several patrons laughed loudly, but most turned their attention to their tables.

"Did you give him what he deserved, Red?" another man asked.

The red-haired man grinned. "Let's just say the ealch won't be coming around here anymore. I ..." More laughter drowned out whatever was being said. Sinccah shook her head as she looked down at her table.

The door to the tavern opened with a loud creak, and a middle aged woman with short black hair entered. She walked purposefully through the room toward the counter. Her clothes were of a remarkably high quality, and she carried herself with obvious confidence. As the lady approached, Red turned from the counter.

The woman started speaking, but Sinccah couldn't make out the words over the noise of the tavern.

"Yeah," Red boasted. "I met Ucksil's rat in the woods just now. He'll be returning to his master with a few more bruises than he had before."

Sinccah's eyes widened. Dreekadack had told her this town wasn't particularly friendly toward Ucksil, but she hadn't expected such active hostility.

The woman gave a short reply to Red and handed him a small bag. She started to turn away, and Sinccah caught a glimpse of her face. It looked emotionless, almost lifeless. The lady's eyes, in particular, appeared to be gazing at a far away object that they had no desire to focus on. Instead, they just stared forward blankly. Sinccah shivered at the sight.

"Is your offer still good?" Red asked, causing the woman to turn back to him. "I doubt the ealching lord will take kindly to this. Make sure your people are ready for a fight."

The woman gave another short response which seemed to satisfy Red. She then turned and started walking toward the door. Her eyes met Sinccah's but passed over without seeming to register her presence. Sinccah sunk her head into her shoulders. The blank gaze was unsettling. Sinccah stole quick glances at the lady, who continued toward the exit. After the strange visitor had left, Sinccah continued to stare at the door. It felt wrong. Something was wrong with that woman. Questions began to dance around in her head. Who was she? What was wrong with her eyes? And why was she helping Red strike out against Ucksil?

"Need anything, traveler?" a rough voice bellowed from beside Sinccah.

She startled and turned to see the large man from the counter standing over her table. "Uh, yes," she said softly. "I need a—"

"Speak up!" the man nearly shouted.

"I need a room for the night," Sinccah said louder than she felt comfortable doing. "And some hot food if you have any."

The man nodded. "I can do that for you," he said loudly. "We've got some soup going, and I'll have a room prepared for you."

"Thank you," Sinccah said softly. The man cocked his head toward her and opened his mouth. "Nothing," Sinccah said loudly as she waved the man off. He nodded and walked back to the counter. Sinccah looked back at the red-haired man, who was loudly relaying the humiliations he'd forced onto the man Ucksil had sent. Periodic bouts of laughter told Sinccah that his limited audience was thoroughly enthralled. Sinccah turned back to her table and began to nervously trace the grain of the wood. Ideally, she'd be able to quickly eat her soup and get out of here.

She cringed as she caught pieces of the red-haired man's gristly exposition. As much as she tried to ignore it, the brute's description of the bloody torture he'd forced upon the Ucksil's man forced itself into her mind. Part of her wanted to flee, but her more rational side told her she'd do better blending into the crowd. She certainly couldn't let this man know she was working for Ucksil.

"Here ya are, miss," a deep female voice said.

Sinccah looked up to see a plump middle-aged woman standing over her with a wooden bowl. "Thank you," Sinccah said as the woman placed the bowl in front of her. As Sinccah reached for the bowl, the woman grunted. Sinccah cringed before reaching into her pouch and producing a small copper coin.

The woman took the coin. "Ya got a room for the night also?"

"Yeah," Sinccah said as loudly as she dared.

The woman looked her up and down. "You'll be want'n the private room," she muttered as she turned away. "This'll cover everythin'."

Sinccah smiled as the woman walked away. She'd been worried about the cost of the room, but apparently the copit was adequate payment. Another bout of laughter shook the room. Sinccah grimaced. Hopefully, this soup would be good. She picked up the fat wooden spoon and began to peck at the contents of the bowl. It certainly didn't look that appetizing, but at least it was hot. For several minutes, she worked through the steaming soup as the red-haired man finally finished his story. She'd nearly finished eating when a large arm planted itself firmly on the side of her table.

"Hello there, miss!" a slurred voice bellowed.

Sinccah squeezed her eyes shut. In another minute she would've been able to escape the distasteful situation. Why did this have to happen now? She looked up to see the red-haired man standing over her with a stupid grin. "Yes?" she growled.

Red pulled his head back. "Oh," he said as he turned his shoulder to look back at three men who were standing behind him. He quickly pivoted back around and planted the other arm on the table. "You're a rude one."

Sinccah frowned. "I wish to be left alone," she said flatly. The men behind Red snickered.

"Oh, come now," Red said as he leaned closer. "It never hurts to be friendly."

"Get away from me," Sinccah said with grim calmness.

"Now, now," Red said as he stuck out his neck and leaned closer. The rancid stretch of his breath wafted into Sinccah's face. She curled her lip into a disgusted snarl. If she'd wanted to show dainty manners to brats, she could've stayed with Lady Dove.

Red kept moving closer. "I was just thinking—" His voice was cut short as Sinccah slapped him across the face. He recoiled at the strike as his face contorted in anger and confusion.

Sinccah could feel the room grow silent as eyes locked onto her. "I said," she growled as she slowly rose from her chair, "I want to be left alone."

"Oh, is that how it is," Red said as he turned to walk away. Suddenly, he spun back around and pulled back his arm to throw a punch. Sinccah reflexively cast a shield spell that caught his arm before he could begin swigging it. Red lurched forward, but his arm didn't follow. Instead he lost his balance and awkwardly flopped forward onto the table.

"You alright there, Red?" one of the three nearby men said as the group burst out laughing.

Red pulled himself off the table, his face rapidly approaching the color of his beard. He glared at Sinccah, eyes blazing. "I'll—" he started to say.

"Hey!" the taverner shouted. "We'll have none of that here!"

"Ealched mage," Red muttered to Sinccah as he walked to the far side of the room. His three friends chuckled as they followed closely behind.

Sinccah glanced quickly around as the patrons turned back to their own affairs. The noise of conversation quickly filled the room once more.

"Sorry about all that, miss," the plump woman said as she appeared behind Sinccah. "I'll get ya another bowl of soup."

"I've had enough, actually," Sinccah protested. The sooner she could get away from this room the better.

"Naw, I insist," the woman said forcefully. "Can't have people thinking this place ain't generous."

Sinccah lifted her hand in an attempt to protest. She wanted desperately to get out of here, but she did still need information about the mage she was looking for. She frowned. No information was worth staying in a room with a thug like Red. Besides, she could always ask more questions in the morning. "I can't stay," Sinccah said forcefully.

The woman eyed her suspiciously. "Very well," she said flatly. "I'll get the key to yer room."

"Thank you," Sinccah said as she slowly sank back into her chair. She folded her hands together and looked across the room at Red. He eyed her scornfully as his companions mockingly reenacted his awkward punch. Sinccah looked around for the woman, but apparently, she'd vanished. She glanced back at Red. It was unlikely that he'd try something again, but she didn't want to stick around to find out. Fortunately, it appeared the taverner and the plump woman would have her back if he did.

As she was waiting, the door opened again, and a short hunched-over figure entered. Sinccah eyed the new visitor with great interest. He was bent like a crippled old man and completely obscured by a heavy cloak. Even his legs were hidden behind the thick cloth. She suddenly noticed that the other patrons had gone silent again. They were also staring at the new arrival. Red and his companions, in particular, eyed the figure with extreme suspicion. The figure hobbled up to the counter and dropped a scrap of paper from his oversized sleeve.

The taverner looked at the note briefly. "You got payment?"

The figure produced a couple of silver coins and tossed them onto the bar.

"Just two this time?" the taverner said disdainfully. "That isn't enough."

The figure recoiled slightly and tilted his head to the side.

"Prices have gone up," The taverner said flatly before setting a small bag on the bar. "This is all that'll get you."

Sinccah furrowed her brow. The taverner had already had the bag waiting there, and it didn't appear he knew how many coins the hunched traveler would have. What sort of business was taking place?

The figure opened the bag and dumped its contents onto the counter. It was just some food, most of it dried, with a couple loaves of fresh bread. Sinccah was taken aback. There was no way the contents of the bag were worth even a single siv.

The figure reached for the two coins, only to have the taverner snatch them away. "I told you to stop coming by," the taverner said forcefully.

"Yeah," Red said as he walked up behind the cloaked figure. "I told you to stop coming around here."

The figure turned slowly toward Red but offered nothing in reply.

Red snarled at the figure. "I'm in the mood to give out another beating." He glanced at the men around him. "What do you all think?"

Red's friends let out a series of chuckles to signal their approval.

Sinccah quickly scanned the room as questions raced through her mind. Was everyone just going to let this happen? Her face hardened. This must be another one of Ucksil's men.

Red grabbed the back of the figure's cloak and yanked him backward. The figure twisted as he fell, catching himself with his hands. A smirk formed on Red's face. "What's wrong, ealch, not even going to bother fighting back?"

Sinccah's eyes widened. She needed to do something! Her mind lurched back to the description Red had given of his previous beating. She wasn't about to let that happen in front of her. Particularly not when it came from a thug like Red. "Hey!" she shouted as she leapt to her feet, knocking her chair over. The men ignored her and quickly surrounded the figure.

Red stepped forward, grabbed the hunched man's cloak, and rammed his knee into his face. As the figure recoiled from the blow, his hood fell and revealed a single semi-transparent amber tentacle instead of a head. Sinccah gasped. This wasn't one of Ucksil's men. This was a mygnus. She'd never even seen one before. According to the stories, they lived in the mountains and hated all humans. Why was one here? What in the world would cause it to come this far for food?

The mygnus pivoted as three more tentacles emerged from the top of his cloak. One of these tentacles lashed out at Red's hand.

Red gasped in pain as he jerked his hand away. "You'll pay for that!" he yelled as he dove forward. The mygnus lurched aside to avoid the blow.

"Hey—" the taverner bellowed.

"Be gone freak!" one of Red's companions interrupted as the three of them rushed at the mygnus and grabbed the edges of his cloak.

Sinccah stood with her mouth agape as Red and his companions tried to wrestle the mygnus to the ground. Had she just made a giant mistake? She looked over the other patrons, who were staring at the mygnus but otherwise remained motionless. Words instantly formed in her mind and escaped her lips before she had time to consider them. "Leave the mygnus alone!" she shouted as she stepped toward the men. A grimace formed on her face. Was she really about to defend a mygnus?

One of the men turned to her, gave her a look of disdain, then returned his attention to the mygnus.

Sinccah suddenly heard a wispy voice in her head. "Help," it said without emotion.

Was the mygnus talking to her? Was he offering her help? Was he asking her for help? She made up her mind. "I mean it!" she called out.

"Shut up, wretch!" one of the men said as he pulled back his fist to strike at the mygnus. Sinccah projected a quick shield spell that prevented him from swinging. The man twisted around as he brought his weight forward. He fell to the floor with a loud thud. The mygnus took advantage of the opportunity and slipped out of his cloak. He dashed over the fallen man and hopped onto a table amid a murmur from the other patrons. The mygnus jumped off the table and landed smoothly on the side nearest Sinccah.

She marveled at the strange creature for the few seconds the shock had bought her. He was composed of six identical tentacles that surrounded a central sphere. Each tentacle was roughly the length of Sinccah's legs, but none of them were held straight. The sphere itself was covered in metal plates and had a diameter similar to the length of Sinccah's torso. The base of each tentacle was also covered in a few bands of metal, but most of the length was bare. He stood on three of his tentacles, which raised the top of the sphere to the height of Sinccah's chest.

"Hey, ealch!" Sinccah heard Red screech. She startled from her dumbfounded observation and turned to see him pointing at her. "You think I can't see what you're doing!" He started charging at her. "You'll pay!"

Sinccah winced. What'd she gotten herself into? As Red rushed at her, she projected a shield at his feet to trip him. He fell forward onto Sinccah's table. As he stood back up, Sinccah drove her shoulder into his chest and he stumbled backward. She projected another shield behind his ankles, causing him to trip and fall onto his back.

Meanwhile, the mygnus was evading the attacks of the other men. He hopped around the room as the men fumbled after him. As Red struck the ground with a loud thump, one of the men turned to see what had happened. The mygnus darted forward and wrapped himself around the man's calves. The nimble creature reached up a pair of tentacles and yanked the back of the man's shoulders. The man shrieked in pain as he fell backward and knocked his head on a chair. As the man crumpled, the mygnus jumped from around the man's legs and started to scramble to the far side of the room.

The final man dove at the mygnus, grabbing one of the creature's tentacles. The mygnus rolled his sphere forward, switching out the tentacles he was using for walking, and yanked the captured tentacle free. "You ealch-brained fool!" one of the fallen men shouted at Sinccah as he pulled himself to his feet. "You—"

"Enough!" the voice of the taverner called out. Sinccah turned to see him pointing a large crossbow at the mygnus. "You, mygnus," he said slowly. "Take your purchase and get out. Never come into my tavern again!" The mygnus hobbled slowly to the counter, shoved the food back into the bag, picked it up, and headed for the door.

"Thanks," Sinccah heard the wispy voice in her head say. She turned to see the mygnus wave at her as he walked out the door.

"You four," the taverner growled as he gestured toward Red and his companions. "Out."

"What!" one of the men exclaimed. "You're kicking us out! That ealching woman was aiding the creature!" He pointed at Sinccah. "She should be executed for such treason!"

"Out I said!" the taverner shouted. "And if I ever catch one of you starting a fight in my tavern again, I'll personally make sure Ucksil tans your ealched hides."

"Very well," one of the four men growled as the group of them finished picking themselves off the floor and exited the tavern.

Sinccah wished she could suddenly disappear. The taverner turned to her. "Miss," he said crossly, "you have your room for tonight. After that, never come to my tavern again."

———— ◆◇◆ ————

Sinccah gazed up at the shoddy wooden ceiling. The bed wasn't comfortable. Honestly, it wasn't really even a bed, just a pile of cloth and straw on the floor. Even so, she lingered on it out of apprehension for the new day. She combed her hands through her hair. Why had she helped the mygnus? Sure, the poor creature was being attacked for no discernible reason, and sure, the thugs had it coming. She let out a soft groan. She really couldn't afford to make enemies so quickly. Her mind reflected on what the taverner had told the thugs. These people were no friends of Ucksil. Perhaps it didn't even matter. She pulled her hands down her face and tugged on the skin under her eyes. A sigh escaped her. There wasn't really anything else to do. She needed to get to Beilbauk. She felt a familiar ache as she instinctively reached for her missing pendant. Her hand curled around the empty air, and she shook her fist. Thoughtful times like these hurt the most. She shook her head as she sat up. It was time to get off this shabby bed, get the information she needed, and get out of here.

She walked slowly downstairs to the main room, her lack of motivation clearly showing in her steps. Once there, she noticed the plump woman prodding at something in the hearth. Sinccah gazed around. The taverner didn't appear to be around at the moment, so maybe she could still talk to this woman before she left.

"Excuse me, ma'am," Sinccah said as she jogged to the fireplace.

"Hum?" the woman snorted in surprise and she straightened up and turned to Sinccah. "Ah, the feisty one. Did you have a pleasant sleep?"

"It was good," Sinccah lied in the sweetest voice she could manage. The night had honestly been pretty awful, but she still needed information.

The woman grunted, "That's nice."

"I was hoping I could ask you a question before I left," Sinccah said optimistically.

"Mmmm," the woman hummed to herself. "Afraid I can't answer it."

"What do you mean?" Sinccah questioned.

"You 'ave many enemies," the woman said flatly as she turned away from Sinccah and resumed prodding the coals.

"I don't—" Sinccah started.

"You oughta leave," the woman said without turning around.

"Ah," Sinccah grunted before turning and walking to the door. Upon reaching it, she turned back toward the plump woman. She wanted to say something friendly before she left, but it didn't seem like it would be appreciated. The door opened with a sharp creak and Sinccah had to hop aside to avoid being hit. The taverner entered carrying a large sack. He glared at Sinccah as he walked past her. Sinccah sunk her head into her shoulders before slipping silently out the door.

She walked briskly away from the tavern. Apparently, her actions the night before had soured these people's opinion of her, but she could probably ask one of the other townspeople.

As she walked, she glanced up toward the distant mountains, vague and foggy in the overcast sky. She frowned. It was better than the misting rain from the night before, but she could've really gone for some sunlight.

Her eyes returned to the buildings. In the morning light, she could see the town much more clearly. It wasn't very large. Her eyes caught sight of a giant pile of crumbled stones poking out from behind the house she was walking past. Why hadn't this large stone structure been repaired? With the constant threat of dragons, wooden houses were an extreme liability. A dull creak sounded softly behind her. She turned to try to catch a glimpse of the source, but nothing looked irregular, save the fact that the street was empty. She shivered slightly. Something was wrong with this town.

She quickened her pace and walked briskly down the road. As she did, the sun peeked out from behind the clouds. Sinccah glanced down at her shadow as it mimicked her movements. The sun slipped behind another wisp of cloud, and the shadows vanished. Shouldn't the people who lived here be out on the streets already? It wasn't that early; they certainly wouldn't all still be in bed. The sun freed itself from the cloud and once again caused shadows to appear. Sinccah's eyes widened as she saw two more shadows on either side of her own. Someone was behind her. She spun to see two of the thugs from the night before.

One grinned menacingly at her. "What is it, little mage?"

"Do we need to go through this again?" Sinccah asked sharply.

"Is the little mage still feisty?" the other man said mockingly. "I don't think you understand," he said, gesturing behind Sinccah. "We're in charge here."

Sinccah glanced over her shoulder to see Red standing behind her. "This doesn't need to get violent again," she said with more confidence than she had.

"I think it might," Red said as he took a step toward Sinccah. "Wretches like you need to be taught a lesson."

"You know," Sinccah said slowly. "I was just thinking the same thing."

Red's face filled with rage. "You dare say that!" he screeched.

"I do," Sinccah said flatly. She was trying her best to stay calm and project power. Power she didn't have. She only knew spells for healing and shielding. It wasn't like she was going to toss out a fireball or a shatter orb. Her best chance was running away. If only she could make even a wisp of fire! At least then she could bluff knowing a more dangerous spell. She fought back a grimace. It wasn't like she could heal them to death. A scream threatened to escape her, but she suppressed it. Instead, she walked confidently past Red and continued swiftly down the road.

"Hey, ealch," Red said as he recovered from his shock and caught up to Sinccah. "I didn't say you could leave."

"I don't care what you say," Sinccah said flatly as she quickened her pace.

"Hey!" a man shouted. Sinccah looked up to see the fourth thug from the night before. He was standing a few dozen steps in front of her. However, her eyes were quickly drawn even farther down the road, where a familiar hunched figure hobbled along.

"Look what we have here," Red said with a chuckle. "If it isn't your ealched friend." He turned to Sinccah with a fiendish grin. "It looks like we're going to have a rematch," he said excitedly. "But this time, we aren't going easy."

Sinccah caught movement out of the corner of her eye and turned slightly to see six men exiting a nearby building. Each of them was wearing an incomplete smattering of armor that ranged from cloth to mail. "I see," Sinccah said calmly as she tried to hide her genuine fear.

"Still trying to sound tough, eh?" Red said mockingly. "Doesn't matter," he continued as he pulled a hand ax from his belt. "There isn't going to be enough of you left over to be tough when we're done here."

The men surrounding her started chuckling.

Sinccah's mind raced. What could she even do in this situation? She was alone against ten men. Sure, she could use some spells, but she was still doomed.

A familiar wispy voice spoke into her head. "Help," it said softly.

Sinccah looked down the road at the mygnus. He was sprinting toward her. Apparently, she wasn't quite alone after all.

"Ready to die, little mage?" Red jeered as he stepped toward Sinccah.

Sinccah's face hardened as she drew her dagger and pulled her arm back. She breathed in deeply before suddenly dashing toward an opening between two of the men. They moved to close the gap, but a pair of twangs pierced the tense air. The men collapsed, screeching as crossbow bolts sank into their thighs. Sinccah leapt over their writhing bodies and sprinted down the street.

"Get her!" Red bellowed. The remaining eight men surged after Sinccah. She glanced over her shoulder and quickly projected a pair of shields along the ground. The two leading men tripped over the shields and collapsed into the dirt. The men behind them stumbled as they tried not to trip on their fallen companions.

Sinccah looked up at the mygnus. He had thrown off his cloak and pack and now blazed a deep red. Two pairs of tentacles each worked to wind the crossbows, and another tentacle brandished a sword. Even though the mygnus would've only come up to Sinccah's chest, she was glad he was on her side.

"Got ya!" a man called out from right behind Sinccah. He lunged forward and grabbed Sinccah's shoulder. She shrugged her way out of his grip, but staggered in her run. She pivoted around to face her attackers. The next man stumbled over the man who had just grabbed her, and tumbled forward. Sinccah tripped him with a shield. As he fell in front of her, she slashed across his arm with her dagger. The man screamed as he fell to the ground, clutching his arm.

As Sinccah was recovering from her swing, she caught a glimpse of two spears racing toward her. Each of the men wielding them was met with a sharp twang as bolts struck their shoulders. They cried out and toppled forward.

"You think you can get away!" Red roared as he jumped over his fallen companions and chopped at Sinccah. Sinccah grimaced as she cast a shield that deflected the blow. Red stumbled to the side as his ax bit into the hard ground. Sinccah staggered at the shock of the strike and wobbled back before catching herself on a knee.

Another man pulled back a sword to stab at Sinccah, but she caught his arm with a shield before he could begin his strike. He twisted as he fell forward, and Sinccah sliced across his back, but her dagger failed to cut through the thick cloth jacket he wore. Sinccah shoved her hand against the ground and pushed herself back onto her feet. As she rose, a knife flashed in the corner of her eye, and she jumped back to dodge the attack. Her attacker recovered from his strike and tried to stab up at her. She threw up a shield against the man's elbow, forcing his arm to bend and stab the knife into his shoulder. He howled as his momentum carried him forward and he slammed into Sinccah, driving her to the ground.

Two more screams sounded as another pair of bolts tore into another pair of thugs. Sinccah struggled out from under the thug who'd fallen on her. She freed her leg and kicked him in the face, which allowed her to squirm away. She looked up; her eyes locked onto an ax as it rushed toward her face. She tried to project a shield, but she knew it was too late. Even if she blocked this attack, the drain from the shield would probably kill her. She squeezed her eyes shut. Suddenly, a sickening metal clank filled the air. She felt a gust of air sweep over her before a blood curdling scream pierced the air.

Sinccah's eyes shot open to see that the mygnus was standing above her. His tentacles blazed with a deep red color as he held his now-bent sword over top of Sinccah. A glint to Sinccah's right caught her eye, and she glanced over to see Red's ax laying on the ground, the base of the handle covered in specks of blood. She looked past her feet to see Red writhing on the ground clutching his bloodied hand.

"Ealch on you!" Red screeched through gritted teeth. The mygnus pulled a crossbow forward and quickly began winding it. A few more thugs were still standing, but all bore wounds and didn't seem particularly inclined to continue the attack. The mygnus raised a tentacle and began to move it quickly through the air. As he did so, the tip of the tentacle left a thin line of floating red energy.

Apparently the mygnus was writing something. "Let us go. Enough of your blood has been spilled," the lines now spelled.

Sinccah's eyes widened. Was this how magnus normally communicated? What was the voice in her head from before then? No answers were forthcoming, but the thugs did begin to slowly pick each other up and hobble off the road.

As Red walked away, he turned back and shook a bloody fist at Sinccah. "You'll pay for this, little mage!" he growled. "You'll see!"

The mygnus stepped off of Sinccah and held out a tentacle. With another he wrote in the air once more: "Thank you for your help, miss."

"Uh," Sinccah fumbled as she grabbed the tentacle and the mygnus pulled her to her feet. "I think I should be the one thanking you."

"Perhaps," the mygnus wrote. His tentacles turned a dull green and he continued, the new text taking on the same green color. "Regardless, I appreciate your assistance, ..." he paused, slowly rotating the tentacle that had been writing in a small circle as though waiting for Sinccah to interject.

"Sinccah," she stammered as she suddenly realized what the mygnus was asking.

"Spelled?" the mygnus asked as his uncompleted sentence faded.

Sinccah methodically spelled her name. The mygnus wrote each letter in the air as she said it.

After the name was finished, he quickly moved his tentacle in front of her name and completed the three word sentence: "Thank you, Sinccah," the mygnus wrote. "Your kindness yesterday was certainly noticed."

Sinccah nodded. Her eyes darted from the text to the mygnus, but she couldn't quite decide where to focus her attention. It didn't seem the creature had anything resembling a face, or even a front, which made looking at his sphere feel like staring into the back of someone's head. Her gaze twitched to the ground. "It seemed like you needed a hand."

The mygnus tilted his sphere slightly. For a second he stood motionless before quickly straightening out. "Indeed."

Sinccah glanced around awkwardly. "Do you have a name?"

The mygnus rotated his central sphere and switched one of the tentacles he was standing on. "It seems I lack that," he wrote. "However, you may call me the Wanderer."

Sinccah's brow furrowed. What kind of strange creature didn't have a name? And who would call themselves a wanderer? "Alright, Wanderer," Sinccah said slowly as she glanced between the tips of his raised tentacles. "What brings you to Rivvairt?"

"What brings me to a human town?" the Wanderer wrote before walking back to his fallen cloak and picking it up. "Perhaps you will find out," he continued as he shook the dust off the cloak. "I presume you also intend to leave before the thugs return, yes?"

"Oh," Sinccah said in surprise. She glanced over her shoulder. "Yeah, I suppose I'd better get out of here."

The Wanderer shoved his cloak into a pack that had been hidden under it. He grabbed the pack with two of his tentacles and strapped it onto his central sphere such that it obstructed Sinccah's view of the metal ball. "Very good," he wrote as he gestured southward. "I have some friends I need to visit. I have arranged to meet them nearby. You are welcome to come."

Sinccah's eyes widened. A mygnus was inviting her to join him? She took an excited step forward before realizing what she was doing. This was a freak creature she'd never even seen before. She certainly shouldn't trust him. A grimace formed on her face. If he'd wanted to hurt her, he could've just left her to Red. Still, it felt wrong to blindly follow him. She shifted her jaw to the side. It couldn't hurt to join him for a minute. Besides, it wasn't like she would ever get another chance to talk to a mygnus.

The Wanderer tilted to the side, then started to raise a tentacle.

"Alright," Sinccah said suddenly. "Let's go find your friends."

Chapter Six

Sinccah jogged alongside the Wanderer as he headed south, away from the village. Questions danced through her mind. There was so much she wanted to ask this mygnus, who had gradually turned a teal color. She opened her mouth but caught herself just in time. Her companion was a mygnus. With his dependence on writing text in the air, it'd be quite difficult for him to walk and talk at the same time. He'd probably find it rude if she tried to make conversation. Instead, she watched him carefully as he walked. At least with the pack on, he gave the impression of facing some direction, not that he seemed to care which way that was. She glanced over the tips of his tentacles. Three of them hovered aimlessly above his sphere, and he used the other three to cleanly glide across the ground. She thought back to the hobbling he'd done in the tavern. That must've been an act to hide the fact that he wasn't human. Sinccah frowned thoughtfully. She'd been fooled at first, so she couldn't question his methods.

The pair soon made it to the edge of the stump field, passed between the crumpled remains of two stone towers, and entered the forest. The Wanderer continued walking just long enough that the trees mostly obscured Sinccah's view of the town. He stopped abruptly, standing motionless on the three tentacles he'd been walking on.

Sinccah glanced around nervously. "Is everything alright?"

The Wanderer raised a tentacle. "Yes."

Sinccah pulled her ponytail over her shoulder and began to comb her fingers through it. "It's just that you stopped so suddenly," she said awkwardly as her gaze snapped between the Wanderer's sphere and the text he'd just written. "I thought something might be wrong."

"Oh," the Wanderer wrote as he shuffled his walking tentacles around slightly. "In case you missed it, we are now hidden in the trees. We could be more hidden if we went farther. However, I would then be unable to perceive what people are doing in the town."

Sinccah looked back at Rivvairt and squinted. From here, she could hardly even see the buildings, much less the people around them. She turned back to the Wanderer with a confused look. "You can still see those people?" she asked incredulously.

"If that is what you want to call it," the Wanderer wrote. "As far as I can tell, I am unable to actually see anything." After finishing his sentence, he twitched his tentacle back to the word "see" and drew a quick underline.

Sinccah studied the mygnus. His assertion seemed correct. Nowhere on his body did he appear to have any eyes or even ears. She tilted her head slightly as she stared into the fading text. "How exactly do you, uh, *perceive* anything?"

"That is complicated," the Wanderer wrote. "I can simplify it somewhat. Humans use their frail eyes and ears to take in their surroundings. I simply sense all objects around me all the time."

Sinccah's eyes widened. "And can you still sense the people in the town?"

"Obviously," the Wanderer wrote quickly. "The far side of the human town is just outside my range of perception."

Sinccah glanced back at the obscured buildings. If this mygnus was telling the truth, he could see things that no human realistically could. "And you can still make out details?"

"I can sense that the group of thugs we fought earlier are tending to their wounds as they gather more of their men."

"What?!" Sinccah exclaimed before continuing more quietly. "Doesn't that mean we should get out of here?"

"Certainly," the Wanderer wrote. "However, I am waiting for my friends."

"Right," Sinccah said slowly, feeling less certain about her decision to join this strange creature. "Won't they also be in danger? Magnus clearly aren't welcome here."

The Wanderer twisted sharply. "I think you misjudge the nature of my friends," he wrote quickly, such that the text was jagged and hard to read.

Sinccah recoiled at his sudden movement. "I guess I just figured ..." her voice drifted off as the Wanderer raised his tentacle to continue writing.

"Maintain confidence," he wrote. "They are in far more danger if they fail to meet me than they could ever be because of me."

Sinccah furrowed her brow. She had no idea what this mygnus was talking about, and his comment had done nothing to soothe her. Just what kind of danger were these friends in? Would that lead her into another fight? She didn't feel like his answers would make sense, so she didn't bother to ask. She briefly considered bidding the strange creature farewell, but her curiosity held her in place. Seeing as her new companion wasn't moving, she took a moment to settle down at the base of a tree to catch her breath.

Her eyes darted back toward Rivvairt as a thought pushed itself into her mind. Should she tell Ucksil about all this? He'd certainly be interested in what she'd heard. Her face pulled into a frown. She could always fill Ucksil in when she returned with Beilbauk. Her eyes drifted past the Wanderer to the forest beyond. She needed to get moving. Every minute that passed gave the bandits a greater chance to pawn off her pendant. The corner of her lip curled upward. Not that she had any idea where Beilbauk lived. She glanced at the Wanderer, who had remained entirely motionless. Was he really just planning to wait here?

Several minutes passed in relative silence. Sinccah spent all of that time vainly trying to avoid staring at the mygnus. The creature was so strange yet incredibly interesting. A nearby bird let out an optimistic call, and Sinccah briefly searched for it but quickly gave up. She was starting to get restless. Red and his thugs might come after them at any time. She leaned forward and looped her arms around her knees. "Do you know how long it'll take your friends to get here?"

"No," the Wanderer wrote slowly. "I suspect it will be slightly less than an hour."

"Right," Sinccah said as she shifted awkwardly. Almost an hour. As if she could wait that long. Questions or otherwise, she needed to get to Beilbauk. "I need to get going."

The Wanderer tilted slightly. "Your existence is so tumultuous that you are unable to pause for a few minutes?"

"Yes," Sinccah grumbled as she pushed herself to her feet. She didn't care for the implication the Wanderer was making, but it didn't matter. She wasn't going to wait for Red to come kill her. She let out a sharp sigh. "I was supposed to ask around at the tavern to figure out where the mage Beilbauk lived. I need to see if he'll come help Ucksil—" she stopped suddenly as she noticed the Wanderer turning a bright orange color.

The Wanderer wrote rapidly on the air between them, the text becoming increasingly sloppy as he wrote. "What do you want with this mage?!"

"Uh," Sinccah stammered. What had she done? Clearly this mygnus didn't care for Beilbauk. How would he respond to her telling him about her quest? For a few seconds her mind raced, but eventually she decided to be honest. After all, this mygnus had saved her from Red. "I need to talk to him to see if he'll join Ucksil's men in a journey north. A group of bandits have been attacking caravans that travel over the mountains, and Ucksil wants them dealt with."

The Wanderer tilted his central sphere to the side. "You are trying to recruit this mage for a quest up north to go after some humans?"

"Yes," Sinccah answered.

"How long will this quest take?" the Wanderer wrote as his body became a brighter shade of orange.

"I don't know," Sinccah said as she glanced upward. "I'd guess at least two months, both to track the bandits down and to get the needed men up there to deal with them." Sinccah paused briefly. "Assuming Beilbauk agrees to it."

The Wanderer's tentacles quivered slightly. "Do you think it is likely he will join this quest?"

"I hope so," Sinccah said nervously. "He does owe my family a favor." Her lip twitched upward. Was she telling this creature too much?

"Excellent!" the Wanderer wrote, turning a bright green color. "I will help you find him!"

"Really?" Sinccah exclaimed. She instantly regretted revealing her emotions. It wasn't like she knew what caused the mygnus to make such an offer. She forced a calmer expression onto her face and looked down toward her companion, finding her eyes resting on the fading text he'd written. "Do you know where he lives?"

"Naturally," the Wanderer wrote. "He lives in a ruined tower to the south of here. I can take you there after I finish a few errands."

Sinccah raised an eyebrow. "What kind of errands?" she asked with a hint of disgust. "I'm on a pretty tight schedule."

"Simple ones," the Wanderer wrote. "After we meet with my friends, I need to direct myself southwest to converse with some goblins, but that is basically on the way. After that, I was already planning to head farther south."

"Sure," Sinccah said with measured excitement. She didn't appreciate the distractions, but it'd be worth it if she got a guide. Besides, the mygnus still intrigued her. She raised an eyebrow dubiously. "Am I going to owe you anything for this?"

"That would be irrational," the Wanderer wrote. "You have already helped me enough. This will be no problem."

"Sure," Sinccah said as a thin smile formed on her face. "It appears we're partners now."

The Wanderer flashed a dull blue color before turning teal. "Yes," he wrote quickly. "It seems we are."

Sinccah grinned as she settled back down against the tree. Finally something was going right. Up to this point, she'd been assuming that her actions at the tavern had ruined her chances of quickly finding Beilbauk. However, it seemed they'd actually won her a guide. A guide that wanted to wait around for the next hour, but a guide nonetheless.

She glanced at the Wanderer, who was once again standing motionless. His motives were certainly unclear, but perhaps she could trust him. He had saved her from Red and his thugs, after all. She frowned. This was a mygnus. Technically, the kingdom was at war with this creature. Her lips twitched to the side. Perhaps such politics didn't really matter here in Ucksland.

The Wanderer suddenly tilted, and Sinccah glanced away as though she'd just been caught staring. Her eyes were slowly drawn back toward the strange creature. If she was going to be waiting, she might as well ask this mygnus some questions. "I always thought magnus needed to live around a big crystal," she said softly. "How are you able to journey among humans?"

The Wanderer straightened. "I am unique."

Sinccah tilted her head, unsure what to make of this response.

"Do you know what maggni are?" he wrote quickly.

"Of course," Sinccah answered. "They're large gems used to store magic energy."

The Wanderer flashed a dark red color. "Wrong."

Sinccah's eyes widened in horror. "I, uh," she quickly stammered before words failed her. She'd mindlessly given the same answer she would've given any human who asked her. However, she wasn't talking to a human right now: she was talking to a mygnus.

"What kind of mage are you?!" the Wanderer wrote in harsh, jagged text before edging closer.

Sinccah cringed at his advance. "A failed one," she whispered sorrowfully as her eyes drifted downward.

The Wanderer's color lightened into a fiery orange. He waved his tentacle through the air but didn't write anything. After a few seconds he started writing cleanly and slowly. "You are distressed." He paused. "Sorrowful."

Sinccah read the text out of the corner of her eye but didn't look up. Instead, her head slumped forward and she focused her gaze on the ground. She didn't want to look at him. Didn't want him to see her pain. She squeezed her eyes shut and started to shake her head. What was she doing? He could see her no matter what she did. She fought to force a calm expression onto her face, but regrets continued to crowd her mind and force her face to contort. Why was she such a failure?

She heard the Wanderer shuffle toward her and saw him waving a tentacle near the ground. She finally looked up to see he had turned a light blue. "It's …" she started before her face twisted in despair. She'd tried so hard, but she could never do it. She could never pass her classes. She could never make her aunt happy with her. She hadn't even been able to save Vistimmot. Even this mygnus thought she was a poor mage.

"I seem to have hurt you," the Wanderer wrote calmly. "Unfortunate."

Sinccah glanced over the text to read it but didn't look up.

The Wanderer shuffled awkwardly. "I am sure you are very skilled." He paused, rocking gently side to side. "I am sorry to imply that you were anything else. My intentions were more noble than that."

Sinccah bit her lip as she read the text. "What do you mean?" she asked, struggling to keep her voice level.

"My passion was too great," the Wanderer wrote. He took a short step backward. "Your pack and person seem devoid of maggni."

"Yeah," Sinccah said softly. "I never got far enough in my classes to be awarded one." She frowned. "And none of the more experienced mages ever bothered to take a simple scribe as an apprentice."

"You have never used a maggni yourself?" the Wanderer wrote.

"I tried once," Sinccah sighed. "Some of the other students had stolen one, and they all worked out how to tap into the energy. I …" her voice drifted off. "I couldn't get it to work."

"That is quite fortunate for you," the Wanderer said as his color took on a subtle green.

"Huh?" Sinccah questioned.

"If you are ignorant in how to use them, you are disincentivized to collect them," the Wanderer wrote. "That means we can still be partners."

Sinccah's face twitched. Perhaps her past failures were more fortuitous than she'd thought. It was certainly helping her avoid getting stabbed by a mygnus in the wilderness. The faintest smile formed on her face. "I suppose it sounds better when you put it that way."

"Indeed," the Wanderer wrote.

Sinccah glanced into the sky, then back at the Wanderer. Her eyes darted over his tentacles for a few seconds before twitching to his sphere. "If you don't mind me asking, where do maggni actually come from? I know magnus make them, but what do you actually use them for?"

"You are unaware?" the Wanderer wrote as his color briefly flickered to red before changing back to a subtle blue.

Sinccah shifted uncomfortably. "No, I only know what humans use them for."

"Maggni are more than a mere gem to store magic in," the Wanderer wrote quickly, the text becoming increasingly red. "Each mygnus forms around a maggni. They are empty shells that hold our energies and allow us to manifest our individual forms. Over time, we carefully harvest them from our progenitor crystal." The Wanderer slashed a tentacle through the text as he turned a deep red. "Only to have them stolen by humans for their foolish experiments!"

Sinccah stared into the rough text as it slowly dissipated. "I had no idea," she whispered.

The Wanderer's tentacles flopped to his side as he turned increasingly blue. "Humans and their secrets."

Sinccah shook her head in disbelief. "I never thought we were stealing your corpses."

"Calling them corpses would be simplistic," the Wanderer corrected. "All magnus form around a maggni, but some maggni have never been inhabited by a magnus. The progenitor crystal can grow new maggni faster than new magnus are formed."

"So you have extras?" Sinccah asked innocently.

"Yes," the Wanderer wrote as his color flickered to red. "We need them."

Sinccah cringed slightly.

"We need them for when humans pour into our villages like locusts," the Wanderer wrote quickly. His color flashed blue for a second but returned to red as he kept writing. "We need them when we are senselessly cut down!" His color flicked again. "We need them to reform our bodies when vile humans kill us!"

Sinccah's mouth slid open.

The Wanderer's color lightened but remained a shade of red. "We need them to save our crystal from the corruption of foul magic."

"Ah," Sinccah said awkwardly as silence fell between them.

A rustle sounded as a small rodent scrambled up a tree. For its new perch, it let out a disgruntled squeak. Sinccah glanced down and started to pick at the bark on a nearby root. She had no idea what to say. The Wanderer clearly held humans in contempt. Yet he was helping her. She glanced up at him. Did he have some ulterior motive? It didn't seem right that he'd help her. She needed to be careful.

The Wanderer twitched slightly as his color turned blue again. "Sorry for the outburst," he wrote quickly. "I become impassioned when discussing the vessel of magnus life."

Sinccah nodded slowly. "I understand," she said softly. "Maggni make a lot more sense now. They're a catalyst. You have one inside you, and your village has extras waiting in case you die."

The Wanderer shifted awkwardly. "Actually, no," he wrote. "My body contains a void where the maggni should be."

Sinccah's brow furrowed. "Didn't you say that all magnus have them?"

"They do," the Wanderer wrote slowly as his color took on a blue tinge. "I am ..." he paused, waiting for the text to fade completely before he continued. "I am different."

"What do you mean?" Sinccah questioned.

"I am a wanderer," the mygnus wrote.

"A wanderer?"

"A homeless mygnus," the Wanderer wrote. "A mygnus with neither a maggni nor a crystal. A strange anomaly."

"What's holding you together then?" Sinccah questioned.

"It is unknown," the Wanderer wrote. "Such is the way of wanderers."

"So some magnus just form around nothing?" Sinccah said as she shook her head. "Why?"

"That too is unknown," the Wanderer replied. "Many believe that wanderers like me are formed to address particularly dire situations. The crystal creates us to deal with threats."

"So you were formed during such a time?" Sinccah asked as she leaned forward.

"Perhaps," the Wanderer wrote.

Sinccah pulled her head back. "What do you mean? You just said that wanderers form in times of turmoil."

"That is what many believe," the Wanderer wrote. "However, when I first formed, nothing seemed to be amiss. To this day, I have never found the great turmoil that I was formed to resolve."

Sinccah nodded. "I see," she said softly. Her face twisted slightly. Wasn't this mygnus saying too much? They'd only just met, yet he was willing to explain all of this to her. She shifted slightly as her mind turned inward. Was this mygnus like her? Stuck with a constant feeling that he was formed for greatness but never quite being able to figure out what to do. She tilted her head. "Do you ever feel like you somehow missed it?"

The Wanderer rocked back and forth on his tentacles. "No," he wrote firmly. "The crystal did what was best. I am no mistake."

"I guess that's a good attitude to have," Sinccah admitted.

The Wanderer stood motionless for a few seconds, then started writing: "It is the attitude I must have. The life of a wanderer is a lonely one."

"Why's that?" Sinccah asked. "You're far freer than the other magnus. They have to stay around their crystals, but you can travel wherever you want. Certainly you could stay with other magnus if you wanted to."

"You simplify the situation too much," the Wanderer wrote, turning a dark blue. "Those who share a crystal share a bond. As a wanderer, I am devoid of that bond. I am able to travel the land freely, but I can never truly be a part of a village." He paused, his tentacles drooping slightly. "I can never truly have a home."

"Oh," Sinccah said sympathetically. "I'm sorry."

"You may maintain confidence," the Wanderer wrote as his color turned teal, though a hint of blue still remained. "The crystal that formed me did so for a reason. My path may be a lonely one, but someday I will discover what I was made for."

Sinccah nodded as silence fell between them. She began to think about her own life. What had she been born for? Was she destined to become a great mage? Or perhaps she was doomed to live her life in irrelevance, striving toward something she could never attain.

After half a minute, the Wanderer started writing again: "Earlier, when you talked about the bandits, you seemed to have strong feelings about them. Would it be rude of me to ask why?"

"No," Sinccah said softly. "Honestly, if we are going to travel together, I should probably tell you."

———◄○►———

Sinccah leaned against the tree she was sitting under. She'd just finished telling the Wanderer about her time in Ucksland. The mygnus had stood nearly motionless for the entire story. Periodically he'd changed colors, but he never attempted to write anything in response. Now that Sinccah was finished, the Wanderer lifted a tentacle, but instead of writing, he just waved it through the air in random circles. Sinccah tapped her fingers against one of the roots she was nestled between. She looked up into the sky. The morning was fading fast. She'd been sitting against this tree for over an hour already.

The Wanderer suddenly started writing in a light blue text: "I am sorry to hear of the loss of your pendant."

Sinccah tilted her head. Of all the items in the story, this was what the Wanderer chose to fixate on, even though she'd barely mentioned it. In fairness to the strange creature, it was the part that was most responsible for her continued pursuit of the bandits. She wondered if he somehow knew that or at least understood something about her she hadn't told him.

The Wanderer continued, "It sounds like whatever your mother had hidden in it could be quite useful for you."

"Yeah," Sinccah said hesitantly. "I've been wondering if the message was about her research or just a personal letter to me."

"Either way, it would be useful," the Wanderer wrote as he changed to a teal color.

Sinccah lifted an eyebrow. "I'm not sure how useful it'd really be if it's just a personal letter." She paused, then continued with a dismissive tone. "My mother is almost certainly dead. What difference do her opinions make?"

The Wanderer lifted a tentacle but paused for a few seconds before writing, "Perhaps none, perhaps a great deal."

"Well," Sinccah said as she shifted uncomfortably, "I guess it depends on what it says."

"And also the person reading it," the Wanderer wrote.

Sinccah eyed him curiously. Did he know something she didn't? Was he just plying her for information? She decided not to play along. "I don't suppose you knew my mother?"

The Wanderer shifted slightly. "Based on my knowledge of the requirements humans have to produce offspring, I would consider that impossible."

"Uh ..." Sinccah said awkwardly.

"I have met very few humans on friendly terms," the Wanderer clarified. "None of them are old enough to have been your progenitor."

"Ah," Sinccah grunted. "I suppose that makes sense."

"Indeed," the Wanderer wrote before silence fell between them.

A few minutes passed in irritating silence. Sinccah glanced toward the Wanderer impatiently, but her eyes couldn't decide where to settle on his strange body. She frowned as she turned away and watched a small rodent scramble up a nearby tree. Upon reaching the top, it let out a shrill squeak that instantly became annoying. This waiting had been going on far too long. Sinccah grumbled slightly as she stood and stretched. She looked down at the mygnus. "Shouldn't your friends be here by now?"

"Ideally, yes," the Wanderer wrote. "It is likely they have been delayed."

"Right," Sinccah said with a frown. "Do you think they're still coming?"

"Certainly," the Wanderer wrote with calm and rhythmic strokes.

"I'm starting to doubt that," Sinccah said, irritation beginning to flavor her voice.

The Wanderer fidgeted. "They will be here."

"Well, I'm getting tired." Sinccah said flatly. "I can't keep waiting like this."

The Wanderer tilted his central sphere, switching one of the tentacles he used for standing. "Is your remaining lifespan that pitiful?"

"What?!" Sinccah exclaimed. "What are you even trying to imply with that?"

"I ..." the Wanderer wrote before shuffling his tentacles along the ground, "was just asking a question?"

Sinccah's head lurched forward as her mouth slipped open. "You do realize how silly that sounds?"

"My knowledge is inadequate," the Wanderer wrote. "You said you were unable to wait any longer. I always assumed that humans lived longer than that."

Sinccah's eyes widened. "Well ..." she started.

The Wanderer continued writing, far more rapidly than before. "I suppose you might have one of those diseases that humans get, but if that is the case, it would probably be better to avoid running around through the wilderness, and—"

"No, no," Sinccah said as she waved her hand through the text the Wanderer was writing. "I'm not dying or anything," she said as she tried vainly to fight back a grin. "I was just saying that I'm sick of waiting."

"Is that one of your—" the Wanderer started

"Tired of waiting that is," Sinccah said quickly.

"Oh," the Wanderer wrote. "So you are neither sick nor dying?"

"Correct," Sinccah said as she shook her head in amusement. "I just want to get out of here before Red comes looking for us."

"And your remaining lifespan is sufficient?" the Wanderer asked.

Sinccah nodded her head. "Unless we wait here long enough that the thugs kill us."

"Point taken," the Wanderer wrote. "It is good to know you are currently free from sickness."

"Yeah," Sinccah snorted, "it'd be rather unfortunate otherwise."

The Wanderer tapped a tentacle against the ground. "I have always wondered what it would be like to be the member of such a short-lived race. Always worried about some sickness or famine sweeping in and ending you. Are you frightened by it?"

"Not really," Sinccah mused. "I don't really think about it."

"Fascinating," the Wanderer wrote. "You are very interesting."

"Right," Sinccah said, now feeling somewhat self-conscious. "Don't magnus have their own issues? Certainly you have diseases of some kind."

"It would seem we have avoided that struggle," the Wanderer wrote calmly, "unless you count the plague that is the human race."

Sinccah lifted her hand slightly. She wanted to protest, but the mygnus did have a point. Besides humans, she wasn't aware of anything that killed large quantities of magnus. Perhaps goblins or dragons, but the magnus always seemed to be allied with those races. "Yeah," she said awkwardly. "Sorry about that."

"At least your responsibility in that regard is fairly minimal," the Wanderer continued as he turned a shade of green.

"Right," Sinccah said slowly as her jaw tensed. Fairly minimal. As if. She hadn't been involved at all. She'd never even used a maggni and certainly never hurt a magnus. Granted, she wasn't that far removed from the issue. Had she done better at the academy, she would certainly have been awarded a maggni. Then she'd be another one of the mages who senselessly exploited the magnus, but as it was, she hadn't done anything.

"I have good news for you," the Wanderer wrote quickly as his color deepened.

"Oh?" Sinccah mumbled as she pulled her thoughts back to the present.

"Yes," the Wanderer wrote, "my friends are nearby. I sense them heading this way."

Sinccah perked up. "Where?"

The Wanderer pointed east. "They are coming through the woods over there. We should go meet them." He promptly glided into the underbrush.

Sinccah shook herself slightly, then followed after the Wanderer. It was about time these friends showed up. As she crawled through the thick foliage, she began to wonder what kind of friends a wandering mygnus would keep. He'd said they weren't other magnus, so presumably they were goblins. She couldn't imagine any humans being receptive toward a mygnus. Ucksil and his people didn't seem too fond of them, and the people in Rivvairt seemed downright hostile. A grimace formed on her face. She certainly wasn't looking forward to meeting goblins. She looked up to see that the Wanderer had stopped in a small clearing. As she stepped out of the foliage and straightened herself, she could hear the soft rustle of underbrush from the far side.

"Uncle Wandi!" a shrill voice suddenly exclaimed. A young girl jumped into the clearing and ran toward the Wanderer with arms open. Sinccah recoiled. The friends *were* humans? Or they'd kidnapped this girl! Sinccah glanced awkwardly back and forth as she fought the urge to backpedal. This girl couldn't be more than six years old. How did a young child like this get to know a mygnus? She even had an endearing name for him!

"Hello, dear," the Wanderer wrote before the girl threw her arms around him in a hug that pinned his three free tentacles to his sphere. He wiggled a tentacle free of her grasp and continued. "It is pleasant to be with you again."

Another rustle sounded beyond the clearing, and three more children walked out of the foliage. Sinccah eyed them suspiciously, and they returned the favor. One of the three newcomers was an older girl, perhaps twelve. The other two were boys who had to be around the age of nine.

"Who is this?" the older girl asked dubiously as she pointed at Sinccah.

"This is Sinccah," the Wanderer wrote. "She is a friend of mine. We are going on a quest together."

Sinccah glanced toward the mygnus, an eyebrow arched. Friend?

The two boys stared at the floating text. The shorter one slowly followed the text from left to right, then turned and smiled at Sinccah. The taller boy looked clueless as he leaned forward with squinted eyes. The youngest girl glanced at the floating text, then looked expectantly over her shoulder at the other girl, who flashed a quick smile before reading the message out loud.

The children's expressions brightened, and they waved at Sinccah, who cringed slightly as she awkwardly waved back. Her mind started racing. These couldn't be the friends, right? They were just kids. Probably annoying little brats as well. Her eyes darted to the edge of the clearing. Maybe she should just get out of here. No. She needed the Wanderer's help. She could deal with children.

"What kinda quest?" the taller of the boys asked.

"It's uh ..." Sinccah started until she noticed the Wanderer was already writing.

"A very important quest," he wrote. "We need to make sure some bad people stop doing mean things."

The shorter boy's eyes widened, and he started nodding. He moved his mouth rapidly, but no sound was produced.

"Yes," the Wanderer replied, "it is very exciting."

As the oldest girl began reading the messages aloud once again, Sinccah glanced between the boy and the floating text. She raised her eyebrows as she realized that this boy could actually read the Wanderer's writing, and the mygnus could, in turn, read the boy's lips. She tried valiantly to force a sweet smile onto her face as she scanned the clearing. Were these four children the friends? Had she just waited an hour so that the Wanderer could say hello to some kids?

"Did you bring us a gift, Uncle Wandi?" the youngest girl squeaked as she finally released the Wanderer from her embrace.

"I did indeed," the Wanderer wrote as he reached into his pack and handed the oldest girl a tattered bag. "I am afraid I was unable to get much, but hopefully this helps."

Sinccah's eyes widened. This was the bag the Wanderer had bought from the tavern. The one he'd been overcharged for and nearly gotten killed over. He'd done all that just to give it to these children? Sinccah shifted awkwardly as the oldest girl opened the bag and looked inside.

"This is amazing," the girl said with a smile. "Thank you so much."

"You're the best, Uncle Wandi!" the younger girl exclaimed.

"I have a little more," the Wanderer wrote as he pulled a handful of dull gray coins from a pocket in his pack and offered them to the children. Sinccah tilted her head to the side. She'd never seen coins like this before. The face of each coin appeared to have a shape cut into it, but the quality was far too poor for her to be able to tell what it was.

The silent boy took the coins from the outstretched tentacles. He looked down at them with wide eyes. The other boy stepped over to inspect the metal disks. "Goblin coins!" he exclaimed.

"I know their food is inferior when compared to human food," the Wanderer wrote, "but it will at least keep you full."

"Yay, Uncle Wandi!" the younger girl exclaimed as she hopped up and down in a small circle.

Sinccah winced at the excessive excitement. Particularly since the oldest girl hadn't even read the text yet. Her expression morphed into a frown as she looked into the woods. No one else was coming. This was it. These were the friends she'd been waiting an hour for. She glanced at the older girl, who was holding the bundle close to her chest. A tear slipped from the girl's eye as she turned to look at Sinccah. Sinccah quickly forced a smile back onto her face.

"Is your quest going to be long?" the taller boy asked the Wanderer.

"It should be fairly short," the Wanderer answered. "I intend to return in a little over a week."

The silent boy started moving his mouth, but once again, he made no sound.

The Wanderer shook his body slightly. "I will miss you all as well." He stepped toward Sinccah. "Now, we must be off."

The taller boy glanced at the older girl, who wiped the tear from her eye before reading the text.

"Already?" the taller boy asked.

"Unfortunately, yes," the Wanderer wrote. "Some mean people from the town will soon be searching for me."

The older girl's face warped into a look of concern. "You got attacked again?"

"Yes," the Wanderer wrote, "but you can maintain confidence; Sinccah kept me safe."

Sinccah tried desperately to avoid cringing as another few seconds of vocal reading resulted in the younger children staring at her with awe. She wanted to turn around and run, but she remained frozen. She fought through her awkwardness and tried to maintain a smile. The youngest girl ran up to her and held out a small purple rock. "Thanks for keeping Uncle Wandi safe!" she shouted.

"What's this?" Sinccah asked as she crouched to inspect the rock.

"It's a pwesant!" the girl declared.

Sinccah gave the girl a forced smile and took the rock. "Thank you so much," she said as sweetly as she could manage. She stood and looked at the Wanderer. "Shall we?" she said, sweeping her hand toward the south.

"Of course," the Wanderer wrote. Then he stopped, reached into his pack, and pulled out his cloak. "Here," he said, handing it to the oldest girl. "It seems I no longer need this."

The girl nodded as a pained smile crossed her face. "Thanks."

The Wanderer waved at the children. "Goodbye everyone!"

A chorus of goodbyes sounded from the children as Sinccah walked briskly out of the clearing with the Wanderer following slowly behind her. She exhaled deeply as they entered the trees. At least that was over, even though the experience had left her with more questions than it had answered.

CHAPTER SEVEN

Sinccah walked briskly after the Wanderer. They'd been heading south for over an hour. The thick forest made rapid movement difficult, but hopefully, if the thugs came this way, they'd be equally hampered.

The Wanderer suddenly stopped and started writing. "It seems the thugs have given up their search."

Sinccah looked down at the text. "You can still sense them?"

"No," the Wanderer wrote. "That is why it seems they have given up."

"Ah," Sinccah grunted sheepishly.

"I was only able to sense them briefly," the Wanderer wrote. "They seemed to be searching around the town for our trail, but it appears they failed to find it."

"Well, that's good at least," Sinccah sighed before looking up into the trees.

"Is something bothering you?" the Wanderer asked.

Sinccah startled. "I'm fine," she said cautiously. "Why do you ask?"

The Wanderer tilted his central sphere. "You seemed rather uncomfortable earlier."

"Oh that," Sinccah said awkwardly as she tried to compose her words. "I just ..." her voice drifted off. Did she really want to tell this mygnus how annoyed she was? Waiting over an hour just to talk to some children wasn't exactly her favorite activity. Still, she needed a guide, so she couldn't afford to offend him. Her lips twitched back and forth as she tried to cobble together a response. Finally, she came up with something that sounded reasonable: "I just didn't expect your friends to be children."

"Indeed," the Wanderer wrote. "I suppose that was quite a surprise."

"Yeah," Sinccah said softly as she dug into her pouch and pulled out the purple rock. She held it out to the Wanderer.

"What are you doing?" he asked.

"You'll appreciate this more than I will," Sinccah sighed.

The Wanderer tilted his sphere slightly. "You disparage the gift?"

"I guess so," Sinccah admitted.

"You should still keep it," the Wanderer wrote as he turned a light blue. He put a tentacle on Sinccah's hand and closed her fingers around the rock. "It was given to you in appreciation."

"Maybe," Sinccah murmured as she pulled her hand away. She opened her hand and stared at the rock. Her face contorted as images of Lady Dove's children invaded her mind. "I don't want it." She closed her hand around the rock and squeezed tightly as she tried to block the images from her mind. Her fingers turned white as her hand started to tremble.

The Wanderer's color darkened. "Very well," he wrote slowly. "If it hurts you, I can take it." He held out a pair of tentacles toward Sinccah.

Sinccah grimaced as she put the rock into the gap between his outstretched tentacles. He slowly retracted them and transferred the rock into a pouch on the side of his pack. Sinccah turned her gaze southward as her face softened.

"We should continue," the Wanderer wrote with a subtle gesture.

"I was meaning to ask you something," Sinccah whispered.

"Oh?" the Wanderer wrote, turning a dull orange.

"That bag of food you gave the kids," Sinccah said slowly. "That was the food you purchased from the tavern right before the thugs attacked you, right?"

"Indeed."

Sinccah shook her head. "So you almost got yourself killed just to buy some overpriced food that you were just going to give away?"

"Indeed," the Wanderer wrote again. "The humans living in that town have decided to become the typical brutes that humans tend to be. Therefore, my friends are no longer allowed to buy anything themselves."

"You have the same problem now," Sinccah said flatly

The Wanderer shifted his tentacles slightly as his color took on a hint of red. "Yes, my deception has expired. They know what I am now. They will hunt me like the ravenous beasts they are." He paused as his color returned to teal. "Even so, the children always did love fresh bread. I am pleased to know I was able to give them some enjoyment once more."

Sinccah's eyes narrowed. This creature didn't make any sense. One moment he was talking about how all humans are evil, and the next he was risking his life for a few kids. What sort of plan did he have? She turned toward him with a suspicious look. "Don't they have someone else who can take care of them?"

"That is something they lack," the Wanderer wrote. "Ever since their caretaker died from one of those human diseases, they have been on their own."

"Caretaker?" Sinccah questioned. "You mean their parents?"

"An old lady," the Wanderer corrected. "My friends tell me she was kind, but I never encountered her myself. She ran an orphanage several years ago."

"Oh," Sinccah said softly. That made sense, but it didn't feel right that a mygnus was taking care of them. "Surely they have some other family? Perhaps an aunt or uncle?"

The Wanderer turned a shade of light blue. "Perhaps," he wrote. "However, there is no way to find them. Presumably, their residences are beyond the mountains in the human-infested lands. Regardless, even if the families could be located, it is unlikely any of the children would be able to identify them anymore."

"Oh," Sinccah said sorrowfully. She felt awkward for being so annoyed with the children. "So you're their caretaker now?"

"As much as I am able," the Wanderer wrote. "My ability to help is fairly restricted, since most humans are hostile, but I can at least make sure they have sustenance."

"That's quite kind of you," Sinccah said softly.

"Perhaps," the Wanderer wrote. "I do wish I could do more."

Sinccah furrowed her brow. "Couldn't you just take them in yourself?" she questioned. "You could probably even take them back to a magnus village and raise them there."

The Wanderer pressed two of his tentacles together. "My kin would certainly reject that."

"Sure," Sinccah sighed, "but you could at least have them live nearby?"

"Humans need humans," the Wanderer wrote. "As wretched as humans are, my friends need something from that vile race. I can care for their obvious needs, but they will eventually go through things I will be unable to understand."

Sinccah nodded. She didn't really know what to say, but after a few seconds, the silence grew awkward. "Sure," she offered in an attempt to move the conversation along.

"Someday, I hope to find something better for them," the Wanderer responded. "However, the rest of the pesky humans make it quite hard."

Sinccah frowned. She was getting a bit sick of being insulted in such a casual manner, but it probably wouldn't help to point that out. "So you're just going to care for them in secret?"

The Wanderer straightened up. "Perhaps it is the purpose for which I was formed."

Sinccah recoiled slightly as she tilted an eyebrow. "Didn't you say you were made for dire situations?"

"I did," the Wanderer wrote calmly.

"I'm not sure their plight really qualifies," Sinccah said dubiously.

"That is how it would seem to you," the Wanderer wrote. "However, for these children the situation is quite dire."

Sinccah squinted. "I get that, but wouldn't the crystal need more than a few human children to form a wanderer?"

"Perhaps," the Wanderer wrote. He suddenly turned bright orange, raised a tentacle, and began writing quickly. "It seems I was wrong."

"About the children?" Sinccah questioned.

"The thugs," the Wanderer wrote. "They found our trail."

Sinccah straightened. "They're coming?"

"Yes," the Wanderer wrote in jagged text, "and they brought a hound to pick up our scent."

Sinccah's eyes darted between the nearby trees. "So we're running?"

"Yes," the Wanderer wrote before bolting from his position.

Sinccah started running after him. Orphans or not, giving these thugs an entire hour to collect themselves had been a colossal mistake. She grimaced. If those thugs caught up to them, she was probably dead. She looked up at the Wanderer, who darted easily through the trees. Her lip curled upward. At least he'd be fine. He seemed quite agile, able to duck and dash through thick underbrush. Her face formed into a snarl. Not that his abilities would help her at all.

Sinccah stumbled on an outstretched root. She grabbed a low hanging branch to stabilize herself, but her hand slid along the rough bark. A short cry escaped her as she slid to a stop. She grimaced. This wasn't going to work. She pushed herself back to her feet and looked down at her hand. Sure enough, she had scraped off the skin, and it was starting to bleed. She clenched her hand and pounded her fist into the nearby tree. There was no way she'd be able to run through the woods like this.

"Follow," a wispy voice said in her head.

She looked up to see the Wanderer standing on a fallen tree. He had turned a light blue and was gesturing to the west. Sinccah shot him an angry glance and held up her bleeding hand.

"I will lead to flatter land," the Wanderer wrote rapidly as his color turned orange again.

Sinccah could hardly read the rough text, but she nodded. At least this mygnus hadn't abandoned her. Sure, he had gotten her into this entire mess, but at least he hadn't decided to run off. She jogged to the Wanderer, who hopped onto the ground and dashed past a few dozen trees. He then stopped and waited for Sinccah to approach him before dashing another short distance.

Sinccah scrambled after him, her mind whirling. He was helping her. Again. But why? He seemed to dislike her? Maybe? His actions didn't make sense. One moment he'd denounce humans, and the next he'd risk his life to save her. It didn't sit right, but it wasn't like she had a better option.

For almost an hour, they continued methodically: the Wanderer identified terrain that would be easy for Sinccah to pass through, and Sinccah jogged briskly behind him. Over this time, the trees had become thicker, but the underbrush had grown increasingly sparse. The Wanderer suddenly turned a bright amber color.

He started writing quickly. "There is a goblin nearby."

Sinccah leaned against a tree, breathing heavily. "Do we care?" she said with gasping breaths.

"He is in danger," the Wanderer wrote.

Sinccah's face curled into a snarl. "We're in danger!"

"True," the Wanderer wrote rapidly. "However, I am compelled to support him. He is being pursued by three mages, and I must save him from their capture."

Sinccah's face twisted in anger. "You're going to get us both killed!"

"You have no obligation to follow me," the Wanderer wrote, his tentacles gaining a twinge of red. "However, I must do this." He darted off to the west.

Sinccah threw her head back and looked up into the sky. Sure, she didn't have to follow him, but there was no way she'd be outrunning anyone without him. She started running after him. If the thugs were going to catch her, it'd be better if the mygnus were still around. Perhaps they'd have a chance in a fight.

As she ran after the Wanderer, she began to hear voices. "You idiot!" a familiar voice exclaimed. "You let it escape!"

Sinccah furrowed her brow. Where had she heard this voice before?

"Sorry, master!" another voice sounded. "The wretched creature is tricky!"

"Or you're an idiot!" the first voice screeched. "We've had this set up for weeks! But *you* managed to let it escape! At this rate, the client is going to buy from someone else!"

The Wanderer suddenly stopped and started writing to Sinccah. "I need you to distract them."

Sinccah ran up and stopped beside the mygnus. "Distract who?"

"Those three men," the Wanderer wrote as he gestured through the trees.

Sinccah squinted in the direction he was pointing and caught some movement. A tall man in royal mages robes was digging through the foliage. She recognized him as one of the mages she'd run into the day before. "What do you want me to do?"

"Wait here for a minute so that I can get into position," the Wanderer wrote, "then I need you to cause a distraction."

"How do you suggest I do that?" Sinccah hissed.

"You could just talk to them?" the Wanderer suggested

Sinccah eyed the Wanderer doubtfully. "What do you think that'll do?"

"These mages will think that you are a simple traveler," the Wanderer wrote, "and you will be able to make idle conversation long enough for me to save the goblin."

"One problem," Sinccah said quickly. "I've already met these mages, so they're going to recognize me."

"Is that bad?" the Wanderer wrote.

"Somewhat," Sinccah admitted. "We definitely didn't get along when we last spoke."

"What did you do?" the Wanderer asked as his color took on a hint of red.

Sinccah glanced around awkwardly. "I was a bit flippant with them."

The Wanderer quickly curled his writing tentacle. "Why would you do that?"

Sinccah frowned. "They were mocking me."

"Unfortunate," the Wanderer wrote rapidly. "However, I still fail to grasp why that would prevent you from talking to them."

"It's complicated," Sinccah grumbled.

"Why are you being so selfish?" the Wanderer asked.

"What?!" Sinccah hissed.

"We are saving this goblin from a life of slavery," the Wanderer wrote as he turned red, "and all you care about is yourself!"

Sinccah curled her hands into fists. "If our roles were reversed, do you think the goblin would help me?!"

The Wanderer quickly raised a bright red tentacle, then slowly lowered it as he turned orange. "I suppose that is a fair point." His central sphere sank a little. "I would still ask that you set that aside for now. Please lend your aid."

"I—" Sinccah started.

The Wanderer started twitching. "We are out of time," he wrote with incredible speed. "Do what you must, but please distract these men."

Sinccah sighed. "Fine," she said forcefully. "You have one minute."

The Wanderer fidgeted. "Thank you," he wrote before dashing away.

Sinccah threw her hands into the air as she watched him scramble away. Just what she needed. She shook her head and began breathing in and out deeply, counting her breaths. This was a really bad idea. If only she'd just gotten out of here when she could. Actually, she should've just stayed silent in the tavern. Had the Wanderer really needed her help? Probably not. He could've handled the four thugs who were attacking him. Her mind drifted back to the scene, and she pictured the robed mygnus being pulled around as the men tried to strike him. Maybe not. Perhaps he'd actually needed her help. She frowned. Besides, he had only been there to get food for the orphans. He seemed like a kindhearted person. Well, a mygnus actually. Did they even have hearts? Probably not.

Had a minute passed yet? It was probably close enough. She glanced toward the men. She really didn't want to talk to them again. An idea formed in her mind. She breathed in deeply before screaming as loudly as she could. She held the scream for a few seconds, then dashed southward.

"What was that!" one of the apprentices called out.

"Don't get distracted, you idiots!" the familiar voice bellowed.

"It could have been the goblin!" another voice exclaimed.

"Yeah!" the first apprentice shouted. "We finally got it!" Sinccah heard the two apprentices running toward her.

"Idiots," the master loudly grumbled. "If this is a bird again ..." he muttered before his voice trailed off.

"We need to split up," one of the apprentices suggested. "I'll go north, you take the south."

"Got it," the other apprentice responded.

Leaves crunched as this apprentice ran in Sinccah's general direction. She peered out from behind a tree and watched him pass the location where she'd screamed. He continued running southward, getting closer and closer to where she was hiding. Sinccah frowned. She hadn't run far enough. At least the leading mage hadn't come this way.

As the apprentice neared her, she forced herself to start breathing heavily and practically flopped out from behind the tree. "Thank goodness!" she gasped in the most distressed voice she could manage. "I was worried no one would hear!"

The mage glared at her. "You again."

"Yeah, yeah," Sinccah said softly through gasping breaths. "I just saw the goblin you were after! They're such horrible nasty looking creatures!"

The mage's eyes widened. "Where did you see it!"

"Just over there!" Sinccah said as she gestured at a random tree a bit to the east of her. "The creepy thing was spying on me from behind that tree."

"Right," the mage said quickly. "I'll get the others."

"Please get rid of it!" Sinccah cried out.

The mage's lip curled upward, then he turned and sprinted back toward his master. Sinccah's face contorted into a snarl as she fought back the urge to use a shield to trip this brat. She shook herself and started moving southwest; she couldn't afford more enemies. At first, she walked slowly, but as the distance between them grew, she started jogging. Suddenly, a set of barks rang out behind her. Sinccah started running. The hound!

Sinccah heard the mage she'd been talking to call out. "Master I—"

"Shut up!" the master shouted. "We have company."

Sinccah stopped running and spun around to look north. Through the thick trees, she could see the three mages still within shouting distance. She hid herself behind an overturned tree stump and looked on. Beyond the mages, a group of perhaps forty men emerged from the trees. At the front was Red, holding back a vicious looking hound.

"Who are you?!" Red shouted.

The leading mage stepped toward Red. "I don't think you understand," he said flatly. "I ask the questions here."

"Oh," Red said mockingly. "Do we have another nasty mage on our hands?" He turned to his men. "What is it we do to nasty mages?"

The mage snapped his hand upward, and a spike of yellow light shot out. The hound gave out a sharp cry as the spike impaled it. The light suddenly vanished, and the hound crumpled to the ground with a loud yelp. The mage glared at the Red. "What is it we do to mages?"

Red backed away from the three mages. "My apologies, sir," he stammered. "I was, uh, attacked by a mage earlier today." He held up his bandaged hand. "My men and I were—"

"Shut up," the lead mage said dismissively. He held up his hand and made a shooing motion. "Now, get out of here before I lose my temper."

"Of course, sir," Red said as he continued backing away. One of Red's men stepped forward and picked up the whimpering hound. Then the group of them quickly retreated.

The master mage turned to his apprentice. "Now, what were you saying?"

"I found the woman from before," the apprentice said rapidly. "She said she saw the goblin just a moment ago."

"Oh?" the master mage said dubiously, "and where is she now?"

Sinccah ducked behind the stump. The apprentice started talking, but this time he clearly had less confidence. "She was just over there."

"Very well," the master mage groaned. "Let's go find your missing woman."

Sinccah waited a few seconds, then peeked out over the stump. The mages had turned east and were picking their way through the trees. She straightened and started jogging southwest. Hopefully, the Wanderer had done whatever he'd needed to do.

Soon she came to a thin road that snaked its way southward through the trees. A series of unintelligible shouts sounded behind her. Presumably, the leading mage had become upset at the situation and was berating his apprentices. Sinccah started running again. There was no way she could let them find her now. Her mind pulled up an image of the hound crumpling from the mage's spell. If the mages caught her and figured out she was helping the goblin, that'd be her. She shook her head and pushed herself to run faster.

———————◄O►———————

The trees blurred as Sinccah ran down the road. After a few minutes, her pace slowed to a brisk walk. She thought back to the encounter between Red and the mages. Honesty, it couldn't have gone any better. Not only had she avoided talking to the mage who'd been so rude to her earlier, but Red and his men had been driven off. She felt sorry for the poor hound, but now that it was out of the picture, it was unlikely Red would be able to track her down.

A faint voice abruptly sounded in her mind: "Wait."

Sinccah drifted to a stop. Apparently, the Wanderer was talking to her. Had he succeeded in rescuing the goblin? Was he still in trouble? Why was it that he only spoke one word? She suddenly realized that if the Wanderer could speak to her like this, he could probably hear her as well. To whatever degree he heard anything.

"Are you alright, Wanderer?" she said softly.

"Yes," the voice said, even fainter than before.

So he could hear her, but why was the voice growing more faint? It probably didn't matter. He'd asked her to wait, and he was apparently alright, so it'd probably be best to do what he asked. Fearing that the mages might venture southward, she jogged a short distance into the trees, where she found a fallen log, set down her pack, and took a seat. Her face tugged downward. She was waiting for this crazy mygnus again. Not that she had a better option. She still needed him to lead her to Beilbauk. Of course, this assumed the Wanderer was actually helping her and not simply using her to further his own ends. Sinccah frowned. For some reason she couldn't picture the Wanderer as evil. Sure, he never seemed to stop talking about how abominable humans were, but even his most reckless actions seemed to be focused on helping others.

She tapped her fingers against the log she sat on as her mind drifted back to her encounter with the apprentice. She cringed. The entire performance had been fairly bad. Pretending to be a helpless maiden was hardly her favorite activity, and it was unlikely her act had really convinced him. He hadn't even had the confidence to tell his master what she'd said. It probably didn't matter. Red and the mages had both been rather rude. At least they'd gotten what was coming to them.

A soft rustle caught her attention. She turned toward the source of the sound, expecting to see the Wanderer. Instead, she saw a small striped brown bird land awkwardly on a tilted twig. She smiled in amusement as the bird's weight caused the twig to bend, forcing the bird to take flight. It flitted to a slightly larger branch and eyed Sinccah suspiciously. Sinccah chuckled softly as her mind returned to her acting. She shook her head as the words she'd spoken to the apprentice danced through her mind. Had she really been that bumbling? Probably. The frail and helpless act was bound to seem fake, particularly after she'd tried to be so confident with those mages earlier. Oh well, it was over now.

A twig snapped behind her, and she spun to see a goblin stepping out from behind a tree. The goblin froze briefly before a familiar tentacle appeared from behind his shoulder and pushed him forward. Sinccah stood as the goblin stumbled forward. She'd seen goblins before but none so ragged as this one. From head to toe, he was a mess. His bald skin was covered in cuts, some of which appeared to be quite deep. What little of his clothes remained clung in tatters around his slender frame.

Sinccah's eyes darted to some text the Wanderer started writing. "This is Sinccah, the kind lady I told you about."

The goblin nodded. "Hello, Sinccah!" he exclaimed in a remarkably clear, if very high pitched, voice.

"Uh, hi," Sinccah offered in return. She'd never spoken to a goblin before. What was she even supposed to say? She twitched her lips to the side before she settled on an appropriate response. "What's your name?"

"Erdah!" the goblin responded with surprising cheerfulness. He ran up to Sinccah, grabbed her hand, and shook it vigorously. "It's great to meet you!"

Sinccah fidgeted as she fought back a grimace. "Yeah," she said slowly as she pulled her hand away. "Nice to meet you as well."

The Wanderer waved a tentacle between the two of them and gestured to some text he'd written: "Thanks for waiting, Sinccah."

"Oh, right," Sinccah said awkwardly. "I was going to ask you about that."

The Wanderer wrote a single question mark.

"The voice I hear in my head," Sinccah said cautiously. "That's you talking, right?"

"Indeed."

Sinccah nodded. "I thought so, but ..." she paused, trying to figure out the best way of asking her question.

The Wanderer started writing. "Why do I avoid talking that way all the time?"

"Yeah," Sinccah said before pressing her lips together. "Wouldn't it just work better than this writing in the air thing?"

"Generally, yes," the Wanderer wrote. "However, it takes a great deal of my energy to focus my voice into someone's mind."

Sinccah perked up. "So that's why you only say one word?"

"Indeed," the Wanderer wrote. "The voice you hear is the way magnus normally communicate with each other. However, when they are part of the same village, it is nearly effortless."

"Oh," Sinccah said with a twinge of sorrow as she recalled what the Wanderer had told her earlier about the nature of wanderers. "I guess that makes sense." For a few seconds, no one said anything. Sinccah grew restless in the silence and turned to Erdah. "Sorry about the scene I made when I first saw you."

Erdah tilted his head to the side. "You were calm though?"

Sinccah shook her head. "Not just now," she said quickly. "You were the goblin I saw by the river yesterday, right?"

"Oh!" Erdah exclaimed. "I'd forgotten!" he said with a laugh before clasping his hands together. "I oughta be the sorry one. It's not polite to sneak up on people."

Sinccah let out a soft laugh. "I suppose not. Either way, it's good to finally meet you properly."

The Wanderer turned slightly toward the goblin and started writing. "Why were you in such deep trouble with those mages?"

"Oh that," Erdah mumbled, awkwardly kicking at a fallen stick. "I messed up." He shook his head. "I was desperate. They offered to help for a favor."

"What was making you so desperate?" Sinccah asked.

"I lost my gramp's herd," Erdah sighed. His head lurched forward. "Most of it anyway," he continued under his breath.

"And these mages helped you find it?" the Wanderer wrote.

"Yes," Erdah said regretfully. "I was going crazy! I couldn't figure out where the swine had run off to. Then these mages showed up and offered help." Erdah slammed his hand into a nearby tree. "It was a trick!"

"Did they actually help you?" the Wanderer asked.

"Oh yes," Erdah growled. "The dumb beasts had gotten trapped in the mountains."

The Wanderer tilted his sphere as he turned a light blue. "How do you think they got there?"

"No idea!" Erdah exclaimed. "I don't even know how they escaped! One day I was getting ready to separate the yearlings, and the next, the entire herd was gone!"

"That is strange indeed," the Wanderer wrote.

Sinccah felt her heart sink. "I'm not sure it is."

"What?!" Erdah nearly shouted.

"I think the mages did it," Sinccah said softly. "They probably drove the beasts off, or at least spooked them." She sighed. "Then they showed up after you got desperate."

Erdah's eyes widened. "Those ... Those ..." he started, looking increasingly agitated.

"You seem so certain?" the Wanderer questioned.

Sinccah nodded her head. "When I first ran into these mages, they talked about goblins existing to be tricked. They even mentioned setting something up weeks ago. I suspect this is what they were talking about."

"That'd make sense," Erdah said as he started to calm down. "Nothing else does." He glanced into the sky. "It has been a few weeks since they *helped* me."

"That is very cruel," the Wanderer wrote as he turned a light red.

"Yeah," Sinccah sighed. "It's no wonder Ucksil is having problems with the goblins." She shook her head.

"Who's Ucksil?" Erdah asked.

Sinccah looked at the goblin in surprise. "He's the human who rules the lands east of the mountains." She grimaced. "To the degree any human rules them."

"We should get moving," the Wanderer wrote. "Those mages are still looking for Erdah. They may eventually find us if we remain here."

"Of course," Sinccah said as she reached for her pack. Instead of the coarse fabric, she felt smooth flesh. She spun to see Erdah holding his hand over her pack. "Hey!" she shouted.

Erdah jumped back. "Sorry, I was just wondering if you had any extra food."

"Have you considered asking?" Sinccah said angrily.

"Oh, uh," Erdah stammered. "I was only—"

"Do you normally steal from people who help you?!" Sinccah interrupted.

Erdah cowered beside Sinccah. "I wasn't going to steal!"

"You were just going to borrow without permission?!" Sinccah shouted.

A tentacle waved in between the two of them. Sinccah turned to see a block of text the Wanderer had started writing: "He had no intention of stealing from you. Had you been looking at him, you would have realized he was merely gesturing toward your pack. If you had waited another second, he would have asked you."

"Oh," Sinccah mumbled.

"I'm very sorry," Erdah said as he clasped his hands together. He looked up at Sinccah with pleading eyes. "I haven't eaten in forever," he said slowly as the tips of his ears drooped and he shifted his weight from foot to foot. "Can I borrow some food?"

"Uh," Sinccah said awkwardly. "Sure." She reached into her pack and pulled out a pouch of her provisions. "Here," she said as she bent and offered it to the goblin.

"Thanks!" Erdah said excitedly as he took the pouch. "I'll pay you back!"

"How do you intend to do that?" Sinccah asked bluntly.

Erdah opened the pouch and shoved a handful of food into his mouth. He frantically chewed before swallowing forcefully. "We'll have a feast when I get back home!"

Sinccah's face twitched nervously. She straightened up and looked at the Wanderer. "Is that where we're headed?"

"Yes," the Wanderer wrote. "The business I mentioned to you earlier is in Vroklav, his village, so we needed to head there anyway."

"Right," Sinccah said with a twinge of regret as she watched Erdah greedily consume another handful of the food. She certainly wasn't looking forward to a meal with these creatures. She turned back toward the Wanderer. "I'm on a pretty tight schedule, so I'd really rather avoid the distraction."

The Wanderer tilted his sphere to the side. "Are you opposed to being rewarded?"

"No," Sinccah mumbled.

"Then we should head there," the Wanderer continued. "I am confident that Erdah will make it worth your while."

Erdah nodded rapidly, his cheeks stuffed with Sinccah's provisions.

Sinccah grimaced but gave the Wanderer a nod. "Very well."

"Ideal," the Wanderer wrote before gesturing to the west. "If all goes well, we can get there by nightfall."

⎯⎯⎯◆⎯⎯⎯

Sinccah trudged through the forest next to Erdah. The weather had turned sour again, and they were now walking through a light rain. She looked up at the strange shape of the Wanderer, who was leading the way. A frown formed on her face. How much farther away was this village? She shook the rain from her cloak and glanced at Erdah. The poor goblin looked miserable. His tattered clothes offered little protection from the rain, and he was constantly shivering. Sinccah felt sorry for him. She almost wanted to offer him her cloak, but she couldn't imagine giving it up.

Instead, she chose to study the goblin. He was short, barely coming up to Sinccah's waist, and his short stature was further exacerbated by the fact he stood with a slight hunch. She glanced at his arm and watched the rain glisten on his gray-green skin. Her eyebrow arched. Hadn't he had a large cut on his arm before? Maybe it was the other arm. Her face warped as she questioned herself. The cut should've been on this side, just above his wrist. She squinted. There was certainly a light scratch where the large cut had been. Did goblins have healing magic they could use on themselves? Unlikely. To the best of her knowledge, goblins couldn't use magic of any kind. Still, the cut had either healed absurdly quickly or the rain was driving her insane.

Sinccah shook her head and looked at the goblin's hands. They looked wrong, uncanny even. They were similar to human hands, but the spindly fingers were just a little too long. Sinccah glanced away. It was probably rude of her to stare at him. She thought ahead to their destination, Vroklav. Apparently, the Wanderer had some business there. Hopefully, their visit would be quick and she'd finally be able to get back to looking for Beilbauk. She began to question what the goblin village would be like. She quickly found herself looking back at Erdah. He was, after all, the only goblin she'd ever spoken with. This time, she inspected his head. It was roughly human proportioned except for his nose and ears, both of which were pointed and stuck incredibly far out from his head. In fact, his ears were probably longer than Sinccah's hand, and his nose was slightly longer than that. His eyes were probably a bit too big, but it was less dramatic than his other features.

He suddenly turned to Sinccah. "Got anything for this rain?"

Sinccah startled. She felt caught. "I could give you a blanket," she fumbled, to her instant regret. She only had one, and it'd be much harder to sleep that night with a soaked blanket.

"Really?!" Erdah asked excitedly. "That's so generous!"

"Yeah," Sinccah muttered awkwardly as she stopped under a large tree and untied her bedroll. She couldn't really refuse him now. She glanced up at the Wanderer. He liked helping people. Why didn't he offer this goblin something? Probably because he didn't have anything. Didn't he have his own cloak? She frowned. He'd given it to the orphans. She tried to suppress grumbles as she pulled the blanket out of her bedroll and handed it to Erdah.

The goblin's eyes widened as he gently grabbed the cloth. "You're so kind!" he exclaimed as he wrapped the blanket around himself. "This'll be way better!"

"Right," Sinccah said with a hint of bitterness as she pulled her pack back on and continued walking.

Erdah jogged up beside her. "Don't worry, I'll pay you back."

Sinccah nodded grimly. "I sure hope so," she muttered under her breath.

"What?" Erdah asked.

"Oh nothing," Sinccah said quickly. "The rain is getting to me."

"Yeah," Erdah grunted, taking a few quick steps to avoid falling behind. "Once we get home, we'll have a nice warm fire."

"That'd be nice," Sinccah said mirthlessly.

"Yeah!" Erdah exclaimed. "And we'll have a nice hot meal!"

"What'll that be?" Sinccah said softly as she tried to avoid sounding disrespectful. She really wasn't looking forward to whatever it was goblins ate.

Erdah looked up thoughtfully, sticking out his lips. "I'm not sure," he eventually said, "but it'll certainly be fancy!"

Sinccah nodded. "I don't want to sound dumb," she said slowly, "but what do goblins even eat?"

"Oh!" Erdah exclaimed. "I suppose you don't know."

"Correct," Sinccah said flatly.

Erdah nodded rapidly. "Mostly meat. Sometimes fresh, sometimes dried. Beyond that, we grow mushrooms and a few simple vegetables."

"What exactly is a simple vegetable?" Sinccah asked dubiously.

"Oh," Erdah said with a chuckle, "a plant that doesn't die too easily."

"Such as?" Sinccah questioned.

"Er …" Erdah said awkwardly as his gaze turned upward. "Radishes … Potatoes … Beetroots?" His eyes suddenly popped open. "My wife makes the most delightful beetroot soup! Maybe we'll have some when we get there, or maybe …"

Sinccah stopped listening as the goblin chittered on about the various foods he liked. She felt a wave of relief. Apparently, she wouldn't be expected to eat bugs or even some strange vegetable she'd never heard of. Her face suddenly twisted into a frown. She glanced at Erdah with a dubious expression. "Where do you get your meat?"

"Hunting!" Erdah said excitedly as he seamlessly switched the topic from whatever vegetable he'd been praising. "All kinds of wild game." He looked up thoughtfully. "Though, for tonight, we'll have a yearling from my gramp's herd."

Sinccah exhaled. Wonderful. No strange meats either. Her eyebrows suddenly arched. She looked down at the goblin, who was vainly trying to brush the water from his bald head. "What exactly do you raise?" she asked slowly. "You said they were swine but—"

"Boarine!" Erdah said quickly.

"Oh," Sinccah said as her eyes widened.

"Yup," Erdah said proudly. "My gramp has the best herd in the area …" his voice drifted off. "Or he did. Who knows what happened to it now."

"How long have you been on the run?" Sinccah questioned.

"Three weeks," Erdah said with a sigh. "They're relentless."

Sinccah glanced around awkwardly. "Doesn't that mean you're still in danger?"

"Very," Erdah said flatly. "We'll be safe at home, but I can't stay there forever."

Sinccah furrowed her brow. "Is there any particular reason why you couldn't stay?"

Erdah turned to her with a confused look. "The herd needs to migrate."

"Oh," Sinccah said stiffly. "I knew that. I just didn't think about it."

Erdah nodded. "Yup."

Sinccah nodded slowly as her feet splashed into a small puddle. "I suppose that is why we never bothered to domesticate boarine."

"Yeah," Erdah said bluntly. "You people do like to stay in one place."

Sinccah wanted to protest, but the goblin was right. "How often does the herd need to migrate?"

"Four times a year," Erdah said sorrowfully. "Though, I'm not sure what I'll do now."

"How long until you need to move the herd again?" Sinccah asked.

"A month or so," Erdah said optimistically. "I'll figure something out. Maybe I can work somewhere else."

Sinccah nodded. "You don't think the mages will give up?"

"Nope," Erdah said as he shook his head. "Even if they did, they'd probably just go after someone else."

Sinccah frowned. "I suppose you're right."

"Besides," Erdah said bitterly. "They'll certainly stick around, so I'll be risking my life whenever I leave home."

"What kind of deal did you make with them?"

"A bad one," Erdah grumbled as he shook the rain off his ears.

"I knew that," Sinccah said with a twinge of annoyance. "I was hoping for more details."

Erdah sighed. "They insist that I become their slave."

"Oh," Sinccah said in surprise. "That seems a bit excessive. All they did was help you find your herd again, right?"

"Well, yes," Erdah grumbled. "But they used powerful magic to locate them, so they need payment for that." He curled his hands into fists and waved them through the air. "Apparently, a maggni is the only other thing they'll accept."

Sinccah glanced at the Wanderer, who had stopped at the mention of maggni. She rubbed her hands together nervously as she turned back to Erdah. "Just so you know," she said slowly. "There's no spell that could help them locate your herd. It simply doesn't exist."

Erdah's eyes widened. "What?!" he exclaimed. "It was all a lie! Tricky mages trying to fool me!"

"Most likely," Sinccah said with a slight grimace.

"Those sneaky—" Erdah started before he suddenly turned to Sinccah with wide eyes. "How do you know this!" he screeched.

Sinccah took a step backward. "I took mage lessons when I was younger—"

"You're one of them!" Erdah yelled as he raised his fists, dropping the blanket. He hopped away from Sinccah and snatched up a large stick.

Sinccah recoiled as he pointed the stick toward her. She glanced nervously at the Wanderer.

"You're helping them!" Erdah screeched.

The Wanderer stepped up, laid an orange tentacle on the stick, and pushed it gently downward. "She is my friend," he wrote. He flickered briefly to blue, then red, then back to orange.

Erdah poked his head forward and glared at Sinccah. "She's a mage."

"I know," the Wanderer wrote as his color turned blue. "Even so, she has proven herself trustworthy."

"Mages hunt magnus!" Erdah exclaimed. "She'll butcher your kin someday!"

The Wanderer's color deepened. "Perhaps," he wrote slowly, "but it would be wrong to judge her on what she may do someday." He shifted slightly. "So far, she has done nothing of the sort."

Sinccah squirmed in discomfort as she read the Wanderer's words. Yet he'd just called her his friend, even though he seemed to hate humans. She breathed in deeply. That had to count for something.

"Maybe," Erdah growled, "but we can't trust her."

"I trust her," the Wanderer wrote. "You should too. After all, her actions prevented the mages from catching you."

"I would've been fine," Erdah insisted as his face curled into a frown.

The Wanderer quickly raised a tentacle. "They almost stepped on you," he wrote in clean text. "In another few seconds, they would have found you. Being fine is quite far from what you would have been."

Sinccah's eyebrows arched. She hadn't realized the situation had been that dire. Sure, the Wanderer had told her that Erdah needed help, but he hadn't filled her in on the details. Apparently, the timing of her distraction had been impeccable.

Erdah's shoulders slumped as he dropped the stick. "I suppose," he sighed.

"Besides," the Wanderer wrote. "She was even nice enough to give you her only blanket."

Erdah looked down at the fallen wrapping, then up at Sinccah, then back to the ground. "I didn't realize she only had one."

Sinccah glanced awkwardly between the Wanderer and Erdah. She watched the rain run slowly down the solemn goblin's face. "It's alright," Sinccah said softly. "After what you went through, I wouldn't expect you to trust mages." She sighed. "Not that I'm much of a mage."

Erdah lifted the blanket out of the mud and held it out toward Sinccah. "Sorry I took this," he said without looking up.

Sinccah put her hand on the blanket and pushed it back. "Keep it," she said softly. "You looked so miserable in the rain. Besides, it isn't going to be dry by tonight anyway."

Erdah looked up at Sinccah with a faint smile. "Thanks," he said as he wrapped the blanket around himself again.

"Ideal," the Wanderer wrote as he turned a teal color. "Shall we continue?"

Erdah nodded. "Yup,"

The Wanderer twitched. "You will both be glad to know that we are nearly there."

Sinccah looked up in measured excitement. "Really?"

"Yes," the Wanderer wrote. "Our pace has been quite slow, but we will reach Vioklav by nightfall."

Sinccah looked up into the stormy sky. "How much longer do we have?"

"About an hour," the Wanderer wrote. "Unless you two get into another spat."

"Sorry about that," Erdah offered.

The Wanderer wrote two small dots with a long curved line underneath. Sinccah smiled as she shook her head. Really? A smiling face? Not what she would have expected from a mygnus. She'd always assumed they were constantly serious. Not that she had any real reason for that. As the group continued, Sinccah thought over the Wanderer's words. Did he really trust her? Or was it all part of an elaborate act? She glanced toward the Wanderer and watched the rain glimmer off his sphere. She'd have to trust him regardless. She'd messed up her relationships with too many people to turn back now.

CHAPTER EIGHT

Erdah tripped and fell into a mud puddle. The dirty water splashed up onto Sinccah. She grimaced before turning around to help the goblin to his feet.

"Thanks," Erdah mumbled.

Sinccah nodded, then turned and continued her slog. The loathsome rain had gotten worse, and they were now walking through a downpour. At least the Wanderer seemed fine. Not that he had any clothes that could be soaked anyway. She squinted with a hint of envy. He did wear metal armor, though. Certainly the rain couldn't be good for that.

Her eyes darted over the rest of his body. Based on the appearance of his semi-transparent appendages, she wouldn't have guessed he'd be able to pick up physical objects. Clearly he could, since he'd been carrying his pack and armor all this time. Her eyes narrowed slightly. Could it be that he was physically stronger than an average human? She thought back to her time with the mygnus. Nothing he'd done made him seem especially strong. He didn't carry much with him, and the one time he'd actually used his sword hadn't made him seem particularly impressive. He was fast though, particularly in rough terrain. Even back at the tavern, he had moved quickly through the cluttered room and avoided several men with apparent ease. Presumably, his ability to sense the world around him in an unusual way had helped him with that.

Erdah stumbled over a protruding root. This time he caught himself by grabbing the tails of Sinccah's cloak. He pulled himself to his feet and looked up at Sinccah. "Sorry," he said quickly, resuming his shamble.

"Do you know how much farther we have to go?" Sinccah groaned.

Erdah looked into the sky. "It'll be dark soon. Not much longer."

Sinccah glanced upward. "It's dark already," she grumbled bitterly.

"Yeah," Erdah replied glumly. "The rain is ruining everything."

"I hope your promise of a warm fire was genuine," Sinccah muttered under her breath.

"It better be!" Erdah exclaimed. "Otherwise we're gonna get sick!"

Sinccah grimaced. This was awful. Honestly, everything that had happened after she'd left Kinscue had been awful. Maybe her aunt had been right. Maybe this adventuring business was too rough for her. Still, she'd made some unlikely connections, and she was still making progress. All things considered, she was holding her own pretty well.

A rumble of thunder shook her from her thoughts. She looked up at the Wanderer. He had stopped at the crest of a small hill and was twitching strangely. "Is everything alright, Wanderer?"

The Wanderer lifted a tentacle as he turned a green color. "Better than alright," he wrote with rain-streaked text. "We have arrived."

Sinccah's face brightened. She jogged to the top of the hill with Erdah scrambling after her. She looked over a dark expanse populated with a handful of large lights. This was Vroklav? It looked so empty. Sure, the lights themselves were quite large, but there were only eight of them. How many goblins actually lived here?

Erdah started jumping up and down. "Finally!" he yelled before running down the hill.

Sinccah glanced at the Wanderer, who made a shrugging motion with two of his tentacles. She exhaled deeply. At least they'd made it.

Sinccah and the Wanderer slowly followed after Erdah, who continued to run recklessly forward. He suddenly tripped and started to tumble down the hill. At the bottom, he splashed into a giant mud puddle and lay motionless. Sinccah picked up her own pace slightly. Was he hurt? The goblin abruptly sprang to his feet and sprinted enthusiastically through an opening in a rough wooden palisade.

A tentacle flashed in front of Sinccah's face. She turned to the Wanderer, who had written a message: "He seems to be alright."

Sinccah squinted at the letters, which were hard to read in the dim light. "Apparently," she said quickly. "He seems really excited."

"Indeed," the Wanderer wrote before continuing down the hill.

At the base of the hill, the two travelers crossed the puddle and walked toward the palisade. It was a remarkably shoddy construction and was peppered with small gaps that Sinccah could probably squeeze through. Not that she had any intention of sneaking into a village filled with crazy goblins. She followed the Wanderer through the opening Erdah had run through. On the other side, they were met by a pair of goblins. Each of these goblins carried a long spear and was covered in armor that seemed to consist of chunks of leather tied haphazardly together with the occasional metal plate strapped on.

One of the goblins pointed his spear at Sinccah. "Who's 'dis," he demanded, stabbing the spear forward menacingly.

The Wanderer placed a tentacle on the spearhead. His color briefly flickered to blue before returning to teal. "A friend of mine."

The goblin widened one of his eyes. The other eye appeared to be stuck in a squinted state. "Is she now?" he asked gruffly. "You with Erdah?"

"Yes," the Wanderer wrote. "I also have a delivery for your chieftain.

"Good," the goblin said with a nod. "She's been expecting you." He lowered his spear and gestured toward the rest of the village. He and his companion then spun away and walked over to a sagging wooden structure built into the wall. Its crooked posts barely managed to hold up a leaky roof. The two goblins carefully positioned themselves on either side of a large metal disk, sitting in the only two dry spots that could be found.

Sinccah frowned as she took in the shoddy construction. If all goblin buildings were like this one, there wasn't much hope for getting out of the rain. The Wanderer gestured her farther into the village, and she followed. They passed a few more structures, each of which appeared empty and on the verge of collapse. Sinccah shuddered. It wasn't looking good. She looked deeper into the village at a large building they seemed to be approaching. Signs of a blazing fire flashed through occasional gaps in the vertical logs that made up the wall. At least Erdah had been right about that.

A flash of lightning lit up the village, and Sinccah could see another building just in front of her. As the boom of thunder shook the scene, she rephrased that thought. She could see what *used* to be a building. It had apparently collapsed. She was only able to see it for a moment, so she couldn't quite tell how long ago it'd happened, but the sight caused her to walk more apprehensively.

Half a minute later, Sinccah and the Wanderer came to the large building they'd been walking toward. A loud ruckus of goblin voices could be heard issuing through the coarse wooden walls. The Wanderer lifted a fur flap that hid the doorway and gestured for Sinccah to enter. She bent nearly in half and entered the building in a crouch. For a moment, she was blinded by the bright light. She straightened herself, reaching upward to make sure she didn't hit her head on anything. The gesture proved unnecessary, as the inside of the building proved to be much higher than the doorway.

She glanced into the ceiling, which consisted of long strips of dark brown bark lashed to flimsy rafters to form a conical roof. In the center, a large hole had been left to allow the smoke from the fire to escape. Fortunately, it didn't appear this roof had any active leaks. Something brushed against her leg, and she looked down to see the Wanderer slipping past her. She stepped out of the way awkwardly and suddenly realized the room had gone silent. She finally looked at the floor of the building. Around seventy goblins sat on the ground around a fire, all staring at the newcomers. For a moment, she stared back at them. It didn't seem like any two goblins were alike. Some were almost as tall as she was while others wouldn't even come up to her waist. Several had bulging muscles, but many looked to be little more than skin and bones. Even their faces weren't consistent. Most faces were humanlike, but the sizes of their ears, noses, chins, and brows all varied in size. All these strange goblins were staring at her with eyes as wide as their facial structure allowed. She felt the sudden urge to flee from their gazes but suppressed it. They were Erdah's kin, so they'd presumably treat her kindly. The image of Erdah shaking a stick at her forced itself into her mind. She frowned. The goblins didn't seem to be trying to attack her; besides, the warmth of the fire was remarkably pleasant.

"Wandi!" a shrill chorus rang out. A dozen or so tiny goblins surged at the Wanderer. They quickly crowded around him and began to pepper him with questions, though they never seemed particularly interested in his answers. From what Sinccah could tell, they asked mostly about his travels, hoping to hear if he'd encountered anything truly exciting. The Wanderer tried valiantly to write answers to their questions, but his writing was frequently broken by the excited ball of goblings that'd formed around him.

Sinccah breathed a sigh of relief as she stepped away. Groups of human children were dreadful enough. Getting accosted by goblings would certainly have been worse. She breathed in the distinct smoky scent that filled the room as she cautiously leaned against the outer wall. The din of goblin voices quickly resumed, drowning out even the sound of the flames. She turned back to the fire, where the adult goblins had remained. Most of them appeared to have gotten over their initial shock at the new visitors and had turned their attention to several stacks of carefully piled stones that stood on the left side of the fire.

Sinccah took in the rest of the building. The floor space was mostly circular, but it clearly hadn't been designed with much precision. The very center of the room had a dirt floor, with the rest of the floor being composed of wooden floorboards that'd been worn smooth. On her right, a larger doorway seemed to also lead outside. To the left of that, on the far side of the fire, she could see an enclosed area with a balcony on top and a small set of rickety stairs that ran up the left side.

Sinccah felt a tug on her sleeve. She looked down to see a short female goblin. "You're Sinccah!" the goblin yelled in a high-pitched voice.

"Uh, yeah" Sinccah mumbled as took in the sight of this new goblin. She looked similar to Erdah but was a bit shorter and had a softer face. Her clothes instantly drew Sinccah's attention. They weren't anything fancy, but they were remarkably more sophisticated than the scrappy attire that every other goblin seemed to be wearing.

"I'm Kacksa!" the goblin exclaimed, her large eyes seeming to bug out slightly. "My husband tells me you saved his life!"

"Oh," Sinccah said awkwardly. "It was mostly the Wanderer's idea, I just—"

"Come along!" Kacksa declared as she grabbed Sinccah's hand and pulled her forward. "You're soaked. We'll get you somethin' dry."

The goblin walked around the edge of the building, pulling awkwardly on Sinccah's hand such that she had to bend over slightly as she walked. The skin on the goblin's hand was rather smooth and wasn't at all slimy like Sinccah had feared. The pair walked to the enclosed area, and Sinccah ducked through the doorway. Here the ceiling was incredibly short, and she walked in a crouch. Kacksa led her farther forward and through a wooden door.

"Here you are," Kacksa said merrily as she gestured around the room, which was dimly lit by a few beams of firelight that slipped through cracks in the wall. Sinccah looked up. This room was actually tall enough for her to stand in. Besides that, it was tiny, with a small bed taking up most of the room. Next to the bed stood a small wash basin filled with clean water.

"Thanks ..." Sinccah said awkwardly, not quite sure what was happening.

"Welcome to your room!" Kacksa exclaimed as she danced forward. She hopped over to the bed and picked up a dull shirt. "Hopefully this'll fit you," she said as she held it out toward Sinccah.

Sinccah took the shirt. It wasn't in as bad of condition as she would have expected. It wasn't really that nice, but compared to everything else she'd seen in this village, it was clearly high quality. At least it wasn't covered in holes or filled with some disgusting smell. "Thanks," she offered. "It'll be good to get into something dry."

Kacksa nodded. "There's a skirt here as well!" she exclaimed as she pointed out a folded piece of cloth that was set out on the bed. "My finest work!" She dashed toward Sinccah and slipped past to reach the doorway. "Let me know if you need anything else," she said as she opened the door, which bumped into Sinccah's back in the tight space. "The meal will be ready in an hour or two. You're not gonna wanna miss that!" Kacksa bounded out of the room before gently closing the door.

Sinccah exhaled deeply as she dropped her pack next to the bed. She looked at the clothes that'd been laid out gently on the bed. They weren't the nicest looking, but they'd do. She dug into her pack and pulled out her extra set of clothes. Soggy, as expected. She shook them out and hung them on a low rafter. At least her provision pouches had stayed dry. She frowned; presumably this had been at the cost of her clothes. Maybe if she hadn't given Erdah her blanket, these clothes would still be dry. Not that it mattered anymore; she'd make the most of it.

———◆○◆———

Sinccah emerged from the low hallway and stepped back into the boisterous main room, where she once again felt the full force of the goblins' rowdy conversation. She cringed slightly at the excessive noise as she straightened up. A few of the goblins noticed her entrance and looked at her excitedly. She glanced down to avoid eye contact and walked briskly to an empty space near the fire on the opposite side as the stone piles. Here she found a log that had been set up as a stool and sat down. For a few seconds, she stared into the roaring fire as she listened to the clamor of the goblins socializing. It was probably dangerous to have such a large fire in this building, but the goblins didn't seem terribly concerned. Sinccah shrugged, then leaned closer. The fire's warmth was a welcome change from the cold rain.

After a few seconds, Sinccah leaned back and began to scan the room. The goblins seemed to be congregating on the far side of the fire. From the bits and pieces of conversation she could make out, it was clear the boarine Erdah had promised had been butchered and was being cooked on the stone piles. Sinccah breathed in the luscious aroma of roasting meat that had begun to fill the building. She smiled. This would likely be her best meal since leaving Kinscue. Sure, it would be made by goblins, but it didn't seem that goblins ate that differently than humans, so it couldn't be too bad.

She glanced at the Wanderer, who was still being assailed by the questions of the goblings. It didn't seem like he minded. In fact, the elegant movements of his bright green tentacles implied that he actually enjoyed it. Sinccah shuddered. It was good the mygnus was here; otherwise, she'd be the one beset by goblin children. She ran her hand through her damp hair until her fingers caught on a snag. She reached her other hand up and began trying to detangle it.

"You look lovely in those," a high-pitched female voice said softly.

Sinccah turned to see Kacksa standing behind her with a cheerful smile.

"The clothes are quite nice," Sinccah mumbled, trying to be polite.

"You really think so!" Kacksa exclaimed as she plunked herself on the floor beside Sinccah. "I worked on them for so long; I'm glad you like them!"

A roar of laughter boomed from the far side of the fire.

"Yeah," Sinccah said softly as she tried to avoid sounding flustered. For a second, she tried to figure out what the goblins had found so funny, but the answer wasn't forthcoming. She pulled at the snag in her hair one last time before giving up and lowered her arms. "Why make human-sized clothes?"

Kacksa beamed as she looked up at Sinccah. "In case we have guests!"

"Oh!" Sinccah exclaimed in surprise. "Do you normally have a lot of visitors?"

"Not really," Kacksa lamented. "You're the first human I've seen in months."

Sinccah glanced at the goblin, who'd stuck her lip out in something of a pout. "Were humans more common before?"

"Oh yes!" Kacksa exclaimed. "Several times a week we'd have some stop by." The goblin frowned. "That was before all the nasty ones showed up."

Sinccah nodded as she recalled her own experience back in Rivvairt. "That's certainly fair," she said slowly as another bout of laughter sounded from the far side of the fire. She glanced up briefly but returned her attention to Kacksa. "What's your option on humans?"

Kacksa turned to her with wide eyes. "I think you're nice!" she said quickly. "I didn't mean to say that you were nasty or anything!"

"No, no," Sinccah said as she waved her hand. "I wasn't talking about me. You haven't run me out of your village yet, so I assume you don't have a problem with me. I meant other humans, like the ones who used to visit this village."

"I used to like humans," Kacksa answered cheerfully. "They'd bring all kinds of exciting things. But now ..." her voice trailed off as she hung her head. "They're always mean."

Sinccah nodded. "I understand," she said softly before silence fell between the two women. The rest of the goblins continued to make a ruckus, talking and laughing loudly as they bustled around the room. Sinccah turned to watch a group of goblins scurry behind her.

"Do you have a husband?" Kacksa suddenly asked.

Sinccah turned stiffly toward the goblin, who wore a friendly smile. "I do not."

"Oh!" Kacksa exclaimed with renewed excitement. "Do you have anyone in mind?"

"Uh, no," Sinccah said awkwardly. She wanted to explode at this goblin for asking such prying questions, but she held back. She couldn't afford to make a scene.

"Is it normal for humans as old as you to still be single?" Kacksa asked with an innocent smile.

Sinccah inhaled sharply as she sucked her lips inward. "Not necessary," she said through clenched teeth. "However," she continued before the goblin could begin talking, "it would be considered rude to ask that question."

Kacksa's eyes shot open. "I'm sorry!" she exclaimed. "I didn't mean to be rude!"

"It's alright," Sinccah said before exhaling deeply.

Kacksa fidgeted awkwardly for a few seconds, tapping her fingers on the floorboards. "Did you grow up around here?" she suddenly asked.

"I didn't," Sinccah said with a smile, welcoming the change of topic. "I grew up in Kinscue."

"Where's Kinscue?" Kacksa asked, excitement returning to her voice.

"A ways west of here," Sinccah said before closing her eyes to try to visualize the city's location in relation to Vroklav. "If it weren't for the mountains, it'd probably be less than a week's journey."

"That isn't that far away," Kacksa asserted.

"I guess so," Sinccah admitted before her voice trailed off. For a few seconds, she looked into the fire, listening to its loud crackling. She glanced back at Kacksa. "Where are you from?"

"G'dask!" Kacksa shouted before jumping to her feet. "It's a city up north! My gram is an Elder there!"

Sinccah's eyes narrowed; she wasn't entirely sure what being an Elder actually meant, but the mention of northern goblins instantly turned her mind to her mother. "When you were younger, did you get any human visitors up north?"

"No," Kacksa moaned as she stuck up her lip. "They don't get any now either. In the letters my family sends me, they never mention visitors." She sighed. "The only visitor we ever had stopped coming before I was born."

"When was that?" Sinccah asked with forced calmness as her hands started shaking.

"Are you asking how old I am?" Kacksa questioned.

"Uh," Sinccah stuttered awkwardly. "I was actually—"

Kacksa smiled broadly and held up her outstretched fingers. She slowly pulled in one of her thumbs.

"Nine?" Sinccah asked.

"Yeah!" Kacksa exclaimed. "I've been nine for two whole months now!"

Sinccah struggled to maintain her composure. The goblin's excessive excitement wasn't helping anything. A frown threatened to form on her face. Her mother would've disappeared long before this goblin had been born. Still, Kacksa had mentioned a human visitor. "Do you know much about the human who used to visit your home?"

"Oh yes!" Kacksa exclaimed. "My gram told me lots of stories about her."

Sinccah's eyes shot open at the use of the word "her." She breathed in sharply as she tried to contain her own excitement. "What stories have you heard?"

"The visitor was a nice young lady," Kacksa said quickly. "I don't remember her name, but apparently, she could do all kinds of fancy magic tricks."

"Do you know what she looked like?" Sinccah pressed.

Kacksa stuck out her lip and pressed a finger into it thoughtfully. "Nope," she said dismissively. "The magic stuff was way more interesting."

"Ah," Sinccah said slowly as she attempted to hide her disappointment. "Do you know when the visitor stopped showing up?"

"Uhhhhh," Kacksa droned as she looked up into the roof. "It would've been around the time my pop was born."

Sinccah leaned closer as she mentally worked out the math. "How many years do you think that would be?"

Kacksa pulled up her hands and started raising and lowering her fingers in an attempt to count. She shrugged and let her arms drop to her sides, then held up her hands with all her fingers extended. She curled her hands into fists and then extended her fingers again.

Sinccah nodded. Twenty years. This visitor had to have been her mother. "Do you know what happened to her?"

"Sorta," Kacksa said proudly. "She stopped coming after the attack."

Sinccah leaned even closer. "An attack? What happened?!"

"A fish village got attacked," Kacksa responded. She stuck out her lip and glanced upward. "I don't remember the name."

Sinccah's eyes narrowed. "Who would do that?"

"Don't know," Kacksa admitted.

"How do you not know who attacked you?!" Sinccah exclaimed.

Kacksa bit the side of her lip as her face contorted into a frown. "There weren't any survivors," she whispered without releasing her lip.

"Oh," Sinccah said softly as she looked into Kacksa's sorrowful face. "I'm—"

"I guess there were some survivors," Kacksa interrupted. "But none of them were able to think straight. I guess they'd all gone insane."

"I'm sorry," Sinccah said softly. "I didn't realize—"

"That was long before I was born," Kacksa interrupted again. "I guess the magic lady didn't want to come back after that."

"I see," Sinccah whispered. For several seconds, the two women stopped talking. The other goblins in the room continued to prance around and yell loudly, but Sinccah's thoughts fixated on what Kacksa had told her. It reinforced the stories Vistimmot had heard about goblins going crazy up north. Sinccah frowned. Had her mother been killed in this attack? Her stomach suddenly dropped. Had her mother been involved in the attack?

"Have you been around here before?" Kacksa questioned.

Sinccah startled. She returned her attention to Kacksa. "No," she said with a frown, "the mountains make it a bit too tricky."

Kacksa tilted her head. "I've never been over the mountains. Are they that hard to cross?"

"Not really," Sinccah answered. "Well ..." She paused. "They aren't physically hard to cross."

"Huh?" Kacksa asked, her wide eyes squinting in consternation. "What's that mean?"

"Humans don't come to this side of the mountains very often," Sinccah explained. "People have only been settling in Ucksland for the last thirty or so years. That was when Ucksil founded the city of Sillburg. Before that, everyone assumed the eastern side of the island was too dangerous to inhabit."

"Why's that?" Kacksa asked as she leaned forward with wide eyes.

"At first everyone was afraid of the Witherome," Sinccah answered with a hint of apprehension. "People assumed that, if they lived too close to it, it might expand to kill them."

"Really?" Kacksa asked as she squinted her eyes. "You humans are all afraid of a patch of barren land?"

"Well," Sinccah replied carefully, "I wouldn't call an area that actively siphons your life force away simply 'barren.'"

"I suppose so," Kacksa admitted. "It's easy to avoid though. My family has been doing it forever."

"Yeah," Sinccah said with a nod, "but it took humans a long time to realize that."

Kacksa moved her hand up to her mouth and placed a single finger thoughtfully over her puckered lips. "Why are there still so few humans here, then?"

"Dragons mostly," Sinccah said somberly.

Kacksa tilted her head. "What's wrong with dragons?"

Sinccah's eyes widened. She wanted to scream all the terrors the dragons had inflicted on the kingdom. Instead, she breathed deeply, then answered calmly. "The dragons have been at war with humans for centuries."

"Oh," Kacksa said awkwardly. "Why?"

"I ..." Sinccah started before her voice trailed off. She knew a great deal of history, but the actual cause for the dragon war had never been firmly established. Most people agreed that the war had truly started when some dragons betrayed an important general. However, tensions had to have been simmering long before that. "I'm not quite sure," Sinccah finally answered.

"That's a shame," Kacksa said decisively. "They're awesome. They always have the most interesting things to say." Her eyes suddenly widened. "And! And!" she continued as she started to bounce with excitement. "They can breathe fire!"

Sinccah glanced nervously at the goblin. "You've met dragons?"

"Yeah!" Kacksa exclaimed. "You just missed one! She came with a delivery a few days ago."

Sinccah's eyes shot open as she inhaled sharply. She hadn't thought through her actions at all. Of course dragons and goblins were allies, so it'd make sense for dragons to visit goblin villages. If a dragon showed up and learned that she was here—

"You alright?" Kacksa asked.

Sinccah turned to see the goblin staring at her with concern.

"I'm fine," Sinccah managed. "Just ..." she paused, letting the ruckus of the room fill the air. She didn't really want to keep talking about dragons, but her curiosity got the better of her. "What did this dragon look like?"

"Oh," Kacksa said cheerfully, "she's the most lovely shade of blue, with a really pretty black at the very top of each scale and ..."

Sinccah stopped listening. Her mind rushed back to what Iszailliah had told her about the dragon that had been flying over the caravan. A dark-blue female dragon. That's what Iszailliah had described. Sinccah's mind quickly flipped to the grave look that'd been on Dreekadack's face when she'd told him about the dragon. He'd been so concerned as he explained the dire situation she'd been in. Apparently, that dragon had been on her way to the very village where Sinccah was now planning to sleep. The thought brought her nothing but dread. Was she even safe here? What would happen if this dragon returned? Did the goblins already have plans to give her to the dragons?

"Hey," Kacksa said as she waved her hand in front of Sinccah's face. "You listening?"

Sinccah shook herself. "Yeah," she said, turning to Kacksa with a forced smile. "I'm fine."

Kacksa lifted an eyebrow. "Are you sure about—"

A dull metal clang sounded on the far side of the fire. The majority of the goblins stood and rushed toward the sound. Sinccah eyed her companion inquisitively.

"Food's ready!" Kacksa exclaimed. She hopped to her feet, grabbed the hem of Sinccah's skirt, and started pulling her around the edge of the fire.

Sinccah smiled in spite of herself as she followed her guide. Hopefully, the food would be good and then she could finally sleep. Assuming she could calm herself enough to make that possible.

Kacksa led Sinccah to the far side of the building, where the rest of the goblins had clustered together. Sinccah looked over the piles of rocks, which apparently had bits of metal placed among them to serve as some sort of cooking surface. Out of the corner of her eye, she saw Erdah, now changed into clothes similar to Kacksa's. He was straightening a short log near the fire. After setting it upright, he hopped onto the top and struck a large metal disk with a stick. The dull metal clank sounded again, and the goblins turned to him.

"Hi everyone!" Erdah shouted. "It's time to eat!" An excited rumble sounded from the gathered goblins. "But first," Erdah continued. "We have guests!" He gestured toward Sinccah. "My rescuers, Sinccah and Wandi!" Sinccah looked toward the Wanderer, who was slowly extracting himself from the gaggle of goblings. Erdah gestured forcefully toward the Wanderer, and the log he was standing on started to wobble. He overcorrected in his attempt to balance himself, and the log tipped over, sending Erdah tumbling into the fire. Sinccah gasped as he screeched in pain. Several nearby goblins rushed toward the flames and pulled him out.

Sinccah ran to the ash-covered goblin. "Are you alright?!"

Erdah opened and closed each eye alternately as he let out a short groan. He suddenly hopped back to his feet and shook himself. "Oops," he said sheepishly. The rest of the goblins started laughing.

Sinccah recoiled. This was no time for laughing: Erdah might have serious burns. She knelt next to Erdah and caught a whiff of burnt flesh. She fought through the urge to gag. "Erdah," she said softly, "are you—" She stopped suddenly as she saw that Erdah was grinning.

The blackened goblin looked at Sinccah with a crazy expression. "How exciting!" he declared.

Sinccah raised an eyebrow. "You just fell into a giant fire," she said sternly. "This's no time for jokes."

Erdah eyed her curiously. "Why not?"

"You could be seriously injured!" Sinccah hissed.

"I'm fine," Erdah said as he craned his neck to inspect his shoulder, which bore obvious burns. "I'll be patched up by tomorrow."

Sinccah's eyes widened. "You have healers?" she asked dubiously.

"Hmm?" Erdah grunted.

"Magic users that'll heal you," Sinccah clarified.

"Nah," Erdah said with a chuckle. "I don't need magic for this."

"Oh," Sinccah said softly.

Erdah twitched. "I should wash this ash off," he said quickly before darting away.

Sinccah stood back up. Apparently, he was fine. She shook her head in disbelief. How durable were these goblins? A familiar flash of teal caught her attention, and she turned to see the Wanderer standing next to her.

"Have you enjoyed the hospitality so far?" he asked.

"It's been surprisingly nice," Sinccah admitted. She lowered her voice before continuing. "I expected goblins to be a bit more savage."

"Indeed," the Wanderer wrote.

"Do goblins not feel pain or something?" Sinccah asked as she looked into the crowd of goblins in an attempt to locate Erdah.

The Wanderer twitched. "They feel less pain than humans do," he wrote slowly. "Additionally, their natural regeneration is quite fast."

"I see," Sinccah said softly. "So that's why no one was bothered by Erdah falling into the fire."

"Correct," the Wanderer wrote. "This type of thing happens quite a bit with goblins. Their dull sense of pain and rapid healing makes them reckless."

Sinccah nodded. "But Erdah will be fine?"

"Yes," the Wanderer wrote. "He should recover completely by tomorrow."

Kacksa's voice sounded over the busy room. "Sinccah!" she called, hurrying toward them with a large wooden plate.

"What is it?" Sinccah asked.

"You're a guest," Kacksa said as she reached Sinccah and lifted the plate over her head so it was even with Sinccah's chest. "That means you go first."

Sinccah looked down at the slab of tan meat and small heaps of roasted root vegetables. "Thanks." She took the plate and glanced around the building. "Do you have any tables?"

Kacksa stuck her lips out abashedly. She suddenly perked up and darted to the log Erdah had been standing on. She flipped it back up and brushed the top with her hand. "Will this do?"

Sinccah furrowed her brow. Apparently, the goblins did not, in fact, have tables. "That'll be fine," Sinccah said as sweetly as she could. This goblin was trying after all. She sat down next to the log and set her plate on it.

"I could wash it for you," Kacksa offered.

"It's alright," Sinccah said with a smile. "You don't need to serve my every whim."

Kacksa rubbed her hands together nervously. "I want you to feel welcome."

"You've already done that," Sinccah said kindly. She gestured toward the piles of rocks. "You should get some food for yourself."

Kacksa nodded. "Let me know if you need anything," she said before turning and jogging toward the other goblins.

Sinccah turned to the Wanderer, who hadn't moved since Kacksa had arrived. "Are you going to get anything?"

The Wanderer twitched. "If by 'anything' you mean food, then no."

Sinccah tilted her head. "You're not going to eat?"

"How would I accomplish that?" the Wanderer asked.

Sinccah's eyebrows arched. In hindsight, her questions hadn't made a lot of sense. If the Wanderer could neither hear nor see, it wasn't that likely he could taste either. "Do magnus not need any sustenance?"

"Normal magnus do," the Wanderer wrote. "Though it would be inaccurate to call it food."

"What is it then?"

"A chitinous substance that helps keep our energies focused around our maggni."

"Oh," Sinccah said with great interest. "Do you have any of that with you?"

"My body is devoid of maggni," the Wanderer wrote, "so no."

"Ah," Sinccah said awkwardly. "Does that mean you can survive forever without consuming anything?"

"Perhaps," the Wanderer wrote. "No wanderer has ever lived that long, so it is unknown."

Sinccah shook her head. Of course he would take her question literally. "Sure," she said slowly, "but you don't regularly consume anything to keep yourself alive, right?"

"Correct."

Sinccah nodded as a few seconds passed in silence. "Are you meeting with the goblin chieftain tomorrow?"

"Yes," the Wanderer wrote. "I need to complete my delivery."

"Do you think I could talk to her while we're there?"

The Wanderer shuffled his tentacles. "It seems like a harmless endeavor."

"Great," Sinccah said with a smile. "I'm hoping I can get a better understanding of goblins, particularly their leadership."

"Oh?"

Sinccah nodded. "Things aren't going well between Ucksil and the goblins. I'm hoping I can get a better look at what the goblins are experiencing."

"A noble goal," the Wanderer wrote. "I will assist you as I am able."

"I appreciate that," Sinccah said, smiling warmly. If she could help resolve some of the conflict with the goblins, Ucksil would be more willing to send men north to find the bandits. It wasn't all that likely she'd be able to do anything, but it was worth a try.

The Wanderer started twitching. "I need to talk with several others in this village," he wrote slowly. "I will be waiting for you in this room tomorrow morning. Then we can talk to the chieftain."

"Did they give you your own room to sleep in?" Sinccah asked.

"I have no need for sleep," the Wanderer wrote quickly. "I will return to you tomorrow." He skittered away and exited the building.

Sinccah looked down at her plate. It must be nice to be a mygnus, not needing food or sleep. She shook her head. The food looked appetizing at least, and the smell of burnt flesh had finally dissipated.

It turned out that the food was remarkably good. It didn't really compare with the delicacies that Lady Dove had served, but it was satisfying all the same. As Sinccah finished her meal, she looked into the crowd of goblins and saw Erdah and Kacksa making their way toward her. As they drew close, Erdah extended a semi-transparent tan slab that was wrapped in thin cloth. He wore an exceptionally large smile and stared at Sinccah expectantly.

Sinccah furrowed her brow and glanced awkwardly between the two goblins.

Kacksa leaned forward. "Break off a piece!" she whispered loudly.

Sinccah grabbed a corner of the slab and broke off a tiny piece. Erdah quickly spun away and began offering the slab to the surrounding goblins.

Kacksa stepped closer and clasped her hands together.

"What is it?" Sinccah questioned.

"Candy!" Kacksa cried. "Magnus make it, and it tastes amazing!"

Sinccah cautiously slipped the sliver she had broken off into her mouth. Her eyes widened. It was delightfully sweet, almost too much so. She shifted it around in her mouth. "Thanks," she mumbled.

"Enjoy!" Kacksa called out as she spun away and ran back to Erdah.

Sinccah sucked on the treat as she watched the two goblins distribute the candy among the gathered crowd. She smiled. She would have to come back to Vroklav someday.

⊷◦⊷

Sinccah groaned as she rolled over in the small bed. It'd been a restless night. She'd left the main room as soon as she'd finished eating and had returned to her room. Even so, the goblins had made an excessive ruckus for several hours, making it impossible to sleep. Even after the goblins dispersed, her mind got caught up thinking about dragons, and sleep continued to elude her. It didn't help that her extra set of clothes had still been slightly damp when she put them back on. Her paranoia had forced her to change before trying to sleep. If a dragon showed up and wanted her dead, she wanted to have some sliver of a chance of escape. It'd likely only been four or five hours since she'd actually fallen asleep. However, the light of dawn was already glimmering through a small crack in the wall.

She squeezed her eyes shut in a vain attempt to block out the morning. Her mind darted back to her conversation with Kacksa. The human visitor all those years ago had to have been her mother. She reached toward her chest but caught herself. She squeezed her hand into a fist as she lowered it. Her face contorted in sorrow. She was finally learning about what her mother had been like, but the new knowledge only brought her pain. Tears threatened to form in her eyes as her mind raced back to the loss of her pendant. She grimaced before suddenly sitting up. This wasn't the time for such thoughts.

Sinccah shook her head before running her hands down her face. She peeked through her fingers at the washbasin, which had been refilled at some point during the night. She reached into the lukewarm water and splashed it into her face. As the water dripped off, she noticed her blanket hanging on the rafter where her damp clothes had been. Apparently, Erdah had remembered to return it. She stood and brushed the fabric with her hand. Kacksa must have washed it, as there was no muddy residue. The clothes she'd been wearing on her way to Vroklav had also been washed. She pulled her blanket off the board. It was quite dry. She smiled. It'd been a simple gesture, but she couldn't help but feel more at ease due to it.

A light knock sounded on the door. "Come in," Sinccah called out.

The door opened and Kacksa waddled in, carrying a large pouch. "Good morning!" she shouted as she smiled up at Sinccah. "Did you sleep well?"

"It was alright," Sinccah replied, not wanting to offend the goblin.

Kacksa nodded. "Sorry if we kept you up."

Sinccah laughed softly. "It's fine," she said as she tossed her blanket onto the bed. "I had a lot on my mind, so I probably wouldn't have slept much anyway."

"That's too bad," Kacksa sighed before holding out the pouch. "I brought you some boarine jerky. Erdah told me you shared your food with him, so this is payment for that."

"Thanks," Sinccah said as she took the pouch and shoved it into her pack. "Where's Erdah?"

Kacksa gestured behind her. "Talking to Wandi."

Sinccah's eyes widened. She'd forgotten that he'd said he'd be waiting for her. Hopefully, he hadn't been waiting too long. She reached for her hanging clothes before stopping suddenly. She turned back to Kacksa. "I suppose you'll be wanting those back," she said as she gestured to the shirt and skirt that she'd left next to the bed.

Kacksa waved her hand. "Keep them," she said with a smile. "They probably won't fit anyone else anyway."

"But you worked so hard on them," Sinccah protested.

"No worries," Kacksa said with a chuckle. "I was looking for a new project anyway!"

"I won't need them," Sinccah insisted. "Besides," she continued, "I'll want something nice the next time I come here."

Kacksa's eyes widened. "You'll come back some day?!"

"I'll try to," Sinccah said with a smile before grabbing the shirt off the floor. She carefully folded it and placed it on the bed.

"Here," Kacksa said as she stepped forward and grabbed the other loose shirt. Mimicking Sinccah's movements, she folded it and held it out toward Sinccah's pack. "I wanted to thank you again," she said softly.

"For what?" Sinccah asked as she placed the garment gently into her pack.

"For saving my husband," Kacksa said. Her voice turned sorrowful. "I don't know what we'd have done if those mages got him."

Sinccah frowned. It felt wrong. This goblin was so appreciative of her, but she'd only helped Erdah because the Wanderer had pushed her. Guilt crowded into her mind, and she turned away to pick the skirt off the floor. "I'm glad I could help," she said softly, not really sure how genuine the sentiment was.

Kacksa nodded. "I wish we could do more to thank you."

Sinccah shifted uncomfortably as she set the folded skirt on the bed. "You should really thank the Wanderer. He was the one who noticed your husband needed help."

"Erdah has that taken care of," Kacksa replied. Sinccah folded the last article of clothing and placed it in her bag. She then stood and pulled the pack onto her back.

"Don't you want to take that?" Kacksa asked as she pointed to Sinccah's blanket. "I went through a lot of fuss washing it."

"Oh," Sinccah said as she looked down sheepishly. "Yeah, I do." She tossed her pack onto the bed before grabbing her blanket, rolling it back into her bedroll, and tying it onto her pack.

"Ready?" Kacksa asked.

Sinccah glanced around. "Yeah."

The two women left the room and walked slowly through the low hallway into the large room. Erdah was leaning against the wall on the other side of the fire pit. Beside him, the Wanderer was balancing his newly straightened sword on one of his tentacles. He gave it a twirl before slipping it into a loop on his sphere.

Erdah noticed their arrival and waved enthusiastically. "Good morning, Sinccah!"

"Morning," Sinccah replied politely as she stepped up to the goblin.

"Are you ready to go?" the Wanderer asked.

"Yeah," Sinccah responded. "We're going to talk to the chieftain, right?"

"We are," the Wanderer wrote before gesturing toward the doorway. "Shall we?"

Sinccah nodded, then turned to Erdah and Kacksa. "Thanks for everything."

The two goblins smiled. "We're glad to do it," Kacksa said cheerfully.

"Save travels!" Erdah exclaimed.

Sinccah waved at the goblins, then she and the Wanderer exited the building. She squinted in the bright morning sunlight. In the light of a new day, Vroklav looked less foreboding but no less rickety. In fact, as Sinccah studied the small squat buildings that made up the majority of the village, she became increasingly concerned that they might suddenly collapse as she walked past. She breathed in deeply. Taking in the fresh post-rain smell. At least the weather promised to be pleasant today.

The Wanderer led the way around the large building. Upon reaching the other side, Sinccah caught sight of the mountains that towered above the trees on the far side of the village. Her eyes narrowed. She shouldn't be this close to them. She scanned the horizon. How far west had they come?

Her thoughts were interrupted as she noticed the Wanderer hadn't slowed with her and was continuing farther into the village. She jogged to catch up with him and soon found herself wading through a swarm of goblins. Due to Sinccah's comparatively tall height, she could see what must have been hundreds of them. As the two travelers continued over soggy dirt roads, Sinccah took in the sight of the goblin construction. There were several hundred small buildings that Sinccah guessed were goblin houses. Most of these small buildings were built together in small clusters around blocks of crumbled stone. In many cases, it would have been impossible to tell quite where one building ended and the next started. Interspersed between the houses were twenty or so larger buildings like the one where she'd spent the night. Based on the events of the previous evening, she assumed these served as some sort of gathering palace where collections of goblins got together to socialize. Around all the buildings, a short wall stood, with rickety towers placed at haphazard intervals along the length. The wall primarily consisted of rough wooden palisade, like she'd seen earlier, but large portions were made of cracked stone.

The Wanderer waved a tentacle in front of Sinccah and gestured toward a ruined stone tower, which looked very similar to the unrepaired towers in Sillburg. It was about half the size of the meetinghouses and seemed to be held together by periodic bits of wood. Apparently, that was to be their destination.

As they continued through the village, they were regularly greeted by goblins. Some met them with excited waves, but most gave Sinccah awkward looks. Some looked suspicious, and a few looked clearly hostile. The Wanderer would wave back to each goblin they passed, often waving toward several goblins at once. Sinccah kept to herself, feeling more awkward than friendly. Goblins were still strange to her. Even though Erdah and Kacksa had been very kind, she was still dubious of the rest of the goblins. After a minute or so, she and the Wanderer came to the base of the ruined tower. Now that it was closer, Sinccah could see that the vast majority of the stonework was ancient. Presumably dating back to before the Withering. Around these stones, the goblins had constructed rickety wooden structures. In particular, a low wooden hut encircled the base of the tower.

The Wanderer walked confidently up to a slightly taller section of this wooden skirt, which apparently served as the door. Here a half dozen goblins stood at something that vaguely resembled attention. Each held a spear and shield, and had a short sword at their waist. They were all clad head to toe in armor. However, no item quite matched what the other goblins had. The spears were all different lengths, the shields were not quite round, and the armor was, like the armor of the goblins at the gate, a random mishmash of leather and metal. Additionally, none of the goblins were the same size as each other. The shortest of them was quite bulky but was around the same height as Erdah, coming up to Sinccah's waist. This was contrasted by the tallest goblin, who came up to Sinccah's shoulders but scarcely seemed to have any muscle. The sight made Sinccah want to laugh, but she controlled herself. They certainly wouldn't appreciate how funny they looked.

The tallest of the six goblins stepped toward Sinccah. "Stop!" he yelled in an absurdly high pitched voice.

Sinccah's eyes widened as she tried not to chuckle. She stopped moving and looked at the Wanderer.

"I have a delivery for your chieftain," the Wanderer wrote as he held up a small leather pouch.

"You're welcome here, Wandi," the goblin responded. He pointed his spear at Sinccah. "She isn't."

The Wanderer flickered briefly to a light blue. "She is my friend."

"Perhaps she is," the guard said gruffly. "Humans are no longer welcome."

Sinccah glanced awkwardly at the Wanderer, who continued to write rapidly. "She is here because she—"

The goblin waved his hand through the text. He shot the Wanderer a disapproving look before eyeing Sinccah suspiciously. "I have orders," he squeaked. "You," he said, pointing at the Wanderer, "go on." He stepped back to the side of the doorway and gestured for the mygnus to enter.

"Sorry," the Wanderer spoke into Sinccah's mind as he stepped forward.

Sinccah stood still and watched as he disappeared into the low hallway. Letting out a sigh, she turned and looked over the village. One of the nearby buildings caught her attention, as it seemed to be swaying in the light breeze. She furrowed her brow. A building shouldn't sway like that. She looked closer. This building looked somehow worse than the others, and was far taller. Was it even inhabited? The building suddenly let out a sharp snap and collapsed in front of her eyes. She glanced awkwardly at the guards, who didn't seem to notice.

She waved her hand at the tall guard. "Do buildings normally just collapse like that?" she asked, gesturing toward the rubble.

The guard glared at her. "That one's been abandoned for weeks."

"So you were just waiting for it to tip over?" Sinccah questioned.

"Yeah," the goblin answered with a scowl, his voice becoming increasingly agitated.

"Wouldn't it be better to repair it?" Sinccah pressed.

"Wouldn't it be better if you left me alone?" the goblin droned mockingly before turning away.

Sinccah recoiled at the goblin's rudeness. Maybe it was reasonable for the chieftain to reject her, but why was this random goblin so hostile? She shook her head and walked toward the fallen building, which had attracted a small cluster of goblins. By the time she reached it, most of the goblins had dispersed, and those that remained didn't seem particularly interested in conversation. She inspected the fallen logs that had once held up the roof. This house really had been doomed, even though it probably hadn't been built that long ago. It must have been constructed so poorly that it only lasted a few years. Was this common for goblins? She ran her hand across one of the shattered logs. A small splinter stabbed her and she jerked her hand away. She looked at the small dot of blood that now formed on her finger. Touching the shoddy construction hadn't been her brightest idea.

A squeal sounded on the far side of the rubble, and Sinccah walked briskly around. On the far side, the land sloped gently away, and at the base of that slope she saw a herd of unfamiliar creatures. They immediately reminded her of pigs, except they had long tapered noses instead of snouts and had fairly long tails, similar to those of cows. Additionally, these creatures were covered in remarkably thick, coarse hair that hung down from their rounded bellies, partially covering their stubby legs. They also didn't have distinct necks, so much so that Sinccah questioned if they were capable of turning to look behind them. The vast majority of them were roughly the size of full grown pigs.

Presumably these were boarine, the creatures that Erdah apparently ranched. Around the edge of the herd, a few larger boarine stood, each a bit smaller than a horse, and each with a single goblin riding it. The goblins held large poles that they seemed to be using to guide the smaller boarine. On the far side of the herd was a massive boarine that would've made even a large horse look small. Long leather straps stretched between this immense creature's nose and a pair of wooden boxes that were strapped to either side of its rounded body. Apparently, each box also contained a goblin who pulled alternately on the straps to steer the creature.

Sinccah marveled at the display. Nearly all of the smaller boarine followed after the massive one; the goblins on pony-sized beasts merely had to round up stragglers. Apparently, this was how boarine were relocated. She continued watching as the herd rumbled through the village, letting out periodic grunts and squeals. This did explain how a small goblin like Erdah was capable of tending to such large animals. It seemed that they were agreeable to sticking together and really seemed devoted to following the massive one.

Her mind drifted back to the stories of the goblin war, in which boarine charges had become infamous. The same herding system had been deployed to great effect on the battlefield, where hundreds of pony-sized boarine could be guided by a few of the massive ones. In fact, the crown prince had been crippled by one of these charges, and he was far more fortunate than the rest of his men. Sinccah shivered as she pictured the beasts charging headlong into a battalion of the king-dom's finest soldiers. It was good the days of war were behind them.

Out of the corner of her eye, she spotted the Wanderer coming around the side of the collapsed building. "Enjoying the herding?" he wrote, gesturing toward the boarine.

"Yeah," Sinccah said softly. "I presume you have finished your business with the chieftain?"

"Indeed," he wrote quickly. "I completed my delivery and asked if she would be willing to speak to you."

"And?" Sinccah asked with a hint of hope in her voice.

"She refused," the Wanderer replied. "After hearing what happened to Erdah, she was in no mood to speak with a human."

"Ah," Sinccah sighed.

Sinccah and the Wanderer started to walk briskly back the way they'd come. They walked for a few seconds in silence before the Wanderer stopped. "I apologize for her hostility," he wrote, turning a darker shade of blue. "It was unexpectedly strong."

Sinccah paused to read the text, then exhaled deeply. "Yeah ..." Her voice drifted off as her head sank.

"Take comfort," the Wanderer wrote as his color lightened. "Goblins are quite emotional creatures. If you come back later, you may find the chieftain in a better mood."

Sinccah read the text without looking up. "I don't know," she said glumly.

"Give it some time," the Wanderer suggested. "Goblins are quite poor at holding grudges."

"Sure," Sinccah said with a sigh. "I just don't know if I'll ever return."

The Wanderer twitched. "I am sure Kacksa would appreciate you coming back. Maybe you can stop by after you find that mage of yours."

Sinccah nodded. "That'd be nice," she said optimistically. "I suppose it's worth a try."

"Indeed," the Wanderer wrote, returning to a teal color, "but first we need to find him." He gestured toward the south. "Shall we?"

"Yeah," Sinccah said as she glanced back at the chieftain's tower. "Let's get out of here."

CHAPTER NINE

Sinccah and the Wanderer walked through the village to the opening where they'd entered the night before. The gruff guard and his companion had been replaced by a pair of larger goblins, who waved enthusiastically at the travelers as they passed. Sinccah followed the Wanderer to the top of the hill that stood outside the walls. As she reached the top, she drifted to a stop and turned to look over Vroklav. From this vantage point, it was clear that the goblins built their buildings in the most random places they could find. Though the village was fairly large, the buildings were scattered aimlessly. She shook her head. Goblins were such strange creatures.

The Wanderer tapped Sinccah's arm and pointed to some text he'd written: "Did something disrupt you?"

"Not really," Sinccah said slowly. "I just wanted to see what the village looked like during the day."

"Indeed," the Wanderer responded as he slowly tilted his sphere. "Try to avoid being too hard on yourself about the chieftain. Her anger rests on other humans."

Sinccah eyed the Wanderer with a hint of suspicion. Why was he so fixated on the topic? "Sure," she said dismissively. "It's not that important."

"Goblins are simple creatures," the Wanderer continued. "They often get in trouble by being too emotional. That is why their chieftains exist: to hold back their reckless behavior."

Sinccah narrowed her eyes. "What does that mean?"

"Cleverness is somewhat rare in goblins," the Wanderer answered. "However, a few of them are born with dramatically more logical minds. These goblins are made into Elders who are responsible for picking new chieftains from among themselves. This way the ruling goblins are chosen from those who are less rash and more intelligent."

Sinccah arched an eyebrow. "Is that how all the goblin villages work?"

"No," the Wanderer replied, "just the functional ones."

"Uh ..." Sinccah said awkwardly.

"Some goblin's rule by force," the Wanderer explained. "The largest goblins rule the others. However, those villages tend to be short lived. Perhaps lasting a few decades."

"Oh?" Sinccah questioned.

"They tend to get themselves killed," the Wanderer wrote with flat text. "These goblins must show up quite often in human stories. They were more common before humans returned to this island. However, many of them were wiped out in the war the humans fought with them over a half century ago."

Sinccah nodded. The Goblin War had been costly for the kingdom and had set the stage for the even bloodier Son's Rebellion. She looked intently toward her companion. "So after the war, the more intelligently-run goblin villages thrived?"

"Indeed," the Wanderer replied. "Those who were able to make peace and keep it were rewarded, particularly during the war humans fought among themselves. During that time, the more savvy goblins were able to make advantageous deals with the humans around them. The human kingdom simply lacked the needed cohesion to stop them."

"Do you know of any warlike villages that still exist?" Sinccah asked.

"I know of several," the Wanderer responded. "In fact, many of them are in the south, relatively near where your mage lives. Some of those villages won't even tolerate magnus. They would attack me on sight."

Sinccah frowned. "The Rakniv?"

"Indeed," the Wanderer replied.

Sinccah nodded. So that was why these villages were causing problems for Sillburg. "Do you think they'll bother us on our journey?"

"Unlikely," the Wanderer wrote. "They are quite a bit farther south than we need to go. However," he paused, curling his tentacle, "they sometimes come north to raid humans."

"How comforting," Sinccah grumbled.

"The two of us should have no problem avoiding them," the Wanderer wrote.

Sinccah nodded. "Sure." She stopped nodding as a frown formed on her face. "How do you think Beilbauk avoids them?"

The Wanderer's color flashed a fiery orange before returning to a teal. "It is unlikely he avoids them at all."

"Wouldn't they attack him?" Sinccah insisted.

"Only if they wanted to die," the Wanderer wrote quickly as he started to turn red. "Your mage is powerful and unlikely to be worth attacking. These goblins might be comparatively foolish, but they do think. Their motivations go beyond simple anger. They are raiding. Raiding the one person capable of fighting back is remarkably illogical."

"Oh," Sinccah responded as she looked down. Clearly her companion was quite passionate about mages. It would've been better to avoid bringing Beilbauk up.

The Wanderer stood still for a few seconds as his color returned to teal. "We should get going," he wrote quickly. "It will take a few days to reach the tower where your mage lurks."

Sinccah nodded and the two started out in a southeast direction. For the first couple of hours they traveled through thick trees, where the rains from the night before had made the footing treacherous. They were following some kind of road, but it was presumably maintained by goblins, so it wasn't really maintained at all. Sinccah spent most of that time complaining to herself. She wanted to speak her complaints out loud, but she doubted the Wanderer would be interested.

As they pushed forward, Sinccah noticed a flash of movement ahead of them. Further inspection revealed it to be a large bird. It noticed the travelers and promptly ran down the road. However, after a few minutes, Sinccah and the Wanderer caught up and sent it fleeing once more. Sinccah couldn't help but chuckle at the bird's foolishness. It could easily slip into the woods and be safe, but instead, it insisted on staying on the road. The accidental pursuit continued for another fifteen minutes, with each sighting of the bird bringing Sinccah fresh amusement.

Finally, they came to a crossroads where several small roads came together. Here, the bird fled north. The Wanderer selected the largest of the roads and led the way southward. This road was comparatively pleasant and hadn't been turned into a complete mudhole. Even so, the cobblestones were worn and cracked, and the surrounding forest was threatening to overtake the road entirely. Sinccah's gaze drifted into the trees. Now that her mind wasn't as preoccupied with the sorry state of the road, she began to take in her surroundings. The trees were becoming thinner as they traveled, but she would still call the area a forest. Periodically, she noticed the sights and sounds of small woodland animals, but she didn't focus on any of them. Very little changed with either the road or the terrain for the next several hours.

She moved her hand across the space her pendant would have otherwise occupied, hooked her fingers into the collar of her shirt, and let out a sigh. Her time in Ucksland had allowed her to learn so much, but somehow she felt worse. A shudder rippled over her body. At least she knew her mother had been trying to get back to her and that she'd disappeared after some sort of strange attack on a goblin village. Her face twisted into a frown. This new information merely brought more attention to all the details she still didn't know. What had really happened in that village?

As the sun neared the peak of its daily travels, the Wanderer suddenly stopped. He twitched awkwardly in the middle of the road for a few seconds, then dashed into the trees. He waved for Sinccah to follow, and she jogged over and crouched next to him.

The Wanderer started writing. "There is a human on the road ahead of us and another at the upcoming crossroads."

Sinccah glanced down the road. She couldn't see anyone, but presumably the mygnus was correct. "Do they look hostile?"

"No," the Wanderer wrote. "The one we were following just waved to the other human."

"What are they saying?" Sinccah asked.

"They are exchanging pleasantries at the moment," the Wanderer answered. "It would seem the two are brothers."

"What do you think they're doing here?" Sinccah questioned.

"Probably trappers," the Wanderer wrote. "They seem to be discussing related topics."

"Should we talk to them?" Sinccah asked.

"That would be foolish," the Wanderer responded. "They would never respond kindly to the presence of a mygnus."

Sinccah's eyes narrowed. "Sure," she said slowly, "but I could talk to them."

"Perhaps," the Wanderer responded. He gestured to a hill that rose on the western side of the road. "We should slip through the woods. Then you can hear them before they see you. If they seem friendly and you want to speak with them, you can go ahead. I will remain hidden either way."

Sinccah nodded and followed the mygnus up the hill. As they reached the top Sinccah started to hear voices.

"... hear what happened to Red?" a deep male voice asked calmly.

"Nah," a higher voice answered. "Did he finally get what was coming to 'im?"

"Sure looks that way," the deep voice answered. "Some mygnus creature really messed him up."

Sinccah glanced at the Wanderer with wide eyes. He twitched slightly but didn't start writing. She crept toward the source of the voices.

"Serves 'im right," the other man said disdainfully.

"Yeah," the deep voice responded. "He lost a couple of fingers. Couldn't find a mage willing to patch him up in time."

"He always was a fool when it came to mages," the other man scoffed.

"For sure," the deep voice said with a chuckle. "But that's not even the crazy part. Apparently, a young mage was helping the mygnus."

Sinccah's eyes shot open.

"Naw!" the higher voice exclaimed. "Now you're making things up! No sane mage would help a mygnus."

Sinccah cringed slightly. Apparently, she wasn't going to be talking to these men.

"That's what I was thinking!" the deeper voice blurted out. "But it's all true. The mygnus and the mage woman took out a whole group of Red's men."

"Insane!" the other voice responded. He lowered his voice before continuing, "Almost too crazy to be true."

"I know," the deep voice sighed, "but these are strange times,"

Sinccah snuck down the other side of the hill and finally caught sight of the men. They were standing in the crossroads shaking their heads. Each man was dressed in weathered clothes and carried a large pack.

"Yeah," the man with the higher voice said before turning to gaze down the southern road.

Now that Sinccah could see them, it was clear the man with the deep voice was the older of the two, likely in his early thirties. The two men continued their conversation as they started walking southward but changed the topic to a camp where they were apparently headed.

After a few minutes, the Wanderer appeared beside Sinccah. He lifted a tentacle and started writing: "It seems we made the right decision."

Sinccah nodded. "Do you think they're from Rivvairt?"

"Perhaps," the Wanderer replied. "Though, their respect for the thug was clearly nonexistent, as they lacked significant sympathy for his wounds."

"I can't say I blame them," Sinccah muttered.

"He is a disagreeable type," the Wanderer wrote, his text turning a light blue. "It is unfortunate I maimed him though."

Sinccah tilted her head. "Why? The brute had it coming to him."

"Indeed," the Wanderer wrote slowly. "Even so, a tricky human like him is almost certain to spin the story. Soon a tale will spread of a valiant hero who saved the town from a rogue mage and an evil mygnus." His tentacles drooped slightly. "It will only cause humans to hate magnus more."

"Yeah," Sinccah said softly.

"You may be harmed by it as well," the Wanderer continued. "If word of this gets around, you may lose your reputation with your people."

"I don't think I have to worry about that," Sinccah said with measured confidence. "I'm already working for Ucksil, and Red clearly isn't."

"Ah, yes," the Wanderer wrote. "The barkeeper did imply that when we first met the thug leader."

Sinccah raised an eyebrow. "Didn't he say that after you left…" her voice drifted off as she awkwardly remembered she was talking to a mygnus. "You could still hear him, couldn't you?"

"Yes," the Wanderer answered. "My perception was more than adequate to discern what he said after I had departed."

Sinccah let out a soft snort. "Maybe Ucksil will even reward me for striking out against a thug like Red."

"Possibly," the Wanderer wrote. He promptly started walking down the hill, apparently intending to continue the journey.

Sinccah jogged to catch up and then fell in behind him. A frown formed on her face. What would Ucksil think of her actions in Rivvairt? Had helping the Wanderer been a giant mistake? What if Ucksil got angry with her? What would she do? She shook her head. It didn't matter. She needed to get her pendant back, and getting help from this mygnus was the fastest way to do it. There'd be time for regrets later.

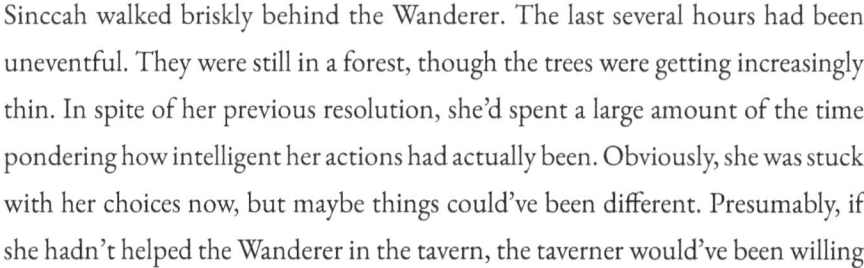

Sinccah walked briskly behind the Wanderer. The last several hours had been uneventful. They were still in a forest, though the trees were getting increasingly thin. In spite of her previous resolution, she'd spent a large amount of the time pondering how intelligent her actions had actually been. Obviously, she was stuck with her choices now, but maybe things could've been different. Presumably, if she hadn't helped the Wanderer in the tavern, the taverner would've been willing to tell her where Beilbauk was. Perhaps she could've even tagged along with the trapper. He'd just come from Rivvairt, after all. Maybe he'd even been in town while Sinccah had been there.

A loud rustle sounded in the woods by the road. Sinccah's head snapped to the source, and she caught a glimpse of some large animal fleeing deeper into the trees. She shook her head. Everything hinged on how Ucksil would see the situation. She wouldn't have any problems as long as the lord of the land sided with her. However, he might harbor a deep hatred for magnus, which would be disastrous. Ideally, no matter what he thought about magnus, he'd appreciate what happened to Red. The thug clearly had too much power over Rivvairt. Ucksil would probably appreciate this blow to his small-time rival. A faint smile formed on her face. It was good to see Red put in his place.

She suddenly frowned. Why was she doing all this? She'd come to Ucksland for adventure and maybe to figure out what had happened to her mother. None of that required talking to a mygnus. She shook her head. Had she known all the crazy things she'd have to deal with, she would've stayed in Kinscue. Instinctively, she reached for her pendant. As her hand closed around empty space, she felt a deep longing. It'd been such a part of her, a constant her mother had never been. Her face twisted in sorrow. The pendant was gone now. Her face hardened. It was gone *for now*, but she wouldn't let some bandits take the only thing she had left from her mother. She started breathing more heavily as she pictured the bandits' faces as they'd stood over her to gloat. Squeezing her eyes shut, she tried to regulate her breathing. It was no use getting worked up about it now. Finding the bandits was still a long way off.

Sinccah's eyes drifted to the Wanderer as he glided forward. Such a strange but somehow elegant creature. He seemed good-natured enough, perhaps even too much. Her lip twitched upward. Was he hiding something? She frowned. He seemed to genuinely care about the folks he met, assuming they weren't actively hostile. Still, she couldn't quite feel at ease with him. The event with the trappers hadn't helped. Sure, she probably wouldn't have wanted to talk to them anyway, but it felt wrong. If his companionship meant she could never get help from other humans, then it was going to make things harder. Her face pulled downward. Did he think similar thoughts about her? She was a mage, after all. A failed mage, but a mage nonetheless. He'd spoken favorably about her to the goblins, particularly when Erdah had gotten aggressive. Had he really meant that? It was hard to know. On one hand, his color seemed to change based on his emotions, but his lack of facial expressions still made him difficult to read. What was really going on inside his mind?

The Wanderer, as if on cue, stopped suddenly and started to twitch. He slowly started writing: "How much farther do you want to go today?"

Sinccah squinted her eyes and looked up at the sun, which was already starting to sink into the leafy embrace of the trees. There would still be another few hours of daylight, but she was getting tired. "We can go a bit farther."

"Alright," the Wanderer wrote. "I only ask because your pace has slowed."

Sinccah inhaled sharply. She hadn't noticed. Thinking back, her pace had probably been slowing over the last hour or so. Apparently, the mygnus had noticed and slowed his own pace so subtly that she hadn't noticed. A grimace formed on her face. She was tired, and it wasn't like she'd slept properly back in Vroklav.

The Wanderer took a few steps forward before stopping again. "You are uncertain," he wrote quickly.

"Yeah," Sinccah mumbled. "Maybe we should stop for today."

"Very well," the Wanderer wrote before pointing into the trees on the western side of the road. "There is a small clearing over there. We will use it for our camp."

"Sure," Sinccah said with a nod. The two travelers left the road and slipped into the trees. After a minute, they came to the predicted clearing.

Sinccah dropped her pack and glanced around. "Do you mind if I start a fire?"

"I would approve of it," the Wanderer replied. "Fire always fascinates me."

"What do you mean?" Sinccah questioned as she pulled her dagger from her belt and set it against her pack.

"As I understand it," the Wanderer responded. "You humans can see the fire leaping from the wood and even feel some sort of warmth. That is beyond my capabilities, but I can still sense the energy of the heat escaping."

Sinccah raised an eyebrow. She really had no idea how a mygnus would perceive heat escaping something. "Do you want to collect some wood?"

"Sure," the Wanderer said before darting into the trees.

Sinccah rummaged through her pack and pulled out a trowel. She kicked the dead leaves away from her desired fire pit and started digging a small hole. The roots running through the dirt made the digging nearly impossible, so she gave up after creating a hole just large enough to be considered usable. She kicked the previous year's dead grasses a little farther away and sat next to the pit. The Wanderer appeared a few seconds later with his tentacles wrapped around a pile of sticks. He unceremoniously dumped them beside the pit.

"Will these do?" he asked, gesturing.

"Yeah," Sinccah said as she grabbed the sticks and started to arrange them in the pit. "Do magnus ever build fires for themselves?"

"Never like this," the Wanderer replied. "Heat is unnecessary for our survival, so fires have different utility. Naturally, we use fires for forging and other similar tasks, but I would never make one if I were traveling alone."

"So you'd never build a fire just to enjoy it?" Sinccah questioned.

"No," the Wanderer replied. "I would consider it strange to do so."

Sinccah grabbed another set of sticks and started adding them to her stack. "So you've never built a fire?"

"I did once," the Wanderer responded. "While I was visiting a village of my kin in the northern mountains, they gave me the opportunity to start a small fire."

"Was that fire just for enjoyment?" Sinccah asked.

The Wanderer pushed the remaining sticks closer to Sinccah. "No," he wrote calmly. "I was building a fire to warm the village neksi."

"Neksi?" Sinccah asked, tilting her head.

The Wanderer tapped his tentacles against the ground. "They are hard to describe," he wrote before pausing for a few seconds. "I suppose they look something like large ..." He twirled the tentacle he'd been writing with in a small circle. "I forget the name," he wrote quickly. "The shelled creatures that tend to live near the sea and walk sideways."

"Crabs?" Sinccah asked.

"Yes," the Wanderer replied with snappy motions. "I would describe the general shape of neksi as several crabs stuck together. They produce the chitinous substance that we use as sustenance."

Sinccah furrowed her brow. The image that appeared in her mind didn't make any sense. "What color are they?"

The Wanderer slowly wrote three dots. "Others have described them as black."

"Ah," Sinccah said awkwardly as her mental image of the creature continued to be hazy. She mostly pictured a shiny black beetle. Her face scrunched up in disgust. "So you eat bugs?"

"That would be an imprecise description," the Wanderer wrote. "There is no eating involved, and the chitin can be collected without harming the neksi."

"Ah," Sinccah said as she tossed the last stick into the pit. "How big are these creatures?"

"That depends," the Wanderer wrote slowly.

"On?" Sinccah questioned.

"If they are properly cared for," the Wanderer answered. "In the wild, they grow to be around the length of your forearm and hand."

Sinccah's eyes widened as she pictured such a large bug. "And in magnus care?"

"They can get as large as horses," the Wanderer replied. "Actually, they produce far more chitin when they are larger, so it is desirable for them to grow very large, and ..." The Wanderer paused in his writing as he noticed Sinccah had taken on a look of shock. "You are distressed."

"Yeah," Sinccah mumbled. "I guess I was thinking they would be a bit ..." She paused, moving her hand in a circular motion as she tried to select the right word.

"Smaller?"

Sinccah nodded. "Something like that."

The Wanderer bobbed slightly. "You have no need to fear them. They are quite docile. Besides, you are unlikely to find one still living in the wild, and you will never encounter a large one outside a magnus village. They only get that big after many years of domestication."

"I see," Sinccah said somewhat thoughtlessly before holding her hand over the wood. It'd been a while, but it was time to try to cast the spell Vistimmot had taught her. She closed her eyes and tried to focus on the steps. Surprisingly, the rhythm of casting it felt somehow natural. Before, everything had felt so forced; now it flowed freely. She smiled. The old mage hadn't wasted his time on her.

She suddenly felt a stab of pain in her chest and lurched forward as the spell fizzled. Had she messed something up? It'd been going so well. She touched the stick she had been trying to ignite. It was cold. Not the slightest hint of heat.

"What are you doing?" the Wanderer asked.

Sinccah shot him an angry glance. "Starting the fire."

"By holding your hand over it?"

"I'm going to cast a flame spell," Sinccah said with determination. She closed her eyes and tried the spell again. A dull pain slowly seeped into her chest. She felt herself being drained; the spell was threatening to siphon all her energy away. Her eyes shot open, and she lurched forward, gasping for breath.

"You should light the fire the normal way," the Wanderer wrote stiffly.

"I can do this," Sinccah insisted. Once more she tried to cast the spell. Failure. Again. She planted her hands on either side of the fire pit as she started to wheeze.

The Wanderer tapped her on the shoulder. "I am sure you are very skilled, but magic is unnecessary for this," he wrote. "We can start the fire without."

Sinccah glanced at the bright orange tentacle that rested on her shoulder. "Just one more try." She closed her eyes. Another tentacle looped around her other shoulder, and the Wanderer started shaking her. She opened her eyes to glare at the mygnus.

"Stop," he wrote in blazing red text. "I accepted your magic when you used it for self-defense. This is different."

"What's your problem?" Sinccah hissed.

The Wanderer recoiled, stepping back slightly from Sinccah. "Magic is evil," he wrote in harsh text. "You are letting it corrupt you just to light an irrelevant fire!"

Sinccah opened her mouth to yell back, but at the last moment, she thought better of it. "You wouldn't understand," she muttered to herself.

The Wanderer fidgeted. "Explain."

"Someone taught me this spell. Someone I cared about." Sinccah bit her lip as she tried to suppress her emotions. "I need to do this—for his sake, if nothing else."

"Fine," the Wanderer wrote in remarkably level text. "I am going to explore. Try to avoid killing yourself with your vile practice." He darted off into the woods, leaving Sinccah alone with her thoughts.

Sinccah slapped a stick off the top of the pile. She threw her hands into the air before pounding her fists into the ground on either side of the fire pit. Her lips started trembling as she struggled to hold back tears. Dejected, she closed her eyes and hung her head. She couldn't cast this spell. Perhaps she'd forgotten the required sequence, or maybe her skills with magic were actually abysmal. It'd been almost an hour, and the drain from failing to cast the spell so many times had exhausted her. Vistimmot's face appeared in her mind. He was wearing his silly grin as he encouraged her to try again, insisting that she could do it. Sinccah shook her head as she clenched her fists. He was wrong.

She let out a slow sigh. No, he wasn't wrong. It would take more practice and a significant amount of diligence, but someday she'd do this. A thought popped into her head. Maybe she should take a break—figure out the bits she must be missing from the casting sequence. Perhaps she could find the book Vistimmot had mentioned or someone else willing to give her some pointers. Her face hardened with determination. No, she could do it herself. She leaned back and reached her hand over the piled sticks once again. As she did so, she felt something touch her hand. Her eyes shot open and she saw the Wanderer standing on the far side of the fire pit.

Some light blue text floated above the unlit twigs: "Are you alright?"

Sinccah nodded her head slightly. "I can do this," she insisted before closing her eyes to focus.

The Wanderer tapped her hand again. She turned her head away in an attempt to ignore him. The tapping increased in frequency until she gave up and looked back at the mygnus. He had turned a deep shade of blue.

"You must stop," he wrote. "You are exhausted."

Sinccah glared at him. "I'm fine," she said stubbornly.

"At least take a short break," the Wanderer wrote quickly. "It can aid focus."

Sinccah frowned. At least he wasn't trying to forcefully stop her any-more. Perhaps a quick stretch would actually do her some good. "Fine," she growled. She pulled herself to her feet. It instantly became apparent that this had been a horrible mistake. Her vision darkened, and her legs wobbled. She stumbled forward as she felt herself fading from consciousness. The Wanderer darted to her side to stabilize her before slowly lowering her back to the ground.

"I ..." Sinccah started before her faintness overtook her.

The Wanderer laid her onto her back. "You are skilled, but you are pushing yourself too hard."

Sinccah grimaced. "I just wanted to ..." her voice drifted off as her head started to throb with pain.

"It is alright," the Wanderer wrote with gentle motions. "There will be time to try again later. You are exhausted."

"Yeah," Sinccah admitted and she closed her eyes and laid her head against the hard ground. She heard a soft rustling and opened an eye to see the Wanderer digging in her bag. After a few seconds, he pulled out the pouch of fine tinder that Sinccah had bought in Sillburg.

He stepped toward Sinccah. "May I borrow your dagger?"

Sinccah's brow arched slightly. But then her eyes fluttered closed. She didn't care. "Sure," she mumbled as she leaned over, drew the blade, and handed it to her companion.

He took the dagger and scurried to the fire pit. Here, he stopped to pull the flint out of a pocket on the side of the tinder bag. Sinccah let out a sign as she closed her eyes again. She listened to the rhythmic striking of metal and stone. A dozen or so strikes sounded before everything became silent. For half a minute the silence persisted; then it was broken by the soft crackle of the tinder catching flame. After a few minutes, Sinccah felt a gentle tap on her leg. She opened her eyes and leaned her neck forward.

The Wanderer was standing at her feet, next to a low fire. He had returned to his normal teal color and was slowly writing some text: "You should move a little farther away."

Sinccah sat up and pulled her legs away from the fire, looping her arms over her knees. The Wanderer bobbed slightly as he grabbed a few sticks and tossed them onto the fire. Sparks leapt from the flames and rained down onto the upturned dirt. The Wanderer walked slowly over to Sinccah, then gradually curled up the three tentacles he was standing on until his central sphere nearly rested on the ground, only being propped up by the coiled tentacles. He set two of his remaining tentacles on the ground.

He used his final tentacle to start writing: "The fire is nice."

Sinccah stared at him. Was he sitting down? She'd never seen him look like this before. He'd always been standing, even when he seemed otherwise relaxed. Their earlier spat forced itself into her mind, and she turned back to the fire. "Yeah," she said softly.

Silence fell over the small clearing, save for the periodic crackling of the fire and the distant calls of the evening wildlife. For a few minutes they sat together, neither moving nor attempting to speak.

"Sorry for getting angry with you," Sinccah whispered under her breath. The Wanderer's upright tentacle twitched, but he made no attempt to start writing. Sinccah frowned before continuing. "Thanks for stopping me," she said as quietly as she could manage. "I got carried away," she continued, her voice getting louder and more sorrowful. "I just wanted to cast the spell." She turned to the mygnus. "I'm glad you came back."

The Wanderer slowly wrote three dots in the air, waiting several seconds between each dot. "Who was this person you cared about?" he asked with sudden speed.

"Vistimmot," Sinccah answered. "He was my mentor." She frowned. "Not really," she said as she shook her head. "I only knew him for a few hours. He was the mage the bandits killed when I first came to Ucksland. I guess I never really knew him, but the time I spent with him meant a lot to me."

"Why is that?"

Sinccah closed her eyes. "He," she said softly, "unlike everyone else, believed I could be a great mage someday. Ever since I failed out of the royal mages, I've felt like no one really believed in me." She sighed. "Honestly, one of the reasons I came to Ucksland was to prove them all wrong."

The Wanderer turned a light blue. "Are you succeeding?"

"I ..." Sinccah started as her lips started quivering. "I don't really know," she admitted. "Sometimes it feels like it, but ..." she paused, inhaling deeply. "I can't help feeling that I'll never make it."

"Never make it where?" the Wanderer asked as the fire let out a subtle pop.

"I'm not sure," Sinccah said with a sigh as she looked into the shower of sparks. "I guess I'm still trying to figure that out."

"Reasonable," the Wanderer wrote calmly. "Perhaps you have a companion in that pursuit."

Sinccah raised an eyebrow. "What do you mean?"

"Feeling lost is normal for any sentient being," the Wanderer wrote quickly. "Or at least it should be considered so. If you exist for a purpose but that purpose is particularly uncertain, it is only natural to feel somewhat lost."

"Yeah," Sinccah said as she slowly nodded. "I just wish my future was clearer."

"Perhaps," the Wanderer wrote slowly.

Sinccah furrowed her brow. "What do you mean? You want your future to be vague?"

"I am unsure," the Wanderer wrote before pausing for several seconds. "I often fear that knowing more would be unhealthy."

"I don't understand," Sinccah said softly.

The Wanderer curled his outstretched tentacle. He then uncurled it and started writing. "Perhaps by knowing so little of what we are meant to do, it allows us to do more good along the way. Perhaps it saves us from a single-minded focus that would only ruin us. We are saved to do what is truly best."

Sinccah shifted uncomfortably. "Such as?"

"Caring for those around us," the Wanderer replied. "Whether they need food or ..." He paused. "Someone to talk to."

"You think helping the orphans is your purpose?" Sinccah asked dubiously.

"Presumably," the Wanderer replied. "At least it is part of it. I think too many beings scramble around trying to find a grand reason for their existence. However, very few beings find their purpose doing obviously great things."

Sinccah frowned. "So you think the purpose of existing, for most people, is to do simple acts of kindness?"

"That would be imprecise," the Wanderer wrote. "I think all beings are created with a true and significant purpose. However, since we are often unaware of how to fulfill that purpose, I think it is best to spend our time of uncertainty helping those around us." His tentacle drooped slightly. "I think too many beings waste their lives focusing on only themselves."

Sinccah nodded as silence fell between the two once again. She wasn't sure if she agreed with what the mygnus had said, but it was certainly thought provoking. Her brow furrowed as she questioned why he'd said so much. It wasn't as though he trusted her. Why be so vulnerable? Her lips twitched. Still, it felt nice to have someone to talk to.

After a few more minutes, the Wanderer started writing again. "You implied you had other reasons for coming to Ucksland; what are they?"

Sinccah stiffened. "I'm trying to figure out what happened to my mother."

"As yes," the Wanderer wrote quickly. "That is why the loss of your pendant was so hard for you."

Sinccah bit her lips. "Yeah," she said as the image of her lost pendant flashed into her mind. She felt her fist clench. "I suppose that is part of the reason I'm going through so much trouble to find them."

"And because they killed your mage friend," the Wanderer quickly wrote.

Sinccah frowned as she tilted her head back and forth. "That too."

"Your response is reasonable," the Wanderer wrote slowly, "though I suspect the task will consume you."

Sinccah grimaced. "Yeah," she grumbled, "but I can't let them get away with this."

The Wanderer fidgeted. "That is a poor attitude."

Sinccah slumped her shoulders. "You're probably right," she sighed. "But it's not like I have anything better to do."

"Perhaps," the Wanderer responded. "Maybe this is what is best for you, but I must warn you that becoming so fixated on this task might cause you to neglect things that may matter more."

"What do you mean?" Sinccah questioned.

"Single-mindedness can be dangerous," the Wanderer wrote. "Much like magic, it can lead you to dark places and cause you to miss what truly matters."

Sinccah frowned as sarcastic thoughts jumped into her head. Apparently, this mygnus was an incredible expert in magic. So very knowledgeable, even though he couldn't even cast a spell. She beat back those thoughts. What he said had some truth. A headlong pursuit of the bandits was certainly dangerous, and she had firsthand experience of seeing other mages take their single-minded pursuit of magic too far.

"Maybe you're right," Sinccah said softly. "I really want to see them brought to justice, though."

"Indeed," the Wanderer wrote calmly. "It is reasonable to become passionate when evil goes unpunished. However, allowing that passion to be your sole guide can only be a mistake. It will lead you into all kinds of vile things."

"I know," Sinccah sighed. "I don't want this to consume me either."

"Ideal," the Wanderer wrote before nestling down into his coiled tentacles and wrapping the remaining three around his central sphere.

Sinccah stared into the fire, watching the embers slowly crumble into a heap. She turned back to the mygnus. "I had a question for you."

The Wanderer unwrapped his tentacles. "Oh?"

"Why does everyone call you Wandi?" Sinccah asked. "You told me to call you the Wanderer, but no one I met has ever called you that."

"Indeed," the Wanderer responded. "My friends call me Wandi."

Sinccah's brow furrowed. Hadn't he called her his friend? Her eyes darted to the Wanderer, but she quickly glanced back into the fire. What did this mean?

The Wanderer, apparently noticing her glance, suddenly shuddered as he turned a light yellow. His color flickered momentarily to a deep blue but returned to teal as he lifted a tentacle and started writing. "I would allow you the same, but our time together has been too brief."

Sinccah narrowed her eyes, not entirely convinced of his sincerity. "I'm not sure I understand."

"One day you will," the Wanderer wrote quickly. "Until then, I would prefer you continue calling me 'The Wanderer.'"

"Alright," Sinccah said softly.

The Wanderer wrapped his tentacles around himself again. "You should sleep. You are very tired, and we have a great deal of ground to cover tomorrow."

Sinccah nodded before leaning back and grabbing her pack. As she untied her sleeping mat and blanket, she mused over everything the Wanderer had said. Was he right about purpose? Would she be better off spending her time trying to help the people around her? Would it be better than being some great mage? She shook her head. Why did he even tell her all that? She was a mage, and he hated mages. Didn't that mean he hated her? It was too much to think about. She rolled out her sleeping mat and crawled onto it. Pulling her blanket over herself, she looked up into the darkening sky, where the moon Ahkia shone out alone. She had waned slightly but still appeared as an oval. At least the view here was beautiful. She glanced at the Wanderer, who had wrapped his remaining tentacle around his central sphere. Something felt off about him still. He was a strange creature, and his request for her to keep calling him the Wanderer made her feel awkward. Certainly he had a reason, but it didn't make a lot of sense. Sinccah rolled over. She'd have plenty of time to think about that tomorrow.

CHAPTER TEN

Sinccah awoke to the harsh caws of a flock of large birds flying overhead. She groaned as she rolled over and sat up. The dim morning light flooded into her eyes and forced her to squint. She rolled her shoulders, trying to work out some of the stiffness, before glancing around the makeshift camp. The Wanderer was gone, which was expected, seeing as he didn't need to sleep. He'd presumably left shortly after she'd drifted off. Nothing else appeared different from the night before. She reached for her pack and started to dig through it in search of food. Her hand bumped a small leather pouch. Apparently, the Wanderer had returned her tinder bag sometime during the night. A quick glance outside the bag revealed her dagger, back in its sheath. She returned her focus to the inside of the pack. After a few seconds, she located the jerky Kacksa had given her and pulled out a few strips. A quick inspection of the meat revealed nothing of particular concern. She tried a small nibble and found it surprisingly good. Sure, it was made by goblins, but the flavor was genuinely enjoyable.

A soft rustle caught her attention, and she turned to see the Wanderer entering the clearing. "Sleep well?" he asked.

Sinccah nodded as she took a large bite of the dried meat.

"Ideal," the Wanderer wrote. "The remaining distance is fairly short, we can probably make it to your destination by nightfall."

Sinccah's eyes widened slightly, but she continued chewing. "Really?" she asked after a few seconds.

"Indeed," the Wanderer replied. "Assuming our travel remains free from additional complications."

Sinccah shoved the rest of the jerky into her mouth as her gaze wandered over the clearing. A moment later she nearly choked. Rising over the trees was a distant column of thick black smoke. She hurriedly gulped down the meat before pointing. "Do you see that?!" she exclaimed.

The Wanderer fidgeted slightly. "No. Seeing is quite beyond me."

Sinccah glanced toward the mygnus, who stood motionless. "I know that!" she cried. "But you can sense that, right?"

"Sense what?"

"The smoke?!" Sinccah nearly shouted.

"Ah," the Wanderer wrote as he awkwardly tapped two of his tentacles against the ground. "No," he continued. "No smoke is within my perception."

Sinccah's head snapped back to the black column and she narrowed her eyes. The smoke was so obvious. How could he not sense it? Her eyes quickly widened as she realized the way he saw the world probably didn't allow him to notice things over such long distances. She turned back to him. "There's a giant column of smoke billowing in the south."

"Oh!" the Wanderer wrote quickly as he turned orange. "What do you suppose it is coming from?"

"No idea," Sinccah said as she tied her dagger back onto her belt and started to shove her belongings back into her pack. "We should probably investigate it."

"Or flee," the Wanderer suggested.

Sinccah glanced back at him and raised an eyebrow before standing and slinging her pack over her shoulders.

"A large fire could be quite dangerous for you," the Wanderer continued as he read Sinccah's expression. "If so, we should probably try to escape."

Sinccah shook her head. "It's just a single column, probably not a widespread fire."

"Ah," the Wanderer wrote quickly, "then we should explore it. If we get closer, I will be able to determine the source."

"That's what I was thinking," Sinccah said as she walked briskly toward the road. She paused. "The road continues south here, right?"

"Yes," the Wanderer wrote before dashing ahead.

The two companions started to jog southward as soon as they reached the road. After a few minutes the Wanderer stopped. He wrote rapidly, barely finishing the words. "I can sense cries of distress." He paused. "And shouting."

"What's making those sounds?" Sinccah asked quickly.

"Humans," the Wanderer wrote, his writing slowing considerably. "As few as four and as many as ten."

Sinccah started running, and the Wanderer quickly joined her. Sinccah's mind was racing. Who were these humans? What'd happened to them? Did they need help? Her spirits suddenly sank. Would they be hostile toward her? She glanced at her mygnus companion. What would they think of him?

The Wanderer suddenly stopped, leaving Sinccah to skid to a halt. He started writing. "It appears to be the trappers from yesterday. Their camp is ablaze, and several of them appear to be injured."

Sinccah looked down at the motionless mygnus. "Do they need help?"

The Wanderer fidgeted slightly. "Yes," he wrote slowly, "it seems they could use some help."

Sinccah turned away and took a handful of steps. She glanced back at the Wanderer, who still hadn't moved. "Aren't you coming?"

"It seems I have no desire to do that," he replied.

Sinccah forcefully tilted her head. "Really?!"

"Yes."

"You don't get to back down now!" Sinccah declared. "I helped you with the goblin, so you're helping me with these people!"

The Wanderer raised two of his tentacles and tapped them together. "In that situation, you were more secure. I am at considerable risk."

Sinccah glared down at him. "You can't be serious!"

The Wanderer tapped his walking tentacles against the ground in a series of quick circles. For several seconds his color flashed among various shades of orange, blue, and yellow. "Fine," he eventually wrote as his color flashed briefly red, "I will aid you."

Sinccah nodded and the two hurried toward the smoke. Soon Sinccah could make out loud shouts, likely someone giving orders. They were punctuated by distressing screams of pain.

The Wanderer pointed off the road, down a small footpath. "Here," Sinccah heard in her head. She raced down the path, the shouts were becoming clearer and the cries of pain more harrowing.

"Someone give me an ealching hand!" a deep voice roared.

"Coming!" another voice responded.

"Hurry!" the first voice called out.

The path Sinccah was running on took a sharp turn between two small hills, and she was finally able to see flames dancing through gaps in the trees. She pushed herself harder, trying desperately to get to the scene in time. The Wanderer, now a dark shade of orange, glided behind her, clearly not pushing himself too hard.

The two broke into a large clearing populated with a few small wooden buildings. One of them, the largest, was on fire. A group of men clustered around the burning building, which belched out thick clouds of smoke.

One of the men turned toward them. "Who are you?" he called out apprehensively.

The men around him turned toward the Wanderer and shot each other nervous glances.

"We're here to help," Sinccah declared as she tried to level her breathing. "What happened?"

"Listen, girl," the man answered as several other men began to whisper to each other. "I don't—"

"Get over here!" the deep voice interrupted.

The loud command pulled Sinccah's attention to the edge of the fire, where one of the men from the day before was standing. He wore a horrified look as he bellowed another order, "Move!"

Sinccah quickly scanned the rest of the men, searching for the man's brother. He was missing. Her eyes darted back to the burning building. The nearest corner had collapsed, and one of the large roof-beams had pinned the man against the floor. He struggled limply, barely conscious. The fire hadn't consumed that portion of the building quite yet but was racing toward the helpless man.

The Wanderer darted to the end of the beam which protruded from the rest of the building. He tapped on it rapidly. "Lift," he wrote.

The men gave Sinccah a dubious glance.

"Do what he says!" Sinccah exclaimed.

Most of the men remained motionless.

The deep-voiced man rushed to the beam and started to push against it. His companions shot each other disgruntled glances but moved to help. They heaved upward with all their strength. The beam moved up slightly as they strained against the weight. The Wanderer rushed into the flames and grabbed the man. A sharp jerk moved the man from under the beam. Then a plank snapped, and the mygnus tumbled out of the rubble, tentacles flailing. The man with the deep voice dropped the beam and charged into the fire. He grimaced as the heat threatened to ignite his clothing, but he pressed on, grabbing his brother and dragging him from the rubble.

Sinccah sprinted to the two men as they collapsed. She knelt and quickly assessed the man who had been trapped. His breaths were harsh and raspy, but he was still breathing. She rolled him onto his side and pressed her hand against his chest. She wasn't well practiced in the healing magic used to treat choking, but she figured it was the most applicable thing she knew. She closed her eyes and started to focus. She breathed out deeply, as though she could impart her own actions into this man's mind. She breathed in again, trying to focus on her spell. After some of the longest few seconds of her life, the man started coughing.

"Is he alright?" one of the men asked.

"Let her work!" the man with the deep voice yelled as he pulled himself upright and brushed debris off his clothes.

Sinccah nodded. "I think he'll be fine," she said softly.

The hacking man opened his eyes. He groaned faintly.

"It's alright," Sinccah whispered. "You're safe now."

The man nodded weakly before closing his eyes as another fit of coughing set in. Sinccah looked over his body. He had some fairly serious burns and a large gash running down his leg. Nothing life-threatening but still pretty nasty.

The deep-voiced man knelt next to her. "Thank you, miss," he said softly as his face contorted in sorrow. He looked up at the Wanderer, who'd recovered from his tumble and now stood nearby.

"Thank you as well," the deep-voiced man said awkwardly. "That was some quick work."

The Wanderer bobbed slightly but didn't move to write anything.

One of the other men started whispering, "This's the mage and mygnus who stood up to Red."

"Shhh," another man hissed, "they'll hear you!"

The deep-voiced man glared at them. "Don't you have something better to do?"

The men murmured to themselves as they slowly backed away and continued their conversation beyond the reach of Sinccah's ears. The burnt man finally stopped coughing and tried to sit up. He was initially successful; however, another bout of coughing sent him back to the ground. Sinccah once again put her hand on his chest and cast her spell. He coughed even harder before finally stopping. He flopped back onto the ground and began breathing deeply.

A loud crash sounded as the building finished collapsing. Sinccah looked up into the fresh column of fire. It was a good thing they'd arrived when they had.

The deep-voiced man shook his head before turning to Sinccah. "Is there anything I can do?"

Sinccah glanced toward the fire. "Can you explain what happened here?"

The man's face darkened. "Arson," he said flatly. "We knew those pesky goblins were starting to get riled up, but I didn't think it'd get this far." His lip curled upward. "I figured we had a few more months."

"That is unfortunate," the Wanderer said as he turned a dull blue.

The man looked awkwardly at the mygnus. "We should've just packed up and left, but the trappings were good, so we needed to stay." He looked over the blazing building before bowing his head and slowly shaking it.

Sinccah glanced at the other men, who seemed increasingly agitated as they kept talking. "I'm sorry this had to happen to you," she said and she leaned over and started to heal the burnt man's wounds.

The burning building let out a long crackle as the fire discovered a new item to consume.

"It's alright," the deep-voiced man sighed. "I just got back from selling most of our stock, so we didn't lose much." He grew silent as his gaze drifted into the fire.

"I guess you couldn't take that with you anyway," Sinccah offered as she moved to heal the large cut on the burnt man's leg.

"Yeah," the man with the deep voice said bitterly. "If only the cursed goblins didn't exist."

"Their attack was reprehensible," the Wanderer wrote quickly as he turned a shade of light red, "but you are wrong if you assume all goblins are like these."

The man eyed him curiously. "You a friend of goblins?"

"Yes," the Wanderer replied. "The ones who attacked you are an exception. Very few goblins want war more than peace."

The man glanced at Sinccah as if to ask for her thoughts on the topic.

She shrugged. "He's right. I've met some of those goblins."

The man nodded slowly. "Sure," he growled before glancing at the rest of the men. "If you say so."

"Unfortunate," the Wanderer wrote as he returned to a shade of orange.

Sinccah stood and offered the burnt man her hand. He took it, and she pulled him to his feet. He staggered slightly but kept his footing. The other man rose to embrace his brother. Sinccah smiled as she stepped away.

The burnt man pulled himself away from his brother and inspected his body. He glanced at Sinccah. "That's some fine magic you got." He bent down and rubbed his leg. "Even took the pain."

Sinccah nodded. "It is my pleasure," she said with a smile as she recalled Vistimmot saying those exact words. If he could see her now, he'd certainly be proud
of her.

The Wanderer flickered to a yellow color as he slowly started to edge back
toward the road.

"I suppose you two want to be on your way," the deep-voiced man said quickly.
"Many thanks for what you did here." He paused as he glanced toward the rest of
the men, who appeared to have gotten into a hushed argument. "Is there anything
we can do for ya?"

"There is nothing I need," the Wanderer wrote rapidly before continuing to
edge farther away.

The man nodded and turned to Sinccah. "You?"

Sinccah glanced awkwardly at the Wanderer. She also didn't really need anything, but she wasn't exactly fabulously wealthy either. "I don't want to take
anything from you," she offered. "You lost enough as it is."

"Fair enough," the deep-voiced man responded. "Even so," he continued as he
gestured toward one of the buildings. "I have a few things you could use."

"What do you—" Sinccah started.

A voice in her head interrupted her. "Leave."

Sinccah bit her lip. She glanced at the Wanderer, whose color was darkening
into a deep red. What was going on with him? Her eyes darted to the arguing men,
who were getting somewhat more spirited. Maybe she'd be better to follow the
Wanderer's lead. "Actually," she said quickly as she turned back to the brothers.
"We'll be fine."

"It's the least we can do," the deep-voiced man insisted. "Season was good. We
can spare a few things."

"It's alright," Sinccah said as sweetly as she could manage. The Wanderer's
behavior was irritating, but perhaps he knew something she didn't.

"Very well," the man replied.

The Wanderer started walking back toward the road.

Sinccah smiled at the two men. "I'm glad everyone is alright," she said quickly.

The deep-voiced man gave her a kindhearted smile. "Your friend looks to be leaving without you."

Sinccah glanced at the Wanderer, then back at the two men. "May you have good fortune in your future adventures."

"You too," the men called out, and Sinccah turned away and jogged after the Wanderer.

As they reached the road, Sinccah shot the mygnus an angry look. "What's this about?!" she growled.

"What are you referring to?" the Wanderer replied calmly before continuing to walk.

"They were going to give us stuff!" Sinccah exclaimed. "Potentially stuff I could use!"

The Wanderer paused in his step. "Perhaps," he wrote quickly before resuming his gait.

Sinccah raised her hands to chest height and extended her fingers forcefully. "We didn't need to leave so quickly!"

"That may be true of you," the Wanderer wrote quickly.

"What do you mean?!" Sinccah exclaimed.

"I am unwilling to explain," the Wanderer wrote. "Perhaps more can be said later. For now, we need to cover ground." He paused. "Quickly."

Sinccah frowned but didn't say more. If he wasn't willing to talk, she wasn't going to convince him. Still, she couldn't help scowling at his retreating form. Sure, he'd helped, but she couldn't help but feel like it'd been the most begrudging thing he'd done in his whole life. She grumbled to herself as she followed after him.

———◆○◆———

The two travelers continued southward for several hours. During this time, Sinccah's mind danced through the possible rewards that the trappers might have given her if only the Wanderer hadn't been so prickly. Over time, she calmed

down somewhat and watched the Wanderer turn increasingly blue. Eventually, the trees gave way to a flat plain. Sinccah paused to look over the area. The
ground sloped gently away from her such that the plain seemed to stretch on
forever, only interrupted by periodic hills and trees. The road here was wider,
presumably due to the lack of encroaching trees. Even so, the rugged stones
were easily lost in the rippling grass that surrounded them. Sinccah breathed
in the warm air as a breeze wafted over her. It felt good to finally be out in
the open again. A large flightless bird startled and jumped out in front of
the Wanderer. The mygnus kept walking as though he hadn't noticed, nearly
bumping the bird with his tentacle. The bird panicked and raced into a dense
patch of grass. Sinccah watched the tall grass rustle as the bird fled from the
new arrivals.

The Wanderer drifted to a stop and started writing. "You pause."

"Yeah," Sinccah said softly. "The view here is quite lovely, don't you think?"

The Wanderer rhythmically tapped two of his tentacles against the ground.
"If you say so."

"Come now," Sinccah started, "you can see so far and—" she bit her lip.
Of course. He was a mygnus: he couldn't see anything. This view was entirely
wasted on him.

The Wanderer bobbed slightly. "Do you think this area looks lovely?"

"It does," Sinccah said awkwardly. "It's a shame you can't see it."

"Perhaps," the Wanderer answered. "I perceive other things." he paused for
a second. "At least I, unlike humans, am able to avoid overlooking everything
around me."

"Uh huh," Sinccah grunted. Her lip curled into a snarl. "At least we can see
giant pillars of smoke."

The Wanderer turned a light yellow. "Indeed," he wrote quickly. "I had
intended to bring that up to you again."

"The smoke?" Sinccah growled.

"Sort of," the Wanderer wrote as his color took on a hint of red. "More so
the trappers. We left rather suddenly."

"Yeah?!" Sinccah said with a heavy dose of accusation. "We could've gotten help from them."

"I would normally agree with you," The Wanderer replied as the shade of red deepened.

"Oh really?!" Sinccah growled.

The Wanderer fidgeted. "If you had known what the other four men were discussing, you might have followed me more quickly."

Sinccah tilted her head, her scowl deepening. "And what was that?"

The Wanderer's three upper tentacles twitched higher, then he started writing rapidly: "They were deciding if it was worth it to kill me for my maggni."

"What! You just helped save their friend!" She waved her arms randomly as she struggled to figure out what to say next. Finding no appropriate response, she threw her hands into the air. "You don't even have a maggni!"

"Indeed," the Wanderer wrote, more slowly now. "But they were ignorant of that."

"That seems so heartless," Sinccah said in disbelief.

"It certainly was," the Wanderer wrote as his color became more blue. "Only one of them was really set on the idea of attacking me, but it would have been foolish for me to give him time to convince the others how rich they could become."

Sinccah shook her head and blinked rapidly. "I know maggni are valuable, but there's no way it'd be worth betraying someone for."

"I am glad you agree," the Wanderer wrote slowly. "Even so, we should continue our journey. I would prefer we find your mage friend as soon as possible."

"Right," Sinccah grunted as she started walking again.

As they continued down the path, Sinccah's mind couldn't escape the confines of what the Wanderer had said. There was no way. She grimaced. There certainly was a way. It wasn't like she knew these trappers, and maggni were incredibly valuable. But such an act was so obviously evil, particularly when the Wanderer had just helped them. How was the man who brought it up even tolerated?

For the next several hours, the topic continued to torment her. Humans and magnus had never gotten along. In fact, they'd been in some state of effective war as far back as history recounted their interactions. She shook her head. What a disaster. She let out a sigh as she thought back to what the Wanderer had said about the Rakniv goblins being an exception. Perhaps he suffered from a similar belief as the trappers—but for humans instead of goblins. Maybe he thought all humans were evil, even though most humans would probably enjoy talking with a mygnus.

Her lip twitched upward. That conclusion didn't work. The Wanderer had accepted her. He'd led her all this way to help her find a man who he had every reason to hate. Why would he do that if he thought she was evil? Nothing quite made sense. She looked up and watched the Wanderer glide down the road, flanked on either side by the tall grass. He'd never been particularly friendly toward her. They'd shared a lot of conversations, but none of it quite felt right. But what about the orphans? He didn't think they were evil. He invested a great deal of his time into helping them and likely risked his own life just to help them more effectively.

She wasn't a child though. Perhaps that made the difference. The orphans were friendly toward him and had no obvious intention or ability to hunt magnus. She was different. She certainly didn't want to hurt magnus, but she'd always wanted maggni. Did she still want them? Was she actually just as bad as the trapper? Would she be willing to betray a creature who'd just helped her? She frowned. No. She was different. She'd be better. After everything the Wanderer had done for her, it was really the least she could do.

She began to think forward to their destination, and as the day wore on, her enthusiasm grew. It'd be good to talk to another powerful mage. Hopefully, he'd be like Vistimmot and help her learn more magic. She didn't know Beilbauk, but he'd been a close friend of her father. She grimaced. Her father had hardly been an exemplary man. What kind of company had he kept? Would this mage turn out to be some old creep? Dreekadack hadn't had anything nice to say about him. Perhaps coming all this way had been a giant mistake. She shook her head.

Even if it was, it was far too late to turn back now. Her gaze swept slowly over the open plain. In the distance, a small patch of trees poked up into the otherwise flat horizon. She looked up at the sun, which had already begun to dip in the western sky. The whole day had passed already?

She looked up at the Wanderer, who'd come to a stop. He lifted a single tentacle and pointed farther down the road at the patch of trees. Sinccah squinted at the trees but didn't see anything peculiar on her first glance. She suddenly noticed something different. On the far side of the trees, an old tower rose just above the treetops. The tower was remarkably short, only two stories tall, with the stones near the top appearing jagged and broken. The roof looked out of place. It'd clearly been built recently and would've matched a house much better than an ancient stone structure. At the top of the tower, a small light flickered warmly through an arched window. Beneath the window, a large pile of stones could be seen trailing away from the tower.

"We are here," the Wanderer wrote quickly.

Sinccah nodded. "Thanks for guiding me here," she said excitedly.

The Wanderer turned a deep blue. "Yes," he wrote slowly. "You are welcome."

"Is something wrong?" Sinccah asked.

"Perhaps," the Wanderer answered, continuing to write each letter slowly. "This is where our paths must diverge."

"Oh," Sinccah said sorrowfully. "I suppose you're right."

"Indeed," the Wanderer responded. "I hope that your mage helps you and you one day track down the bandits you are looking for." He paused for several seconds, writing small dots as if to say he was thinking. "May you find your purpose someday."

"You too," Sinccah said with a sigh. "I don't suppose I'll ever see you again."

"Unlikely," the Wanderer wrote more quickly. "If this mage turns out to be what you had been hoping for, then I suspect neither of us will soon desire our paths to cross again."

Sinccah frowned. She honestly didn't know this mygnus very well, but he'd helped her, and he'd shown her a lot about the world she wouldn't have learned otherwise. She almost regretted her dream of becoming a great mage. "Thanks ..." she said slowly, then paused. "For everything you showed me along the way."

The Wanderer's color brightened slightly. "I am glad to be of help," he wrote rapidly before he started to drift away. "I must get going." He quickly took a few more steps away. "Farewell, Sinccah."

"Farewell," Sinccah called after him before lowering her voice. "Wanderer." She watched as the mygnus dashed away, moving far more quickly than she would've expected. Perhaps that was reasonable. If Beilbauk was nearby, the poor mygnus would certainly want to disappear as quickly as possible.

As the Wanderer vanished into the tall grass, Sinccah turned away and started toward the tower. She pondered anew why the Wanderer had bothered to take her here. He seemed so sad about her goal of becoming a great mage, and he certainly wouldn't want her to learn more magic. He'd gotten upset at her for even trying. She shook her head. That was all in the past. It was time to focus on the future.

As she neared the tower, a figure was exiting through a small door at the base. It was an older man, perhaps in his mid-sixties. "Beilbauk?" she called out.

The figure stiffened. "Who er you?" he called out in a disgruntled voice. "An' how you know me name?"

"My name is Sinccah, and I'm told my father Ekkmund was your assistant for a time."

"Ekkmund?!" Beilbauk nearly shouted. "That fool nev'r 'ad a kid!"

Sinccah's shoulders slumped. This wasn't how this was supposed to go. She paused in her step and glanced backward. Maybe the Wanderer was still close. She could probably catch up to him if she left now. No. She couldn't abandon everything now. She turned back to the old mage. "Do you remember the ambush in the Gasping Caves?"

Beilbauk leaned back slightly. "So it's true," he said stiffly. He suddenly straightened. "Don't just stand there!" he shouted with a sudden hint of cheerfulness as he dropped his strange accent. "Come on in! It's nearly night already!"

Sinccah tilted her head as she stared at the old mage, who now wore a friendly grin.

Beilbauk let out a short chuckle. "Only the real daughter of Ekkmund would respond like that. I had to make sure you're genuine."

"Oh," Sinccah said awkwardly as she continued toward the tower. "I thought the two of you must have had some sort of falling out."

"In some ways, we did," Beilbauk said with a grin. "I suppose that happens when a person sails into a storm. It turns out he really was a fool." He chuckled. "But he always was a good assistant. It's a shame he got himself killed like that."

"Yeah," Sinccah mumbled as she reached the base of a small staircase that led up to the base of the tower. She glanced quickly over the area as she started to climb toward the small stone platform where Beilbauk stood. Now that she was closer, she could better see the area around the tower. The crumbled stones beside it were almost certainly left over from when the top of the tower had collapsed, which must have been centuries ago. Beyond the tower, ruined walls rose just above the tall grasses. They encased what appeared to have once been a stone courtyard. However, the long years of abandonment had caused it to become quite overgrown. Attached to the far side of the tower, a rough wooden shed made up part of a fence that held a pair of horses.

"Now," Beilbauk said cordially as Sinccah reached the top of the stairs, "what brings my old friend's daughter to my humble abode? I don't suppose you're here for a friendly chat."

"I am not," Sinccah said quickly. "I was hoping you could help me with a few things."

Beilbauk nodded. "I suppose that's expected. I did owe your father a favor before he sailed off to his death. What can I do for you?"

Sinccah's eyes widened. She hadn't expected Beilbauk to seem so agreeable. Hadn't Dreekadack called him crazy? "Well," she said carefully, "I need some help dealing with some bandits."

Beilbauk cocked an eyebrow. "Are you sure you don't need Ucksil? He rules these lands."

"I've already talked to him," Sinccah replied. "Unfortunately, the bandits have a couple mages leading them, and Ucksil didn't have mages to spare to go after them."

"Ah," Beilbauk said before sticking out his lip and taking on a thoughtful look. "I suppose you want me to run all over Ucksland until we find them."

"Not exactly," Sinccah said as she tried to retain her composure. "Ucksil promised to lend me some men, assuming I could secure a mage."

Beilbauk nodded. "So I'd need to agree to help, then wait until Ucksil's men find the targets?"

"Yeah," Sinccah said optimistically.

"And I suppose I'd have to come right away," Beilbauk muttered to himself.

"Ideally, yeah," Sinccah said as cheerfully as she could manage.

Beilbauk lifted his hand and started tapping it on his chin. "I'll need to think about it," he said as he opened the door to the tower. "Is there anything else you need?"

"Well," Sinccah said awkwardly. "I was also hoping you might be willing to teach me some magic."

"Oh?" Beilbauk said as he turned around and leaned against the doorframe, crossing his arms in front of his chest. He eyed Sinccah suspiciously for several seconds before he started nodding. He tilted his head upward and stuck out his lips thoughtfully. He suddenly returned his gaze to Sinccah. "What spells do you know?"

"I know healing and shielding spells," Sinccah answered confidently.

"That's it?" Beilbauk said flatly.

"Uh," Sinccah stammered. "Yeah, I was trying to learn some fire magic, but it hasn't been going very well."

Beilbauk unfolded his arms, pressed his palms together, and started tapping his fingers against each other. "You have potential," he said slowly before gesturing through the door. "Come inside. We have things to discuss."

Sinccah stepped through the door. She wasn't sure if she should be excited or apprehensive. Regardless, this was her opportunity. She just needed to take it.

Chapter Eleven

Sinccah stepped into the musty old tower. She squinted in the dim light as she tried to make out her surroundings. Beilbauk walked confidently across the room to the base of a set of spiral stairs, which were dimly lit from above. Sinccah tried to follow him but found herself tripping over small wooden crates that littered the floor. After stumbling around for several seconds, her eyes finally started to adjust. She glanced over the room and could now see that the entire lower level of the tower was covered in rubbish. The only place free of junk was a small path that meandered its way from the door to the staircase. She kicked a few boxes out of her way and walked along this path until she also reached the stairs. By this time Beilbauk had already ascended, so she jogged up the stairs after him.

Upon reaching the top, Sinccah was greeted by a bit more light, which emanated from a small lantern that hung from a cord in the middle of the room. She slowly lowered her pack to the floor. Beilbauk was sitting at the room's single chair, digging through a pile of papers on the table. Sinccah glanced around awkwardly. This room was also a giant mess, with various stacks of paper and loose cloth littering the entire floor. Barrels and crates poked out of larger mounds of heaped up junk. She fought back a grimace as she turned her eyes upward. The walls had a handful of shelves, but each of them was overflowing with massive stacks of seemingly random items. She glanced at her feet. Directly adjacent to her was a small cot which was as disheveled as the rest of the room.

Beilbauk looked up from the papers. "Have a seat," he said as he gestured to the other side of the table. He straightened and peeked over the far side of the table. Muttering something to himself, he stood and dug a small stool out of one of the piles and set it next to the table. He returned to his chair and gestured again.

Sinccah sat gingerly. She half expected the stool to suddenly collapse under her weight, but it somehow held.

"Alright," Beilbauk said cordially as he pulled a blank piece of paper out from under a pile of other papers. He picked the quill out of a nearby inkwell and held it over the paper. "What did you say your name was again?"

"Sinccah."

Beilbauk nodded, "Great," he said as he started writing, only to find that the inkwell had run dry. He curled his lip at the small glass bottle before standing up and walking to the far side of the room, where he started to dig through another pile of rubbish. Sinccah rocked uneasily on the stool, still thinking it would break. She bit her lip and started to tap her fingers against the table.

"Stop," Beilbauk commanded without looking up from his search.

Sinccah cringed slightly before clasping her hands together and setting them on the table. It wasn't comfortable, as the stool was so short that her shoulders rose only just above the tabletop. She alternated raising each shoulder as she looked up into the ceiling, which was made out of roughly-cut boards. The ridgeline didn't quite look straight, and the boards appeared to be warping slightly. She returned her focus to the table. Best to just ignore it. Her mind started to bombard her with doubts. Beilbauk was entirely disorganized. What kind of person was he? Did she really want to become this man's apprentice?

Beilbauk returned and flopped into his chair. He uncorked a small glass bottle and poured the contents into the inkwell. Dipping his quill into the fresh ink, he looked up at her. "Name."

"Sinccah," she answered politely, even though she'd just told him that a moment ago.

"Mhmm," Beilbauk mumbled as he started writing. "Known magic."

Sinccah glanced at the paper, which now featured her name at the top, though spelled entirely incorrectly. "Healing and shielding," she said quickly. Had he forgotten everything already?

Beilbauk shifted to position his arm above the paper, blocking it from Sinccah's view. He moved the quill over the paper without actually looking at what he was writing. "Reason for wanting magical instruction."

Sinccah bit her lip. She wasn't prepared for this question. At least he'd remembered something this time. "I want to become a great mage." She cringed slightly at her response. It sounded weak, selfish even.

"Right," Beilbauk said flatly as he moved the quill in small loops over the paper. "It seems I can help you with your goal. However, I need to know what you can do for me."

"Sure," Sinccah said with forced cheerfulness. She hadn't expected this to be free, but she was suddenly concerned with what this mage had in mind.

"What kind of work have you done?" Beilbauk asked.

"I used to work as a nurse-mage," Sinccah answered.

Beilbauk's eyebrows shot upward. He leaned forward and quickly started writing. "What were your responsibilities?"

Sinccah frowned as memories from that time in her life came flooding back. "My main responsibility was taking care of the Lady's children. I made sure they were safe, and I healed any injuries they might get. I was tasked with cleaning up after them and sometimes aiding the Lady herself. Before that, I used to transcribe shield magic manuals for the royal mages."

Sinccah could see that Beilbauk was smiling now, but his arm was still obstructing the paper, so she couldn't see what he was writing. Purely based on the movements of the quill, it appeared he was writing with far more detail than before. Her mind started racing. What did this mage have planned?

"Excellent," Beilbauk said loudly as he looked up from his writing. "Do you have any experience with horses?"

"Not much," Sinccah admitted. "I've never cared for one, but I have some experience riding."

Beilbauk stuck out his lip and twitched his head side to side. "That's alright," he muttered to himself. "I have a couple of them. An old friend of mine brought them here for some hunting. He left them behind after he ... uh ..." He glanced awkwardly to the side. "Never mind him." He suddenly pierced her with a fierce gaze. "Last question," he said slowly. "Do you have any experience with magnus?"

Sinccah's eyes widened slightly before she got herself under control. "Why do you ask?" It wasn't clear what this mage wanted with magnus, but she suddenly felt suspicious of his motives.

"Now, now," Beilbauk chuckled as he leaned closer to Sinccah. "We can get to your questions later."

Sinccah frowned. "I don't know much about magnus."

"That's not quite what I asked," Beilbauk said with a hint of friendliness. "I asked if you had *experience*."

"Would it make a difference if I did?" Sinccah asked.

Beilbauk laughed. "Of course," he said with a chuckle. "I've been doing a great deal of research on the creatures. If you have any experience interacting with them, it would be invaluable."

A pained look flashed on Sinccah's face. She didn't want to tell this mage everything, but if it was going to be the difference between her learning magic or being doomed to a life of nothingness, then she'd do it. Her face hardened. She needed Beilbauk's help. This was no time for cowardice. "Well," she started softly. "I actually talked to a mygnus rather recently, he was—"

"Really!" Beilbauk exclaimed as he leapt from his chair in excitement. "That's splendid! You found one willing to talk to you!"

"Sort of," Sinccah responded awkwardly. "He actually found me."

Beilbauk waved his hand dismissively. "Whatever. The important thing is that it didn't consider you a threat."

Sinccah's gut started to tie itself into knots. The use of the word "it" sent a shiver down her spine. "Why's that important?"

"To catch them off guard obviously!" Beilbauk exclaimed as he started to practically prance around the room. "This is perfect. So perfect. Normally, those dratted creatures are so hard to attack. What with that pesky crystal of theirs always bringing them back to life. But this is perfect! We won't even need to risk the attack! You can gain their trust and then I can swoop in and eradicate them." He looked up at Sinccah with wild eyes. "You can consider yourself my new apprentice," he said quickly. "We're going to be so very rich!"

"Well, actually ..." Sinccah started before drifting off at a sharp glance from Beilbauk.

"Actually what!" Beilbauk exclaimed.

"I don't really want to spend time going after magnus," Sinccah said diplomatically. Her hand curled into a fist. "The bandits took my mother's pendant, and I want to get that back as soon as—"

"Don't mind that!" Beilbauk cried. "This's the opportunity of a lifetime! With your help, we'll be able to harvest the entire cluster of them! Even once we split the profits from selling the maggni, you'd still have enough money to just buy everything the bandits ever had."

"Uh," Sinccah mumbled. She tried desperately to think of something to say, but words eluded her.

Beilbauk rubbed his hands together gleefully. "It's even better than it sounds!" he declared. "Some folks came by the other day offering men to help take the nearby cluster! Sure, they had a strange look about them, but they didn't even want the maggni, merely the land the creatures inhabit!"

"Sure," Sinccah said awkwardly as she stood. Her mind was racing. She wanted to learn magic, and this mage was willing to teach her. He was also willing to give her what must be a few hundred maggni. Still, it wouldn't be right. She couldn't hunt magnus. Not after everything she'd been through with the Wanderer. She breathed in deeply and locked her eyes on Beilbauk. "I don't think I can do that."

Beilbauk tilted his head as the excitement drained from his body. "Look," he said flatly. "This's what's best for both of us."

"You might be right," Sinccah said softly, "but I can't do it."

"Why not?" Beilbauk questioned.

"I ..." Sinccah's voice drifted off. She remained silent for several seconds trying to figure out what she wanted to say.

"Well?!" Beilbauk asked impatiently.

"I don't think it's right," Sinccah said resolutely.

"Hmmm," Beilbauk said as he started tapping his hand against his chin. His face warped into a sly smile. "In that case, I don't think it would work for me to teach you anything."

"I understand," Sinccah said with more confidence than she felt. She was throwing so much away. Sure, this mage was slightly crazy, but she could've learned so much. It didn't matter. She wouldn't betray the Wanderer like this. She turned away and started to walk toward the stairs. "Thanks for your offer," she said with a quick glance back at Beilbauk, who wore a look of surprise.

"Wait," Beilbauk said flatly as Sinccah reached the stairs.

Sinccah turned back. "Yes?"

"Do you actually think I don't see what's going on here?" Beilbauk said as anger started to rise in his voice.

"What do you mean?" Sinccah asked wearily.

"You talk to magnus," Beilbauk said slowly. "You're their friend." His face hardened. "You're going to warn them."

"I don't even know your plan!" Sinccah exclaimed.

"You know too much," Beilbauk said as he turned away and started walking toward the window. Suddenly, he spun and released a blast of white light. Sinccah let out a pained yelp as she dove over the top of Beilbauk's bed. The spell sailed just above her and struck the stone wall of the tower. The bricks cracked and a large section of the tower wall crumbled away, revealing the evening sky. She looked frantically up at Beilbauk, who was now seething in anger.

"Wait!" Sinccah called out as she stood back up. Beilbauk ignored her cries and threw another spell, this time a small red sphere. Sinccah projected a shield just in front of her, and the spell erupted into a ball of fire. The fire reflected harmlessly off the shield and ignited a stack of papers. The large pile of junk next to Sinccah erupted in flames, blocking her view of Beilbauk. She glanced down the stairs, but another shatter orb sailed through the flames and struck what was left of the wall behind her. Large chunks of the wall collapsed into the stairwell, making it impassable. She dodged a falling stone and turned to see Beilbauk stepping around the burning heap.

"Look what you made me do," he growled disdainfully.

"I didn't want any of this!" Sinccah cried. She took a deep breath, but the air was laden with smoke, and she coughed.

Her cries fell on deaf ears as Beilbauk once again summoned a fireball to throw at her. She projected a shield just in front of him, causing the fireball to erupt in his face. Sinccah's gaze darted to the opening in the wall. It would be quite a fall, but certainly better than being trapped with this crazy mage. She took a short step toward the opening, but Beilbauk lunged forward, blocking her path, the fading wisps of a shield spell dissolving from around him.

"Did you really think that would work on me?" he chuckled before tossing another fireball at Sinccah.

She blocked this one as well, but it was quickly followed by a shatter orb that struck her shield. The shield let out a sharp crack before Sinccah dispelled it. Even so, the drain from the block drove her to her knees. She couldn't fight him. She struggled to her feet only to jump aside as another set of spells flew at her. The shatter orb raced past her and hit another portion of the tower's wall, causing it to crumble.

Sinccah crawled around the flaming pile of debris just in time to dodge another set of spells. However, the fireball still exploded near her feet and set her pants on fire. The shatter orb then hit the floor, causing the smooth wooden boards to explode into hundreds of splinters. Sinccah rolled onto her back, trying to smother the fire on her legs with shield spells. She glanced up just in time to throw up another shield, blocking Beilbauk's attack. Two shatter orbs collided with her shield, crushing it and draining most of her remaining energy. She cried out in pain as hopelessness set in. It was pointless to resist anyway. He was going to kill her! Why hadn't she kept quiet about the Wanderer?!

She looked up sorrowfully at Beilbauk. He stepped forward and glared down at her. "Still glad you rejected my offer?" he growled. "We could've done so much together." He glanced around the burning room and shook his head. "Next time, die faster." He threw out another shatter orb, but Sinccah instinctively blocked it.

Her vision was blurring, and her body cried out in pain. Still, she pushed herself onto her elbows and struggled to back away from the mage.

Beilbauk snorted. "Still haven't given up?" he scoffed. "That'd be admirable if you weren't a snitch." He took a step forward, his frame stark against the darkening sky that could be seen through the gap in the wall behind him. A light breeze drifted through the tower, blowing smoke into his face. He staggered backward as he coughed on the fumes. Sinccah struggled to her feet, clutching a nearby crate for balance. Her legs wobbled, and she glanced despairingly toward the nearby window. It was no use. She was too weak. She shuddered as she turned to give Beilbauk as fierce a look as she could muster. He was still going to kill her, but at least she'd make him remember her.

Beilbauk let out a chuckle. "Amusing," he coughed as he stepped out of the smoke. He projected a small white ball in his hand and examined it carefully as he stepped toward Sinccah, mocking her helplessness. "Now die," he said as he slowly rotated his hand toward her. A sharp snap sounded, and Beilbauk cried out in pain. His spell sailed out to the side as he stumbled forward, revealing the end of a small crossbow bolt, now embedded in his shoulder. Another snap rang out, and Beilbauk whirled to project a shield, deflecting a second bolt.

"Jump," a voice said in her head.

Sinccah's eyes widened, and she spun toward the window. She threw herself onto a stack of rubbish and crawled to the opening. Pushing herself up, she shoved her legs outside and pulled herself onto the windowsill. She grabbed the stone lip and made an attempt to lower herself gently. Her arms suddenly gave out and she lost her grip, falling onto the pile of stones that rose against the side of the tower. She landed on her feet and tried to soften the impact by bending her knees. It partially worked, but her legs were already exhausted; her knees collapsed, and she tumbled to the bottom of the heap of stones. Everything hurt, but she pulled herself back to her feet and started to shuffle toward the far side of the tower. The Wanderer had come back for her! She couldn't leave him to this mage! As she reached the far side, she saw him, the Wanderer, blazing a fiery orange. He was darting around the courtyard in front of the tower with his two crossbows, both of which were reloaded.

"Got you!" Beilbauk hollered. He was standing in the broken section of the tower with a shield projected over his torso and head. He tossed a flurry of spells at the Wanderer, who leapt to the side before making a misstep in the rough terrain. As the mygnus tumbled to the ground, Beilbauk cast a final spell. It was a large fireball, clearly timed to catch the Wanderer after he dodged the previous spells.

"Look out!" Sinccah cried, but she knew what she had to do. The fireball exploded an instant before reaching the Wanderer. Sinccah gasped in pain as she fell to her knees, her energy spent on the small shield.

"Still alive, snitch!" Beilbauk screeched. "Not for much longer!" He cast a pair of fireballs at Sinccah, but she managed to barely throw up a shield in time. "Ealch on you," he growled as he formed a shatter orb in his hand. He turned his hand toward Sinccah, but a crossbow bolt struck him in the arm as he was releasing it. He jerked his hand in pain, causing the spell to fly sideways into the tower wall. The wall crumbled, causing the tower's roof to creak sharply. The main beam snapped, and the entire roof collapsed into the gap in the tower wall.

Beilbauk screamed as one of the roof beams struck him in the back and carried him off the tower. Sinccah squeezed her eyes closed as she pressed herself against the wall. The remains of the roof hit the ground with a sickening crash, which brought a sudden end to Beilbauk's scream. Sinccah kept her eyes closed as she panted. Was it over? She cracked open an eye and looked through the cloud of dust that had formed. The dust quickly filled her eye and she started blinking rapidly. She pushed herself to her feet and pressed her hands into the smooth weathered stones of the tower. Feeling her way, she slowly stumbled around the outside of the tower.

"Here," she heard in her head as she felt a light tap on her shoulder. She opened her eyes and turned around. Through the tears that had formed, she saw the Wanderer standing calmly next to her. He had turned a deep green color and had raised a tentacle to write a message.

"Are you—" he wrote.

Sinccah threw her arms around him, pinning the tentacle to his sphere. "You came back!" she cried out. "You actually came back!" Sinccah smiled as the tears slipped from her eyes and ran down her face. She felt two tentacles wrap around her as the Wanderer returned the embrace. A third tentacle started tapping her shoulder. She opened her eyes to see what he was writing.

"Are you alright?"

Sinccah nodded. "Barely," she said with a wince, "but yes. How about you?"

The Wanderer pulled away from Sinccah. "I am fine, thanks to you."

"What happened to Beilbauk?" Sinccah asked as a sudden feeling of apprehension swept over her.

"The mage is dead," the Wanderer replied. "The main beam of the roof crushed his torso."

Sinccah's shoulders flopped as she breathed out a sigh of relief.

"This is going to thwart many of your plans," the Wanderer wrote rapidly.

"Yeah," Sinccah said softly. "I guess there are some things I have to refuse."

"Indeed," the Wanderer responded.

"Why'd you come back?" Sinccah's legs gave out and she stumbled backward against the tower wall.

"There will be time for explanation later," the Wanderer wrote as he helped lower Sinccah to the ground. "For now, you need to rest."

Sinccah nodded as her vision threatened to go dark. A pained smile formed on her face. Everything had gone wrong with Beilbauk, but at least she wasn't dead. Maybe something worthwhile could still come of this.

⋇⊷◉⊶⋇

Sinccah became aware that she was awake again. She hesitated to open her eyes, instead choosing to feel around with her hands. She was lying on her sleeping mat with her blanket over the top of her. The ground underneath was smooth and hard. Probably some sort of stone. The air felt damp. Too damp. She opened her eyes to see that she was lying in the bottom of Beilbauk's tower. Above her, she could see two large patches of light: one from the staircase, which had been cleared of rubble, and the other from the hole that had been blasted in the floorboards. She was lying just inside the door, where a handful of crates had been shoved aside to make room for her. The scent of smoke still lingered in the air.

She sat up and brushed her hair out of her eyes. As she did, she noticed her pack sitting against the wall. Rummaging through it, she grabbed a pouch of her provisions. For a few minutes, she sat on her mat, eating the food and chasing the drowsiness from her body. Eventually, curiosity overcame her weariness. She needed to figure out what had happened since she'd passed out. She stood gingerly and walked out the door. As she exited the tower, she was greeted by a dim morning light. To the west, mountains loomed in the distance. A quick glance east revealed a rich red sky that heralded the sun's imminent escape from the horizon. She looked around thoughtfully as she walked to the fallen roof, which had crumpled into a pile of shattered boards. Walking cautiously around the rubble, she found a large bloodstain. Presumably, this was where Beilbauk had died. A large heap of loose dirt confirmed her suspicion. She inspected the wood over top of the blood. All the ends were flat, sawed off sometime during the night.

A light rustle sound behind her, and she turned slowly to see the Wanderer shuffling around the rubble. "Good morning," he wrote quickly.

Sinccah nodded. "You took care of Beilbauk's body?"

"Yeah, no sense leaving it out to rot."

"Better than he deserved," Sinccah grunted as she snarled at the bloodstain.

"Perhaps," the Wanderer wrote. "Even so, there is no sense being brutal. He may have lived a cruel life, but it would be wrong for us to despise him in death."

Sinccah eyed the Wanderer curiously. "You're a strange creature."

The Wanderer fidgeted awkwardly. "Certainly, but what, in particular, causes you to think that?"

"You know he was planning to attack a magnus village, right?" Sinccah said, shaking her head.

"Of course. He has been planning it for years."

Sinccah's eyes widened. "Then why'd you bring me here?!" she exclaimed. "You knew what he'd want me to do!"

"Honestly …" the Wanderer wrote before his tentacles went limp. He turned a shade of light blue. "I had hoped you could convince him to go after your bandits."

Sinccah's mouth slid open as her lip started to quiver.

The Wanderer's color darkened. "It was wrong for me to do it. My actions served my own ends."

"You just wanted me to get rid of your mage problem," Sinccah said slowly.

"Yes," the Wanderer wrote slowly as his color continued to darken. "For that, I am sorry. I helped you, but ultimately, I only did so because it was convenient for me. If you could convince this mage to leave, then it would spare my kin from his attack." He shook himself. "At least for a time."

Sinccah nodded as her face started to twitch. "You never cared about me."

"That is true," the Wanderer wrote before his tentacles flopped again. "If you led this mage north, at least one mage would die. I understand it was selfish, I—"

"You led me here to die!" Sinccah screamed.

"I …" the Wanderer wrote before trailing off. "You are a mage. Mages are my enemies." His tentacles started shaking. "At least, that is what I thought when we first met."

Sinccah's face twisted into a snarl. "You …"

"I am sorry," the Wanderer wrote in quick, sloppy text. "I made a mistake. I thought all mages were alike." He paused, the dark blue practically dripping off the text as it slowly dissipated. "By the time we got here, my opinion was altered, but I was unable to turn back. I convinced myself that you would be fine. You would be safe." His tentacle started to shake again. "I was wrong."

Sinccah glanced at the bloodstain as her breathing became heavy. That's why the Wanderer had helped her. Her face curled into a snarl. He'd never cared about her! Her face suddenly contorted in sorrow, and her breathing started to level. He'd left her, but he had come back. That had to count for something. He might have tricked her and led her into danger, but at least he hadn't left her to die.

"I never imagined it would turn out like this," the Wanderer wrote quickly. "I figured this mage would be more friendly toward a fellow human."

Sinccah widened her eyes slightly as she nodded her head. "So did I," she said before inhaling sharply. "I guess he only cared about maggni."

The Wanderer bobbed his sphere. "Certainly," he wrote. A silence fell between them. The Wanderer continued to shuffle his tentacles awkwardly as though he wanted to say more, but he didn't make any attempt to start writing.

Sinccah stared down at the bloodstain as tears threatened to form in her eyes. This had been her chance. Beilbauk had been her last real hope for magical training, as well as for getting her pendant back. She'd thrown it all away, and for what? A village full of magnus she'd never meet? They'd probably attack her on sight if she ever came near them. She'd doomed herself with her actions. The bandits would sell her pendant long before she reached them. Her face contorted in sorrow. She'd never learn what her mother had to tell her. She'd never be a great mage. Her head flopped forward as she squeezed her eyes shut. Maybe she'd done the right thing, but she'd lost everything doing it.

She glanced up to see some text the Wanderer had written: "I suppose this ruins your plan for getting your mother's pendant back."

"Yup," Sinccah said with a hint of rage as tears threatened to form in her eyes. "I failed—again." Her face twisted as she squeezed her eyes closed. It had all gone wrong. By the time royal mages answered Ucksil's summons, it'd be too late. Her eyes shot open. What would she even tell Ucksil! She glanced at the pile of loose dirt as a grimace formed on her face. She was supposed to get a mage, but now that mage was dead. She let out a slow sigh before continuing with a faint whisper. "I ruined everything."

"I am very sorry," the Wanderer wrote. "You were vulnerable, so I exploited you. It was vile of me to do so."

Sinccah glanced toward him with a pained look. She wanted to yell at this mygnus for bringing her here. For making her care about his kind. For leading her to make such costly decisions. Her lip started to curl involuntarily and she turned away and started walking back to the entrance of the tower. She'd still done the right thing. The Wanderer had helped her see the truth. Without him, she would've been ignorant, unaware of the evil she would've helped Beilbauk commit. She couldn't be mad at him. He was only doing what he thought was best, and ultimately, it had saved her from becoming the monster that he feared. She stopped at the doorway of the tower and looked up at the distant mountains. Her face continued to contort in pain once again as her mind turned to the future. What was she even supposed to do now? Out of the corner of her eye she noticed the Wanderer writing.

"Is there anything I can do?" the Wanderer asked.

Sinccah she sat down on the small platform outside the door and glanced at the text he'd written. "No," she grumbled as she leaned forward and buried her face in her hands. "It's not like you're going to get my pendant back."

"I might," the Wanderer wrote rapidly as his color changed to a light orange.

Sinccah read the text through the gaps between her fingers. "Really?" she asked, straightening back up. "Why?"

"You repaid my selfish actions with selfless ones. For that, I must repay you," the Wanderer wrote. "You did help me with my mage problem after all."

"Sure," Sinccah said awkwardly. She eyed the mygnus up and down. It'd be foolish to trust him again. Sure he'd come back to save her, but that didn't wipe away all the lies he'd told. She breathed in deeply. "I'll be fine."

The Wanderer tilted his sphere. "Even if you reject me, I will still do my all to aid you."

Sinccah's brow furrowed. What was this creature saying? It didn't matter. She would go on alone. She exhaled forcefully. "I don't think there's anything for you to do."

"I have allies," the Wanderer wrote as he bobbed excitedly. "If these bandits live in the far north as you said, then I know a lot of goblins who would be able to help us."

Sinccah tilted her head in suspicion. "What are you trying to do?"

"I am trying to show appreciation," the Wanderer wrote slowly. "I refuse to let your last memory of magnus be one of betrayal." He shivered as his color shifted to blue. "Particularly after you sacrificed so much for the sake of my kin. I want to make things right."

"It wasn't that big of a deal," Sinccah said dismissively. "Beilbauk wanted me to help him wipe out an entire village. There's no way I could do that."

"You say that," the Wanderer wrote, "but how many mages in your situation would have acted as you did?"

Sinccah thought back to her time at the academy. She mentally offered her classmates the same offer Beilbauk had given her. "I guess not many," she admitted.

"Indeed," the Wanderer wrote. "You have sacrificed much to do what you thought was right. I want to repay you for that sacrifice."

"Sure," Sinccah said as she nodded. She sighed as she realized how desperate her decision had made her. Did she really have a choice? It wasn't like she had any chance of getting her pendant back otherwise. Still, she couldn't trust him. Her lip twitched upward. She could always have him escort her back to Sillburg. It didn't seem like he wanted to hurt her, so it would probably be safe to travel with him. When she reached the city, she could always leave him. A faint smile appeared on her lips. "Very well," she said. "I could certainly use the help."

The Wanderer bobbed rapidly. "Ideal, we can head north as soon as you are ready."

"Alright," Sinccah said as she stood and looked back toward the tower. "You still didn't answer my question from last night."

"Why did I come back?"

Sinccah glanced back at the Wanderer to read his response. "Yeah."

"I had stayed in the area to eavesdrop," the Wanderer replied. "I wanted to know if you would succeed in convincing this mage to leave. Otherwise, I was going to head to the nearby village and warn them of the potential attack. When I noticed he was getting aggressive ..." His writing trailed off as his color became increasingly blue. "I knew I had made a mistake. I had led you to danger. I might as well have sentenced you to death."

"So you came back out of guilt?" Sinccah asked.

"Partially," the Wanderer wrote as he used one of his tentacles to pick at a nearby rock, "but I also learned a lot from you. I learned that some humans who use magic are able to resist its corruption. I learned that some of you are genuinely trying to do what is best. Some of you do truly care about the lives of my kin." The mygnus paused but kept moving his tentacle as though he was going to write more. "I came back because you proved here that you were a friend of magnus, and magnus save their friends from death."

Sinccah arched an eyebrow. Was he just trying to make her feel better, or did he genuinely appreciate their time together? Either way, she could play along for now. "You're welcome," she said with a slight smirk, "and thank you."

The Wanderer bobbed slightly as he turned a dark shade of green. "Indeed," he wrote quickly. "Shall we be on our way?"

"Yeah," Sinccah said softly before taking an excited step toward the doorway, "but first I want to have a look around this tower."

"What for?" the Wanderer wrote quickly.

Sinccah stepped into the base of the tower. "Books," she said quickly as she continued walking. "He might have had some magic manuals."

Sinccah walked to the staircase and climbed to the second story. By the time she got there, the Wanderer had joined her. She looked over the mess that the upper level had become. Naturally, there was the hole in the floor along with the giant heap of burnt junk near the stairs. The far side of the room was in slightly better shape, but the morning dew and a light breeze had thrown everything into disarray. Not that it'd been particularly organized before.

"You put out the fire last night?" Sinccah asked.

"Yeah," the Wanderer replied. "I figured you would appreciate having some shelter for the night, so I prevented everything from burning down."

Sinccah laughed softly. "I suppose I should thank you for that."

"If you want to," the Wanderer wrote quickly. "What kind of books are you looking for?"

"All kinds," Sinccah responded. "Though, books teaching magic are likely to be stored someplace ..." her voice trailed off as she glanced around the room, "safe."

"Sure," the Wanderer wrote before hopping onto one of the junk piles. He pushed a pile of clothes off a shelf, picked up a book that was hidden under them, and returned it to Sinccah. "Like this one?"

"Maybe," Sinccah said with a smile as she took the book and looked it over. It was certainly convenient to have a mygnus around when searching a room. She opened the book and read a few pages. "This is just a catalog of plants in the area." She set the book down. "Are there any more?"

"There are several," the Wanderer answered as he scurried around the room and collected more books. As he did so, Sinccah meandered over to the table. She scanned it aimlessly until she noticed the paper with her misspelled name. As she read through the notes Beilbauk had been writing, her face contorted in disgust. Instead of jotting down her magical skills, he had simply doodled on the page until writing "nurse-mage." She angrily crumpled up the paper and tossed it across the room.

The Wanderer appeared at her side and started writing: "The contents upset you?"

"Yeah," Sinccah growled before continuing under her breath. "Exploitative old fool."

"Unfortunate," the Wanderer wrote before offering Sinccah two more books.

Sinccah looked through both of the books, but neither of them were related to magic. As she was glancing through them, the Wanderer found three more books. Sinccah grimaced as she grabbed the first two. They had been caught in the fire, so most of the pages had been turned to ash. A brief glance told her they had once been magic manuals of some sort, but there was no way she'd be able to get anything out of them.

The third book looked more promising, but as she cracked the cover open, a wave of nausea swept over her. She tried not to gag as she slammed the cover closed and hurled the book across the room.

"Something offensive about that one?" the Wanderer asked as he appeared beside her.

Sinccah let out a short cough. "Yeah," she wheezed. "It's covered in mold."

"Oh," the Wanderer wrote quickly. "I had wondered about the moisture in it." He dropped a massive volume onto the floor. "Unfortunate."

Sinccah startled slightly at the thump. Her eyes snapped to the tome's cover, which bore a faded title: *A Systematic Treatise on Abstruse Stamina.* She perked up. This had to be magically related. She crouched and lifted the cover. The book wasn't in great shape, but it was readable. She started to scan the text. It was definitely talking about magic, but even the simple descriptions on the opening pages went right over her head. She flipped through to some of the later chapters, but these were even more confusing. This might be useful to her in ten years, but it was currently worthless. She might as well wrap it up and hide it someplace safe in case she ever came back this way, but there was no sense taking it.

She let out a sigh as she delicately closed the tome and stood. "Are these all the books he had?" she asked dejectedly.

"One more," the Wanderer wrote before stepping over to the table. He lifted one side and pulled a dusty book from under one of the legs. He dropped the table and held the book toward Sinccah. The table tilted awkwardly, and the inkwell slid onto the floor and shattered. Sinccah jumped back as shards of glass hit her foot.

"Oops," the Wanderer wrote as he hopped over the spilled ink and handed the book to Sinccah. She took it in her hands and ran her finger down the spine. The dust gave way to reveal the book's title: *A Maze Ablaze.* She nearly dropped the book in shock. This was the book Vistimmot had told her to find. She eagerly opened the book and flipped through the first few pages. It certainly looked like a magical manual.

"Is that what you were looking for?" the Wanderer asked.

"Yeah," Sinccah mumbled in disbelief. "It's exactly what I was looking for." She shook her head. "It's perfect."

"Fascinating," the Wanderer wrote. "However, I would hardly call the floor under the table leg somewhere safe."

Sinccah looked up at the tilted table. "Huh," she grunted. "I guess Beilbauk didn't find much value in this volume."

"He also seems to have some organizational problems," the Wanderer wrote as he swept his tentacle over the heaped-up junk. "Is there anything else you need?"

"Did he have any maggni?" Sinccah asked.

The Wanderer's color quickly changed to red and he started to fidget rapidly. He lifted a tentacle to start writing.

"Not for me," Sinccah blurted out before he could start. "I was thinking you could return them to your kin."

The Wanderer turned a light green color. "Ah," he wrote slowly. "Sorry for the outburst."

"I understand," Sinccah said in relief. "Next time I'll word the question better."

"That would be ideal," the Wanderer replied. "He had five maggni on his person. I have already reclaimed them."

"Good," Sinccah said as she glanced around the room again. "I don't think there is anything else I need." She frowned. "Did he have any money?"

"None that I could locate," the Wanderer answered.

"That's probably good," Sinccah admitted. "It'd feel weird taking a dead man's money." She looked slowly over the rest of Beilbauk's possessions. Did she need anything else? Food perhaps? She grimaced as she glanced between the piles of rubbish. Probably best to avoid whatever a man like this had been eating. She took a deep breath, then turned toward the Wanderer. "I suppose we should start heading back to Sillburg. It'll be a long walk."

"Yes," the Wanderer responded. "However, I would recommend we take the horses."

Sinccah perked up. She'd forgotten all about the horses. "Of course!" she exclaimed excitedly as a smile formed on her face. Apparently, her journey back to Sillburg would be much less tedious than she'd expected.

———————◄O►—————————

Sinccah and the Wanderer walked purposefully out of the tower. Slipping around the smashed roof, they came to the southern side of the tower and looked past the squat shed into a large pasture. On the far side of the enclosure, under the shade of a large tree, Sinccah saw two horses: a silver dapple and a blood bay. Each horse was tall and clearly powerful. They eyed the newcomers with interest but didn't make any attempt to move.

"There is tack in the shed," the Wanderer wrote.

Sinccah glanced at him. "Great, do you want to get that? I'm not sure how the horses will feel about a mygnus."

"Sure," the Wanderer wrote before dashing into the shed.

Sinccah climbed over the fence and tentatively approached the horses. They continued to stare at her as she walked up to them. They twitched their ears but once again didn't move. Sinccah walked up to the bay, which was the closer of the two horses. Stopping just outside of arm's reach, she held her hand toward the horse, who glanced at her outstretched hand before stepping closer to her. Sinccah shifted back slightly but stopped after she noticed the calm look in the bay's eyes. The horse took another step toward her and extended his neck to touch her shoulder with his nose. Sinccah froze. What was happening? She glanced back to see if the Wanderer had returned, but he seemed to still be in the shed. The bay took another step and pressed his head into Sinccah's arm as he closed his eyes.

"Hey," Sinccah whispered. She felt awkward; she'd never had a horse act so friendly toward her before. Not even horses she'd developed some sort of a relationship with. She noticed a mark on the horse's shoulder, some sort of brand. As she leaned in to inspect the mark, her eyes widened. This was no normal horse.

"So you're a dragon charger," Sinccah said softly as she reached her hand out to touch the brand. "That explains why you're so calm."

A loud clatter sounded behind Sinccah, and she spun to see the Wanderer stumble out of the shed. He was struggling to carry a saddle, which was clearly too large for him to hold properly. The bay pulled his head back but otherwise remained motionless. The mygnus tossed a saddle onto the fence, then waved to Sinccah. "You two seem to be getting along."

Sinccah glanced back at the bay, who had withdrawn slightly and was looking at the Wanderer with great interest. "Yeah," Sinccah called out. "This one is a dragon charger. I still need to check the other one."

The Wanderer raised a tentacle, curled it, then let it drop. "Nice," he wrote quickly before darting back into the shed.

Sinccah turned back to the bay. "Should we go check on your friend?"

The horse ignored Sinccah and continued looking toward the saddle that now sat on the fence.

Sinccah smiled at the bay before turning her attention to the other horse, who was about a dozen steps away and didn't seem particularly concerned by the appearance of the Wanderer. She walked slowly toward the dapple and held out her hand. "How about you?" she whispered.

The second horse took a couple of steps toward her and pressed his head against her arm. His shoulder also had a mark. She reached out and pushed the hair away, revealing the distinct flame pattern of a dragon charger. She exhaled slowly. This was incredible. She'd always wanted to own such a magnificent creature, but she'd never expected to find two. Seeing as Beilbauk was dead, these horses were effectively hers to take.

Another clatter sounded from the shed, and Sinccah turned to watch the Wanderer stumble awkwardly out with the other saddle. Sinccah made a series of short clicks with her mouth and started walking toward the Wanderer. The two horses perked their ears up and followed behind her.

As she reached the Wanderer, he started writing: "You already have them following you on command!"

Sinccah glanced back at the horses with a smile. "Sort of," she said with a laugh. "These are dragon changers, so they're trained to follow humans who give them a voice command."

The Wanderer tilted his sphere. "That is what the clicking was for?"

"Yeah," Sinccah responded with a nod.

"Do you have much experience with horses like these?" the Wanderer asked.

"Not really," Sinccah answered softly. "When I worked for Lady Dove, we visited a ranch where these kinds of horses are trained." She sighed. "I don't actually remember that much, but I remembered the trainer always made that clicking sound to get the horses to follow her."

"Fascinating," the Wanderer wrote. "Why are they called dragon chargers?"

"Oh," Sinccah said calmly. "They get their name from their level of training."

The Wanderer fidgeted. "But humans hate dragons, right?"

"Well, yes," Sinccah said awkwardly. "They're trained to be able to charge dragons. Most horses would spook at the sight of a dragon, but these have been trained so well that they would literally run into dragon fire, assuming they were told to do so."

The Wanderer flickered to a light orange. "That is quite impressive."

"Yeah," Sinccah continued. "They're normally incredibly expensive to buy, seeing as the training takes so long."

"So the mage here must have been really wealthy," the Wanderer wrote.

"He got them from a friend of his," Sinccah replied quickly. "I doubt Beilbauk would ever buy them himself."

"Ah," the Wanderer wrote slowly. "His friend simply left them here?"

Sinccah shook her head. "Honestly," she signed, "I think the friend died." Her lips tugged downward into a frown. "Maybe Beilbauk even had something to do with that."

"That is plausible," the Wanderer wrote. "This mage did seem disagreeable. Regardless, it is quite convenient for us now. Which one would you like?"

Sinccah glanced at the horses, which were standing right behind her. "I'll take the bay."

The Wanderer tapped his tentacles against one of the boards that made up the fence. "I am unsure how that answers my question."

"What do you mean?" Sinccah asked.

"It is fine if you want to possess some nook of coastline," the Wanderer wrote quickly, "but I hardly think that applies to which horse you intend to ride."

Sinccah's eyes widened. "Oh no," she said with a laugh. "Bay is the coloration of the horse. In this case, it's the one with the solid coat."

"Sure," the Wanderer wrote tentatively. "Which one is that?"

Sinccah glanced at the two horses. The dapple clearly didn't have a solid coat. How was he confused? She turned back to see him writing.

"Is the solid-coat one the shorter one?"

Sinccah looked back at the horses. She really couldn't decide which one was taller. "Uh," she said awkwardly. "The bay is this one," she said with a gesture.

"Ah," the Wanderer wrote rapidly, "the taller one."

"Can't you see their coats?" Sinccah questioned.

The Wanderer tapped his tentacles against the boards, creating a rhythmic thunk sound.

Sinccah bit her lip. "You can't see colors, can you?"

"Correct," the Wanderer answered, "but now that I know the shorter one is mine, the situation is resolved."

"Right," Sinccah said awkwardly. "I can't actually tell which one is taller."

The Wanderer tilted his sphere. "Really?" he asked. "The one you call the bay is quite a bit taller."

Sinccah looked back at the horses, who were calmly eyeing the Wanderer. They still looked exactly the same height to her. "Sure," she mumbled. "How much taller would you say he is?"

The Wanderer held up two tentacles such that there was a tiny gap between the two. Likely not even enough for Sinccah to pass her hand through sideways.

"Ah," Sinccah grunted. She glanced back at the horses. "For your reference, you're going to have the dappled horse. In case that ever comes up."

"Alright," the Wanderer wrote. "Do you have any idea how to attach these saddles?"

"Not really," Sinccah admitted. "I've never done this before."

"That is unfortunate," the Wanderer wrote. "The goblins put saddles on boarine, though, so I think I can work it out." He climbed over the fence and grabbed one of the saddles. "Do you know what these blanket things are for?"

Sinccah glanced awkwardly at the two saddle pads still resting on the fence. "Those go under the saddle," she said as she grabbed one and tossed it lightly onto the bay's back. She turned back and grabbed the other saddle. She gently set the saddle onto the bay and noticed the Wanderer struggling. He'd gotten the blanket onto the dapple but was clearly way too short for his horse and realistically couldn't get the saddle on without something to stand on.

"Here," she said as she stepped over and took the saddle from him.

"I will take care of fastening those straps," he wrote before slipping under the bay.

Sinccah's eyes widened. She cringed slightly as she waited for the horse to spook. The bay slowly turned his head and looked at her, seemingly oblivious to the strange creature that now stood underneath him. Sinccah let out a soft sigh of relief. It was a good thing these were dragon changers; otherwise, the bay would almost certainly be halfway across the pasture by now. She heaved the saddle onto the dapple and looked back to see the Wanderer stepping out from under the bay.

"How tight do you think this needs to be?" he wrote as he held up a strap.

"I'm not sure," Sinccah admitted. "It should probably be fairly tight; otherwise, we're going to fall off."

The Wanderer fidgeted with the strap. "It seems the leather is somewhat worn, so I should probably fasten it there."

"That assumes we matched the saddles to their horses," Sinccah said with a frown.

"Indeed," the Wanderer wrote as he fastened the saddle on the bay and moved to the dapple. He fiddled with the strap for a while before finally getting it snug. "It seems we choose correctly."

Sinccah tilted her head.

"Both of the saddles seem to fit with the same amount of tightness," the Wanderer clarified.

"Ah," Sinccah said and she glanced between the horses. "I honestly can't tell."

"I suppose that is fair," the Wanderer wrote, "but I think this is correct."

"Alright," Sinccah said slowly. "Where are the bridles?"

"Bride whats?"

"Bridles," Sinccah repeated. "Harnesses for the horses' heads. You use them to steer." She glanced around quickly. "We're also going to need some brushes to rub them down with."

"Oh," the Wanderer wrote quickly. "I was wondering what those things were for." He scurried over the fence and returned with two bridles and a leather pouch. He opened the pouch and held it up for Sinccah to see.

She nodded as she pulled out two remarkably fancy brushes. "These will work," she said as she dropped them back into the pouch.

The Wanderer bobbed slightly, then handed one bridle to Sinccah before walking over to the dapple and tying the pouch onto the saddle. As Sinccah held her bridle toward the bay, the horse bent his head down to help her put it on. She tightened the straps and then climbed into the saddle. "Are you ready to ride?"

"Yeah," the Wanderer wrote quickly before struggling up the dapple's side into the saddle. His awkward ascent once again reminded Sinccah of how fortunate they were to find such fine horses. Upon reaching the top of the saddle, it became clear he didn't fit properly. To compensate for this, he looped four of his tentacles under the edges of the saddle. "This will work."

Sinccah rode briskly to the gate and climbed down to open it. She turned back to the Wanderer, who hadn't started moving. "You alright back there?"

"How do you get it to move?" he wrote quickly.

"Tap him with your ankles ..." Sinccah said before realizing how useless that instruction was. "Er," she fumbled. "Tap him on the side, around where my ankles would be."

The Wanderer reached back his tentacles and gave his horse a soft squeeze. The horse started walking away from the gate toward the pasture. The Wanderer pulled on the reins, and the dapple slowed as he walked in a slow circle that eventually reached the gate. Sinccah watched with amusement as the Wanderer rode through the gate. His tentacles were stiff and he was constantly twitching.

"You've never ridden a horse before, have you?" Sinccah asked.

"I suppose that is accurate," the Wanderer wrote after bringing his horse to a stop. His tentacles shivered slightly. "These creatures are quite unmaneuverable."

Sinccah arched an eyebrow. "Not really?"

"They can only move one direction," the Wanderer wrote as he tilted his sphere. "Very inconvenient."

"Sure," Sinccah said awkwardly. "Have you never ridden anything before?"

The Wanderer tapped a tentacle against the saddle. "Magnus have very little need to use animals for this sort of thing."

"Would you do better if you just ran alongside?" Sinccah questioned as she mounted the bay and rode up to the Wanderer. "You seem pretty fast."

"I would be inadequate," the mygnus replied. "The needed pace would become unsustainable over the course of a day."

"Ah," Sinccah said softly.

Together, they rode slowly around the tower. Upon reaching the door, Sinccah stopped. She jumped off her horse, stepped into the tower, and grabbed her pack. She walked back to her horse and fastened her supplies onto the back of the saddle. Finishing this, she mounted the bay and turned to the Wanderer. She lurched forward as she nearly laughed at the sight. He'd also grabbed his pack and had set it on top of the saddle under his sphere, effectively using the pack as a cushion, the pressure of his body keeping it in place on the saddle. In spite of how silly it looked, it was probably quite a lot more comfortable for him.

"Something funny?" he asked.

Sinccah smiled. "I never thought I'd see a mygnus riding a horse."

"I never thought I would ride one," he wrote as he turned a green color. "I suppose this will make the journey far more interesting."

"Yeah," Sinccah said with a chuckle, "and faster."

Acknowledgments

Thanks to everyone who helped me with this journey. In particular:

My brother Luke, who encouraged me along the way, aided in worldbuilding, and served as my alpha reader.

My sister Sirah, who edited the book, helped me craft the nuance of the story, and calmed my fears about publishing.

My mom, who created the art for the cover.

Ben Gabriel, Amanda Rand, and my parents, who served as beta readers and provided invaluable feedback.

You, who made it far enough to bother reading an acknowledgments page.

www.ingramcontent.com/pod-product-compliance
Lightning Source LLC
Chambersburg PA
CBHW020317200626
46814CB00006BA/2291